ACKNOWLEDGMENTS

Like most people these days, my life is oft-times crazy and chaotic. But every once in a while, the stars align and problems melt away, and I am given the clarity of thought and vision that I need in order to get through the current work-in-progress. Here are a few people who helped me along the way:

My wonderful editor and agent, who are my touchstones within the publishing industry and can always be counted on to share in the excitement of the moment.

My boys, both big and small, for at least pretending to pick up after themselves, even though every last one of them claims not to see the messes.

My family, for always being interested in how things are *really* going.

The whole Pyrotek gang, for their constant encouragement, and occasional harassment.

GB and all the girrrrls at GB.Net for the

giggles and distractions . . . you all know who you are.

And finally, you, the reader . . . this book wouldn't exist without thoughts and dreams of you on the receiving end.

A Charmed Death

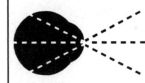

This Large Print Book carries the
Seal of Approval of N.A.V.H.

A Charmed Death

Madelyn Alt

WHEELER PUBLISHING
An imprint of Thomson Gale, a part of The Thomson Corporation

THOMSON
——————★——————™
GALE

Detroit • New York • San Francisco • New Haven, Conn. • Waterville, Maine • London

THOMSON

GALE

LIBRARY OF CONGRESS CATALOGING-IN-PUBLICATION DATA

Alt, Madelyn.
   A charmed death / by Madelyn Alt.
     p. cm. — (Wheeler Publishing large print cozy mystery)
   ISBN-13: 978-1-59722-473-4 (pbk. : alk. paper)
   ISBN-10: 1-59722-473-1 (pbk. : alk. paper)
    1. Witches — Fiction. 2. Indiana — Fiction. 3. Murder — Investigation — Fiction. 4. Large type books. I. Title.
   PS3601.L45C47 2007
   813'.6—dc22
                                          2006101166

Published in 2007 by arrangement with The Berkley Publishing Group, a member of Penguin Group (USA) Inc.

Printed in the United States of America on permanent paper
10 9 8 7 6 5 4 3 2 1

This book is dedicated to my family, who put up with an awful lot when I'm on deadline. But most especially it's for Steve, because he's always believed in me, even when I couldn't believe in myself.

The power of accurate observation is commonly called cynicism by those who have not got it.

— GEORGE BERNARD SHAW

CHAPTER 1

I had been thinking for some time that things weren't quite right in my little Indiana town. Strangely enough, it had nothing to do with the witches living practically in my backyard.

Let me back up. Maggie O'Neill here, at your service. I'm coming up fast on my thirtieth birthday, just your average small-town girl, and I've lived all my life in the somewhat nondescript Hoosier town of Stony Mill, population 6,841. For those of you picturing the corny hats-off salutes on *Hee Haw,* you're probably not far off the mark. Life is simple here. At least on the surface.

For two and a half months, I've been working at Enchantments, an upscale gift shop located in the trendy string of antique stores down on River Street. That's where the witches come in.

It's not what you think.

The store is owned by Felicity Dow, an English expatriate and follower of the Old Ways — but please don't hold that against her. I honestly have never met another woman like her. In a way, I owe her my life, though she insists she had nothing to do with it. But more than that, more than anything, it was Liss who opened my eyes and senses to the . . . *unusual* energy that could be felt in the area, hovering in the shadows, if one but paid attention.

For better or for worse. There would be no going back.

I am Maggie O'Neill, and this is my story.

December in Indiana is never predictable, and when Saturday greeted me with sudden temps in the fifties, I knew this day would be no different. I was opening the store that morning, so after my usual routine of a quick shower and a simple updo with a giant hair clip, I surveyed my closet with an eye toward the weather.

Here unseasonal weather might best be compared to a fickle lover — it never sticks around for long. A Hoosier born and bred, I knew as well as anyone that the real key to comfort meant dressing in layers, so I threw on a pair of navy wool slacks, a thin mock turtleneck, and a nubby sweater in a medium peacock blue that brought out the green in my eyes before I grabbed my coat, purse, and the stack of receipts I'd been working on over the weekend, stuffed a bagel between my teeth, and headed out the door.

I was in a hurry. I'd almost come to terms with the strange things that had been happening in my three-room basement apartment in the aging Victorian on Willow Street. Almost. Lately, the faint thrumming I heard all around me as I lay quietly in bed at night had grown so reliable that I no longer questioned whether it was real or imagined. I knew. Just as I now recognized all the other signs that I was not alone. The flickering lights. The sudden scent of lavender. The fingerprints that appeared on windows and mirrors from the inside after a good cleaning. The way the tuner on my old, beat-up stereo always seemed to roll over to an oldies station best known for its big band sound, no matter that I preferred soft rock. This weekend, however, the high jinks had been so frequent that it had begun to eat away at my hard-won acceptance of my newfound powers as an empath. That's right, people, I'm sensitive to the feelings of others, as well as a whole host of other phenomena that sometimes spooked me senseless. I closed the door to my apartment behind me that morning with the feeling that I had escaped.

Just. In. Time.

In time for what, I didn't know. I could only hope that whatever was causing the increase in activity would find some kind of harmless release — and soon — so that things could go back to the way they were. Before everything started to go wrong.

Because then maybe I could go back to normal as well.

It was a lovely, impossible dream, and I knew it. And to be truthful, I couldn't swear that was what I wanted. For it all to end. I sighed as I started up Christine — my cherished but slightly unpredictable 1972 VW Bug — and began to maneuver my way through quiet residential streets. That was part of the problem. I didn't know what I wanted at all. Some days, I thought it might be better to be oblivious to the threads of magic I sensed weaving their way through my life, quietly and without fanfare. But a part of me thrilled at my newfound ability. A part of me wanted to believe that for some reason I had been chosen to receive this strange gift, and I could not deny a growing desire to know the why and how of it.

Patience . . .

The word floated into view inside my head, focusing my attention and soothing me at once. Yes. Patience. As Liss would say at her most Confucius, there is a time for everything, and everything a place. And I *was* learning. In the last two months, with my boss's blessing and occasional guidance in the selection, I'd inhaled more than twenty books on the supernatural. Yet in spite of all the unexplainable things I'd experienced myself, live and in person, I'd considered the concepts ridiculous at first and still found myself snickering and rolling my eyes over some of the more "Out There" notions. Until the morning I'd chanced into Felicity Dow's world, high school science class had pretty much served to kill any vestiges of awe I felt for the workings of the everyday world. To go back to such an archaic way of thinking, that magic and the strength of a person's will could affect the natural order of things, seemed so . . . backward. So superstitious. And yet, the more I read, the more I recognized bits and pieces of my own past experience. Little things. Things I'd never before thought to question.

So I wasn't normal. I guess deep down I'd always known that. It was just that I thought it had more to do with the real me, the everyday me, than with experiencing the Otherworld. How was I to know that the two would turn out to be so intimately connected?

Shaking off the uneasiness that had settled down around my shoulders, I turned onto River Street and popped Christine out of gear, allowing her to coast downhill toward Enchantments. There were a few cars ahead of me, other shopkeepers making their way in to open their stores in preparation for holiday shoppers, but it was still too early for the marauding hordes. Thank goodness. There were a few finishing touches I wanted to put on the new window display before we opened, and then there were the boxes of new stock that had come in the day before yesterday that I hadn't gotten around to unpacking. If last week was any indication, there would be still more unpackaged inventory by the end of this week. The Christmas season meant nonstop sales and return customers, as I was fast learning. Good for the store's bank account, but awfully hard on the feet. Not that I was complaining.

Felicity had been out for several weeks, taking some much-needed and much-deserved time off. For personal reasons, she'd said. Grieving was probably closer to the truth. Mere months ago, Felicity's sister, Isabella Harding, had been murdered. At first, the police had suspected Liss — an outrage if there ever was one. But the killer had turned out to be Felicity's niece Jacqui, so angry at her own mother for sleeping with her fiancé that she'd taken her life.

Losing two members of her family in such a terrible way can't have been easy. If it meant working double shifts to see that things got done, I was happy to do it, so long as it allowed Felicity the healing time she needed.

I parked Christine in the usual place behind the store and stepped out onto the crushed limestone. A brisk wind picked up the instant I did, lifting my hair off my neck and pushing it in my face. I shivered in spite of the weather broadcast and clutched my jacket closed at the throat while I unlocked the back door and stepped inside.

The scent of cinnamon closed around me, spicy sweet as always. Breathing in deeply, I fumbled for the wall switch, blinking at the sudden transformation of the back office space from shadow to light. A light that also revealed a stack of corrugated boxes four deep and five high. Without further ado, I hung my coat and purse in the closet and pushed up my sleeves. Time to get to work. Well . . . maybe a cup of English Breakfast first.

I deftly performed my morning ritual of filling the water vat in the industrial-sized coffeemakers at the coffee bar. Though our customers, many of whom worked in bustling downtown Stony Mill, favored the various specialty teas, lattes, and cappuccinos we offered, I took delight in the tried-and-true. Earl Grey, English Breakfast, Orange Pekoe. Simplicity at its best and most comforting.

While I waited for the water to heat, I wandered through the unlit aisles, straightening glossy-papered books, plumping up froufrou pillows, testing the many shelves for dust. Though I'd worked at Enchantments only a couple of months, I derived great personal satisfaction from tending to the store and its inventory. I couldn't have felt prouder had I owned it myself.

Assured that the orderliness of the stock had not degenerated overnight, I wandered to the front of the store and gazed out at the nearly empty street. Directly opposite, Randy Cutter was out, sweeping the sidewalk in front of his antique store, Something Olde. He nodded when he caught sight of my upraised hand, but didn't pause in his undertaking. If tea was my morning ritual, sweeping the sidewalk with all due diligence was Randy's. Out with the old, and in with the new.

The only other person in sight was a boy, a half block away, chasing after a giant red ball. I smiled to myself as I watched him. His baseball cap flipped backward off his sandy blond head, falling unheeded to the freshly swept sidewalk, yet no matter what he did, the ball bounced along just out of his reach.

His laughter floated in on the morning breezes, audible even through the same closed front door that I'd fallen through just a few months back. Ah, to be eight again. He belonged to one of the shop owners, I supposed. Still, it was awfully early for an eight-year-old to be out on the street alone, wasn't it?

I frowned as my heart suddenly chugged to life. Enchantments stood in a strand of reclaimed warehouses on the last block of River Street, the oldest thoroughfare in the county. River Street teed into the Wabash River. The ball showed no sign of stopping, and where the ball went, the boy seemed to follow. What if he wasn't paying attention to where he was headed? What if he chased the ball right into the river? My hand opened, splayed against the cool glass in supplication. Too quiet a gesture that would help no one. I thundered my knuckles against the glass, then my fist. Much better.

"Randy! Mr. Cutter! The boy! The boy!"

Cutter looked up at the sound. Too slow! I gestured frantically toward the boy. Cutter turned toward the river, then looked back at me, his brow furrowed. My heart in my throat, I looked myself. The boy was right there, still running, still . . .

He blinked out. The boy, the cap, the ball all just faded away, right in front of my eyes. And from the look on his face, Cutter hadn't seen a thing.

Damn it.

Knowing I must look like the world's biggest idiot, I gritted my teeth into some semblance of a smile and gave Cutter a sheepish shrug. He looked puzzled when he went back to his sweeping. As for me, I slunk over to the coffee bar and made myself the fastest cup of tea in the history of Enchantments. I drank it down even faster, my hands trembling.

It had been happening more often. The creepy sensation of being watched. That heart-stopping, get-away-fast feeling. Trouble was, the episodes weren't relegated solely to my apartment anymore. I couldn't be sure that they ever had been.

And I wasn't quite sure what to think about that.

Turning my back on my confusion, the front of the store, and the possibility of another unwelcome view of the disappearing boy (*Neat trick! Impress your family! Wow your friends!*), I made my way back to the storeroom-cum-office, determined to immerse myself in my work and, with any luck, distract myself from my otherworldly woes.

I had just found the box cutter when Evie Carpenter walked in the back door. A delicate blonde with the face of an angel and a temperament to match, Evie was also the youngest member of the N.I.G.H.T.S., more formally known as the Northeast Indiana Ghost Hunting and Tracking Society, a group I had joined back in October at Felicity's urging when all the trouble started. The N.I.G.H.T.S., with Felicity at the helm, had undertaken the burden of educating me in all things metaphysical.

Forewarned is forearmed, I always say.

Well, I say that lately, anyway.

"Morning, Evie. You're here early."

Felicity had hired Evie to help out during the holiday season, since she herself had been spending so much time away from the store. Evie was still in high school, so that meant after school until eight and Saturdays when the store opened at ten.

"I thought you might need help," Evie said, hanging up her coat.

I smiled at her as I slid the razor carefully down the line of box tape on the uppermost carton and flipped the flaps open to reveal a treasure trove of newsprint-wrapped mysteries. "Sweet of you."

She shrugged and collapsed into the antique barrel-backed desk chair. "Not really. Mom's having her church group by this morning. You know, the Ladies of Perpetual Devotion. Anything is better than that." She stopped suddenly and bit her lip. "I didn't mean it like that. You know I love being here."

"Of course I do."

"Can I help you with that?" She gestured toward the carton.

"Dig in."

In no time, the two of us together had made short shrift of unpacking, logging, numbering, and pricing the delicate crystal that had come all the way from Ireland. We set them carefully to one side, in awe of their beauty. Most residents of Stony Mill would never think twice about the repeated spirals, knotwork, and beautiful silverwork adorning the goblets, bowls, candleholders, and plates that shot sparks in all directions in even the dimmest light. The spiritual symbols of Celtic-based Goddess worship simply wouldn't register. To the initiated, however, the patterns etched into the glassware gave testimony to the religious leanings of the Irish vendor. Like many in the witching community, Felicity liked to patronize other witches whenever possible. Though it wasn't something she required of her suppliers, the ones she did endorse were some of the finest artisans I'd ever seen.

"Once the holidays are over," I mused aloud as I set the glassware out on an antique sideboard, "I think a window display of this crystal would be lovely. Look at the way they catch the light."

"Why not now?"

"And abandon Santa Claus and all of his reindeer?" I asked, holding my hand to my heart in feigned shock and dismay. "Sacrilege!"

Evie grinned. "It's nearly ten. Want me to unlock the front?"

"Is it? How time flies. Yes, thanks. I'll just finish up here."

When I had wiped the last glass clean of fingerprints and positioned it with the others, I stowed my cleaning supplies in the closet and headed back up front. Evie was standing by the front window, her arms crossed over her chest. Something about her stance, a tension I felt more than saw, made me veer away from the counter and head in her direction.

"Anything wrong?" I asked as I went to stand behind her. A shiver ran through me as I did. *Easy, old girl,* I told myself. *You're on familiar ground here. Nothing to be afraid of.*

For a moment, Evie said nothing. Her eyes had that extreme unfocused look that I had come to associate with moments of the otherworldly. Unfocused on anything in particular, but seeing *something.* Her silence made me even more nervous. Suddenly my chest felt tight, constricted; the air, thin. My fingers opened and closed by my thighs, clawing at something unseen. I gasped once, twice. There was a light in the darkness, a mere pinprick, teasing me, taunting me. I couldn't get air, I couldn't breathe, the blackness was too much, too thick, it was smothering me . . .

CHAPTER 2

My grasping fingers closed over something and I seized hold of it, willing it to pull me out.

"Maggie?"

My breath coming in short gasps, I felt my eyelids flutter open. "I — Evie?"

Evie's sweet china doll eyes stared into mine, probing deep. Her hand squeezed mine, and it was only then that I realized I'd grabbed hold of hers. *My lifeline.* "Are you okay?"

I shook myself, searching my memory for the helpful hints Felicity had given me for shaking off residual energy. Deep breaths, in through the nose, out through the mouth, and let the energy ground, or flow, down into the earth. "I'm okay," I managed at last. "Really. You?"

She nodded. "I thought I saw something, down the street."

"A little boy?" I asked, my voice fainter

than I'd hoped.

"Little boy, red ball. He disappeared into the river."

"I saw him this morning." I tried not to shiver. This morning was the first time I had actually *seen* anything, as opposed to merely sensing a shift in energies. To have it corroborated as more than imagination . . . well, I felt a little like I'd tumbled down the proverbial rabbit hole. Any minute now, I'd spy a big fat cat perched atop the far bookshelf or something, eyeing me with a maniacal grin.

Her pale eyebrows stretched ceilingward. "Wow. Two sightings. It must mean something."

I didn't want to think about what it might mean. I cleared my throat. "Not necessarily."

"Hmm. Well, I guess it might have been an energy imprint. An echo of a memory. You felt something?"

I squirmed, saved from answering in the nick of time by the tinkling of the front door chimes. A teenaged girl slouched in, her dark head bent low, shoulders hunched in the indolent stance of the perpetually misunderstood. With kohl-smudged eyes, chunky shagged hair, a jumble of the kind of costume jewelry guaranteed to attract glares from conservative Stony Millers, and clothes that were black, black, and more black . . . all signs confirmed my first impression. A beatnik reincarnated in the Modern Goth tradition.

I smiled at her as she wandered near, but she drifted past without meeting my gaze. Instead she moved aimlessly among the stacks, picking up the occasional tchotchke, running her finger along the edge of a shelf, always with that same faintly bored sneer.

Evie edged nearer before speaking. "Hi, Tara," she offered shyly, raising her hand with a halfhearted wave.

Goth Girl scarcely flicked a gunked-up eyelash. "Hi. Evie, right? You working here?"

"Just helping out. You know, Christmas?"

"Sweet."

Goth Girl went back to her disinterested browsing. I raised my eyebrows at Evie. Evie cast a cautious glance toward her school-mate's retreating back, then unobtrusively reached for a scratch pad and pen and scribbled out a message in her precise schoolgirl script. *Tara Murphy,* the note read. *New to town. Eleventh grade. Kind of a loner, but never bothers me . . .*

I wasn't so old that I had forgotten what it was like to suffer through teenage angst and insecurities — poised as I was on the cusp of the Big Three-Oh and feeling the pain, angst was something I was all too familiar with. Unlike Tara Murphy, I now possessed experience to either talk me down or back me up when I felt like thumbing my nose at the world. What I was looking at here was pure Grade A rebellious youth. I could deal with it, even though her bored procession through the store I took such pride in seriously rankled. The myriad lotions and soaps rated only a cursory sniff. Antique linens, soft as butter after decades of weekly launderings, were bypassed without a second glance. Books, china, teas, chocolates . . . nothing. I had begun to wonder why she'd ventured into Enchantments at all when she scuffed unexpectedly to a halt before the scarred antique counter.

"Yo." She looked me up and down. "I've never been in here before, so I'll bite. Where do you keep it?"

I masterfully retained my patience. "It?"

"You know. The witch stuff."

The implied *Duh* was pretty hard to miss. But in the last two months I'd fielded quite a number of less-than-friendly overtures from certain female members of Stony Mill's up-and-coming leisure class — you know, the ones with the bony asses, brittle smiles, and sharp glances who customarily stormed the store en masse like fashionably dressed lemmings — so I could certainly manage a single sarcastic teenager. I was a professional. I could handle it. Besides, at that moment I was more interested in how a teenage girl, new to town, had come by her awareness of Enchantments' behind-the-scenes purpose. We didn't exactly advertise.

"Which . . . stuff?" I echoed, purposely obtuse.

She sized me up a moment before attempting a meaningful smile. "You don't have to worry about me. I won't blow it for you. My cousin clued me in that this was where I needed to go for supplies. So, wouldja mind telling me where to look? Got some secret stash somewhere, or what?"

She made it sound like we were trafficking in illegal substances, for heaven's sake. I opened my mouth to steer her away gently, but Evie appeared at my elbow again.

"I'll show her. Come on, Tara. This way."

I wasn't sure I was comfortable with it, but I didn't have time to worry much. The stairway door had just closed behind the two girls when the front chimes sounded again. I looked up and broke into a grin. "Gen! What a surprise. Doing some shopping this morning?"

Like Evie, Genevieve Valmont was another member of the N.I.G.H.T.S. She was also a former nun who had left the church for reasons unknown, which gave her a unique perspective when it came to the spiritual theories behind the afterlife. As big as a man, and usually dressed like one, Gen was never to be found without a dog-eared romance novel in the back pocket of her oversized overalls. If that seemed a contradiction, well, we all knew the truth of the matter. Genevieve Valmont's heart was as vast and deep as the mighty Great Lakes, and after her many years spent worshipping at the feet of Christ, she now secretly yearned for a flesh-and-blood man to fill the void. I couldn't say that I blamed her. I'd been preoccupied with that topic myself of late.

"Hello, sweetie. Thought I'd pop into town for a bit of Christmas cheer. My, the store looks good!" She beamed over all the sparkling white lights, silver ribbons, and fragrant evergreens. "I've been rattling around that old bait store for days, waiting for the weather to cooperate so ice fishing can finally kick in. Thought maybe I'd get a bit of the Christmas list pared down."

"Well, you've come to the right place. Have any idea what you're looking for? I could point you in the right direction."

"No need. I think I'll just peep about a bit, if it's all right with you. Maybe something you have in here will spark some ideas."

"Take your time. Want a cup of tea?"

"Mmm, you talked me into it. Yes, please."

"Chai?"

"Pekoe. Plain."

"You got it."

She followed me over to the snack counter. "So . . . how's that young man of yours?"

I made a face as I strained the steaming water over the tea sachet. "If you mean Tom Fielding, he's not mine. In fact, I haven't even spoken with Deputy Fielding since Felicity was released from custody. And when I ran into him the other day at the grocery store, he ducked behind the frozen foods and pretended he didn't see me. I don't know about you, but I just don't think that screams Lasting Relationship."

Tom had caught my eye in October, but following a difference of opinion, he had disappeared faster than I could say, "I'm sorry." What's a girl to do when she falls for a guy who has closed himself down to the experience? I was still working that out for myself.

Gen trailed her work-roughened fingertips

31

over the brightly hued canisters of gourmet teas that Felicity liked to import from her native Britain. "Hmm. Well, never say never, hon. From what I hear, there was a real spark to him when he talked to you. Sparks like that don't just go out without some doing."

Considering that his last words were filled with hurt and suspicion amid the shattered glass of Enchantments' skylight windows and the red-blue strobe of police lights, I rather doubted that.

I was saved from further conjecture over my love life (or absence thereof) by the arrival of a group of girls who breezed into the store on a swell of giggles and squeals. I'd had enough experience at Enchantments to know their group's presence probably wouldn't mean a sale, but at least it would serve as a distraction. Leaving Gen with steaming cup in hand, I stopped by the cash register to don my Shopper's Helper hat. Literally. Everyone loves a Christmassy atmosphere this time of year, so Evie and I had adopted fuzzy green Santa hats, complete with a fluffy pompon dangling from the tip that lit up with multicolor lights powered by a hidden battery pack. Snicker if you like, but Enchantments had seen a steady flow of paying customers despite the flagging economy, and I liked to think the atmosphere here had something to do with it.

The girls had their backs to me, purses slung casually over their shoulders. Unlike Goth Girl, these three wore fashionably flared low-rise jeans and pretty leather jackets that just skimmed their narrow hips. I moved into their side view. "Can I show you girls something?"

The tallest turned in my direction. I recognized her as a girl my sister Mel used to baby-sit, years ago. Only then she'd been just a kid, a doctor's smart-mouthed daughter with freckles across the bridge of her nose and hair the color of the sun. The young woman she'd turned into was polished and obviously self-assured as she turned to me. I saw her gaze drift northward to take in my hat, and for a moment her lips twisted in a smirk. "Yes, actually. My mother saw an antique clock in here the other day. Wendy Roberson?"

"Yes, of course I remember Mrs. Roberson. And you must be Mandy Lynn."

The smirk transformed into a chilly smile. "Amanda, actually."

Oh. Okay. "You probably don't remember me. My sister used to watch you during summer breaks."

"How nice." She didn't even blink.

Her mother had been a lot nicer. It appeared Mandy — er, Amanda — had grown up in more ways than one. I pasted on my best Difficult Customer smile. "You'll be wanting to see the clock. I believe it was just over here, if you'll follow me?"

The clock, a delicate Moroccan-influenced mantelpiece in deep reds and golds, was a specialty piece imported from Spain. It clocked in at just under five hundred dollars.

"I don't like it," said a petite thing with sleek chin-length hair, crinkling her nose. The blond highlights in her light brown hair were so artfully done, it was hard to tell what was natural and what was not. "It's too dark and too old. I mean, couldn't they even fix the face? It's all cracked and wrinkled."

"*You* don't have to like it," Amanda told her bluntly. "This little baby is guaranteed to get me out of the doghouse. Trust me — my mom is dying to have this on her bedroom mantel. And besides, it's an antique. The face is supposed to be wrinkled. It's not like they have Botox for clocks, you know." To me she said, "Wrap it up, please. I'll take it."

I tried very hard not to show surprise

when she opened her purse and took out a wallet brimming with green. What on earth was a seventeen-year-old girl doing with that much cash? I mean, sure, it was Christmastime, and people would be more likely to have money on them, but . . . *wow.* I carried the clock to the counter. "Would you like to select a wrapping paper?"

She scarcely looked at them and fluttered a hand at me. "Oh . . . anything. Whatever you think my mother would like."

Evie and Goth Girl Tara emerged from the hall as I made my way behind the counter. "Oh, good. Evie, would you mind grabbing a box out of the back for me? A one-by-one-by-two should do just fine. We'll just fill in the spaces with popcorn and bubble."

I was so preoccupied with my task of preparing the clock for its nest that I didn't even realize the atmosphere in the shop had shifted until Amanda spoke.

"Well, what do we have here, girls?"

Distracted, I glanced up to find Evie hadn't moved an inch, while before my wondering eyes a standoff worthy of the Old West was unfolding. Tara Murphy was standing frozen in place, books clutched against her chest, her dark-rimmed eyes narrowed dangerously while the three Junior

Miss candidates circled like sleek wolves around her. Amanda, in what I could only assume was the usual lead position, stalked closer to her, her face alive with predatory anticipation. She grabbed the books out of Tara's hands. "*To Ride a Silver Broomstick? The Witch's Book of Spells and Power?*" She looked up at Tara in surprise. "You've got to be kidding."

Tara stared her down, but said nothing.

Amanda laughed. "A witch. Evidently we have a witch in town, girls. Right here, under our very noses, in fact. What next? Vampires? Werewolves? Leprechauns?" She made a *booga-booga* flare of her fingers at Tara's face. "Spooky."

Had it been turned my way, Tara's face would have scared me to death. "Back . . . off!" she growled.

"Or what?" Amanda countered with a daring born of a lifetime of knowing exactly who she was. "You'll put a spell on us? Hex us? *Please.*" She held one of the books up by the corner as though it was a pair of dirty underwear. "Where do you get books like these?"

Well, now. Time to step in. "Excuse me. Evie? Box. Please. Ms. Roberson, I need your approval of a gift card."

Evie snapped out of her daze and scurried

away. Tara yanked her books out of Amanda's hands. Each narrowed her eyes at the other, two cats sizing up an adversary and getting ready to let the claws fly. Tara's pale face was high with color. Amanda curled her lip in a cruel sneer. Then she laughed and turned back toward me, an all-too-obvious dismissal. Behind her, Tara's face burned even brighter.

"I'd like the card to say, '*Merry Christmas from your most brilliant daughter, with love . . . Amanda,*' " she told me. "My mom will just die when she gets this."

Under her breath, Tara muttered, "Too bad it couldn't be her '*brilliant daughter*' instead."

The other girls exchanged amused looks and sang out in unison, "*Oooh.*"

Slowly Amanda turned. "What did you say?"

With the situation sinking quickly in the direction of debacle or worse, I was relieved when Evie reappeared with the box. "Thanks, hon. Why don't you take Tara back to the office while I finish up here? Do you mind?"

Evie shook her head. "Tara?"

For a moment I thought our Goth customer would refuse. She whipped her head toward me in wordless fury, her eyes shooting sparks. It occurred to me that she assumed I was in league with the three, that I was banishing her from the room as I might a naughty child. Knowing that the others could not see, I closed one eye in a quick wink. A flicker of surprise cooled the heat of her glare, but my countermovement worked like a charm. With a rude sound, Tara turned on her chunky boot heel and stalked off toward the purple velvet curtains that separated the storefront from the office in the rear, leaving Evie to scurry along in her wake.

"What a little bitch. Or should I say, witch?" Amanda was saying to her friends, just low enough that Tara was certain not to hear. "Can you believe that?"

"Not worth the time or the trouble," the perky brunette chimed in, tossing her curls. "She's just jealous, you know."

"Well, of course she's jealous," Amanda sneered, causing her friend's cheeks to flush prettily. "You know, I could almost feel sorry for her, if she wasn't such a head case. I can't believe they let people like that walk the streets without attendants. I mean, anyone can get Prozac nowadays. It's obvious she's completely mental."

The dark-haired girl laughed quickly with Amanda, but for a moment the sleek-headed blonde hesitated. "Maybe," she almost whispered, "but . . . you know . . . maybe we should just leave her alone. It's not worth —"

Amanda silenced the blonde with a nail-sharp gaze, and she lowered her eyes immediately. I had a feeling things were rarely calm in Amanda Lynn Roberson's neck of the woods. Probably she'd never heard of that old adage, Live and let live. Amanda seemed more the type to seek and destroy.

Before another catfight could erupt, I decided to forgo a fancy ribbon and slapped a large bow on the package instead before turning to the register to ring up the sale. Out of the corner of my eye, I caught sight of Gen at the lotions display shelves. From her stance, I could tell she was listening in. "That'll be four eighty-nine ninety-two."

Amanda pulled the cash from her wallet. I couldn't help noticing that the purchase was nowhere near to cleaning her out. I sighed, wistfully.

With her change I included the receipt, which she carelessly tucked into her pocket. "Thank you. Happy holidays," I told her. Ignoring me, she picked up the box and her friends headed for the exit. I breathed a sigh of relief when the door closed with a jangle that parodied my nerves.

Gen headed over almost immediately. She set two glass pots of Herbal Treasures hand cream on the counter, as well as a soft wrap in a shade of deep rose. "I couldn't resist this," she said, running the back of a work-roughened finger along the downy fabric. "Reminds me of my granny's shawl. Hers was crocheted, of course. I used to wrap up in it on cold winter days and lie on her divan for hours, reading and daydreaming. Lordy, that was a long time ago." With a tip of her head, she indicated the door, where the bell was still swinging wildly back and forth. "What was up with all that?"

"The usual petty teenage power wars. Egos run amuck. Pay no attention."

She nodded sagely. "That girl's sure got her mean on."

Truth be told, I was feeling a bit uneasy as well, but I was more willing to write it off as that stale bagel I'd eaten that morning. "You mean the little Goth girl?"

Gen shook her head. "Not her. The other one. I've seen it a thousand times, if I've seen it once. There's trouble there. Bad trouble. I could smell it."

"She's a real piece of work, that's for sure. A diva in the making."

"Making? Something tells me she's already there." She wrote out a check while I packed up her purchases. "Listen, honey, I know I don't need to tell you, but be careful, 'kay? There's something in the air lately."

So Gen was feeling it, too. And Evie. I did not need to know that.

When she had gone, I took a few deep, calming breaths to clear out any residual negative threads that might still be lingering before making my way to the store office . . . good psychic hygiene is always important, as I was beginning to find out. At least Evie had been able to keep Goth Girl, a.k.a. Tara, in the back until I could chase the girls from the store. Thank God for small favors. That much chaotic energy in one room was just a bit too much for me to handle at this stage of the game.

I pulled the velvet curtain aside. The sudden movement startled Evie, who nearly fell out of her chair when her elbow slipped off the edge of the desk. She righted herself quickly, looking sheepish. The laptop was open on the desk, angled away from me. Surfing the Web, I supposed. Tara was nowhere in sight.

"Hey," I said, smiling at her. "Where did our Dark and Dangerous friend go?"

"Oh, she left," Evie said, reaching out a hand to quickly press the laptop shut. "Out the back. The girls really got to her, I think. I mean, Tara and I, we're not what I would call friends or anything, but I kind of feel sorry for her."

I glanced around the office. "Did she leave the books somewhere?"

"Ohmigosh." Evie looked stricken. "She still had them when she left."

I sighed. "Well, don't worry about it. It's not like she's going to leave town over something like that."

"I'm really sorry, Maggie. I should have thought —"

"Hey, no worries. It'll all work out." Not that it was any of my business, but I couldn't help wondering what else Evie knew about the feuding girls. Their exchange had been so heated, it took catty to a whole new level. Clearing my throat, I said, "So, what was all that about? Someone steal someone's boyfriend?"

"You mean those girls? I don't think it's anything that complicated. Amanda is always picking on Tara. Well, she picks on a lot of people — she kind of thinks of herself as SMHS royalty, you know? — but I think she likes to torture Tara best of all. The other day at lunch, it was so bad that Tara totally lost her cool and Amanda's boyfriend had to peel her off before she pummeled her." She shook her head. "It's awful, really. Tara never stood a chance when she moved to town."

I'd been through much the same scene myself in school. I decided to cut Tara some slack. It sounded to me like she could use it.

CHAPTER 3

If Saturday came in with a bang, at least the
rest of it went off without a hitch. We'd done
a brisk business the entire day, owing in
part, no doubt, to the fact that Christmas
was less than three weeks away. Since I
needed to reconcile the books for Felicity's
upcoming meeting with the accountant, I
took the store laptop home with me, along
with a portable case full of files. I figured if
I was going to be working on a Saturday
night rather than enjoying a hot date with
(a.k.a. interviewing) a prime candidate for
the role of future father of my children, at
least I could do it in my PJs and bunny slippers with Thomas Magnum, PI (a.k.a. the
love of my life) to keep me company.

Hey, it's my life, and I can cry if I want
to.

Dusk had more than fallen by the time I
pulled Christine to a halt at the curb beside
the Willow Street Victorian I called home. It

44

had dropped toward earth like a hungry predator dive-bombing its dinner. Little more than a sapphire glow glimmered in the soft fringe of the horizon; the rest of the night sky was a void, a black so dense even the stars couldn't seem to penetrate. I shook off that vague sense of uneasiness the night never failed to instill in me as I lugged the file case, the laptop, and my purse toward the sunken entrance.

Now, a basement apartment might not fit everyone's notion of the ideal apartment for a hip young woman on the go, but beggars cannot afford to be choosy. The apartment had three things going for it: It was semiaffordable, which for a girl who hasn't managed to win the state lottery is a Very Good Thing; its size meant I was never going to have to host my family for dinner; and finally, my best friend Steff lived on the upper level, which made for some really fun times on those evenings when Steff tired of her usual action-packed nightlife. Generally speaking, I was pretty happy there.

The spirit or spirits inhabiting my apartment notwithstanding.

I felt my way step-by-step down the dark stairs, muttering under my breath that I really needed to invest in a motion sensor for my light one of these days. The dead bolt presented a moment's irritation, but it took only a moment of wrestling with the key in the worn lock before the tumblers clicked into place and the door swung soundlessly inward. I took a deep, centering breath and counted to ten.

No fear.

Stepping over the threshold, I dropped everything into a chair and flipped the nearest switch, my eyes touching everywhere in the living room-cum-foyer-cum-kitchen at once. So much for no fear. But the room was empty, the lights shone steadily, and the shadows in the corners were just pockets of darkness and not the hidey-holes of some nameless fear. Relaxing my guard, I decided that dinner was the first order of the evening. That, and the blinking message light on my answering machine. I punched the flashing red button and listened to the familiar warning that I had one new message.

"Margaret, this is your mother speaking," her voice intoned, phone-formal as always. "Not home today, I see. I don't know if you'd received a letter like the one I received or not, but I wanted to be sure to let you know that Dr. Phillips is closing his practice. I wish him all the best, of course, but somehow I don't think he realizes he's leaving all of his loyal patients in the lurch. Anyway, dear, I took it upon myself to schedule your yearly. Dr. Phillips's receptionist let it slip that they'd had a couple of cancellations for Tuesday, and since I knew you probably hadn't thought to do it yourself, I claimed one for myself and one for you. Yours is at eight o'clock. Melanie has a specialist in the city now, so she wasn't an issue. I didn't think you'd mind — it's so much better to get it out of the way with someone you're familiar with, I think. Anyway, call me later to let me know you've received this message. Your father says hello, and Grandpa Gordon says to tell you that his teeth have been bothering him and he's thinking about changing his adhesive. Well, that's all for now. Don't forget, Tuesday, eight a.m. Good-bye."

One new message, and it was a doozy. Only *my* mother would take it upon herself to schedule an annual physical for her nearly thirty-year-old daughter.

I sighed and pressed the DELETE key with a little more force than was probably necessary. To distract myself from my motherly woes, I dialed Steff's number as I rummaged through the refrigerator.

"Hello?"

Steff's voice sounded in my ear, as low-pitched and self-assured as ever. My best friend of nearly twenty years was my emotional opposite. Confident where I was insecure, settled in her career as a nurse, whereas mine had always seemed in a state of flux, and petite and delicate where I was, well, *not,* she represented everything I'd always wished I could be . . . and yet she loved me just the way I was, and I loved her like a sister. "Hiya, neighbor."

"Oh . . . hi, Mags! What's up?"

"I, uh, couldn't help noticing that the good doctor's Jag is conspicuously absent this evening," I said as I hauled a box of processed cheese and a tub of margarine out of my refrigerator. Dr. Danny Tucker was a resident at the local hospital and the latest love interest in a long line of the same that had found their respective ways to Steff's doorstep. The two had been going hot and heavy since October, as evidenced by the ever-present antique Jaguar usually parked at our curbside, and I had the unwatched episodes of *Magnum* to prove it. "In light of that, I don't suppose you'd care to indulge in a little bit of harmless ogling of our favorite guy."

There was a slight pause on the other end of the line. I heard it. "Um, sure. Yeah, I can come down for a little while."

It didn't take a genius . . . "Danny's on his way over," I guessed, knowing I was right.

"Well, yes . . ." Steff admitted. "You know how crazy his schedule is. He pops in for a bite or a little shut-eye whenever he can."

It made sense, really. Our Victorian was only two blocks away from the hospital while Danny's condo was on the south side, across the river. But knowing that didn't stop the little dart of jealousy that accompanied her words. "Oh. If you don't want to . . ."

"No, it's okay. Just let me jot him a note and I'll be down in a sec."

I laid out a pair of plates and quickly put together a matching set of grilled cheese sandwiches with sliced tomatoes. The sandwiches were toasting on the griddle when Steff poked her head inside my door. "Knock knock!"

I held out a plate of the not-so-gourmet fare. *"Pour vous, mademoiselle. Bon appetit."*

Her face froze in a pained grimace. "Oh. Well, that's really nice, honey, but . . ." Her voice trailed off. Finally she shrugged in embarrassment. "You see, I have a couple of steaks marinating upstairs. Hey, why don't I bring you one down later? It's really too much for me, and God knows I've put

49

on ten pounds since I met Danny anyway. All those romantic dinners aren't exactly conducive to feeling the burn. Well, at least not *that* kind of burn."

She tossed her curls with a saucy grin, and I laughed, ready to forgive her. Ah, well. This guy, too, would pass. Unless he was The One. But the likelihood of that . . .

Out of the corner of my eye I caught Steff trying to sneak a glance at the clock on my stove. My heart sank.

I set her plate on the kitchen counter and bustled around the living room trying to look busy. "I think we've missed about eight or ten episodes altogether, but . . ." I peeked back at her while I pawed through the tapes, and my heart sank even further. I turned to face her. "Steff. Your heart's not in this. It's all right, you know. I don't mind if you don't want to do this now."

"Really?" She actually looked relieved. That hurt.

"Really," I said firmly, pushing the green-eyed monster firmly down in the hole he was trying to crawl from. "Really really. The *Magnum* reruns will keep. Danny's important to you."

She bit her lip. "Oh, but you're important, too . . . but, well, to be completely honest, I was wanting to get those steaks on, and it seems like I never have time anymore to get the apartment really clean, and —"

"Consider me the human version of TiVo. I'll be here when you're ready."

She gave me a tight hug. "Thanks for understanding, Mags. What would I do without you?"

I patted her on the shoulder, doing my best not to let her see my misgivings. But damn, she *was* serious about him. Scarily serious. It wasn't that I wasn't happy for Steff — I was, really and truly — but only that Steff falling in love heralded the end to an era. Our entire adult lives had been spent going from one dating experience to the next, taste-testing men, so to speak. Some of them had been the male equivalents of sour milk, some fine wines, and still others faint disappointments, like a failed soufflé. For Steff, at least, that journey might soon be over. And we all know what happens then: Best Friends Forever somehow turn into former best friends who send out annual Christmas cards that are somehow meant to be a substitute for once-a-week lunch dates, promising to *"get together soon to catch up."* Could minivans and soccer mom bleacher butt be far behind?

I watched her go with a troubled heart before making a nest of my favorite chair, a deep-seated monster wingback that once belonged to my grandparents. True, it was barf green in color, but it was the most comfortable chair you could ever hope to sit in. Therefore, it had survived the young adulthood of my twenties whereas my occasional boyfriends had not.

It all came down to proving worthy.

With my grilled cheese on the end table next to me and work files on a TV tray to the right, I plugged in the lap-top's power cord and settled it on my knees, Indian style, before hitting PLAY on the remote.

But tonight I couldn't seem to get into the Hawaiian beaches and tropical waters. Not even Magnum's trademark dimples or sparkling blue eyes could hold my attention. My mind drifted as I sorted canceled checks, marked them in the accounting software, recorded bills of sale against the list of store inventory, and entered the new inventory that had arrived that week. Even my dinner lay forgotten with only two bites taken from it. I didn't know the reason for my jitteriness and lack of focus, but I knew if I waited long enough, the universe would present it to me.

The explanation came in the form of the Internet browser.

I flashed back to this morning, when I'd

surprised Evie after the Troublesome Trio had vacated the building. Evie had been in the office with Tara, the little Goth Girl, presumably surfing the Internet. You know, come to think of it, Evie *had* looked a little funny when I'd pulled back the curtain. She'd nearly fallen out of the chair, and then — was I making too much of this? — had most definitely and purposely closed the laptop before I could see what she was doing. Had the two girls surfed their way into someplace they shouldn't have been?

There was one way to find out.

It was something my mother would have done, but I pushed that thought to the back of my mind. How else was a girl supposed to know what was going on in the world around her? Resolutely I opened the browser to "Work Offline" status, then clicked on the Web History icon. A list of websites accessed that day immediately popped up. I wasn't surprised to find that there was but a single entry under Saturday — we'd had nonstop business the entire day — but I was a little surprised to find that it was only the innocuous and oft-visited www.SunnyStonyMill.com.

SunnyStonyMill.com was a fairly recent development sponsored by the Stony Mill Chamber of Commerce. Part virtual marketplace, part community bulletin board, SunnyStonyMill.com had been instituted by the town council to drag Stony Mill residents kicking and screaming into the twenty-first century. A place where store owners could hawk their wares and connect with potential customers, a place where residents of all ages and with interests that ran the gamut could find others of like mind. Part of Evie's job was to update the store web page with whatever new stock we'd received that week. Maybe she'd been showing Tara her handiwork.

But why had she behaved so guiltily when I'd walked into the office?

I'd earned a break, so I connected the laptop to my phone line (not being a technical girl-wonder, the phone cord to the answering machine caused a moment's confusion, but I prevailed) and clicked Connect, then pointed the cursor at SunnyStonyMill in the history.

That's when things went a bit crazy.

Instead of being taken to the Enchantments page as expected, the screen flashed at me — black, red, black — in quick succession. My eyebrows shot up. Oh, *shit.* I'd read about the ways viruses and hackers can attack your PC, but I'd never actually encountered one. Was that what this was? A virtual highjacking? What should I do? Disconnect? Shut down?

It wasn't that I didn't know how to use a computer. It was just that my know-how was limited to things like downloading e-mail, using various softwares, and the point-and-click atmosphere of the Web. This was different. This was unfamiliar territory. This was intimidating. Staring at this black screen, I felt totally vulnerable.

Come on, Maggie. Don't let some cyber-jerk push you around. It can't hurt to close the window, can it?

Well . . .

Hoping for the best, I slid the mouse arrow up to the X in the corner and tapped the touch pad. Instead of seeing the window close down, however, a message box blipped to life in the center of the screen. *Password?* it prompted, with a blank space and a button each for Go and Close. I selected Close, figuring it had to be the safest choice. To my relief, the window disappeared without any further ado. It also severed my connection.

Talk about coitus interruptus.

I stared at the computer, wondering what just happened. The SunnyStonyMill.com website had never behaved that way before. After a moment's consideration, I decided to reconnect. This time, when I opened the Internet browser, I typed the URL into the address bar myself.

The front page of SunnyStonyMill.com popped up, easy as you please, with its usual brand of down-home corn and country charm. Swiftly I ran through the menus until I picked up the Enchantments pages. Felicity had hired out the website creation to Marcus Quinn, her magical partner who, as it turned out, also knew a thing or two about computers. Picturing the lean, lanky, and darkly sexy Marcus in my mind's eye, I had to admit I would never have believed him to be a closet techno-geek. Funny how appearances can deceive.

The Enchantments page was only a little over a month old, but the website was already making an impressive impact on our bottom line. Was it a true upward trend? Only time would tell, but both Liss and I had high hopes for its success. Thanks to the big-city tax refugees flooding into our housing and market base, retail property values in Stony Mill had skyrocketed in recent months. The extra sales helped to ensure the continuation of a physical brick-and-mortar presence for Enchantments, which as a side benefit ensured my continued employment. Always a good thing in my book.

The elegantly feminine site was at odds with its leather jacket–wearing designer, but that was Liss's influence. Her presence was everywhere, from the lacy background and warm colors to the unexpected details. I selected a few items from the menus. Everything loaded quickly and without incident.

Nothing strange about that.

Finally, as an experiment, I reopened the history and clicked on the exact link Evie had used earlier. And there, once again, was the strange strobing screen, black, to red, to black again.

What. The. Heck?

Something was going on. I could feel it, that prickly skin, hair-on-end sense of trouble not far ahead.

Uneasy now, I X-ed the black window and was again presented with the *Password?* prompt.

So it wasn't a fluke. I didn't think so, but I had to be sure.

I closed the prompt and watched as once more the Internet connection was severed by some unseen directive.

Spooky.

With fingers that trembled from a sudden influx of nervous energy, I removed the modem connection and plugged the phone back in.

I didn't know who or what was behind it, but I had a feeling I'd be finding out. Like it or not.

The phone jangled at my left elbow. Heart pounding, I stared at it and grabbed the receiver.

"Hello?"

"Maggie, thank goodness you're home. Oh my God, did you hear?"

As I'd been half expecting to hear my mom's ever-chiding tone, Evie's breathless voice in my ear confused me. "Hey, Evie. Hear what?"

"It's Amanda Roberson. They can't find her, Maggie. She didn't show up for her shift at the hotel registration desk tonight, so the manager called her mom. Mrs. Roberson's been calling all over town all night long, but no one's seen her."

I stopped breathing. "You're kidding, right?"

"I wish I was."

Evie sniffled, and I could hear in her voice that she was hovering on the edge of tears. And I understood. It wasn't that she was close to Amanda Roberson. It was the threat to her naïve teenaged view of the world. With my own world teetering in those gray areas between myth and reality, oh, boy, did

I understand.

"Hey, don't panic," I soothed. "Is it possible she could have taken off somewhere? Maybe she wanted to be with someone she didn't want her mom to know about? I mean, it's possible she'll turn up tonight after all, right?"

"I guess so. But Maggie, I have a bad feeling about this. Really bad."

Truth be told, so did I. But she didn't need to hear that just now. "I'm sure she'll turn up, Evie."

"I know. But after what happened to Mrs. Harding last fall . . . well, you know. It's got me feeling a little twitchy."

"I know. Tell you what — it's late. Let's just see what happens by morning, 'kay? Keep me posted on what you hear?"

" 'Kay. Oh, and Maggie? Thanks for listening. I know you probably think I'm overreacting, but it's nice of you to let me talk."

"Any time, honey. She'll turn up, you'll see."

But Amanda didn't turn up.

I'd been out of bed since seven, munching on grapes and putting the finishing touches on the bookwork I'd started the night before. By nine-fifteen I was just closing the laptop with a satisfied sigh when my phone rang again.

"She didn't show, Maggie. Tiffany Coleson called me this morning. Her mom heard it from Joline Davis's mom, who's best friends with Mrs. Roberson. The police have been out all night, driving the county roads looking for her. I guess usually the rule for a missing persons case is twenty-four hours, but they make an exception when the person's underage."

Last night Evie's voice had been fearful, breathless with worry. This morning what I heard was grim resignation.

Evie told me she was headed out the door to church with her mom and dad. "Tiffany and I both attend the same church, and we're going to hold a vigil for her with the youth group. Light some candles, pray. You know? I wish we could do more."

My mind was reeling. Somehow it seemed impossible to associate the vibrant, self-assured young woman of yesterday morning with a possible missing persons case. What on earth was happening to this town? "Do they . . . do they know who she was with? What she was doing?"

"I wish I knew. I don't know her well enough to even guess." She paused a moment. "I was wondering . . . Do you think maybe your friend Tom might tell you what's going on? What they know? If we can help in some way . . ."

I knew the way she meant, but I honestly didn't see how psychic reaching could help. Besides, Tom and I had never quite arrived at friendship when he turned his back on me, and he definitely wasn't the type to be comfortable with Evie's kind of assistance. "Er . . . I don't think so, Evie."

"Please, Maggie? I just feel like we should be doing everything we can to help. Please?"

I heaved a sigh. "Oh . . . I guess. I'll try to find out what I can. Okay? But I can't promise anything."

"Bless you. Listen, I'll talk to you later. My mom and dad are waiting in the car, and my dad's pointing at his watch and squinching up his face like he's got indigestion or heartburn or an IRS audit or something. I gotta go."

So that's how I found myself joining the volunteer crew who were out that morning beating the bushes and haunting the back roads for any sign of the missing teen. It was, admittedly, against type for me. Not that I was a girly-girly prima donna, but I would never go so far as to consider myself an outdoorsy kind of girl. Despite the sudden plunging temps that signaled an end to our temporary warm spell, I hadn't even thought to don a pair of long johns and boots, or anything more protective than my favorite wool coat and a pair of fuzzy mittens. The volunteer in charge was PC enough to refrain from open skepticism and gave me the easier (and warmer) assignment of driving up and down a segment of roads on the southwest end of town to keep an eye out for Amanda's missing silver Corolla. Of course, Christine's heater had not worked right in years, so I still found myself having to sit on one hand or the other for warmth while I puttered up and down side street after side street, slowing to a crawl with any flash of silver metallic paint I caught sight of.

A stranger traveling through Stony Mill that morning might have seen nothing out of the ordinary. Tree-lined streets remained mostly devoid of traffic as church bells rang out over the midmorning mists, calling the faithful to come home to worship. It was only upon deeper reflection that some of the elements of strangeness might register: The police cars that roved restlessly en masse rather than sleeping quietly in their usual berths outside of the downtown station house. The sheer numbers of hunters and outdoorsmen, dressed stem to stern in blaze orange Carhartts as they prowled in packs along roadside ditches, shotguns oddly absent. The search crew that operated from the snack trailer at the high school football field. The churches, parking lots full, chapels empty.

And the quiet. A threatening quality in the air. A rumbling of trouble.

Or maybe that was just my stomach.

With the exception of the restaurants, gas stations, and churches, Stony Mill proper had closed down at noon the day before. Around here, Sunday was a day of rest, a day of family, weekend sports, and of course, worship. Church attendance was a given in this town, a custom few dared to rebel against. I was one of the misguided few, much to my mother's everlasting dismay. I hadn't been to Mass in over a year, and my attendance had been spotty for several before that. I just couldn't bring myself to believe anymore, you know? Maybe I'd grown tired of the hypocrisy of the so-called faithful who trotted out their piety for their friends and neighbors, but forgot what it meant when no one was looking.

And yet none of the petty stuff mattered this misty morning, as the town pulled together to search for one of its own.

I'd run through the bulk of my assignment without a sign of the missing teenager or her car. I'd saved the hardest area for last — a run-through of the old backwater Riverside Park. Really, it was little more than a grassy turnaround strip along the edge of the river. Once it had been a popular picnicking spot, but today it boasted nothing more than a couple of rickety picnic tables and a rust-bucket basketball hoop on a crumbling pad. Sure, it was a little on the disreputable side, but it was harmless enough on a winter afternoon.

Somehow the park was the last place I wanted to be today.

I hadn't been down this way in years. Back when I was a bored teenager, in a world slightly less jaded and dangerous, I had on occasion made an appearance at the park with other similarly bored teens looking for a little gab, some crunching rock sounds, and a bit of harmless flirtation. I'd had my first kiss down here (ahh, fond memories) . . . But that was then. Things always seemed to change, didn't they? Over the years, the teen element at the park had become seedier. Drugs had replaced the occasional beer, the music had turned angry, restless, and the harmless flirtations had . . . well, let's just say the things that went on down here were better kept behind closed doors. What was left was more than sad. It was depressing.

This place needed some serious healing energy. There was little I could do for the place today beyond a grimace and a quick prayer. Maybe come spring I could assemble a volunteer cleanup crew to spruce the place up.

Just a quick look, I told myself as I bumped to a halt in the rutted turnabout and set the parking brake with a ratchety creak. Just enough to discharge my duty to Amanda, Evie, and my own sense of conscience. Amanda was probably safe at home by now anyway, after a night of illicit misbehavior with some studly young bohunk. Around Stony Mill, missing teens rarely stayed missing for long.

Thank goodness.

I sat in the car, listening to the engine cool with an occasional high-pitched ping. Waiting. Bending forward over the steering wheel, I peered through the windshield. The morning mists had dissipated, bullied aside by storm clouds that now hunkered over the area like a glowering mother bear. A breath of air twisted a smattering of leaves into a coil that slithered over the broken asphalt and disappeared down the incline into the wooded river's edge. That was where I'd be heading, too. My mind made up, I reached for the door latch and stepped out.

For being early afternoon, the light out here looked somehow wrong. Cold. Hard. Brittle, as though at any moment the façade of reality might splinter away, revealing the awful truth beneath. And as I stood there, frozen upon the edge of awareness, I felt it: that shiver at the nape of my neck. It was subtle at first. Closing my eyes, I turned my focus upon it. Breathing. Searching. Testing.

There was energy at work here. It percolated along on the invisible astral tide, just beyond the structural borders of what most people considered reality.

I wasn't most people. Not anymore.

I stuffed my fists deep into the pockets of my wool coat. With my shoulders hunched up, a ward against lingering forces unseen more than a defense against the cold ribbon of air attempting to worm its way down my collar, I waited for a sense of direction. It didn't take long. From the corner of my eye I caught a flash of movement down by the leaden strip of river water glimmering sullenly through the barren tree branches. It was probably nothing, but I was duty bound to investigate. Maybe I'd hit the jackpot — maybe it'd turn out to be Amanda. Maybe after this we could all go home, stamp the cold out of our numb feet, and joke good-naturedly about the teenagers in our lives and the trials they put their families through.

Lured by the hopefulness of a happy ending, I scuffed carefully forward through an ankle-deep pocket of leaves some stray wind had deposited along the weedy strip of grass. Just ahead a footpath meandered through the spindly, waterlogged trees that inhabited the floodplain. The rubbish caught by the exposed tree roots gave clear evidence of the park's most common use. A tire moldered in the mud to the left of the path, complete with rusting wheel, the old rubber gleaming wetly black. To the right an old lawn mower stood on its side, its once sharp blade as jagged as a gap-toothed grin. Crushed beer cans, cigarette wrappers, drug paraphernalia — the flotsam of an uncaring world — all of it carelessly blemishing the park's natural beauty. And then there were other items I didn't want to get too close to. Things discarded by young men with partying on their minds and better things to do than worry about where they left vestiges of their DNA.

Ick.

As I rounded the last turn, I saw the cause of the movement, but it wasn't Amanda. Seated atop a large boulder that rested half in, half out of the water, long, coltish legs crossed like some kind of modern-day leprechaun, was Goth Girl. Tara Murphy.

The ways of the Universe were mysterious indeed. I'd hoped for Amanda, and instead was given her polar opposite. Go figure.

On second thought, maybe this was my chance to hit her up for the books she'd taken from the store. There was nothing wrong with taking advantage of an unexpected windfall. Could a grouchy teenager be considered a windfall?

"Hey there," I said by way of announcing my presence.

Tara's lug-soled boots flared out comically as she started at the sudden interruption of her solitude. Her head whipped toward me and for one unsettling moment her eyes blazed pure green fire. Almost before it began, the fury eased into puzzled recognition. "Oh. It's you."

I ignored the slam. It was so typically teen that I couldn't help flashing back to my own misguided youth. (*Sorry, Mom and Dad!*) Necessary mental atonements out of the way, I came to a halt beside the waist-high boulder. "Sorry if I scared you."

"You didn't."

"Good. Mind if I join you?"

"Suit yourself." She closed her eyes and settled herself more comfortably on the rock face. Lotus position, leggings-clad legs crossed, palms up.

There was a second, smaller boulder to the left of the path. I picked my way across the muddy grass and leaned a hip against it, watching her. Tara ignored my presence as long as she could while I focused all my concentration on her closed eyelids. When she could ignore me no longer, she slitted one green eye open and scowled. "Look, I don't mean to be rude —"

Of course she did.

"— but —"

There was always a "but."

"— you're messing up my auric field, you know what I mean?"

I nodded with false sympathy. "You'd prefer that I leave you to whatever it is that you're doing."

"Right. Now would be good."

"And what is it that you're doing?" I asked, glancing toward the simple round stone that lay in her palm. It was about the size of a half-dollar and thick enough to have some heft.

Tara rolled her eyes and heaved a long-suffering sigh. "Binding ritual, *hello.*"

I frowned, trying to connect her curt explanation with what I'd read so far. I knew bindings — spells used to control the will of another — were performed only in the direst circumstances, and only with an absolute absence of malice, unless you wanted to risk the same energy rebounding on you. Cosmic justice was known for its capricious nature. But the books on Felicity's recommended reading list were pure Metaphysics 101, more why-to than how-to.

What on earth could a young girl like Tara need to bind?

Tara waited impatiently for me to "get" it, but when it became obvious that wasn't going to happen, she gave me a look of bemusement. "You don't know much about the Craft, do you?"

"Obviously not enough."

"Huh. I did wonder. The other day, you know, when the Mod Squad did their usual Mean Girl act at your store? I mean, your selection there is pretty lame, ya gotta admit. All sweetness and light. When everybody knows you can't have the light without the darkness to balance it." Her eyes raked me. "So what are you, then, just some Fluffy

Bunny pagan?"

I'd never heard the term before, but by her tone . . . "Well, for one thing, what I am is my business, not yours. For another thing, it's my opinion that one can choose to follow the light, or be sucked in by the darkness. Either way, it's a conscious choice that each of us must make."

She curled her lip in a sneer. "Fluffy Bunny. Definitely."

I'd had enough of wallowing in teen angst. "Speaking of those girls at the store, I suppose you've heard that Amanda Roberson has gone missing."

She didn't even flinch. "Yeah. So?"

"Know anything about it?"

She snorted. "Has anyone checked with her boyfriend? Or gee, maybe one of the other brainless guys she leads around by the balls. No one could ever accuse her of being . . . picky. Wow, that was mean, wasn't it? Bad me. Guess I've been sucked down the Drain o' Darkness after all. Should have seen *that* coming."

"I don't know who they've spoken with," I said in a quiet voice, troubled by the vehemence in hers. I'd seen Amanda in action, and yeah, she was a real drama queen. But that was just teenager stuff. Right? "All I know is that the whole town is out looking

71

for her. Me included. I guess that means someone out there feels her absence is significant."

"Why not? Amanda's just one of those perfect girls people can't help paying attention to. Everything she says. Everything she does. Maybe this is another one of her famous power plays. It's exactly the kind of scam thing she'd try." Her fingers closed over the smooth stone, her knuckles white with the force of her grip.

Anger. Pure, unadulterated loathing. The strength of the emotional onslaught made my equilibrium do a quick loop-de-loop. I struggled, wishing I could find the means within myself to learn how to control this confounded gift of mine. Did I say gift? Try pain in the ass. "I wonder," I mused aloud, "whether your feelings toward Amanda might change should we find that she's never coming back."

"Look." Eyes as green as summer corn hit me with a hard, sullen bitterness. "Amanda is a bitch with a capital B. Trust me, she can take care of herself. I have no doubt that she can come out on top of any situation she finds herself in. It's her way. Now if you don't mind, I have some work to do."

I didn't have to stay. I wasn't wanted there. But I couldn't seem to get my feet to move, and Tara didn't seem to care. She turned her gaze to the stone she moved back and forth between her palms, back and forth, while the air around us went thick. Something started bubbling down low in my stomach, something that knotted me up and made me think suddenly of Margo Dickerson (now Craig), my own personal high school nemesis who'd once delighted in showing me my rightful place in the world . . . *soooo* far below her own. As intense as the emotions were, they were too raw to be my own.

The stone was moving faster, and Tara's body began to rock and sway as she muttered her words of power from her perch atop the mammoth boulder. Unintelligible though they were to my ears, the words held me in their sway as surely as if I'd uttered them myself. I could not move and I could not look away. Energy was coiling around us. Building. Crackling. Electrifying the very air we took into our lungs. Empowering our bodies. It wasn't the first time I had felt the rhythm of energy invigorating my blood, and it would not be the last. A more experienced empath would have been able to shield herself from energy workings like this one, from random negativity, from even your outright psychic attack. I could scarcely control my own emotions, let alone be adept enough to protect myself from others. Where were my Wonder Woman magic bracelets when I needed them?

But the power that now twisted in a rising spiral around us was different. It was exhilarating, yes, but somehow intimidating at the same time. My previous experience with energy at Liss's hands left me feeling buzzed with adrenaline, charged with possibility. With Liss I'd felt safe. Protected. Tara was too much of a loose cannon to allow for that much peace of mind. It was up to me to try to take care of myself. With that in mind, I steeled myself against the buffeting waves as best I could until, before I knew it, the spiral of energy reached its shimmering zenith. As energy whirled and buzzed around us at fever pitch, Tara slipped from the boulder and took a single, decisive step toward the water's edge. A grunt of effort came from the depths of her being as she lobbed the smooth stone midriver with as much strength as she could muster.

"So mote it be," she growled, hugging her arms about herself as she watched the stone sink beneath the flow of the river currents.

So mote it be, I silently and respectfully echoed the traditional closing to a witch's prayer . . . then added a sheepish *Amen* for good measure. It couldn't hurt, right?

The last thing she did was to kneel at the water's edge, heedless of the damp darkening the knees of her leggings. Slowly, purposefully, she plunged both hands beneath the murky surface of the water, then withdrew them and held them out before her for the air to dry them. *Water for purification* — her actions clicked into realization in my head — *and currents of air to sweep away.* Tara was borrowing strength from the elements to lend oomph to a magickal purpose (magickal being spelled with a K, I had learned, to differentiate it from the visual deceptions performed by illusionists). I had to admit, I was just the tiniest bit pleased with myself for recognizing the meaning behind her actions. I wondered, however, at the lack of a cast circle. Everything I'd learned had indicated that casting a circle, a magickal workspace between worlds, was necessary for psychic well-being while practicing the Arts.

Her task complete, Tara sat back on her heels, and little by little the world around us drifted back until all was as it should be once more. Blinking away the last vestiges of mist from the corners of my eyes, I tried to pretend I hadn't been affected by what she'd enacted there beneath the pall of a lowering gunmetal sky. Why had I stayed? I didn't have an answer. For a moment I considered Tara, who seemed to think the whole of the world was working against her, and then I thought of Amanda, who behaved as if the whole of the world was hers to command. Yet now she was gone, missing, and no one appeared to know how, or why. And I remembered what I was supposed to be doing with my time.

I cleared my throat and my head. "I have to go."

"Whatever. Hope I didn't scare you too much, Fluffy."

She knew. Dammit. I hate that.

I slid from the rock, preparing to leave. As I did, I remembered the other thing I'd meant to address with her. "By the way," I said, turning back, "about those books . . ."

She had the decency, at least, to look contrite. "Sorry about that. I meant to bring them back. I did! I know you probably don't believe me, but I did."

"Don't suppose you have them with you."

She shook her head. "I'll meet you at the store. Tomorrow. I promise."

As I made my way up the path, I heard her call after me: "I wouldn't worry about Amanda, if I were you. It's a stunt. Trust me on this one. She'll turn up."

I wished I could be as certain.

CHAPTER 4

As it turned out, Amanda turned up sooner than expected.

I spent most of my time Monday morning on the phone with one Ms. Poulson (emphasis on the *Miz*), the County Systems Integrator at Town Hall. Ms. Poulson listened to my story about the strange experience Saturday night on the SunnyStonyMill website before informing me there was nothing wrong with the website itself and in oh-so-patronizing tones inferred it must, simply *must* have been user error.

"Well, I realize you think the website is working properly," I said, counting to ten for patience as I struggled for an answer to that eternal question: Why did all technical people feel the need to treat their customers like uneducated twits, incapable of understanding even the most elementary of computer subjects? "In fact, I hope — I truly hope — that you're right. Considering the cost of the service, I'd like to believe the actual security of the secure server we're using for our online presence is as airtight as we all hope it is. As the operating manager at Enchantments, that kind of thing helps me to sleep at night."

"Let me assure you again," came the same bored, precise tones, "the system is functioning perfectly. I designed it myself. The scheduled security checks have turned up zero attempts to breach our firewall. Everything checked out."

"I mean, we've all heard horror stories about hackers and the kinds of things they can do," I continued, determined to make my point. "All I know is, it was the strangest thing I've ever seen. I don't know whether it was a virus or a virtual attack of some kind or what, but there is something wrong. I know it."

"There have been no attempts. There are no viruses on our server. I suggest you try your search again." Whatever patience she'd started with had begun to unravel, giving way to a bluntness that I suspected was her usual modus operandi.

"Can't you just check it out? I can give you the URL that was in our history." As the pause stretched into silence, I sweetened the deal with, "Please? It really would give me peace of mind."

On the other end I heard an irritated sigh and the crisp rustling of papers. "All right. Give me the specific web address you accessed. I'll test it myself."

"Thank you." I read off the address that I'd written down from the laptop's recorded Internet history.

"I'll let you know the results of my testing, but please understand, I can't promise anything."

I hadn't had a chance to ask Evie about the strange computer problem I'd encountered Saturday night and its connection to her sudden disconnect that same afternoon. Amanda's disappearance had thrown a monkey wrench into my day off, all right. I had gotten nothing done. And as of the conclusion of Sunday's search efforts, there had still been no sign of Amanda. The chilling sense of urgency and watchfulness around town deepened. I have to say this about Stony Mill. My town really sticks together when it comes to the health and welfare of its children.

Most of the time, that's a good thing.

It was just after two that afternoon when I heard the sirens. While my customer-of-the-moment, old Mrs. Bailey, dug around in her wallet for change, I looked up toward the front windows. The clutch in my chest tightened painfully as the wailing grew in both number and intensity before diminishing as the cars pushed north. "I wonder what that is," I murmured, half to myself.

"Hmm? Oh, the sirens. Probably an accident up on the highway. You know how those semi trucks are always running the lights. Think they own the road. A body's not safe in her own town anymore." She clucked her tongue as she poked a strip of BlackJack gum into her mouth. Even from here, the aroma of black licorice overpowered.

"Maybe."

Mrs. Bailey was an inmate, er, *resident,* of the old folks home on the other side of the river. At eighty-one and too wrapped up in the ups and downs of her own health issues to be concerned with the problems of others, she wasn't exactly what I would consider a reliable judge of reality.

With a deftness I had mastered over the last two-plus months of my employ, I wrapped her purchase in tissue paper and tucked it into one of our signature gold foil gift bags. A silver and gold ribbon cascade completed the look. "There you are, Mrs. Bailey. Ready to go under the tree."

"Thank you, dear. Tell Mrs. Dow I was

sorry to have missed her."

"I will. Merry Christmas to you."

Truth be told, I was missing Felicity, too. Liss's sabbatical was much deserved, especially in light of all that had happened in October, but it would be a happy day at Enchantments when she'd at last decided enough was enough. It wasn't that I hadn't learned to handle the store in her absence, but that I missed seeing her on a daily basis. And at times like this, Liss's calm perspective helped to route out the path in a complicated situation.

I could use some calm about now.

Out on the street, people had come out of the stores and had congregated on the rejuvenated brick-and-cement sidewalks, talking animatedly among themselves. Curious, I made my way out of the store to find out what was going on. The store's welcome bell rang out as I opened and closed the door. A cheery sound. A false sound. There was no cheer to be found among the Stony Millers on the street. Bits and pieces of conversations reached out to me as I neared the closest knot.

"What . . . ?"

". . . sounded like all the cars . . ."

". . . found her?"

Wary voices. Frightened voices. In none

of them did I hear hope.

My heart beat out an alarm as well.

Randy Cutter joined us from his antique store across the street. Still handsome in his mid-forties despite the crew cut he'd sported since his days in the Marines, his face today was taut with concern. "I had the scanner on when the call went out," he said, his voice pitched so low next to me that I was forced to turn to watch the movement of his lips to catch it all. "They've gone out along the river, just down from the old Crybaby Bridge."

The trestle bridge rose unbidden in my mind, a hulking monstrosity of rusting steel that spanned the river, a remnant from the days when the railroad was still an active and vital part of Stony Mill industry. Nowadays the trains stopped here only to load grain at the farmer's co-op, then went on to pick up steel from the micromill. The tracks crossing the trestle had been shut down or diverted years ago. The bridge was used mostly by fishing enthusiasts or good ol' boys out joyriding on dirt bikes and four-wheelers through the surrounding fields.

"Did you hear anything else, Randy?" The question came from Joe Terry, the bald and burly owner of the Roots 'N All Hair Salon. At six foot one and a beefy 225 pounds, Joe the Hairdresser was a bit of an oddity in our little one-horse town. It had occurred to me before that Joe might just be gay, but no one that I knew of had ever asked him. Er, would you?

Randy nodded, his thin lips set in a grim line, his eyes full of tragedy. "The code called was a 10-32. I looked it up. *Drowning.*"

A collective groan shuddered through us all. There was only one thing that could mean, and we all knew it.

I went back to the store and turned on the radio. Most of the stations came out of Fort Wayne, but instead I flipped it over to AM and tuned in our old standby. If anyone would break the news first, it would be the boys with NewsTalk 1190 WOWO. And it would be done with dignity and grace, not sandwiched between ads for Viagra and smarmy shock jock wannabes guessing listeners' bra sizes or bragging about the killer party they went to last night, dude.

Amanda Roberson was dead.

Suddenly I felt the need to get in touch with my mom. As much as I resented my mother's overwhelming presence at times, I had to admit that the opposite was not always better. I knew I wouldn't feel right until I heard her voice.

In times of crisis, girls often reached out to their moms. Amanda would never be able to do that again.

My fingers shook as I dialed home. The annoying beep-beep-beep of a busy signal grated against my eardrums. Probably Mom and her cribbage-playing cronies were single-handedly spreading word of today's discovery across town. The marvels of modern communication had nothing on my mom's gossip chain. Faster than an Internet worm and potentially just as destructive, it was a force to be reckoned with. You know what they say about information falling into the wrong hands.

I sat on the stool behind the old wooden counter, tapping the eraser end of a pencil idly on the phone's keypad and willing it to ring. When it did, a moment later, I about shot through the roof.

I took a steadying breath. "Enchantments Fine Gifts, may I help you?"

"Hello, ducks." Felicity's warmth filled my soul as her voice sounded in my ear with its usual flair. "You rang?"

"Hey, Liss. Actually I didn't."

"Hmm. I could have sworn . . ." As her voice trailed off in feigned confusion, I could hear the smile that had spread across her face. How she did it, I still didn't know, but Liss had an uncanny knack for knowing when I needed her most. "I suppose you've heard what has happened."

"I suppose you've heard more," I countered, knowing it must be true. That was another thing Liss had a knack for. Her web of information rivaled my mother's.

"They've found the body of that poor tragic girl."

"Where? How?" Was it ghoulish to want to know details? I didn't even care.

"Two young men were out exercising their dogs when they spotted her car down by that ancient bridge that has fallen into disuse. Apparently she was in the river, just down from there. Poor girl. May the Goddess bless and keep her spirit in her crossing to the Summerlands."

In the river just down from Crybaby Bridge. In an instant I flashed back to the spirit boy I'd encountered so unexpectedly Saturday morning, just before Amanda had visited Enchantments. The timing of it, in retrospect, gave me pause. Was it a warning from the Other Side that I'd been too inexperienced to heed? Was that what it came down to? That the Universe gives you the tools, but it is up to you to decide to use them?

Had I failed?

Liss had obviously heard more than I had, which was next to nothing, so before guilt could strike a paralyzing blow, I asked, "Do they know what happened? Was it . . . well . . . was it an accident?"

"The police haven't released any information regarding the situation that I am aware of."

No, they wouldn't. The last thing they wanted was an embarrassing debacle, like last time. My mind whirred along, testing paths. One thing was certain — freak warm spell or no, she could hardly have been swimming. I supposed she could have fallen in had she been walking along the riverbank, but . . . why would Amanda have been out there alone in the first place? She wasn't the type to embrace the Great Outdoors, so a nature hike seemed highly unlikely.

"What about her car?" I wondered aloud. "Maybe there was something in it that could give them an idea of why she'd been out there alone." I paused a moment, considering what I'd just said. "Wait a minute. Her car was found there, too?"

"That's what led to the discovery of her body. The young men saw the car, and then went looking."

The trestle bridge loomed in my memory. The river itself was at times overgrown along the banks, but the bridge wasn't exactly hiding among the brambles. "That can't be right. With all the search parties out looking for any sign of her, surely the car would have been spotted yesterday." I frowned, trying to remember the map the search captain had consulted when he assigned me my area. "In fact, I could have sworn River Road had been crossed off the list. I covered the Riverside Park area myself." The park was only a few miles from the old trestle bridge. I shuddered at the thought that I could have been the one to find the girl's body.

That strange feeling I was having? I did my best to brush it off. Amanda's death was nothing more than a tragic mishap. The fact that we'd had an actual murder in town two months before pretty much guaranteed that this was either (A) an accident, or (B) the unfortunate end to a young girl's private misery. Stony Mill simply wasn't the kind of place you could expect to see a lot of violence. With one homicide out of the way, I figured we wouldn't be due for a good long time. Kind of like your average hundred-year flood.

"We could easily find out . . ." Liss was saying. "Erlin Price was heading it up, I believe. His wife Nancy is an Enchantments regular, you know."

"No, forget about it. I guess my imagination is running away with me. I . . . knew Amanda. Not well, but I guess this has kind of shaken me up a bit."

"Perfectly understandable. You're human, Maggie."

"She came into the store Saturday morning. To buy a Christmas gift for her mother. Her poor mom." I couldn't stop thinking about it, but at least the information dump was serving to relieve the stress of the last few days. "And Liss . . . I think I might have been given a warning."

"What sort of warning?"

Slowly, guiltily, I described what I'd seen the morning Amanda had disappeared, and the sense that things had been off, somehow. Building up to something. Building up to . . . this?

"Oh, Maggie. You must stop. You're not to blame. Sometimes we as sensitives intercept information that we are not meant to understand. Sometimes we just . . . pick up the signal."

"You mean I was never meant to pick up the spirit energy, I just happened into it?"

"Because you're sensitive to those energies, yes. It's possible."

I closed my eyes and gripped the phone

even harder. I had so needed to hear this from Liss. She was my boss, yes, and my friend, but more than that, she was my mentor in an area in which I felt completely out of my element. Had I been raised to believe in the impossible, I might feel differently now, but as a born-and-bred Catholic, if things like witches, ghosts, and magic had been acknowledged at all, it was with the stern opinion that they were tools of the Devil and to be avoided at all costs. Being a practical kind of girl, I had always gone with the more secular viewpoint as taught in school, that they were nothing more than myths perpetuated by ignorance and fear and human desire. To discover that both viewpoints were wrong had, to put it mildly, thrown me for a loop. Now that I'd grown privy to the misty fringes of a shadow world that existed along with our own, and having seen proof of that world with my own eyes, I was conservatively starting to revise my opinion.

Hey, a girl can change her mind, can't she?

The call from Town Hall came less than an hour after Liss and I said good-bye. "Ms. O'Neill? This is Sandra Poulson from Systems Support."

"Ms. Poulson! Thank you for calling back. What did you find out?"

"Well, it pains me to admit this, but it appears you were right. There is something strange going on. The good news is, it doesn't appear to be anything associated with the SunnyStonyMill site, per se . . . but unfortunately, it does appear that the site integrity has been . . . challenged, shall we say."

"Challenged," I echoed, frowning down at a just-opened box of cheerful, bulbous-nosed Santas. "What does that mean?"

"It's really too soon to say, but I want to thank you for bringing it to my attention. The rogue attack was an extremely subtle one, and it appears to be inventively fire-walled. I will be making the investigation of this situation my number one priority."

A rogue attack. Now, I might not be an expert, but surely that description translated into computer hacking, of some sort. The question was why. Why would anyone hack into the community website for a rinky-dink town in Nowheresville, Indiana? It just didn't compute.

It also didn't sound to me like Ms. Poulson knew any more about the hacker's doings than I did, thanks to the "inventive" firewall methods employed. But I knew someone who did. Two someones, in fact. And the first of them was due here any minute.

I was waiting patiently behind the counter when I heard the back door close with a metallic boom, followed by Evie's breathless voice. "Maggie?"

"Up here."

Evie pushed through the velvet curtains in a rush, the long flaxen strands of her hair catching on the soft fabric and lifting around her into a halo of static electricity. "They've —"

"Found her. Yes, I know."

Evie dropped her book bag to the floor and slumped against the counter. "I don't understand it. I just don't understand any of it. How could this have happened? Here?"

I sighed and rose to my feet, turning away for a moment to make us both a cup of hot chocolate, heavy on the whipped marshmallow cream. Chocolate, the healer of a thousand ills. All hail. "I don't know, Evie. Sometimes kids get into trouble and don't know how to get themselves out. Maybe she was depressed and didn't feel like she could talk to anyone about it. I'm not excusing it, but there has to be an explanation."

"You're assuming she did this herself. Just another troubled teen."

I sprinkled a bit of cinnamon overtop the marshmallow, dropped in a candy cane, and set it in front of her. "Wasn't she? I mean, that was one messed-up young woman I saw in here the other day. On the surface, she had everything to live for: She was pretty, nice parents who obviously have money, a good, solid upbringing. She had a charmed life. I'm sure she was planning to go to college. Everything seemed fine to us, but who can truly know another's inner thoughts? It's heartbreaking to think that someone could be suffering so much without anyone knowing, but . . . it happens."

Sweet Evie's frowns came so rarely that the intensity of this one threw me. "I didn't know her very well — I'm not the kind of girl she'd have chosen as a friend — but I do know that Amanda Roberson was not the type of girl to end her own life. She was kind of a . . . a spoiled princess. She had this power over people like I've never seen before, and she wasn't afraid to use it. She was the kind of person you could see being in charge of a big company someday, or maybe even going into politics. Rule the world, and keep the little people in their place." Evie caught my eye. "People who are into power like that are too in love with themselves to fall victim to self-doubt. Trust me, she thought way too much of herself for that."

I took a sip of the hot chocolate, musing over melty marshmallow. "So what are you saying, Evie? That you think her death wasn't accidental?"

Evie cast her gaze downward to the candy cane she was absentmindedly using to stir her cocoa. "Well, I don't think she just fell in the river. No," she said, looking up again with an expression of pure determination, "I know that she didn't just fall in the river. I don't know who or how or why, but I know. And I think you do, too."

Damn. I didn't want to admit it, not even to myself, but she was right. I did feel it, despite my attempts to talk myself out of it.

I shrugged noncommittally because I didn't yet trust my instincts. It was still too new. I wanted to hear it in an official capacity before I owned up to anything. The fear of being ridiculed was just too strong for me to overcome at this stage of the game. Instead I set down my cup and folded my hands in my lap as I studied her. "Evie, I have to ask you a question, and I want you to be completely up front with me."

"Sure."

Reaching down, I withdrew the laptop from where I'd stowed it beneath the skirted counter, watching Evie's face as I set it on the scarred wooden countertop. "The other day," I began quietly, "Saturday . . . the morning that Amanda and her friends came into the store . . . I sent you and Tara into the back room. Do you remember?"

Something flitted behind Evie's eyes, something unsteady and hesitant. "Y-yes."

"And do you remember when I came back, after the girls had left the store? You had been on the Internet, and Tara was gone. Remember?"

This time I was certain I saw nervousness in Evie's china doll eyes. "I remember."

I nodded, keeping my expression as neutral as possible. "Funny thing happened. Now, I don't want you to think I was checking up on you" — *Ahem* — "but I somehow came across a link that I think you must have accessed while you and Tara were surfing together."

"Oh?" Her voice had faded, ever so slightly.

I cleared my throat and tried to look her in the eye. "Evie, what were you and Tara looking up on the SunnyStonyMill website? Honestly?"

Evie licked her lips as she avoided my gaze, staring instead at the closed laptop. "Um . . . well . . . gosh, this is hard."

I waited for her to go on.

She got up and turned her back to me,

facing the display behind her. "There's a blog on the site. Well, not exactly on it, but . . . You see, it's an underground blog. Tara showed it to me. Everyone's talking about it. I was just curious about it, that's all. I didn't want to be the last kid in Stony Mill to be in on the whole thing. I'm always the last person people think about. The last one picked for the team. Not this time, though."

An underground blog. An inventively firewalled one, according to Ms. Poulson. "Evie, what do you mean, everyone's talking about it? Who is talking about it?"

"Well . . . the kids at school."

I frowned, trying to understand what was going on. "All right. So there's a blog. A secret one. So how is it that everyone's talking about it?"

"People are passing the URL and passwords around to each other, friend to friend to friend. You know."

And evidently, they were reading the blog as well. "What could possibly be riveting enough to hold the attention of a bunch of high schoolers?" I wondered aloud.

A pretty flush colored her cheeks. "*Weeeell* . . . it's kind of embarrassing to talk about . . . I mean . . . geez!"

"Try me."

"It's about . . ." She coughed self-consciously. "Well, actually, it's about . . . um . . . sex."

I felt my eyeballs bulge as I tried to choke back a surprised laugh. "Oh." And then: "Really?"

Okay, I'll be the first to admit that my love life leaves a little to be desired. Well, maybe a lot. Lately. But even I couldn't come up with an acceptable excuse for the flicker of curiosity that riffled through my mind. Shame-y, shame-y.

Still blushing, Evie could only nod.

"Oh. Okay!" I cleared my throat. "So, what kind of things are on this website, exactly? And who writes it? And how did it get on SunnyStonyMill.com?"

"It's kind of hard to explain," Evie hedged. "I didn't see very much of it, you know. And I don't think anyone knows who writes it. It's all very hush-hush."

Evie didn't seem to know much about the subject, and she wasn't the type of girl to lie. By way of omission, sure — she was a kid, after all — but other than that, I just didn't think so. Not about something like this. On the other hand, I wondered how much Tara was privy to what was going on in Sunny Stony Mill. More than was healthy for a high school girl, for sure.

Determined to get to the bottom of it one

way or the other, I unplugged the phone and plugged in the computer's modem cord, powered up the laptop, then rotated the whole thing in Evie's direction. "Listen, why don't you just pull up the site so that I can see what we're talking about."

She hesitated, but for only a moment. "All right."

I watched as she logged on and typed in the mystery web address that I'd passed on to Ms. Poulson, Systems Support, just that morning. The familiar strobing screen came up almost instantly. Pointing the arrow to the X in the corner of the now-black window and receiving the *Password?* prompt in response, Evie typed in a string of characters that showed up as asterisks in the blank space provided, then clicked Go. But instead of immediately being flashed into the website as I'd expected, Evie was required to enter a string of passwords. A total of seven, in fact. She didn't miss a beat on any of them, and without crib notes, a detail that did not escape my notice. Either Evie had a photographic memory she could access at will, or she'd been to this site more times than she'd let on.

My bet was on Curtain Number Two.

At first glance, the blog seemed to be as innocuous as they come, a confection of bubblegum pink background and hearts and flowers. Totally girly. But the chatter on the page was anything but innocent. The most recent entry was date stamped last Friday. My face heated with the very first paragraph: *"Y'know, guys are a lot like lollipops. If you lick them a little, they melt just fine, but if you pop them in your mouth and swirl them around, they disappear soooo much faster . . ."*

Sweet Mother Mary.

I have always loved those nineteenth-century authors who spoke to the hearts of their readers as though they were trusted friends. Jane Austen, the Brontë sisters, Louisa May Alcott. It was a kinder time, a gentler time, and this blog proved it in that in-your-face way so much admired these days. Instead of the sweet and innocent declaration of: *"And so, Gentle Reader, I married him!"* that made a girl's heart go pitter-pat with thoughts of her own One True Love, the diarist of this web journal preferred the more direct approach of: *"And so, Gentle Reader, I bopped his brains out."* In titillating, step-by-step detail.

I read on in silence, my brows stretching higher by the minute. Whoever the author of the page was, she was getting plenty of, shall we say, experience? Of course it was also fairly evident that she had watched way too many episodes of *Sex and the City* — she gave each of her guys an alias, like the Alligator Man, Papa Bear, Chicken of the Sea, the Anteater (I was trying my best not to picture that one), Buzz Lightyear. The funniest? The Mole (because he liked to burrow under the covers, so to speak — ba dum bump).

"Are you going to tell my mom?"

I peeled my eyes away from the laptop screen. Evie was looking at me with worried puppy dog eyes. I wished she wouldn't do that. I'm a real sucker for puppies. "No, I'm not going to tell your mom. It's natural to be curious. Besides, I'm pretty sure your mom would just freak, and you're not doing anything to hurt anyone." I paused a moment, then said hesitantly, "Listen. Evie. The things that are happening on that page . . . they have to be made up. That's not real life, you know?"

Evie nodded. "I know it's not. Don't worry, I'm not going to go out and try to imitate what's going on there. I mean . . . geez! But I do think it's a real diary, Maggie. And I'm pretty sure it's someone from right here in Stony Mill. Everyone else thinks so, too. Besides, some of the guys from school are saying that they're being featured. Like I said, everyone's been talking about it."

So someone from Stony Mill had high-jacked a community website in order to spread news of her sexploits countywide. Was I the only one who saw the weirdness in that?

I wondered what Tara would have to say about the whole thing, being the one, evidently, who had showed Evie how to access the site in the first place. Maybe she would know who put the whole thing together. I'm sure Ms. Poulson would love to get her hands on that info.

"Evie, would you write down the passwords for me?"

"Okay." She scratched them down in her neat, round, schoolgirl hand and passed the paper over to me. "You won't say where you got them, will you?"

"No. I won't tell."

CHAPTER 5

I left Enchantments just after eight. The store had been abnormally quiet, devoid of the usual Christmas crowd that kept us hopping until well past closing. Evie's mom came to pick her up, leaving me to my thoughts, which were admittedly dark. How could they not be? So much had happened . . . so many bad things. It had been a draining couple of days.

I prepared the day's deposit, then went up front to lock the street door for the night. In the alcove I leaned my forehead against the cold glass of the door and gazed out upon the cobbled street and the storefronts lining this section of River Street. Once the buildings had been warehouses for a thriving river shipping industry. Over time they had fallen into disrepair, only to be adopted as a key part of a major town cleanup project several years ago. Revitalized and rejuvenated, the buildings had been snapped up, eventually becoming the picture-postcard ode to Americana that it was today.

The sun had gone down by six that evening as the hemisphere careened toward the winter solstice, the shortest day of the year. Streetlamps burned brightly against the shifting shadows, but if not for the Christmas lights twinkling cheerily within storefront windows, the hollow feeling that tugged at my insides when I looked out at the street would have been much worse. I pulled the café curtains that closed off the window displays from the rest of the store and felt a bit less vulnerable.

What I really needed was time to center myself, to focus my thoughts and energies, a little meditation in a safe place. The loft called to me, but I dismissed the notion out of hand. The loft was Liss's sacred indoor working space as well as being the repository for our witchy stock. The large second-floor room had a presence all its own that even a newbie like me could sense. I felt at home there during N.I.G.H.T.S. get-togethers or when assisting our more, shall we say, *specialized* clientele, but to be there during quiet times, without Liss's knowledge or express approval, just wouldn't feel right. The protective Invisible Threshold spell Liss had placed upon the circle guaranteed that, for the good of us all.

No, I would not use the loft tonight, I thought as I locked down the security door for the evening.

Outside, the air was crisp, still, the sky moonless beneath fitful clouds. Fitful . . . that matched my mood to a T. Once upon a time I might have made my way across town to St. Catherine's of the Cross, the spiritual home of the O'Neill family for decades. But I hadn't been a regular churchgoer for years. Not since I was old enough to understand the kinds of things St. Catherine's revered leader, Father Tom, had been up to during his lengthy tenure. You might say the good Father was at least in part responsible for my spiritual ennui. It was hard to blindly follow when faced with the purposeful betrayal of core teachings and beliefs by the person who should adhere to them the most. Hypocrisy cannot serve faith well.

And yet, in spite of all that, I found myself steering my old Bug along the familiar roads, wondering what the heck I thought I was doing.

At some point in the last few years, St. Catherine's had discovered the joys of landscape lighting. The stately brick church with its twin spires absolutely blazed with lights. Hidden beacons dazzled from the shrubbery, casting obscene shadows onto the coves and corners of the neo-Gothic architecture and transforming the old gravestones in the backyard cemetery into something straight out of a horror flick. I pulled slowly into the rough chip-and-seal parking lot, hesitating at the number of cars already in attendance there. *Crap.* I had hoped to slip in for only a minute to light a candle for Amanda Roberson. It seemed the decent thing to do. But I'd feel ridiculous walking in and disturbing a bunch of regular parishioners. People who in all likelihood knew me or, more importantly, knew my mother, and who would waste no time in passing along the tale of my unexpected intrusion to her perked ears. For all I knew, Mom could be in there, too.

Cowards never win, Margaret . . .

The voice of my conscience butted in with its usual unsolicited advice. Everyone has a conscience — thank goodness for all the rest of us — but for some reason mine came all too often in the disapproving clucks of my late Grandma Cora. Grandma C had been a hard, practical woman of Catholic faith who'd ruled our clan with an iron hand, never mind the velvet glove. I had never been especially close to Grandma — can you get close to an emotional porcupine? —

even though I'd spent loads of evenings with her back when my mom was going through her Tupperware Lady phase. So while Mom demonstrated the correct way to burp plastic lids and tried to entice acquaintances to throw still more boring parties, I baked bread with Grandma C and tried not to do anything that would get woolly worms stuck down my shirtfront. Even in death I hadn't been relieved of her vigilant eye. Irony at its most Murphy.

So cowards never win. Big whoop-de-ding-dong. They never get shot on the front lines, either.

I scowled, tapping my thumbs against the steering wheel as I tried to decide what to do. It was always the same. Once I heard Grandma's nagging from the recesses of my mind, I could squirm and I could wiggle, but in the end, what Grandma wanted, Grandma got. I didn't have much of a choice if I wanted to skip a ride on the Great Guilt Trip on which Grandma C served as engineer, chief conductor, and ticket taker.

A girl's gotta do what a girl's gotta do.

I left the relative safety of Christine's snug confines and crossed the parking lot as quickly as I could toward St. Catherine's arched doors. With a little luck I could get down to business and leave before anyone noticed I had been there. Luck . . . I had never had an overabundance of it. The heavy doors squeaked on their old iron hinges as I pulled open the one on the right. I cringed. So much for subtle. The air outside the church had been so still I could hear the traffic from the highway at least a mile away, but from within, the traffic sounds were muffled by the singsong cant of the Father's homily. It was both familiar and somehow foreign at the same time. A rite for the dead. I gave up straining against the heavyweight doors, took a deep breath, and slipped into the vestibule through the gap I'd created.

The entrance to the main sanctuary was closed. Thank heaven for small favors, I thought as the outside doors closed behind me with a tomblike *phloomph* — I would be able to see to my business in peace. I looked around as my eyes adjusted. Things hadn't changed much. The same oak paneling lined the walls and ceiling, dark enough to be considered black. A truly awful gilt crucifix stood on the wall opposite the main doors, looking like something from one of the home shopping channels. Beneath it was the attendance book, proffered on a chest-high stand. I didn't sign it. If by some miracle my appearance here managed to go unnoticed, I wasn't about to let my signature in the Book of Days tip Mom off.

Off to the right was a painting of the Last Supper, just your average paint-by-numbers church fare. Next to it was a closed door that almost disappeared into the paneling, which I knew from past experience led to the upper gallery and bell tower. (*Helpful hint #191: Never sneak off to the bell tower for an illicit makeout session when your bratty little sister knows your every secret. My ears didn't stop ringing for a week.*) To the left I saw my target — that same low table filled to overflowing with flickering votive candles in cut-glass cups of cobalt and crimson. I walked toward them, my hand outstretched in anticipation of the cup of long matchsticks.

The candle flames flared in unison as I approached them.

I saw them. I know I did.

I froze uncertainly, my focus riveted to the anomaly like the proverbial moth. As I watched further, the flames flickered, dropping in intensity until they nearly guttered, then flared again, one inch, two, higher, higher. It was amazing. It was confusing. It was . . .

Probably a stray air current. From the

door closing, or even as a result of my own movement through the room.

Yeah, that was it. Had to be.

But just to be sure, I knelt and bowed my head before the marble representation of the Virgin Mary before touching a match to an unlit votive and saying a silent prayer for Amanda Roberson and the family she had left behind. Despite my own internal struggle, it seemed the least I could do. And while I knew a simple prayer might not help much, if enough prayers were made, perhaps we supplicants might set into motion a chain of events that would instigate justice. I would do my part, even though the God I'd been raised to believe in had ceased to have much meaning for me.

The Virgin Mother, on the other hand . . .

Mary had shown great resilience and strength in the Bible, and had managed somehow to be one of the few women of regard to be included in that lengthy narrative. I respected that about Her. And so, on the occasions when I did pray, I prayed to Mary, the Great Lady.

The statue of Mary smiled benevolently on. She could always be counted on to listen when you needed Her.

From within the sanctuary, I heard movement, rumblings. Time for me to exit, stage right.

My duty done, I turned to go.

"We've got to stop meeting like this."

The resonant male voice came from nowhere and everywhere at once. To an isolated female the sudden materialization of a man might well be viewed as threatening, but I knew that voice.

"Marcus! What the devil are you doing here?"

He stood in the darkened stairwell to the bell tower, a shoulder leaning indolently against the jamb. A vision in black leather and aging denim. "Funny you should ask that. I was about to ask you the same thing."

It was probably wrong of me to notice the way his jeans clung to his lean hips. I made myself look away. Marcus Quinn was my boss's main squeeze, the May half of their May-September love affair. And no matter how much his bad boy image on occasion piqued my curiosity, he was indisputably off-limits. Period. Besides, despite the fact that I hadn't seen Deputy Tom Fielding since he'd hightailed it out of my life in October, I still harbored a secret hope that I hadn't seen the last of him. It might seem silly, but something told me I shouldn't give up. Not yet.

I shook myself from my reverie. "I asked first. I'm surprised to see you here." A nervous giggle threatened my composure. "Stunned, actually."

"Who, me?" Marcus stepped down off the landing with the nimble grace of a stretching cat. "My aunt goes here. She wanted to come tonight for the vigil for Amanda Roberson, and I came along to lend moral support. Not to mention that I knew Amanda. Besides, I love churches."

Doubtfully I squinted at him. "Really?"

His eyes were dark and shadowy in the dim vestibule, but I felt the weight of them on me for a long moment before he spoke. "There are many paths to the Divine, Maggie. Mine is just one of them. No better than the rest, except that it works for me. And isn't that the most important thing?"

My own thoughts were too muddled to agree, so I simply avoided the question. To fill the silence, I said, "So, your aunt belongs to this church? I wonder if she knows my mother. *Oh*." A sudden uncomfortable thought. "You don't mean your Aunt Marian, do you?"

"You know her?"

Did I ever.

If Marian Tabor was inside, it really was time to get the heck outta there, and fast.

111

As well meaning as she was, Marian was one of the town's most determined match-makers, not to mention my mother's long-time friend. Besides, she'd already made noises about fixing me up with her nephew when I'd met up with her at the library a couple of months back. Evidently she was oblivious to Marcus's involvement with Liss. And if he hadn't told her, I wasn't about to let the cat out of the bag.

"Yes, I know her. Listen, I have to go."

"If you'll wait a minute, I'll go with you. I have something I need to talk to you about."

I glanced nervously toward the door. "Um, sure. I'll just wait outside."

"Be right back."

I wasn't about to stand on the doorstep waiting to be discovered, so I huddled out by Christine in the dark, fists in pockets and shoulders hunched against the lowering temperatures, while the muffled strains of the pipe organ trembled the church's old stained glass windows. The moment might have been peaceful if not for the reality of why I had come in the first place. I thought about Evie's perceptions that Amanda's death was not accidental, and I shivered. We had good people here in Stony Mill, a fact I sometimes forgot. And yet good people have been known to commit really horrifying acts. What would we find about the circumstances surrounding Amanda Roberson's death? Did one of our own cause it to happen? Or had it been an accident after all?

Nervously I eyed the starkly illuminated church and wished that Marcus would hurry.

Finally the doors to the church opened and my wish was granted. Out walked Marcus with his recognizable Lone Cowboy gait. Except he wasn't alone. On the left was his aunt, and — *Oh-Sweet-Jesus* — there was my mother toddling beside him on the right. I knew a moment of cold fear. Alone, each woman was formidable indeed. Together they were like a matchmaking nuclear bomb, ticking away toward matrimonial Armageddon.

Maybe I should have mentioned to Marcus that I was trying not to be seen.

My first thought was to duck behind Christine. My second thought was to get in and take off before they saw me.

It was way too late for that.

CHAPTER 6

Marcus's voice drifted to me across the parking lot: "Aunt Marian, there's someone over here I think you'd like to say hello to."

With a smooth gesture, he ruined my last hope to escape unnoticed. Marian's face lit up like a ten-strand Christmas tree the moment she noticed me skulking on the far end of the parking lot.

"Maggie! Yoo-hoo, Maggie! I had no idea you were here!"

She waved at me across the expanse of gravel at the exact same moment my mother caught sight of me — I could tell by the look of annoyance on her face. Before anyone else could say a word, Marian made a beeline for me, leaving Marcus and my mother scurrying to keep up the pace.

Damn and double damn.

It wasn't that I didn't want to see my mother — I did. I just didn't want to see her there, tonight, with Marcus and the church in the background. It wasn't exactly what I would call neutral ground. My mom and I had a relationship that might best be described as grudging acceptance. I was the black sheep of the family, the child who could not manage to conform to my mother's strict views of the world, no matter how hard I tried, and she had never quite forgiven me for that. Eventually I had given up trying. She'd never forgiven me for that, either.

"Hello, Marian," I said as they drew near. "Hi, Mom."

Marian puffed to a halt, her breath steaming around her in the lowering temperatures. The town's head librarian, Marian defied the conventions of her post with her love for any item of clothing that hearkened back to the animal kingdom for inspiration. Tonight she appeared to be practicing a modicum of self-control in honor of the occasion. Wrapped in her thick wool overcoat, the only sign of her predilection for animal prints was her plush mittens and scarf, both a cheesy faux leopard.

She put her hands on her generous hips and pretended to frown. "Maggie O'Neill. Did I miss seeing you inside?"

"Now, Marian, you know my Margaret has been avoiding the church. Haven't you, dear?" My mother was one of the few people I have ever known who possessed the ability to speak through pursed lips. I've often felt she missed her calling as a ventriloquist. "She's also avoiding her mother and father these days. It's a crying shame how you give your best years to your children, only to be abandoned by them the instant they leave your house."

She tugged on her oh-so-practical Isotoners with undue force. Behind her, I saw Marcus grimace. He met my eye as if to say, *"Oops."* I shrugged. What could I say?

"I'm not avoiding you, Mom," I tried to explain. "I've just been . . . busy."

She shook her head sadly. "I can understand too busy for your parents. Children grow up and grow selfish. But too busy for your church? It's shameful, Margaret. The ladies of the auxiliary ask after you every Wednesday afternoon. What am I supposed to tell them?"

If they did ask, it was only to make my mother feel small, of that much I was certain. I've met these women. A pit of vipers had more compassion, at least when it came to each other.

"I've always thought the truth the best approach," I said, only marginally successful

116

in disguising my irritation. "Tell them I'm busy."

My mother opened her mouth to say more, but Marian elbowed her out of the way. "Oh, put a sock in it, Patty. Give the girl a bit of breathing room." Marian turned to me with a speculative glint in her eye. "I had no idea you knew my nephew, Maggie. Marcus has never mentioned you." She paused to transfer her eagle-eyed stare to her nephew, standing in the background with a grin on his face. "Come to think of it, Marcus rarely mentions anyone. You been holding out on me, boy?"

His answer was the arch of a blackguard brow.

"I knew it! I just knew it. I'm going to have to watch you more closely, I can see that right now. You wicked thing, you." Her gaze flicked back to me. "So. How do you know Miss Maggie here?"

She thought we were an item. I held up my hands, laughing. "Whoa, there. I'm not seeing Marcus. In case you were wondering."

Her face fell, but she recovered nicely. "Well, you can't blame an old girl for trying. I figure if I'm not getting any action, someone might as well be."

My mother made a huffy sound. "Really,

Marian. Can't you rein in that tongue, in light of the occasion?" She stepped forward, positioning herself between Marcus and me. "How is Tom, dear?" she asked.

Her maneuvering was not lost on me. By appearances alone, Marcus was not the type of guy my mother had in mind when she cased out prospective husbands for her oldest daughter. But she needn't have worried. Marcus wasn't the least bit interested in me. And Tom . . . *well.* I cleared my throat and mustered an airy, "Oh, he's fine," while I dug around inside my purse for my keys, which were hiding somewhere between my wallet, credit card receipts, candy wrappers, lint, pennies, and other assorted flotsam in the bottom.

All right, all right, I admit it. I never told my mother that Tom and I had never really gotten off the ground. So I'm the biggest coward that ever lived. Cowardice has its advantages.

Three sets of eyes were watching my hands. I wanted to hide from all of them.

My mother picked a piece of lint off my wool coat. "It occurs to me, Margaret, that we never rescheduled that dinner with you and Tom. I know your father would like to meet him. How about next Sunday?"

Keys, keys, where were the blasted keys?

"Um . . . well, we've both been working an awful lot lately, Mom."

"He does take the time to eat, doesn't he?"

"Um . . . well . . ."

"I'm sure I could get Melanie and Greg to come to dinner that night. You really should see the girls. Little Jenna will be in preschool next fall, and baby Courtney just took her first steps. As their aunt, you should be taking more of an interest."

I felt a pang. I hadn't seen my nieces in ages, either. Mom was right, I was not being the greatest aunt. The girls were sweeties, and it wasn't their fault that their mother went out of her way to remind me that she was the better daughter.

"Hey, Maggie?" Marcus called my name, his voice a welcome interruption to the guilt trip I sensed coming on. "We'd better get going, huh?"

"Right! Sorry, Mom. I'll let you know about Sunday, okay?" I was talking fast, rushed, still trying to find my keys. "The store is open Sundays, of course, so it may not work out anyway. I'll have to check the schedule. Oh, and I think I might have promised to go to a movie with Steff that night. Or maybe it was Monday. I won't feel right unless I check with her, too."

"My. You do sound busy."

And she sounded hurt. And yup, there was the guilt, right on schedule. I turned away, biting my tongue to keep from making a promise I wouldn't be able to keep. Funny how, no matter how irritating our moms can be, we still want to protect them from being hurt by our actions.

"Pleasure to meet you, Mrs. O'Neill," Marcus was saying. "I can see where Maggie gets her pretty face." He gave Marian a peck on the cheek and a friendly shoulder squeeze. "See you later, Aunt Marian."

"Come around sometime, wouldja?" Marian patted his smoothly shaven cheek. "Your poor old aunt gets lonely."

"I'll try to get around more often. You know how things get."

"Don't we all. Oh, and maybe when you get the chance, you can check up on your cousin? Your Uncle Lou tells me she's giving him quite the time. Teenagers. I seem to recall your mother had the same complaints about you, once upon a time. I can't tell you how many nights she called to cry on my shoulder . . . but you seem to have turned out all right." With a final fond smile for her nephew, Marian turned to me and winked.

So incorrigible. I couldn't help smiling back. "See you, Marian. And thanks."

Mom and Marian got into their respective cars and pulled away while Christine was still warming up. Plagued by a sappy mixture of sadness and relief, I watched the taillights on my mother's old station wagon fade into the distance on the roadway. While I'd stopped, for the most part, going out of my way to try to please my mother, the urges still came on strong. Maybe one day we'd be able to make peace with each other. I hoped so. Despite everything, deep down, I knew I still desired my mother's approval. I suppose, deep down, we all do.

"You okay?"

I glanced up to find Marcus watching me in Christine's darkened confines. I nodded and slanted an embarrassed smile his way. "Yeah. Fine. My mom wears me down sometimes, that's all."

"She's upset because . . . well, never mind. You probably don't need to hear this from me."

No. I knew. That was the whole problem. I knew how much of a disappointment I was. It was reflected back at me in my mother's eyes every time she looked at me.

I shrugged to let him know it didn't matter. "I don't really want to talk about it right now."

"Suit yourself."

We sat in silence for several moments until I judged that the oil had thawed enough to flow through the old engine. "Where to?" I asked him. Then, "You know, I never thought to ask. Do you have a car here already?"

"Nah. I rode in with Aunt Marian. Howzabout the Little Nipper?"

The Little Nipper was a country-and-western bar located at a crossroads in the middle of nowhere eight miles to the west of Stony Mill. It was dark and smoky, but always filled to bursting with rednecks and young upwardly mobiles alike, as both flanks found themselves in need of being shown a good time on occasion. Though, to be truthful, some found the occasion more than others.

We parked in the busy lot and entered through a side door, passing through a room lined with pool tables to get to the main area, where a jukebox blared twangy songs about feisty women, faithless men, drinking and deviling and daring all for love, lust, and liberty. I felt my mood lift with the buoyant spirit of the place as I watched a quartet of couples two-stepping around the scuffed dance floor. Lowbrow it might be, but it was honest, it was true, and it was just what I needed on this dismal night.

We found a table in the corner, away from the ruckus of the dance floor. One of the barmaids, a matronly fifty-something wearing jeans and a red sweatshirt shouting the joys of the Christmas season, approached us with a friendly smile, her jaw cracking her gum in time with the music. "What'llya have?" she shouted as she leaned in over the table.

"Beer!" Marcus shouted back with the kind of grin that made women weak in the knees. "Longneck, whatever you have plenty of. No glass."

"You got it, hon!" She turned to me, waiting, brows lifted.

"Just Coke for me, thanks." I was driving, so I figured I'd better keep it simple. Besides, I didn't need anything alcoholic to feel better. It was enough to be in this place, brimming with life and vivid energy. Generally speaking, I avoided crowds like the plague because of their tendency to drain the life from me, but my spirits were already low enough that the power boost was both needed and appreciated.

Marcus looked at me when she was gone. "You sure? I can drive us home, if you'd rather." He paused, then added, "You look like you might need it."

I shook my head. "I'll be fine."

He gazed at me a moment, then nodded knowingly. "You will at that." He held his tongue as the waitress dropped off the drinks at our table. Lifting his longneck, he waited for me to raise my glass of Coke, which the older woman had seen fit to top with a lemon slice and a cherry stabbed onto the thin red plastic straw. "Cheers."

I clinked my glass to the brown bottle. "Cheers."

"It's been quite a night, huh?"

"Quite a weekend, actually."

He turned back to look at me, his blue eyes softly questioning. "Did you know Amanda?"

"Not really. Well, I used to, I suppose. My sister babysat her, once upon a time. A shirttail acquaintance, at best. I hadn't seen her for years until . . ."

"Until?"

I took a sip of my Coke, grateful for the distraction of the chemical burn as it slid down my throat. "Until she and a couple of her friends sashayed into the store Saturday morning and got into a verbal slash-'n'-bash session with another of our customers."

"Interesting timing, but that sounds like Amanda. Amanda was, shall we say, top poodle in the kennel. Was that about the gist of it this time?"

I shrugged. "Typical high school posturing, it seemed to me. Apparently she liked to exert her influence wherever possible."

"Some things about high school never change."

"No, they don't seem to, do they?" I took another thoughtful sip of my Coke. "She also bought a Christmas present for her mom. A clock. Really beautiful. Really expensive. She paid for it herself, like it was nothing. And then Goth Girl came down from the loft with Evie, and Amanda and her friends started in on her like they were a pack of dogs and she was a trespassing little rabbit."

"Goth Girl?"

Argh. I'd done it again. "Sorry. I called her that in my head before I knew her name, and now I'm having trouble thinking of her as anything else. Tara. Tara Murphy. She goes to SMHS with Evie." Marcus laughed suddenly. I tilted my head, questioning. "What?"

"Tara's my cousin. Stepcousin, technically. My Uncle Lou married Tara's mom, my Aunt Molly, when Tara was a wee little thing."

"You're kidding me."

"Small world, huh?" He took a drag on his beer as the jukebox flipped to the next

125

selection with an audible mechanical switching of the gears. "Aunt Marian said Tara's been having a hard time getting used to Stony Mill. Not surprising, considering that Uncle Lou moved the family here from Milwaukee."

I nodded sympathetically. "She doesn't exactly blend in."

"No. And people around here aren't exactly welcoming if they think you're . . . different."

That was for sure. I felt myself warming up to Tara in a way I hadn't before. Maybe she was just a confused teenager, trying to find her way. I could relate. "Especially not people like Amanda Roberson." I let my gaze drift toward the dance floor. Not much going on tonight. A lot of rhythmless men trying to dance with women who actually could. A+ for effort, C for execution. Ah, well. No one said life was perfect.

"Did you want to dance?"

I froze, not entirely sure I'd heard him correctly. Hoping that I hadn't, I lifted my gaze to meet his. "What did you say?"

He slid down in his seat and stretched his long legs out before him, crossing them at the ankle. His clunky motorcycle boots looked even bigger and clunkier for the effort, but it didn't detract from the overall image he made. Bad ass, all the way. "You were watching the floor. I thought you might want to . . ."

Oh, I wanted to, all right. Something told me Marcus was one of those rare men who could move his body with the kind of sinuous grace that could make a woman melt like spun sugar. An experience like that can make up for all the crushed toes of a lifetime. But . . .

I shook my head regretfully. "I don't think so. I'm kind of seeing someone right now." *And so is he, remember?*

"It's just a dance."

Yeah. Just a dance. "I wouldn't feel right."

"Tom Fielding?"

I lowered my gaze to where he cradled his beer bottle in his hands, balancing it against his belt buckle. "Yeah."

There was a pause, and then he said in a quiet voice, "Liss told me things were on hold between the two of you."

Heat flooded my cheeks. I kept my eyes on his hands and the bottle. It was standard fare, as everyday American as the bar we were in. "Liss has been talking to you about me?"

The bottle turned a quarter-spin in his long fingers. "Do you mind?"

Hmm. Did I? "Well. She's right, of course.

I think I scared him off."

The bottle turned again. "I never pinned him for a wise man. And Maggie?" The softness of his voice insisted that I look at him. His eyes held me the instant I did, as blue as a pool of water, clear and inviting beneath a summer sky. "He can't dance, either."

I stared at him, thrown for a loop again. No matter how often he seemed to read my thoughts, the ability surprised me, every single time. I was going to have to be more guarded — if he was able to discern what I was thinking about dancing, maybe he also knew what I'd been thinking about *him.* Not that I meant to, drat it! I just couldn't seem to help myself. I swallowed nervously. "Dancing isn't everything. Tom has lots of good qualities. I haven't given up on him yet."

We fell into a silence that was feeling less and less easygoing by the minute. I squirmed, needing to fill the space, to get the closeness back. "You know, you haven't told me why you needed to talk to me."

"Hmm?"

"You know. The whole '*I have something I need to talk to you about, Maggie*' thing. Remember?"

"Right." He lifted his beer to his lips, tilting his head back far enough to expose his throat. It was such a male thing to do. I couldn't help watching, mesmerized, as the muscles of his throat convulsed with each swallow as he'd drained the rest of the bottle. With a final *ahh* of satisfaction, he set the bottle on the table with a decided thunk before facing me. "I wanted to re-assure you about the upcoming investigation. I know you're a little wary about things, but everything's going to work out. I don't want you to worry. You're ready for this. You are. And I'll be there to watch your back. As a friend. That's all I wanted to say."

Mass confusion. I heard the words, but not a single one was registering. "You mean, Amanda's investigation?"

He frowned. "No. I mean the N.I.G.H.T.S. investigation. Tomorrow night. Didn't Devin call you?"

I frowned, too. "I don't think so. What investigation? What are we talking about here?"

He leaned forward in his seat, balancing his elbows on his knees. His hair looked as dark and glossy as a black cat's coat beneath the dim barroom lights and the intermittent flashing strobes from the dance floor. "It's an active on-site investigation, Maggie."

On-site. My first. A flutter of anticipation tickled at the base of my spine at the thought, playing counterpoint to the sudden rumbling of nervousness in the pit of my stomach. "That's . . . exciting. Where will we be investigating?"

"At a cemetery just outside of town."

In my mind's eye, I had a flash of memory: an angel towering over me, arms reaching out, eyes pupil-less and blind. I shuddered. "Not . . . not Oakhill Cemetery?" I said faintly. I had a teensy little problem with Oakhill. All right, so it's more than teensy. Just between us, I'm a bit of a wuss at times.

He shook his head. "Rosemont. Out on 500 North. Do you know it?"

"No, I don't think so. Why there? What's the story?"

"Rosemont Cemetery borders on Joe Aames's property. The activity on Joe's place has always run kind of high, but lately it's gotten worse."

I toyed with my straw, sliding the lemon and cherry up, then down, against the edge of my glass. "How so?"

"There've always been cold spots. Flashing lights with no sources. Unusual electromagnetic readings that correspond with experiences people have had. Touches. Whispered voices. Orbs. Visual disturbances. It's happening all the time now, and we don't know why. It's amazing. It's a wonderful opportunity to get fresh readings against our base point reading from last summer."

His expression had warmed with the topic, lighting up in all sorts of interesting ways. Of course he was talking about one of my childhood terrors. That kind of put a damper on the whole thrill factor. I cleared my throat. "I'm — um — I'm not very good at cemeteries. They — um — really — *really* — scare me."

He reached out and closed his hand around mine. "Maggie, if I didn't think you could handle this, I wouldn't have mentioned it. I know it scares you. You're still new to all this. It took me years before I could do an investigation without getting nervous."

His eyes were so soft and gentle that I could feel the anxiety easing, just a bit. I licked my lips. "I'm not sure I'm ready, Marcus. My experiences haven't exactly been pleasant."

"Wouldn't you like to learn some ways of reclaiming control over your reactions to those elements?"

"Well . . . yes. Is that possible?"

A mysterious and somehow reassuring smile curved his lips. "Anything is possible. I believe that. Do you?"

Did I? "Sometimes I do."

"Well, then. That's a start." He let go of my hand and leaned back in his seat again, almost languidly. "So you'll come, then?"

I hesitated. It took everything I had in me to nod. "I'll try."

It wasn't so bad, right? I had until tomorrow night to muster my courage. A girl could do a lot in twenty-four hours. Considering that tomorrow morning I had an impromptu appointment for my yearly, the ghost hunt might actually turn out to be the lesser of two evils.

Besides, his grin was infectious. "I knew you would."

The waitress came by to refill my glass. Marcus, to my surprise, ordered a Coke as well. "Just one beer?" I asked.

He shrugged amiably. "Nothing in excess, that's my motto. Nothing in excess."

I leaned forward on my hand, gazing at him. "So. Tell me. What were you *really* doing at St. Catherine's?"

"I told you. I went along with Aunt Marian. Lend a strong arm for support. You know."

"Is that the only reason? Seems a little contrived to me."

He laughed. "Does it? I guess you're right. Would you believe me if I told you I love astronomy and the church tower is one of the best places around for looking at the night sky?"

"Maybe."

"Especially when they turn off those damned landscaping lights. What do you think they use in those babies, halogens?"

"Maybe." I paused. "Did you grow up Catholic?"

"Baptist. My dad's influence. Mom was a Catholic, though. I've been to my share of Masses. I've always kind of liked them. The ritual aspect. The pageantry."

"And yet you ended up . . . what you are."

He laughed. "You don't have to be so polite about it, you know. A male witch?"

"Shhh!" I looked around us for eavesdroppers, inadvertent or otherwise.

"Maggie. I'm comfortable with what I do. With what I am. I don't generally advertise one way or the other because I don't think it's anyone else's business. Now let me ask you a question. Did you grow up Catholic?"

"Yes."

"And yet you ended up . . . uncertain. Searching."

"It was a stupid question, wasn't it. Sorry."

He smiled, shaking his head. "No harm. No need."

I twirled my straw in my glass, causing the melting ice cubes to chase after each other like goldfish in a bowl. "Marcus?"

"Yeah?"

"What do you think they'll find out about Amanda Roberson's death? The police, I mean."

He was silent for a moment as he looked at me. Then his gaze slipped westward, briefly. "Looks like you'll have a chance to pursue the answer to that question yourself. Straight from the horse's ass. Or mouth."

He inclined his head toward the bar. I couldn't resist the temptation to turn and look for myself.

Tom Fielding stood at the bar, one hip perched on a tall stool and his arms crossed over his chest. For one brief blip in time, the rest of the world fizzled into nonexistence. He looked good. Damn good. Jeans skimming over his hips and thighs, a Kelly green rugby shirt, and — be still my heart — the kind of glasses that made a man look all studious and deliciously intense. The pristine white T-shirt peeking out at the neck was just the icing on the cake.

He was staring straight at us.

At me.

CHAPTER 7

I smiled tentatively while my heart did a little Snoopy dance with the excitement of seeing him. It was in the next heartbeat that I noticed he didn't look especially happy to see me. My bubble of joy burst with a big, juicy raspberry.

Small Stony Mill might be, but it was big enough that for more than two months Tom had managed somehow to avoid all the places I frequent. How many times had I thought I'd caught a glimpse of him, a victim of wishful thinking? Only to run into him, *now,* of all times, in a bar, of all places. Not to mention the fact that he found me in the company of Marcus Quinn, when I was supposed to be pining for him.

It just goes to show, Murphy's Law is obviously alive and well.

I turned back to the table and picked up my drink, wishing I had chosen alcoholic after all. I didn't understand what he was waiting for, why he wasn't turning his back on me and walking straight out the door. I mean, he'd avoided me this long — why stop now? And Marcus's knowing smirk made everything that much worse. Was I that transparent? The idea made me feel distinctly green at the gills.

A part of me wanted to sink into the cracked red leatherette booth cushion and disappear. Another part of me wanted to take Tom by the hand and lead him to the dance floor to get, er, reacquainted to the wail of the cheatin' song on the jukebox. Still another part of me wanted to snub him horribly for turning me away for so long out of pure male stubbornness.

"Maybe we should leave," I mumbled across the table.

"Too late," Marcus muttered back under his breath, sliding insolently down on the bench, his knees jutting out akimbo.

"Maggie O'Neill. As I live and breathe."
Or not . . .

"Can't say as I expected to run into you this evening," Tom went on, oblivious to my discomfort. "And what do we have here? If it isn't the mighty Mr. Quinn. Wasting no time. Not that I'm particularly surprised." He lifted his beer to his lips and took a draw from the bottle, his gray eyes never leaving

Marcus's face.

Marcus returned that storm cloud gaze with a steely one of his own. "Fielding. Off duty tonight, I see."

His gaze dipped to the bottle in Tom's hand. I could have sworn I saw a flush creep up Tom's neck.

"Yeah. Off duty. It's been a helluva week."

I could see it in his face, a strain that evidenced itself around his eyes, his jaw, the very coloring of his skin. Something told me Tom was taking Amanda's death just as personally as he'd taken Isabella Harding's. A life taken before its time. "It's terrible, isn't it?" I said softly. "My mother knows her mother."

"Mine, too."

Small world. In towns like Stony Mill, the world was nothing but small. Sometimes that was a good thing, because the problems that plagued more urban areas tended to pass us by. But sometimes that meant pain and suffering flooded in to make up the difference, a product of small, closed minds. Tragedy, though — that was universal.

Marcus stood up abruptly. "I need some air. You be okay, Maggie?"

I smiled at him, grateful that he had picked up on my need to talk to Tom without an audience. "I'll be right here."

He tossed a last look Tom's way, then sauntered away toward the men's room.

I cleared my throat. "Why don't you sit a moment, Tom?"

He hesitated, long enough that I thought he might refuse me. When he set his bottle on the table and sat down, I realized I'd been holding my breath. We sat on either side of the table, warily watching each other and waiting for the other to let down their guard.

I was never good at that kind of contest. "It's been a while since I've seen you around," I offered quietly.

His gaze met mine, then skipped away. "Yeah. Sorry. It's been a busy coupla months."

If I'd thought he was about to give up the ghost, I guess I was kidding myself. That excuse barely even qualified as lame. I should know, I'd just used it myself with my mother. Before I had the chance to consider how I felt about that, I decided to proceed with the next best thing. "So, who was it that pulled her body from the river?"

He snagged his bottle and slouched down in the bench, his head tilted back against the seat as he stared up at the ceiling, where the rafters were hung with old farming implements, license plates, and a variety of throwaway antiques. "Tommy and Harlan Samuels. Stu Samuels's boys. They were out exercising their hunting dogs when one of them found Amanda Roberson's shoe. A little further along the river, they found her body." A muscle jerked at the corner of his jaw. "She's at the coroner's right now."

"Is it . . . was it . . . I mean, I hope . . ." I stopped, unable to get the question out without sounding like a totally insensitive ghoul.

He stared at me between slitted eyelids. "An accident? Hell if I know. There didn't seem to be any outright evidence of foul play, thank God — can you imagine having to relay that kind of information to a seventeen-year-old girl's parents? But . . ."

His voice trailed off, but not before I heard the undertone of uncertainty that lurked in the darker corners of his consciousness. "But?"

He sat up and his eyes met mine, pain and rage merging in the cool gray. "I've seen drowning victims, Maggie. My cousin Martin lost his footing on the drop-off out at Little Long Lake back when I was eight, and we couldn't reach him. By the time they hauled him out of the water, it was too late." He shook his head as if trying to send the memory back to the past where it belonged, then gave a harsh laugh. "I've been haunted by that face ever since. I've seen it again and again, every time there's a boating accident, every accidental drowning. The bloating, the burst blood vessels, the strange color. Amanda's body didn't have that same look. If I was the kind of man to bet on things like that, I'd lay odds against there being water in her lungs. No water, no drowning. Which would mean, of course, that she died elsewhere and her body was dumped into the river. Much as I hate to admit it, my money is on this being no accident."

I nodded, but my mind was racing. "Is that a professional opinion?"

"It's professional speculation. I leave the opinions to the men of science. When the coroner confirms my suspicions, then I'll bite."

And yet I think we both knew that his instincts were dead on. It was that crazy sixth sense that electrified the air and intensified a person's awareness. "How long before they make their assessment?"

"A day. Maybe two. A week, maybe, to get all the results back from the hospital lab. I have a feeling they'll push this through as fast as possible — they want to catch whoever did this as much as we do."

And in the meantime, a killer was free to walk the streets, secure in the freedom of the moment. Life just wasn't fair. I twirled the ice cubes around my glass. "You know, Amanda came into the store on Saturday. A weird coincidence. I hadn't seen her for years — since Mel baby-sat for her, gosh, that was a long time ago — and then boom, there she was, Christmas shopping with her friends."

He laughed. "I could make a comment linking your place of employment and weirdness — but I won't."

I made a face at him. "Thanks."

"Don't mention it."

I didn't want him to get on the subject of Felicity — he had been one of the people who strongly suspected she'd had a hand in her sister's death. It was a sore subject for him, and I was too close to Liss by now to suffer his prejudices lightly. "Don't worry, I won't."

The tension between us was back, and he was eyeing his beer with a renewed interest. If I wanted to keep him within my sphere of influence, and I did, then I needed to steer us back onto neutral ground. "Look, I'm sorry," I said quietly. "I don't want to argue. I think it might be better for both of us if we agreed not to mention Felicity for the time being. Obviously we have different viewpoints where she is concerned —"

He muttered something that sounded suspiciously like *Got that right.*

"— so avoiding the subject altogether seems the best decision, in my book," I finished, plowing right ahead and pretending I didn't hear him. I meant to give him a charming smile, but I was pretty sure all I managed was a twisted challenge. "What do you say?"

He remained silent a moment, assessing me over the top of his beer bottle. Then he smiled at me. It wasn't a perfect smile — it reached his eyes as admiration, but only just — but for the time being, it was enough. "Right. Yeah. Agreed. Sounds like the best plan."

I smiled back, trying to make it a real one. "Good."

We fell silent, each absorbed in our own thoughts, while raucous music and tipsy laughter ebbed and flowed around us. My attention drifted, touching upon the other visitors to the tavern. The large woman at the bar in droopy jeans and an oversized denim shirt who sagged blearily over her near-empty glass. The old man in a scruffy John Deere baseball cap and faded flannel, who was challenging a younger man of the same general dress to a game of darts. The sports junkies who congregated around the muted TV, howling over the scoreboards. The bikers and their babes holding court around the pool tables, who might have looked a little scary but were mostly harmless when left to their own devices. A familiar face at the bar, his usual ramrod posture yielding to the bottle of Jack Daniel's sitting on the bar in front of him — Randy Cutter, I noted with some surprise. He didn't seem quite the type, but I guess everyone needs an outlet on occasion.

Most of the other people in the bar proved to be more of the same. One seemed familiar, a pretty young woman in the corner — except I couldn't figure out why. The guy she was with had his back to me, but he looked like your typical mid-twenties bad-ass. In fact, he looked a little like Marcus from behind, minus the tied-back hair. Tousled hair curling around his nape and ears, tight T-shirt clinging to his biceps, holey jeans. She looked a little out of his league, actually . . . not that that was any of my business. His interest in her was undeniable — I was pretty sure it had something to do with the tight little body she displayed to the hilt in a flirty dress of baby doll pink. The young woman rose to her feet, bending low over the table to lay a warm kiss on the guy's lips. As I watched, he toyed with the neckline of her dress, an openly suggestive touch. She laughed and playfully batted his hand away, then sashayed toward the corner where the restrooms were located.

I racked my brain. I knew her from somewhere. But where?

As she walked past the bar, Randy Cutter's head pivoted to follow her path.

Men.

"I'm gonna get going."

The voice nudged at my consciousness. "Hmm?"

Across the table, Tom rose to his feet. "Got an early day tomorrow. Better hit it."

I looked up at him, my concentration broken entirely. Disappointment hit a sour note in my stomach. "Oh. I see. Well, I suppose if you have to."

" 'Fraid so." He scrubbed his palm against his jeans, then held his hand out to me. "Good to see you again, Maggie. Take care of yourself."

He released my hand almost immediately, which disappointed me even more, then grabbed his leather jacket, and turned to go.

"Good to see you again, too," I echoed faintly as he strode out the main entrance without even a backward glance. Something told me I wouldn't be seeing him again. Not in a dating capacity, anyway, and not at his request. It seemed obvious that our relationship had ended before it had a chance to get started. And somehow I found the thought too depressing for words. I guess I had seen him as someone with a stronger character than that.

The reality of the bar came sifting back in on me, whatever glamour it had held earlier completely worn off. Now it just looked dirty, a little seamy, engulfed in shadow. The people, who earlier had appeared to be everyday people blowing off a little steam, now seemed nothing more than out-of-control drunks and incessant partiers who couldn't deal with life in the real world, a world that had admittedly wandered off course and couldn't seem to find its way back. I wanted to leave, but Marcus still hadn't returned to the table, and I didn't know where he'd disappeared to.

I sat for a moment, staring into my still half-full glass before my thoughts returned to the young woman in the pink dress. Before I knew what I was doing, I found myself leaving my dark corner and following the way she'd gone, toward the ladies' (term applied loosely) restroom.

Another nondecision that transitioned to action, as though my subconscious had taken control of my body.

There is something unsavory about a tavern restroom, and this one was no different. Three stalls stood on the far wall, each painted a bilious green, a color that must have been on sale at the hardware store at some point in time because it covered every bare surface in the room, including the ceiling. The first stall door was latched, so per the usual bathroom protocol, I skipped the middle one and quietly entered the far stall on the left. Trying to ignore the grime, the sticky floor, and the decades' worth of messages etched through the thickest paint layers, I sat down on the closed toilet.

I could hear the blips and beeps of a cell phone emerging from the far stall. It was her, all right. If I glanced beneath the partial stall wall, I could see her feet, delicately shod in whimsical silver sandals. No one else in the bar tonight would have been wearing silver sandals, I guarantee. The young woman swore softly, and then I heard her dial the seven digits of a local number. I held my breath. I didn't quite know why I was eavesdropping, but that didn't stop me.

"It's me," she said to whomever had picked up on the other end. "I got your text message. Don't worry, I'm out with Jason at the Little Nipper. Yeah, I know you don't like it. I don't see why not, though. Amanda's gone. Nothing I can do will help that. But I don't see why that should change things with Jason. I mean . . . Aw, come on, Lily. Don't cry."

Amanda. For the last three days Amanda Roberson had been on everyone's lips. But this was different. The word "friend" floated into my head, and I knew instinctively that the connection was right.

"I know. I know! Don't worry. I'll be careful. Jason wouldn't hurt me or anyone else. He's really, really nice to me, you know that. And I like him. And besides, we don't know what happened to Amanda, right? I mean, it could have been an accident, couldn't it, just like they're saying. Just plain, dumb bad luck? I mean, I know we both wondered if she was seeing other guys and all, but that doesn't mean . . ."

That rolling sound that made her stop talking? It came from my stall. I must have leaned too far to the left in an effort to hear better. The plunger rolled out of my reach and under the next stall.

"Listen, I have to go. Don't worry, I'll be fine. Talk to you later."

Almost immediately I heard the rattle of

the latch, light footsteps on the plain con-
crete floor, a squeak of reluctant taps, and
then water as it gushed down an open drain.
The water went on for a few minutes, longer
than seemed necessary. Finally the squeak
came again as the water was turned off.

Any minute now . . .

I'm not sure when I became aware that
she was waiting for me to come out. Eventually it became obvious she wasn't leaving
the restroom until I made an appearance,
so I cleared my throat self-consciously and
made a few ineffectual tugs on the lopsided
toilet paper roll that some thrifty soul had
squashed to make it harder to unravel.
Inspiration struck — I lifted the lid of the
feminine product disposal bin, tossed the
toilet paper bits in, and let the lid drop with
a bang. It was a sound every woman could
identify that could explain *anyone's* lengthy
sojourn in the ladies' toilet.

I flushed for good measure. When I could
delay no longer, I unlatched the door.

She looked over her shoulder at me in the
mirror as she applied powder from a compact — and *paled*. I didn't imagine it.
Abruptly she closed the compact with a
snick and dropped it into a little silver mesh
bag. Her dark hair fell over her cheek, hiding her face from me, but it didn't matter.

In a series of mental flashes, I realized where I knew her from.

One, Enchantments. *Two,* mantel clock. *Three,* Amanda's friend.

Bingo.

She looked different tonight, her hair a mass of sultry, chin-length curls, tucked back here and there with some sparkling little clips. Expertly applied makeup that gave her a seven-or eight-year edge on her actual seventeen. The pink babydoll dress matched her overall appearance to a T. Youthful, but seductive. A man's fantasy come to life.

Without further ado, she stuffed the rest of her makeup back into her purse. She'd just turned to escape when I stopped her.

"Excuse me. You're Amanda's friend, aren't you?"

Slowly she pivoted back to me. Uncertainty flickered like a shadow in the depths of her eyes. "Um . . . yes?"

Her hand came up to tuck a stray strand of hair behind her ear. Her nervousness was palpable in the air between us, making it vibrate.

I tried a smile. "You came into the store I work in the other day, remember? Enchantments?"

"Yes, I remember."

"I'm so sorry about poor Amanda. Such a terrible, terrible tragedy. The whole town is praying for her family. Were you very good friends with her?"

The girl just stared at me.

I held my hand out to her. "I'm Maggie O'Neill, by the way."

She hesitated only a moment before she took my hand, I'm sure, because she'd been taught it was rude to refuse and she was still too young to realize that was more a guideline than a rule. "Candace Knightley. Yes, we were good friends." She reached for a tissue and began to dab at her eyes.

"It's hard to lose a friend, especially someone so young." My idea of a subtle prompt. "I understand the school has arranged for some special counselors, to help kids who knew her come to terms with it all."

"Yes. No one really knew her, though. Not really. She was a pretty private person."

"But you two were close?"

"As close as anyone could be. I don't think she really trusted anyone, as far as that goes." She shrugged.

I sighed, watching her. "The idea that somebody might have wanted to hurt her —"

She looked up sharply. "What gave you

that idea?"

"Just something I heard somewhere. It makes sense, doesn't it? I hear some people don't think it was an accident. Do you . . . do *you* think that might have been possible?"

"I guess." She bit her lip at the thought. "I guess I think with Amanda anything was possible. Like I said, I don't think she let many people really know her."

"I keep thinking back to the day that Amanda disappeared," I mused. "I suppose you've probably already told the police what happened after you all left the store that day."

There is a fine line between making polite queries and being viewed as a busybody. I was probably in a fair bit of danger of crossing that line, but I pushed on, despite the squeamish nature of my conscience that would under normal circumstances have made me back down in disgrace. Keeping her mind on the move made it less likely that she'd realize I was asking questions she didn't have to answer. And I really wanted to know. I couldn't explain why it seemed so important just then, but for the sense that if I didn't ask the questions now, I might never have another chance. Which didn't make me exactly a nice person, I guess, but at least someone sensitive enough to want to leave that impression.

She leaned back against the door (brave girl) and closed her eyes. "I wish I knew. We shopped until two, and then she was supposed to go home to get ready for an afternoon date with Jordan before heading in to work at six."

"Jordan?"

"Jordan Everett. Her boyfriend. They're — they *were* — pretty tight. But according to him, she never showed up. He's pretty broken up about it."

"I'll bet." I paused, wondering whether I should say anything else. But Amanda's death really had me troubled, and in the end I couldn't help myself. The last thing we needed was yet another teenage girl so intent on living on the edge that she forgot about the lack of guardrails. "You know, Candace, if you don't mind my saying so, I'm pretty sure you're not old enough to be here legally."

She flinched slightly, but youthful bravado saw her through. She tossed her curls. "Well, I'm here with my uncle. His friend owns the place."

"Your uncle knows Jerry Maxwell?"

Her tension eased, ever so slightly. "Yes. And I would hate for anyone to get into trouble because of me. You won't tell, will you?"

I turned off the water. "Candace. The owner's name is not Jerry Maxwell, and something tells me the guy you're with is not your uncle." Not to mention the state law that said no one under the age of twenty-one was allowed to be in a bar. That appeared to be beside the point.

"Yes, he is, he —"

"No. He's not. Look, this is none of my business —"

"No. It's not." She stuffed the tissue into her tiny little purse and jerked herself upright.

"— but you're so young, and if you don't mind me saying so, that guy looks just a little old for you. I know it's tempting to go for someone a little older, a little more knowledgeable, someone who can maybe get you into bars and parties and such. But Amanda is gone, and we don't know why. Or how. You're such a pretty girl. Just, please . . . be safe."

Her expression closed in on itself with the sullen and suspicious undertones of a girl not yet free of her Me years. "You know, lady, somebody ought to tell you to mind your own beeswax, 'cause I sure don't need anyone to mind mine," she smarted off before tossing her dark head at me and sailing out of the room.

I sighed and turned to look at myself in the mirror beneath the restroom's harsh fluorescent lights. My thirtieth birthday was right around the corner, and in a way the thought of it made me cringe. Was it the end of an era, or only the end of my youth? Then again, based on Candace's reaction to my words of caution, maybe my youth was long gone after all.

By the time I followed Candace's example, she had her guy friend by the arm and was headed for the door. Did I really believe her to be in danger with her friend? Not necessarily. The more I thought about it, the more likely it seemed that she was just working the good-girl-gone-bad thing. Trying for independence, but getting it all wrong. It happens to the best of us.

Still, Amanda *was* gone, and I was getting the distinct impression that Amanda had led the charge down that same path. I hoped Candace and other girls like her would see that as a sign to stick to the straight and narrow. To play it safe.

I decided it was time to call it a night, so I motioned to Marcus, who was chatting with a big biker with arms like battering rams and a handlebar mustache that drooped two inches below his jaw.

Marcus caught up with me by the door "Hey. I see old Wonder Bread is gone. All too early, too." He pushed the door open and held it for me. Cold seeped in from the outside, but it was nothing compared to the chill that tightened like a band around my heart. Seeing my woebegone face, Marcus took my hand and tucked it through the crook of his arm, giving it a solicitous pat. "Don't worry, Maggie. I always did think him an idiot, but sometimes it's hell being proven right."

Sighing heavily, I touched my forehead to his shoulder. "Thanks, Marcus. You're a good friend." I paused a moment before pulling back to a *friendlier* distance, and looked up at him. "You really don't like him much, do you?"

"Am I that obvious?" he said, with a self-mocking grin, knowing full well just how obvious he had made it.

"Only just." He took Christine's keys from my hand and unlocked the door. I couldn't help noticing the locks cooperated instantly, knife through butter. Traitorous thing. "Why is that?"

Marcus shrugged. "Not all energies are compatible."

Energies. I took this under consideration.

Was that why some marriages worked and some didn't? The couple's energies revved up their engines, but when all was said and done, they were out of calibration? "Fair enough. But I still feel like you're not telling me everything."

"Everyone loves to maintain an air of mystery, no matter how slight."

He was so good at that, answering a girl's questions without ever truly clearing the air. Marcus kept more than his share of mystery gathered about him. I wasn't even sure what he did for a living now, although I did know he'd left the military only a year or so ago, a fact I'd gleaned from his informative aunt. But he was a supportive friend and Liss trusted him implicitly, so that was good enough for me, too. He'd fill me in on the rest when he was ready.

Funny, though. I couldn't picture Marcus, with his long hair, impudent slouch, and alternative way of looking at the world, as a military man.

We sat in the car, waiting for the engine to smooth out enough to drive. So much for unseasonably warm weather — it was getting colder by the minute. I didn't have my gloves, so I tucked my hands between my legs and tried not to shiver.

I felt a nudge. "Here," Marcus said, holding out a big pair of dark leather gloves, "before you freeze to death."

"Thanks." I put them on. The heat from his hands permeated the soft lining. Instant relief. "Marcus? Did you see the girl in the pink dress at the Nipper tonight?"

He laughed. "Underage hottie? Yeah, I saw. Why?"

"That was Amanda's friend. The one from the store. Remember, I told you they'd been harassing Tara? I didn't tell you this, but they saw the books she'd brought down from the loft and were just really, really cruel about it."

His jaw tightened, but he said, "I've run into a few of those types in the past myself. Tara will be fine. She's a strong one."

"Yes, I know. Very strong willed. She's also very talented."

"What do you mean?"

Briefly I recounted how I'd run into Tara at Riverside Park, and what I'd witnessed. "A binding, she said. She raised quite a lot of power. I'll be honest — it kind of scared me. It didn't feel like the power Liss raises. I . . . I thought I should tell you. It's probably nothing — the difference between Liss's age and experience as opposed to Tara's — but I thought you should know." I paused a moment, then added, "She called me a Fluffy Bunny. Sounds cute, but from her tone I got that it wasn't meant to be."

He shook his head and sighed. "You'll find that even in the Pagan community, differences are not always embraced. Although I think as a general rule, Pagans are more tolerant than most people. Sometimes to a ridiculous extent. Ah, well." He shook his head again. "I'll have a talk with her."

"Um . . . Could you also maybe, possibly, ask her about the books she borrowed from the store?"

He froze. "Borrowed?"

"Well . . ."

"You mean took," he said, his tone as flat as a cast-iron griddle. "She'll be there tomorrow to return them or to pay for them. You have my word."

"No biggie. I'm sure she meant to, but with everything that's been going on . . ." I didn't ask him what he thought Tara might have been binding, there by the river. I didn't want to push my luck. "I think Christine's ready to go. Where can I drop you now?"

"My truck's at the library. I met Aunt Marian there earlier."

"The library it is, then."

The Stony Mill Carnegie Library stood on a quiet tree-lined street three blocks

158

from the Town Hall square, on the fringes of the downtown area that comprised Main Street. I puttered up to the curb behind the only vehicle parked along the street, an old, battered pickup truck that appeared to have hailed from the same era as Christine.

"No bike tonight?" I asked him.

"In this weather? I'm no fool. By the way, thanks for the ride."

"Don't mention it. Tonight was —" My breath caught in my throat. "Oh my God! Someone's in the library!"

He swung around to see what I was looking at. "Where?"

"I saw a flash of light in the basement. It had to be a flashlight." I grabbed his arm. "There it goes again! Did you see it? It must be one of those micro-miniflashlights, the beam wasn't very big, and —"

The tension in Marcus's arm released and he turned back to me with a chuckle. "There isn't anyone in the basement, Maggie."

I frowned at him. "What do you mean? Didn't you see it?"

"I saw it. The light had a blue tint to it, didn't it?"

"Well . . . yes. I guess it did. Why?"

He was grinning by now, even white teeth flashing in the muted light from Christine's dash. "How long have you lived in Stony Mill?"

"I was born here."

"You've never heard that the basement of the library has a resident spirit?"

I opened my mouth, closed it, turned to gape at the library. "I —"

"I'm surprised Aunt Marian never told you about him herself. It's Boiler Room Bertie, or so they say. He died in an accident when the library was young, just after the turn of the century."

"Boiler Room . . . Bertie?" I echoed, dubious.

He held up his hands. "Hey, I don't name 'em. I just investigate 'em."

CHAPTER 8

Tuesday morning arrived on the heels of a sleepless night. I had lain awake for hours, thinking about Amanda, and wondering how her life, which up until that point had seemed so charmed, could have ended so badly. Was it fate that had brought Amanda Lynn Roberson to our doorstep that Saturday?

Busybodying had its downside. I awoke, dazed and confused after too little sleep, to the raucous jangling of my alarm clock going off bright and early at six-thirty. I sat up with a jerk and reached out a hand to stop the horrible ringing at once . . . only to discover I'd forgotten to set the alarm. At the precise moment I remembered that my alarm clock made a *bleep-bleep* and not a clanging jangle, some unseen thing fell to the floor across the room, dropping with a thunderous clap. I leapt from bed, clutching G.T. (Graham Thomas, my dilapidated but beloved old teddy bear) to my breast while I groped for the light switch. But once I had found the switch and light flooded the room far and wide, I could see no reason for the noise itself. Still I knew.

Apparently someone . . . or some*thing* . . . didn't want me to miss my appointment.

It hadn't happened in a while — or perhaps I had been extra successful at turning a blind eye toward the phenomenon — but I had understood all the while that it was not gone forever. A reprieve, yes, but no more.

There was nothing to do but get on with it, then.

"All right, all right, already. I'm up."

Eight o'clock in the morning was an ungodly time to have to think about undergoing the torture that modern science called the feminine annual exam. Especially on such short notice. All the women I knew called it "your yearly," a polite term for the regularly scheduled legal torture that took place in your doctor's medical chamber of horrors. I mean, what else can you call the *feet-in-stirrups-knees-to-chin-spread-'em!* procedure that took a woman's dignity, pride, and money all at once? All in the name of preventive maintenance. Did I mention that Dr. Phillips had the unfortunate tendency to tell jokes while probing about doing his doctor thing? Until a person had been in that position, staring up at the perforations in the ceiling tiles and trying to ignore the terrible jokes that made you clench your teeth to keep from laughing in spite of everything, one had not really lived.

I signed in at the board and set about finding a comfortable seat where I could be sure to avoid stray germs.

"Maggie? Why, Maggie O'Neill!"

I looked up. The blond receptionist had stood up behind her counter and was leaning out the sliding window. "Katie Coolidge?"

"Oh my gosh! It is you! Wow, I haven't seen you since high school."

I waggled my fingers at her. Katie Coolidge had been as geeky as me back in high school — we'd even hung out once or twice — but she'd been far more interested in worming her way into the popular cliques than I had ever been, and our friendship had never grown past a polite affability. Last I heard she'd moved to Chicago with a boyfriend. Seeing as how her last name was still Coolidge, it was a pretty easy guess that that particular relationship hadn't worked out.

"When did you start working for Dr. Phillips?" I asked her.

"Oh, I've been here almost a year now. I guess you've heard Doctor P. is closing his practice, huh?"

I nodded. "My mom told me, and she's none too happy about it, believe me. Tough luck on your part, or are you going with him?"

"I guess I'll be staying on here. We have a new doctor that's going to be taking over the practice." She glanced down at the file folder she held in front of her. "So you're here for your yearly, huh? Lucky you."

Waaaay too loud. I made a small sound in the back of my throat that could have passed for either assent or dissent and went to find a seat as far away from everyone else until my name was called.

Dr. Phillips's waiting room walls were lined with personal photos. I whiled away the time studying them, one by one. Pictures of fish, both ocean creatures and northern lake varieties like trout and bluegill. Some photos of what I assumed to be his family. More fish. It was pretty funny how the pics of the fish outnumbered those of his family.

Men. Ya gotta love 'em.

"Margaret?"

I looked up to find a nurse standing in the open doorway, calling my name at last. She smiled expectantly at me. Rising, my purse clutched against my side, I followed her down the hall, past a bathroom with the usual cubbyhole specimen repository, toward the examination rooms. The nurse measured my weight (*perhaps I had better rethink that bowl of cream of potato soup I had been considering for lunch . . . Maybe a garden salad. No dressing. Sigh . . .*) before leading me into an exam room, where she checked my blood pressure and temperature, jotted a few somethings down in my file, and left.

With a resigned sigh, I scowled at the examination table. The metal stirrups glinted coldly, taunting me. I hated this part. After folding my clothes and setting them neatly on the chair, I wrapped a paper robe around myself.

A knock at the door scared the pants off me — well, they were already off, but you get the idea.

"Everyone decent?" Dr. Phillips's trademark greeting boomed from the hall.

"Everyone being me, then I'll say yes," I replied dryly, turning toward the door as it swung inward and Dr. Phillips's barrel-chested bulk seemed to fill the narrow room. I'd always liked Dr. Phillips despite his corny jokes. He had a no-nonsense way of speaking that let you know he was listening without giving in to fears, and whether young or old, he seemed to really care for his patients.

He consulted the folder he had in his hand. "So you're here for your yearly," he said, unwittingly echoing his receptionist's greeting.

I crossed my arms protectively over my paper-covered chest. "And how are you today, Doctor?"

"Much better than you're about to be, I'd wager," he quipped right back at me — the family practice doctor's equivalent of gallows humor. "Why don't you just climb up there on the table while I fetch Amy."

Amy turned out to be the whirlwind of a nurse who had checked me in. Dr. Phillips returned with her in tow within seconds. All of the necessary instruments had been prepped in advance. Amy the Nurse helped Dr. Phillips with his latex gloves. The snap as she fitted them into place made me wince. Dr. Phillips turned to me, his hands held up before him at the ready. "All right, Miss Maggie, if you'll just lie back, Amy will help you get your feet into the stirrups."

Oh, joy.

The paper crinkled as I slid into place. I felt Amy's blessedly warm hands guide my bare feet into the stirrups. From thereon out, I tried to forget where I was and why.

Focal point. I needed a focal point.

My desperate gaze fell back to the line of photos along the wall. A blurry vacation photo of the Doc in cover-thine-eyes! tight little swim trunks (well, more briefs than trunks), flanked on each side by a beaming friend, the three of them lifting aloft a huge swordfish. And was that a tattoo on the good doctor's shoulder? He didn't seem the type. Then again, he didn't really seem the too small swimsuit type either. Blech. New focal point needed. I turned my gaze to the ceiling.

"So, Miss Maggie, did you hear the one about the woman who took her daughter to the doctor because she was having strange symptoms? Doc examines the girl and says, 'Madam, I believe your daughter is pregnant.' A claim the daughter instantly denies, on the basis that she's never even kissed a man. Well, the good doctor processes this information, then walks over to the window and stares out at the sky. The mother asks him what he's doing. 'Well, madam, I'll tell you. The last time this happened, a strange star appeared in the East. I was just waiting to see if another would show up.' " Dr. Phillips chuckled heartily to himself.

"All done. You can sit up now." He stripped off the gloves that made his hands look like a clown's and stuffed them into the trash marked BIOHAZARD. "Things look pretty good, young miss. Of course, the results from the tests will be mailed to you as soon as they come back from the lab. Any complaints you haven't told me about?"

I shook my head. "Not really. I've been a little tired lately, but mostly thanks to a few sleepless nights."

He chuckled. "Too many late-night escapades, I hope?"

"Worrying, mostly. With Amanda Roberson being found dead, and with what happened in town a few months back, things just feel a little unsettled to me."

Dr. Phillips frowned as he scribbled on my chart. "Well, that sounds normal to me. A girl should feel unsettled, threatened, with everything that's been going on. I shouldn't expect it's anything to worry about unless it continues." He flipped the chart closed and put it in the clear receptacle on the wall for the nurse to file. "Terrible thing to happen to that girl. Terrible, terrible. Don't know what the world is coming to these days."

Neither did I. Neither did anyone, it

seemed. And wasn't that part of the problem?

I spent much of Tuesday mulling over that very notion in between manning the cash register and running the tea and coffee bar. Tuesdays are typically a slow day for us, and this one was no different. It gave me plenty of time to think about everything that had happened, all that I'd learned.

Which wasn't much.

I kept the radio on low, tuned in to WOWO. Much of the time the airspace was filled with the old Christmas classics, familiar voices from my childhood that for the most part had been replaced on other stations by modern-day divas fond of the kind of vocal acrobatics that drove me crazy. Give me a Burl Ives or a Nat King Cole over the self-styled phenoms any day.

When at last they did play a news update, I upped the volume as much as I dared, depending on the number of customers filing through the aisles. But it wasn't until two-thirty that there was actually any new news in the Roberson girl's disappearance.

"According to a statement read by the County Coroner's office, the death of Stony Mill High School student Amanda Lynn Roberson has been upgraded from

169

Death by Unknown Causes to Homicide this afternoon. Roberson had gone missing sometime during the afternoon to evening hours of Saturday, December fourteenth. Search efforts encompassed much of the next two days before her body was found Monday afternoon by two hunters in the shallows of the Wabash River. Stony Mill Chief of Police, Manny Burns, stated this afternoon that the investigation into the circumstances surrounding Roberson's death continue. Any person or persons with knowledge to impart, no matter how insignificant, is encouraged to cooperate with the authorities as soon as possible."

With the news broadcast at an end, I took a deep, steadying breath and turned down the volume as the Christmas carols resumed.

Homicide.

Again?

What was going on in Stony Mill?

I was still worrying over that as I wrapped yet another package for yet another regular when Tom Fielding marched back into my life.

Or should I say Deputy Tom Fielding. I supposed that would be more appropriate, dressed as he was in his regulation dark blues, a black leather jacket added to guard against the returned winter temperatures.

I stood up straighter and sent the customer on the way with a brilliant smile before I turned to greet Tom with a casualness that I could not feel. "Deputy Fielding. Long time no see. What brings you here on this fine December day?"

He had assumed the Good-Cop-Bad-Girl role he seemed so fond of while in uniform. "Maggie. I'm here on official business."

"So I see. What can I do for you?"

He pulled a notebook out of his inner breast pocket and flipped it open with a flick of his wrist. "I need to ask you a few questions about what you told me last night. You stated that Amanda Roberson visited Enchantments on the morning of Saturday, December fourteenth. The day that she disappeared. Is that correct?"

I resisted the urge to roll my eyes. Official police business could be so dramatic. "Keerrect."

"What can you tell me about the purpose of that visit?"

I could be as aloof as he could, if that was the way he wanted to play it. "On the morning of Saturday, December fourteenth, at approximately ten-thirty a.m., Amanda

Roberson entered the store in the company of two of her friends. One blonde, one brunette. All three appeared to be of approximately the same age. Amanda Roberson purchased one very expensive antique mantel clock, ostensibly as a gift for her mother, who had admired the clock on an earlier visit to the store. Paid cash. Left with friends after verbally accosting another of my customers, one Tara Murphy, another high school student. There didn't appear to have been any love lost between them. Typical jockeying for power, if you ask me."

He scratched down a few more words before continuing. "What time did she leave the establishment?"

"Shortly after arriving. By eleven o'clock, certainly. They looked at things for a little while before deciding on the clock for Amanda's mother. She mentioned the gift was going to get her out of the doghouse, so I took that to mean she had had some kind of disagreement with her mother. Nothing unusual there."

"Was there *anything* unusual about the event that you can recall?"

I shrugged. "Just that for a high school senior she carried an awful lot of cash in her purse. The clock wasn't exactly cheap, but buying it didn't even come close to cleaning her out."

"You don't know the names of the two girls she was with?"

"One was Candace Knightley. The other — I'm not sure, but it might have been Lily. No last name, sorry. But I'm sure if you ask around, you'll find out easily enough."

A few more scribbles on the pad. "What about this other girl, this Tara Murphy. What can you tell me about her?"

"Not much. It was her first time here."

Tom looked at me more closely. "Are you sure about that?"

"I'm sure."

I hesitated over telling him the reason for Tara's visit to the store. He was so uptight about the witch stuff already, and besides, it was totally unrelated to the investigation of the case. Then, too, what about the telephone conversation I'd overheard at the Little Nipper? Or what about what Evie had told me, about the fight at school between Amanda and Tara a few days before Amanda's disappearance? Was it my place to tell him something that I hadn't witnessed firsthand? Usually we call that kind of thing gossip, and I'd been the victim of it too many times to count growing up to want to participate in it much myself. Besides, it was something he could find out from any number of Amanda's cohorts in crime. I decided to hold off. For now.

"What about the disagreement you mentioned?"

I busied myself straightening the items taking up a goodly portion of the counter. "Like I said, typical teenager stuff. Tara is a little bit . . . different. Amanda didn't appear to be the tolerant type. After a few insults were hurled, Tara left, much to the amusement of Amanda and her friends. See what I mean? Typical."

"What do you mean, different?"

"Well . . ." I squirmed a little, trying to think how best to explain things in a way he would understand. "I don't know. An outsider, I guess. And she likes to dress the part. It's something a lot of kids go through when they fall through the cracks of the usual pecking order. They grow out of it eventually, once they realize that high school popularity contests mean nothing once you leave school."

"Ah." He nodded to himself. "Square pegs."

"Exactly!" I confirmed, pleased that I'd managed to say something right.

"The school officials will know more," he continued, closing his notebook and sliding it into his jacket pocket again. "I'll be heading over there next."

Which meant he was done here. Now that he was here, I was loath to let him go, despite his high-handed manner. "Tom . . . you will find who did this, won't you?"

His gray-green eyes met mine, hard with determination. "Count on it."

"Do you have any leads?"

"Some." Then, "Well, not many, but it's still early. There's a protocol to investigation, Maggie. Methodical. Logical," he explained. "The first step is to build a timeline of the victim's final days. Who they spoke with. Where they went, and when. Somewhere in the minutia will be the truth, and if it's there, I'll find it."

I hoped so. One murder was enough to rattle the shelter Stony Mill had erected around itself to keep the world at bay. The residents of Stony Mill were no saintlier than the residents of a big urban center with big urban crimes. People are people no matter where you live. Human prejudices, human fears, human failings.

People didn't change.

"You'll . . ." My voice failed me when his eyes shot to mine. I tried again. "You'll be careful, won't you? I mean," I amended in an attempt to make the question sound somehow less earnest, "you will take all the necessary precautions, right? All of you in the police department. Two murders in Stony Mill in two and a half months . . . that's got to be some kind of record, doesn't it?"

And not the kind of record you wanted to go around breaking.

He slipped on a pair of sunglasses. No cutie-geek glasses in sight. Today it was all he-man mirrored aviators. "See you later, Maggie." He made a motion to leave, then paused and slanted a grin over his shoulder. "By the way, nice hat. Brings out the green in your eyes."

I brought my hand up, only to encounter the fuzzy brim and dangling poof ball of the Santa's Helper cap I'd forgotten.

Maybe I should lose the hat.

I refused to allow myself to mourn the loss of someone who wasn't interested in me. This was the Twenty-First Century, after all. A time of enlightenment. I am Woman, hear me flush all evidence of a broken love affair. *Feh.* I had more important things to devote my time and energy to. My job. My friends. My family.

Everything else at this point was gravy.

I knew all of that. My head was giving me the thumbs-up. My heart was dragging its feet, but I figured it would come around soon enough with the right kind of distraction.

Speaking of distractions . . .

The bell jingled. I didn't look up right away. Most of our customers would follow a pattern that began with pausing just inside the door then wending their way between and around the aisles and stacks. And today I was happy to allow them to do just that.

"Hey, Maggie."

I looked up to find Marcus making his way toward the counter, as tall, dark, and lanky as always. "Hey, Marcus."

"I brought someone in to see you."

From behind him peeked a dark, shaggy head, then a slender, spritelike shadow disengaged herself from his lean figure. She stood quietly beside him, meeker than I would ever have expected.

"Hello, Tara," I said to put her at ease. "School out already?"

Her kohl-rimmed gaze lifted, the merest flicker. "Marcus picked me up at the door."

"Expected?"

"Nope." She let her backpack slide down her arm, the strap falling neatly into her hand, and caught her lower lip between her teeth as she began to dig in the bag's hidden depths. "I, uh, brought money. For the books. I did want to buy them, but I guess I lost my head on Saturday."

"That's okay."

Marcus nudged her softly. Tara jumped. "I, um, I'm really sorry. I meant to come in yesterday. The day was a real bitch. Queen-sized."

She slid a twenty across the counter to me with the books.

I rang them up and handed her back the change. "The important thing is that you did come in, Tara."

"I really did mean to. I hope you believe me."

Weird thing was, I did believe her. Maybe she'd gotten sidetracked by Amanda's death the way the rest of us did. To her credit, she did look contrite. A tad slow on the uptake where apologies were concerned, but she had come through. There was hope for humanity yet. "I'm sure you did."

"I mean, we didn't have any homework or anything because of what happened, which was kewl, but great Goddess, all anyone wanted to do was talk about freaking perfect Amanda and how they're so freaking sorry she's gone. And not a single one of 'em had a freaking clue what she was really like, and that's what's so freaking pathetic about this whole freaking town if you ask me."

Marcus sighed. "What my cousin the

Minimalist is trying to say is that the day threw her for a loop and all thoughts of responsibilities flew out of her spiky little head. Right, String Bean?"

She rolled her eyes, looking every inch the typical teen. Well, a typical teen who had dumped a jar of ink over her hair and who had learned her language from the disreputable river rats that had once dominated the old warehouses along River Street before the town set its sights on the title "Antique Capital of the Midwest." Tara was nothing if not colorful. I supposed we should all feel glad she had edited herself for content, minimizing her use of the F-bomb in favor of pretenders to the throne. Not that I don't use it myself when the situation calls for it, but I do try to practice some measure of self-control.

Tara drifted over to a display of Herbal Treasures lotions and soaps. Marcus leaned back against the antique counter as he watched his younger cousin. I leaned back and watched him. My gaze slid easily over his leather biker jacket and dark jeans. His hair was pulled back with a leather thong at the nape of his neck again, a look that lent an air of centuries-old romance to his dark and dangerous edge. If I blurred my focus, I could just see him, a romance novel hero in dark breeches and a flowing white poet's shirt, open at the neck, a rapier held loosely at his side as he watched his defeated opponent flee in shame. Dark and light, hard and soft, enigmatic and yet approachable. Felicity was a lucky, lucky woman.

Too much distraction for this small-town girl to handle. I cleared my throat. "Did I mention that the police came by today to ask about Amanda Roberson's visit to the store last Saturday?"

His only movement was a teensy lift of his brow. "The illustrious Deputy Fielding?"

"How did you guess?"

"I saw his car and figured he must be combing the area for clues. Besides, everyone knows the chief doesn't get his hands dirty. Unless it's for a good cause. Like a good glazed doughnut."

I laughed in spite of myself. Chief of Police Burns was a fixture in Stony Mill. A big, rawboned man with hands that could just as easily palm a basketball as cradle a gun, he had a history that went all the way back to the state basketball championship of 1969. It goes without saying that that one streak of good luck had ensured his status in Stony Mill for time immemorial — we took our basketball very seriously. In short, he was a god among men, and he enjoyed the fruits of his position as often as possible. In the course of any day, he could be seen making the rounds of the town's various eating establishments. His rumored favorite? Annie-Thing Good's plate-sized cherry fritters.

"That was just plain mean, Marcus," I told him.

"Remind me to bring along one of Annie's famous fritters to the investigation tonight, just in case he decides to put in an appearance and we need a little something to grease the wheel."

"*Mar*-cus!"

"There's an investigation tonight?" Tara interjected from afar, nose deep in a strawberry-kiwi concoction that was one of my favorites.

Marcus balanced back on his elbows. "Think we ought to get her hearing checked?"

"I've heard fruit bats have some of the best ears on the planet. Any chance she has one of those in her ancestry?" I deadpanned right back.

"Hey! I heard that!" She put her hands on her leather miniskirted hips.

"It's a distinct possibility," Marcus confirmed with a wicked grin.

Tara stalked in our direction. "Very funny.

I hope you know, I'm coming with you tonight. Where's the meet-'n'-greet?"

"You're not going."

She stared at Marcus as if he'd lost his marbles. "Yeeeeah. Come on. Where's it really?"

"I'm serious. You're not going."

When she set her jaw and jutted out her chin, she looked just like her cousin. "Why not?"

To Marcus's credit, he didn't react to her righteous fury. "Because you weren't invited."

She compressed her lips together. "That's not fair, Marcus. You can't tell me what to do. You're not my dad."

"No. That's true enough. But from what I've been told, you're not listening much to your dad, either."

She pushed her lips into a pout and said nothing.

"Besides, what I am is family, and I look out for you, don't I? Come on, Tara. You have no real experience with this at all, you have far too much curiosity for your own good, and you've been generating a fair amount of energy. Don't deny it, I can feel the traces of it. The three things together . . ." He shook his head decisively. "Too dangerous. You'd be at risk for any darker spirit energy we might come across."

He chucked her under the chin, but she would have none of it. She jerked away with a toss of her head. "I don't need you. I could conjure it myself if I wanted to, and there's nothing you can do about it. I'm not allergic to dark energy, like some people." That must have been meant for me, given the sneer she flicked my way.

Now it was Marcus's turn to jut out his chin. "You'll do no such thing."

"Try and stop me."

She turned on her chunky heel and ran out of the store before he could say anything else.

Marcus puffed out his breath along with the tension that had gathered in his shoulders. "That girl."

He didn't elaborate, but then again, he didn't need to. His frustration and worry were buzzing along my nerve endings already. "She'll be all right, Marcus. A lot of kids go through that at her age."

"I know," he groaned, clapping his hand to his face and scrubbing with his palm. "I did myself. That's why I'm so worried. I *know* what I did. If she takes after me, my Uncle Lou will have a heart attack."

"And what did you do?"

"Ran off and joined the Army."

"Is that all?" He looked so gloomy, I couldn't help but laugh. "That's hardly something to panic about. It's rather noble. Romantic, really. Running off to put your life on the line for the love of country."

"That would have been noble, sure." He nodded sagely. "Of course, I joined up solely to piss my mom off. It worked, too. See, I told you it was stupid."

I tried to picture him in a soldier's uniform, hair buzzed in a high-and-tight above the ears, or even in a pair of camouflage BDUs. Nope, couldn't do it. "What did you do in the Army?"

"Military Intelligence. I could tell you about it, but then I'd have to kill you."

"Wow, that smarts. You know what they say about paranoia."

"You bet your boots, sweet cheeks. Didn't you know, the Army invented the word?"

CHAPTER 9

Paranoia can be a crippling emotion, but nothing is as crippling as a girl's biggest phobia. I'm not talking spiders here. Ever since I was a little girl, I'd had certain . . . *experiences* . . . when faced with funeral homes and cemeteries. Certain disquieting experiences that I'd buried deep into my subconscious by avoiding those places for more than ten years.

Avoidance has its upside. For me, that meant never having to face the truth about what I'd been feeling, and why. Until Isabella Harding. The events following Felicity's sister's death had been my crash refresher course in utilizing what Liss liked to call my "abilities." Disabilities, more like. Most of the time that meant feeling the onslaught of another person's emotions, whether I wanted to or not. Every once in a while, it also meant sensing things from the other side. So far I'd not had to purposely test this new aspect of my personality in an active role. Things had happened to me, sure, things that before Isabella I might have passed off as sheer coincidence. But tonight was different. This evening's N.I.G.H.T.S. investigation was real time. The height of unpredictability.

It was a little intimidating.

Evie had asked for a ride to the meeting, and I was only too happy to have the company. I pulled up to the curb in front of her parents' house, a sprawling brick ranch in a 1950s-era subdivision near the hospital. At one time it was an area filled with doctors, lawyers, judges, the cream of Stony Mill society, but over the years they'd drifted into newer, more extravagant subdivisions, leaving their middle-class homes to the up-and-comings. Evie's parents fit the bill. Middle-class people, middle-class values, middle-class lives.

Mrs. Carpenter opened the door when I rang the bell. A pretty blonde in a white sweater and jeans, she looked like a more up-to-date version of Donna Reed. The briefcase and a pair of kicked-off stilettos, however, proved how deceiving appearances can be — Evie's mom was an HR manager who made the pilgrimage to corporate Fort Wayne on a daily basis.

"You must be Maggie," she said, holding out her hand. "Evie has spoken of little else since she started working at Enchantments."

I solemnly shook her hand. French manicure, I noticed. Very chic. "A pleasure to meet you, Mrs. Carpenter."

"Call me Janet. Everyone does."

Evie appeared from a room just off the foyer. "Hi, Maggie. Thanks for giving me a ride tonight."

"Thanks to your mom for letting you work extra tonight," I said, giving my coached answer with only a little nudge of guilt.

Evie's mom gave her daughter's hair a soft stroke. "You won't be too late?"

"Don't worry, Mom. Homework's done. Dishes are in the dishwasher. I have my cell phone, so you can call me if you get anxious. It's all good. And no, I won't be too late. Promise."

I sensed Janet Carpenter's eyes on our backs as we walked to Christine at the curb. "So, she doesn't know, then?" I asked Evie as we settled in.

Evie gazed up at the house, where her mother stood peering at us from behind a lace curtain. "No. Neither does my dad. And unfortunately I have to keep it that way."

"Because you're a psychic?"

"Because our church is of the opinion that a person chooses this path, and that Satan's leading the way. My mom may look all modern and enlightened, but when it comes to her faith, she's a throwback to the dark ages." She gave her mom a cheery wave as Christine puttered into motion.

"My mom, too," I confided. "Always has been. I've had to learn to be my own person over the years. To listen to myself. Moms mean well, but they had to learn to be their own persons, too." I took a deep breath. "Do you know the way?"

She took a folded piece of paper out of her pocket and, as the sun went down, read me the directions with the aid of my handy-dandy keychain photon light. "Uh-huh . . . okay . . . right here . . . okay . . . okay . . . next left . . . wow, neat barn . . . just a ways down this road, now. There it is, see?" She pointed just ahead.

I couldn't have missed it. There was only a faint glimmer of light left along the horizon, but it was just enough to make out the jagged teeth of tombstones silhouetted against the skyline, the corn in the field behind the cemetery having been cropped to the nubs. In the distance beneath the high-watt glow of a security light, I could make out a small farm. Other than the cemetery, it was the only hub of habitation around. The next set of lights were at least a half-mile distant — although I supposed there might be Amish families in between. We'd passed plenty of farmhouses with nothing more than the dim glow of a kerosene lamp in the kitchen and barn and not an electric pole in sight. "Is that Joe's place?"

"Yup. We've been out here before. Lots of activity, this cemetery. On Joe's place, too."

Lots of activity. Great.

Reaching into the dark corners of my memory, I thought back to my first encounter with the N.I.G.H.T.S., on a dark October night in the loft. The night that Felicity had introduced me to her cohorts and companions in the quest for Truth with a capital T. Two months had passed since that night, eight weeks that I had spent alternately (A) probing into the theory and history of the hidden mysteries of the world around me, and (B) thinking I had landed in the middle of a den of eccentrics. Before that day, I had been an innocent. A bystander in the secular world — never very taken with the paranoid brimstone theories of the world's religious leaders, but equally certain of the truth behind the assertions that things like witches, ghosts, and magic were all a part of the illusions of a world too superstitious to make sense of phenomena that were essentially part of the natural order. Of course it was all Felicity's fault that I had come to this end. How could I not want to discover the truth for myself when faced with a lot of intriguing little hints of things hitherto thought to be nothing more than self-indulgent fantasy?

Of course, it was at times like these that my curiosity got me into big trouble. Hopefully tonight's endeavor wouldn't follow that pattern.

No fear, Maggie, remember?

Tell that to the squirrels and chipmunks currently making a playground of my stomach.

"Remind me again why we're doing this?" I said nervously.

"Because it's active, so we're sure to get readings."

"But we've taken measurements here before."

"Yes, preliminary baseline readings. But since Joe says that activity is actually increasing, we wanted to test current readings against that data."

I guess it made sense.

We bumped into a long-forgotten, rutted drive and pulled off to one side. I paused only a moment beside a faded and peeling sign that stated the cemetery closed at sundown. "Do we have permission to be here after dark?" I asked Evie.

"The cemetery's on Joe's property, and he takes care of it, even though it fell into disuse long ago. There shouldn't be a problem."

So much for last hopes.

We parked beside an old rust-bucket F150, complete with gun rack in the back window. Ordinarily a pickup like that wouldn't draw much attention — except for the fact that its owner was a former nun who now owned a bait-and-tackle store near a string of lakes in the northern part of the county. Gen waved and headed over to greet us.

"Hey, you two. Glad you could make it. Devin's running late — he'll no doubt regale us with a multitude of reasons when he arrives." Devin McAllister, perennial college student extraordinaire for the sole reason that it irritated the hell out of his banker father, was habitually tardy. He also ran one of the largest underground paranormal Internet newsletters in the country, all from his studio apartment on the college campus. Just goes to show what a little ingenuity and a good desktop publishing program can do for you.

"Unfortunately he also has most of the electronics with him," she continued. "We may need to start without him."

"No worries." Marcus came up from behind us and put his arms around Evie's shoulders with an affectionate squeeze. The heated blush that lit her cheeks could be felt even in the semidarkness. "I brought my pocket recorder. Maybe we can get some EVPs while we wait. Not exactly top quality, but we might get something anyway."

EVP was ghostbusting shorthand for Electronic Voice Phenomena, which as I had learned only recently signified the faint voices sometimes to be found on tape recordings taken in spiritually active locations, even when no voices ought to be present. Scoff if you will, but I'd heard samples and, I have to say, found them a little too eerie for my peace of mind.

"And there are always the old standbys," Joe Aames added as he joined the lot of us. A hulking ex-jock whose muscles hadn't yet gone to fat, he had a quiet energy that surrounded him with an aura of warmth and stability. His very presence reassured me. Kind of ironic when you considered the fact that he was the reason we were all there tonight. He nodded in the direction of his companion. "Right there's an old standby if I ever saw one." He laughed at his own joke.

I glanced over to find Eli Yoder walking slowly, purposefully, among the stones, his hand slightly outstretched before him. Something dangled from his fingers.

"What's that he's doing?" I asked Joe.

"Him? Dowsing. Eli's specialty. That man can find anything with that thing. Damnedest thing I ever seen," Joe said, shaking his head in combined bemusement and admiration.

I watched the older Amish man's progress, curious. "What is he holding? I've heard of dowsing for underground water before — most people have heard the old wives' tales — but I always thought that was with an uncoiled wire hanger or a stick or something."

"He made it himself," Marcus said, leaning up against Christine's curved bumper. "Out of a Goddess stone he found on his property and a piece of twine. But don't let him hear you call dowsing an old wives' tale. He swears by it."

"What's a Goddess stone?" Evie asked Marcus, saving me the trouble.

He smiled indulgently down at her. "A stone, usually round, with a smooth hole in its center. They're said to be good luck if you find one."

I couldn't help wondering if there was truth to that after all. An Amish man, plain as they come in both appearance and lifestyle, Eli was still one of the most contented people I have ever met. He ran a furniture-making business out of a barn on his property, filling his days with sawdust and sandpaper, stains and oils, and the solid heft of wood. He lived without electricity or any other kind of modern convenience, drove a horse-drawn buggy, and derived satisfaction in the simple rhythms of life. From the moment I met him, I have thought we could all take a lesson from him. Perhaps it was true that a person made their own luck.

"You want to try?" Eli offered the make-shift device to me with a shy smile. "It is not so hard. You try, *ja?*"

I looked to Marcus for guidance. He shrugged as if to say, *Why not?*

Why not, indeed?

I took the stone from Eli, a little self-conscious with everyone standing around me, watching my every move. The stone was round and surprisingly warm to the touch, despite the cold evening air that was making me shiver. I cupped it in my hand, traced the smooth surface of the inner circle with the pad of my thumb. "What do I do?"

Eli stood behind me and to one side. "Stretch your hand out, like so." He demonstrated holding the end of the string so that it was no more than eight inches long. "Not straight with the arm. You will tire, your muscles contract. Results no good when that happens. Concentrate. You hold your arm still, but relaxed. Then you focus. Breathe deep. Watch the stone. When you feel at peace, you ask to speak with your guide."

I frowned. "My spirit guide?"

Eli nodded.

"How do I know I have one?"

"Everybody have one. Some more than one. That little voice you hear in your head that is not yours, *ja?*"

Soooooo, did that mean Grandma Cora was my spirit guide? And if so, who had been my guide before Grandma crossed over into the netherworld? Of course, knowing Grandma C, she'd probably elbowed everyone else aside the moment she got there. I loved her, as much as she'd let anyone love her, but that didn't diminish the fact that she was probably one of the biggest pains in the patooty I'd ever known.

"Will she talk back to me, when I ask to speak with her?" I asked, half dreading the answer.

"Probably not. Not a voice. Until you develop your inner ear, they save that for very important matters."

"Then how do I know?"

"The stone — it circles. One way is yes, one way, no. Easy, *ja?* Your guide, she show you which is which. You say, show yes answer. She show you. Easy."

While I turned a skeptical eye on the stone, a sleek black car purred into the now crowded lane. I would have known it anywhere. Relief flooded through me as Liss slipped from her car with all the understated elegance being British affords you.

"Hello, loves. How is everyone on this glorious, full moon eve?"

I cast a glance toward the sky, where fitful clouds threaded across the escalating darkness. I hadn't noticed the moon before, but there it was, just above the tree line, big and silvery white and luminous. I blew out my breath and watched as the fog I'd created climbed toward the moon.

"I've brought cakes and ginger beer for all," she was saying. "In honor of the esbat and the Lady." She raised her hand to her lips and blew two kisses to the moon. Then she turned back to us. "Well, don't just stand there. I demand a hug from each of you."

Gen and Evie were the first to encircle her shoulders with a warm embrace. Joe and Eli came separately, shuffling with embarrassment, but their hugs were no less warm. I moved forward immediately after, embracing her tightly and laying my cheek against hers.

"You look good, Liss. Really, really good," I told her.

She squeezed my shoulders. "I feel good."

"Then you have no excuse for not returning to Enchantments as soon as humanly possible. So long as you're ready to come back," I amended quickly with the realization that I was being pushy.

Liss gave a merry laugh. "Slave driver. I'll have you know I've been very busy these last weeks."

We parted with a mutual sniffle, and she took my hands in hers. "Hullo, what's this?" she asked, turning my palm up and exposing the Goddess stone.

"Eli's teaching me how to dowse."

"Smashing. We can cover protecting oneself at the same time."

I felt better already.

Marcus laid his hand on my shoulder. "Are you planning to hog her the whole night, or are you going to let someone else have a shot at the action?" He threw his arm around Liss's neck and gave her a sound kiss on the cheek. Smiling broadly, Liss raised her hand to his cheek, hugging him close. I turned away, allowing them their privacy.

I gazed around the motley crew, friends all, and noticed more than Devin was missing. "Wait a minute. Where's Annie?"

Annie Miller, owner of Annie-Thing Good, a European-style café that was fast becoming Stony Mill's newest favorite stomping ground. A Birkenstock-wearing neohippie, Annie was a little tornado of a woman, her boundless energy rubbing off on everyone she came into contact with. She was also an integral part of the N.I.G.H.T.S., and not just because of her signature triple fudge brownies.

"Couldn't make it tonight," Gen responded. "Annie's acting as labor coach for a cousin of hers. She went into labor last night and is still going strong."

That was too bad. I liked Annie. But on second thought, I remember once being told that spirits were drawn to Annie's bright light like moths to a flame, and that if a place held spirit energy, Annie would ferret it out. Maybe it wasn't such a bad thing that she would be absent on my first active investigation. Whether or not I was ready remained to be seen, but I knew for a fact I wasn't ready for Annie's talent.

Eli came toward me. "So, you ready, Maggie? I show you."

Liss put a staying hand on his arm. "Maggie, since you've never done this before, I'd like you to practice shielding yourself first. Just as I've shown you. As an empath with telepathic tendencies, and being virtually untrained, I would feel better if we took a preemptive stance. We don't want any surprises until you are the one in control." Her gaze swept the group. "It wouldn't hurt the rest of you to practice this, either."

She motioned for us to gather around and lead the group in centering. One on one, she showed me how to create a personal cone of protection made of pure white light. Built in the mind's eye, it was a defense not easily breached by negative forces.

"Maggie, the most important thing is that you keep yourself centered. And *believe.* The light is protection. It cannot be broken unless you break it yourself. Now, I'm going to cast a circle for the lot of us to work within tonight. Marcus, will you assist?"

A circle would create a sacred space that would keep us safe, but it would also protect others outside the circle from possible exposure and hold in any energies that were raised. I'd been part of the group's protective circle before — my first experience with raised energy — and it had been an eye-opening experience.

"Everyone, you'll need to be within the circle. If you would all move in while we take care of this, please?"

Taking a deep breath, I sandwiched myself between Eli and Joe's bulk and followed the trail of Gen's Maglite, with Evie bringing up the rear. The flashlight was almost overkill. All around us, glowing white beneath the full moon, were stones whose carved lettering had faded beneath the battering force of the elements. I shivered, wondering if I could get away with shadowing one of the men for the entire evening.

From her car, Liss took a duffel bag and carried it to where the line of graves began. Marcus followed. No one else moved, preferring instead to stand by and watch the proceedings. From the duffel bag Liss removed two canisters of sea salt, five pillar candles, a small bundle of herbs tied with twine, and what looked like a twisted and gnarled twig. She took a canister of salt and, beginning from the same point, proceeded to draw a large circle of the protective mineral around the perimeter of the small cemetery. Marcus took the bundle of herbs and touched a match to it until it began to smolder and smoke, then followed in her wake. Their low-voiced chants carried on the night breezes as they walked the circle they made three times 'round:

"Lady of the silver moon
Enchantress of the night
Protect me and mine within this circle fairly
    cast.
Earth Mother, mother of the sleeping earth,
Keep safe all who gather here
Within the protective shelter of your arms."

Candles were placed on each of the compass points, each lit in turn as the chant continued.

"By the earth that is Her body,
By the air that is Her breath,
By the fire of Her bright spirit,
And by the living waters of Her womb,
Our circle is cast.
None shall come to harm here,
From any forces,
On any level."

The final candle went in the very center of the cemetery, the light it made casting grotesque, flickering shadows on the stones nearest to it.

"As we will,
So shall it be done.
As we will,
So mote it be."

Was it my imagination? When I closed my eyes, I could almost see a blue light shimmering on the fringes of the circle all around us.

"I can't believe we're here tonight," Evie whispered, huddling up against me in her bubblegum pink parka, her blond hair sticking out in a cute shaggy fringe from beneath a knit cap. She stamped her feet against the cold. "I never seem to get used to these."

"Have you been on many?" I whispered back.

"Enough. Some are more eventful than others." She paused. "Oh! Did I tell you that the police were at the school today?"

"No. What happened?"

"They wanted to talk to a bunch of different kids who knew Amanda."

"Really? Did they talk to you?"

She shook her head. "I hardly knew her. I'm just a nobody at school. Nowhere near *her* league." She gave a self-deprecating shrug. "They did talk to Lily and Candace, though. The girls who came with her to the store that day? They hung out with her most often, so I guess they knew her best."

"Did you hear anything?"

She lowered her whisper to an even more confidential level. "I heard they talked to Jordan Everett, Amanda's boyfriend." She paused, and then added, "I also heard they talked to Charlie Howell."

I wasn't sure who Charlie Howell was or what connection he had to Amanda, but Jordan Everett I'd heard of. Who in town hadn't heard of the Everetts? Transplanted from nearby Fort Wayne within the last five years and rich, rich, rich, they were Stony Mill's version of a royal family, and Jordan Everett was another notch on the old money belt. The captain of the SMHS varsity basketball team, in the last year he'd given more quotes to the *Stony Mill Gazette* (*Established 1852, and published daily, except Monday, Wednesday, Friday, Saturday, and Sunday*) than the mayor himself. "I suppose they always have to interview the people a victim is known to have had relationships with."

"Yeah. Especially when she was supposed to see Jordan that afternoon before heading home to get ready for work. And because they weren't exactly what you would call an ideal couple."

"What do you mean?"

203

"Oh, you know. Always bickering and arguing. Amanda was a bit on the bossy side. Everyone knew it. I kind of felt sorry for Jordan sometimes. She was always getting on his case in front of his friends and the whole school if he didn't treat her exactly the way she thought she should be treated."

Our whispers were interrupted when Eli turned to me. "All ready, Maggie?"

Chapter 10

I started guiltily. I'd almost forgotten about Eli's dowsing trick. "Um, sure," I said, pulling the homemade Goddess stone pendulum out from where I'd stashed it in my pocket.

Marcus and Felicity approached, their protective work complete. "Anyone want to back me up?" Marcus asked.

Evie practically tripped over herself to volunteer. Liss exchanged an amused glance with me over Evie's blond head before saying she would stay at the fringes of the circle, watching for Devin.

Gen and Joe looked at each other, then made quiet arrangements to walk around the circle and make observations. That left just Eli and me alone in the center.

"Okay, Maggie. You right-handed? Okay. You hold the string between thumb and first two fingers. Like holding a pencil, *ja?* Let the stone hang free, and hold your hand very still. The stone will hang, see? Not much movement. Okay. Now, empty your mind. Breathe. Look at the stone. See it? Watch it, but don't watch it. You understand?"

Well, not really, but I was willing to give it a go. It was harder than I thought to keep my hand relaxed. I used that as my focus, breathing deeply and watching the stone to be sure that I didn't purposely exert any influence on the string. If this stone was meant to move, I was determined that it wouldn't be because of anything I was doing.

"Um, Eli? Now what?" I whispered when nothing happened.

"Too tense. You pinch the string. You relax some more, *ja?* I go over here awhile so you don't have to see my ugly face."

Relax. In the middle of a cemetery. In the dark. On a full moon.

Right.

Still, Eli had taken the time to try to teach me. Even if it was bunk, I didn't want to hurt his feelings. I thought about what he had said about getting in touch with one's spirit guardian. How everyone has at least one. *Well, Spirit Guide, if you're out there,* I thought, *come on down!*

"Is there anyone out there?" I asked out

loud, feeling ridiculous. "Anyone at all. Bueller? If there does happen to be someone bodily challenged out there, please show me a yes answer so I can figure out how this thing works."

The stone was vibrating at the end of the string, just kind of trembling on its tether. I squinted at my hand, concentrating. Cold though I was, my hand remained still. I slid my gaze down the string. As I watched, the stone began to move, minutely at first, then more decisively, forward and back. "Um, Eli? Eli, is it supposed to be doing this?"

He hustled back over in his dusty Carhartt coveralls. "*Ja, ja!* You're getting something, sure. Ask a question, *ja?* Ask whether you talk with your spirit guide."

I cleared my throat, my eyes drawn by the back-and-forth motion of the stone. "Okay. Am I speaking with a spirit? If so, show me a yes answer."

Slowly the motion of the stone changed, from a back-and-forth swing to a tiny continuous circle that rotated to the right. It circled several times, then to my surprise slowly reverted to the back-and-forth movement as though waiting for another question.

I darted a glance at Eli. He nodded his head, as though to say, *Go on.*

I tried again. "Am I speaking with my spirit guide? If yes, then please show me a yes answer."

Again the motion of the stone changed until it was circling in a clockwise motion as though in answer to my question. *Coolness.* But what if it was a natural phenomenon? Something with an explanation rooted in physics, probably. Quantum string theory, or some other kind of scientific hooha. Of course, that had to be it. Still, it was interesting to experiment with. One thing I was sure of: I wasn't moving it, even subconsciously.

After experimenting with trying to ask various questions of my spirit guide (*all the easy questions, like: Are you an ancestor of mine? No. Did I know you before you died? No. Can you tell me your name? Yes. Did you die in the winter? No. Summer? No. Are you in heaven? Yes.*), I began to ask a series of questions, the kind with answers that I knew I could check out.

"Are the locks on Christine engaged?" *Yes.*

I didn't remember doing that, but goodness knows that didn't mean anything. Christine had a mind of her own.

"Is Marcus wearing a red shirt?" *No.*

"Is Tom going to call me this evening?"

No. Drat.

"What color of bandana does Grandpa Gordon have tucked into his back pocket? Red?" *No.* "Blue?" *Yes.*

And so on and so forth. Until:

"Are Marcus and Felicity having a torrid affair?" I whispered this one, not wanting them to overhear. Of course, I already knew the answer, but as I said, the point of this line of questioning was to obtain confirmation.

The stone circled strongly to the left. *No.* I frowned. It was the first time the stone had gotten it unmistakably wrong all night. "Maybe you should take this back," I told Eli. "I think I must be getting tired."

"*Ja,* sure." He took it from me. "You maybe want me to show you more next time? Or maybe you want to watch me tonight."

"Sure."

Truth be told, the makeshift pendulum was starting to freak me out a little. As my questions had progressed, the rotations had become stronger, more pronounced, and somehow the stone seemed to grow heavier the longer I used it, as though it was being pulled down by an unseen hand.

Eli had begun to steady himself already. "The energy you tap into with the stone, it is strong. I could see that. If you hold the stone over your other hand, just so" — he demonstrated — "you will feel it. The energy, it shoots down the string and through the stone. Different spirits, different energies. Here — feel."

Hesitating only a moment, I held my hand out, palm up, beneath the pendulum as he worked it. "Is there a spirit here with us now?" he asked in a voice bold and clear, his *Deutsche* accent even more noticeable when he was preoccupied. He didn't have to ask it to show him a "yes" answer. The stone began immediately to rotate clockwise, strong, certain movements. And to my surprise, I did feel it. An electric, tickling path that felt like someone tracing their fingernail lightly in circles on my palm.

"My God," I breathed.

"Ja," Eli said, with a peaceful smile. *"Mein Gott."*

I stared at the stone, in amazement. "Can you ask the spirit who it is?"

He shook his head. "Not here. There is a way, but it is not so easy. But then, you don't want it to be too easy."

"No?"

"No. If *Gott* let it be too easy, all the lower-level spirits come through. That would be bad."

Bad. I wondered what he meant by lower-level spirits. There were levels? What, like a cosmic version of the social register? I sighed, finding it terribly deflating to think that, even in the great beyond, I might feel somehow lesser than my angelic counterparts.

On the road a single vehicle approached, slowing as it neared the cemetery with our roving flashlight beams. Its headlights blinded us momentarily as it turned into the drive. The driver killed the engine and leapt from the car in the same instant.

"Hey, everyone! Sorry I'm late. I'd promised dinner with my mom and of course my father went into his favorite tirade. You know the one — when am I going to get off my ass and get a real job rather than wasting my life with another meaningless degree." It was Devin, the N.I.G.H.T.S.' electronic Boy Wonder. He opened the back door of his car and hauled out a sturdy canvas duffel bag, slinging it over his shoulder before approaching the invisible edge of the salt circle. "Anyone gonna let me in?"

Felicity came over and, using the edge of her hand, cut a slit into the invisible workings of the circle. Devin crossed the threshold, shivering as the vibrations teased his body, then stood aside for Felicity to seal it once more.

Dropping the duffel bag to the grass, Devin squatted down and began pulling out carefully wrapped cords and sundry electronic devices. "Video and audio recorders, digital camera, magnetometers, thermal readers. All present and accounted for."

He began doling out the equipment to the members of the group. Eli was the only one to pass on the technology, preferring old ways over new.

As for me, I declined taking anything, preferring instead to shadow those who knew what they were doing. Gen had taken a digital camera, Evie a laser thermometer. Evie had felt psychically drawn to the far corner of the cemetery, where a number of exquisite markers from the previous century gathered together shoulder-to-shoulder like warrior kinsmen against the encroachment of time, so Gen had followed to take pictures. Felicity was filming the entire proceedings with a DVD camera, a slick little number that fit into the palm of her hand. Eli had changed his method of using the stone pendulum. Before he'd remained in one place and held the pendulum on a short string, holding it over his free hand. Now he walked around, slowly, and had lengthened the string, suspending it out before him. I made a note to ask him what the difference was in the two methods.

Devin held two devices, which he told me were an infrared recorder and a magnetometer to read electromagnetic fields, or EMFs. Joe followed him, a microphone and tape recorder at hand to record wherever the EMF readings were high. That left Marcus, with his ordinary handheld recorder, and me with nothing but Gen's Maglite that measured the full length and breadth of my forearm. I'd decided Marcus would be as safe to follow as anyone else.

We wandered slowly between the gravestones. I kept my light trained to the frozen ground to help identify the graves with ground-level markers — because the last thing I wanted to do was to walk across one — and tried to keep my psychic defenses up. How was that working for me? Touch and go. I'll keep you advised.

Marcus's gravesite of choice for investigative purposes stood at the very heart of the cemetery, one marked by a statuesque granite marker. "There's something here," he breathed to me. Not that he needed to. As soon as I allowed myself to relax, I knew it myself. I just didn't want to acknowledge it.

He stood beside the marker, avoiding the

graves that surrounded it. The marker was a familial stone, the name chiseled into all four sides of it common to the area. "Spirits who have passed beyond the Veil," he murmured aloud, "if there is any among your number who have something to say to us, anything at all, we are listening." The tape recorder *whirr, whirred* in his hand as he paused, waiting for . . . an answer? One that was not forthcoming. "We're here for you. If you have anything to say, speak now. We'd like to hear what you have to say to us."

The air felt close, and intensely cold. I hunched my shoulders up around my ears and jammed my hands into the pockets of my wool coat. I was shivering fiercely. The flashlight I'd tucked under my arm wobbled with the movement, causing the light beam to swing, casting crazy shadows here, there, and everywhere. I pressed my elbow more tightly against my side to steady it.

"We know you're here with us." Marcus's voice was as soft and inviting as a goose-down comforter. "We can feel your presence. Can you speak to us? Can you say something for our equipment? Something we can take with us to remind us of your presence."

I swallowed convulsively. I wasn't sure what to expect. Would the voice come aloud, as a voice we could hear in the air around us? I was certain of one thing, though. Something *was* there. I felt a heaviness crowding around us, a pocket of syrupy thickness that somehow also held a sizzle of unearthly promise. And the cold! From the moment Liss and Marcus had erected the protective circle around the perimeter of the crumbling graveyard, temps seemed to have dropped significantly. Probably the result of the sun disappearing completely beyond the horizon and no more, but my tingling toes couldn't tell the difference.

"We are here to communicate with you. If there is any way we can be of assistance, we ask you to speak to us while we are here in this sacred space between worlds. We ask that you do not follow us to our homes."

Wait a minute. *Follow us?* No one said a word about anything potentially following us.

"Marcus. You getting anything?" Joe called from the far corner.

"Yeah. Yeah, I think so. Of course, we'll have to analyze the tape and clean it up, but there's something here, yeah."

"Gen? You?"

"Some pretty fine clicks of orbs. The buggers are all over the place. Evie had one nearly a foot across hovering around her

215

shoulders. The thing was following her, no matter where we moved."

"The temp around me was a full fifteen degrees colder than when I handed the laser thermometer to Gen," Evie added. "Totally wild."

"How 'bout you, Big Joe?" Gen asked.

"Battery went out on my recorder. It was reading just fine, then nothing. But Devin's magnetometer is working fine."

"You should see the EMFs I'm recording. The levels are spiking. And moving in a trail. I was actually able to track the movements," Devin added. "Not to mention, the infrareds are the coolest I've ever seen — so to speak," he said with a mischievous grin. "Liss, can you point that thing this way? I'll be curious to see what we'll find when we review the tape later."

"Two incredibly handsome young lads skulking about in a dark corner, no doubt," Liss said to the laughter of all. "But with luck, perhaps a bit more . . .."

"Maggie seems to have attracted something, too," Marcus said, casting a grin in my direction.

"I did not!" I whispered, ducking down and looking around up above my head. "It was there already. You said you felt it, too."

Gen snapped a pic in my direction. "You

should see this, Maggie," she said, her tone full of awe. "You have a giant orb like Evie's. But yours has color. Violet! It's beautiful, huge, swirling with energy!"

An orb? *I will not panic, I will not panic, I will not panic!* "What, um, does a violet orb mean, exactly?" I asked.

"It's nothing you need fear, ducks," Liss said, coming up and putting a reassuring arm around my shoulder. Of course, that meant I had to stand upright. "Usually it's just a spirit that's attracted by your aura. The energy you're putting out. How do you feel?"

"Scared," I warbled, feeling like a wuss but not ready to let shame force me into action. Did scared have a color?

"Good. That's your self-preservation instinct kicking in," Liss said, giving my shoulder a motherly rub. "Without it, none of us last long. What else do you feel?"

She wanted me to use my empath abilities *now?* "Is it safe to purposely link in to a spirit you know nothing about?" I asked her.

Her eyes, as wise and old as the hills, held mine. "You are in control of yourself, Maggie. Once you realize that's true, no other energies can affect you without your permission. But you're not comfortable with this yet. That's fine. There's no reason to rush things. You'll be ready in your own time."

I nodded, relieved. There was something about having to test my so-called abilities in front of an audience that made me feel like I was back in sixth grade, stuttering out my first oral report to a bunch of sniggering twelve-year-olds while I squirmed to keep my knees from buckling in terror.

Such a wuss.

Evie drifted near. "You okay, Maggie?"

I nodded. "Yeah. Thanks."

While the male N.I.G.H.T.S. resumed their investigations, their female counterparts gathered around me, a wall of protective estrogen to keep the boogeyman out. "Thanks, everyone, for sticking with me. I know I'm probably putting a damper on things tonight."

"Oh, pish," said Gen, throwing her arm about mine and Evie's shoulders. "Us girls have to stick together. The men aren't gonna do that for us."

"Besides," Liss threw in for good measure, "they live to do all the technical things for us. It is their very purpose in life."

I giggled in spite of myself. "So even Marcus —"

"Is a complete — what do you call it these days, technogeek? — who adores buttons, switches, and flashing lights," she confirmed. "Of course. But don't think he wouldn't also be the first to put himself on the line to protect his friends. As would Joe and Eli and Devin. Our N.I.G.H.T.S. are also our knights. The best of men."

Spoken like a true aficionado.

We watched them work for a few moments. Marcus, his intensity blazing as brightly as any spirit's energy. Devin, who hopped around with the excitement and verve of the Energizer Bunny. Joe, with his sturdy shoulders, slow purpose, and ready belief. And Eli, whose quiet ways married perfectly with the energies of old. I'd never had a net of people I could count on, but the N.I.G.H.T.S. had become that for me, male and female alike. They really had, and it humbled me to think how quickly they had accepted me as one of their own. Every girl could use a safety net as she walked the narrow catwalks of life.

Poor Amanda, as bossy and self-absorbed as she had been, did she once have a safety net to fall into?

"Evie," I whispered as we huddled together, "did you hear anything else today about Amanda and Jordan? You said the police had questioned him."

Evie shook her blond head. "I don't think Jordan did anything wrong. I mean, why would he? He's . . . well . . . popular. And he and Amanda were thick as thieves. Always together, always on top of the world. He had no reason to do anything to her."

Always together. And in today's world that meant . . . "Were they . . . erm . . . close?"

"Well, of course, they hooked up, and . . . Oh. You mean — ?"

At least I didn't have to explain myself. "Yeah."

"Well, um, probably. I mean, yeah, I think so. I mean —"

Of course they were. "Well, then. Jordan is a nice boy, I imagine, wealthy, popular, the world at his feet. But maybe Amanda presented some kind of obstacle."

"What kind of problem could have been that serious? They were made for each other."

"I don't know."

"What about an unplanned pregnancy?"

Evie and I turned as one to look at Gen. Serious, plain, quiet Gen, who had spent the bulk of her adult life as a wife of God.

Good grief. It was true. It *was* always the quiet ones.

Gen shrugged, meeting our open mouths matter-of-factly. "It makes sense, doesn't it? In this day and age? Well? Doesn't it?"

Our mouths still open, we nodded.

Liss jumped into the conversation feet first and took off running. "But if Amanda was pregnant, surely it stands to reason the coroner would have uncovered that little tidbit?"

"Would they have released the information, do you think?" I posed the question to the group at large, thinking aloud.

It was speculation, pure and simple. That was the problem — none of us knew for sure.

Who would have known, other than Amanda herself? And how could we find out?

Our will to hunt for spirit energy momentarily stripped from us, we huddled there in the cold that felt colder still, breaths merging into one frozen cloud and thoughts spinning along the same dark path as we waited for our male compatriots to finish. Above us, the moon slid across the sky, full and high and eerily bright. We were still standing quietly together moments later when the far-off roar of a car engine split the night into two. It wasn't an unusual sound, really. I'm not sure what it was about our isolated country roads that called to the redneck population like a siren singing for a wandering sailor, but there you have it. The pair of headlights swelled bigger, flared brighter as the vehicle charged closer. And with it came the muffled *boom-boom-boom* of heavy bass. Someone was jamming, big time.

No one seemed surprised when the old pickup truck swerved into the cemetery's drive, its arrival accented by a rattletrap clatter and a plume of loose gravel. The passenger door squealed open and Tara half fell, half slid from the cab to the thump and squall of overactive woofers and tweeters.

"Whoopsie-daisy!" She giggled as she picked herself up and dramatically dusted off her knees and behind. "Well, lookie who we have here, Jamie-honey!" she called to the driver. "A bunch of kick-ass ghost-busters. Including my most favoritest and most loving cousin, Marcus. C'mon out here and meet my cousin."

The driver left the pickup with nary a stumble, but his manic grin hinted that he, too, might have partaken of the alcohol that was wafting from the pair in waves. He saluted the lot of us. "Hello, kick-ass ghost-busters."

Marcus appeared at my elbow. "Your mom know you're out of the house, young lady?" he confronted Tara.

She put her hands on her hips. "Why? You gonna rat me out?"

"Nope. I'm going to take you home."

"No freakin' way, Cousin. You don't want me here, that's too bad. Don't think for a minute that you can keep me from staying if I decide I want to be here, too. Last time I looked, it was a free country. You're not the only one who can shitkick a bad boy spirit into the great beyond, ya know." Tara snapped her fingers. "Got the goods, Jamie?"

Jamie of the manic grin pulled a backpack out of his pickup. Digging into it, he pulled out a Ouija board with one hand and a bottle of Jim Beam with the other. "Yes, ma'am."

Tara looked at me and winked. "Doncha just love a man who comes prepared, Fluff? I know I do."

The two of them stood on the other side of the circle of protection Felicity and Marcus had erected earlier, making no move to go farther despite Tara's obvious intentions. I couldn't help wondering if they, or at least Tara, sensed its presence.

"It's too late," Marcus persisted with a calm and patience that truly impressed me. "We're finished here."

"Then you won't mind us moving in on your space," Tara responded. "Right, Cuz?"

"There is nothing here, Tara."

"Marcus, Marcus, Marcus," Tara said,

peacock confidence in evidence as she mockingly shook her shaggy head. "You forget. I'm just as good at this stuff as you are. I'll make my own assessments, *thankyouverymuch.*"

Did I say patience and calm? When Marcus set his jaw, *wowzer.* Look out. "You will do no such thing, young lady."

Tara took one step toward the circle, then stopped, frowning in confusion. *So,* I thought, *she does feel it.* "You can't tell me what to do."

I could feel energy rising, moving around us like invisible zephyrs of air. Nerve-jangling, disquieting energy. Trouble was, I didn't think it stemmed solely from Marcus's rising temper. The very notion frightened me.

I placed a hand on Marcus's arm. "Um, Marcus?"

Distracted, he turned on me. "What?" he snapped.

I took a step back, surprised. I'd never seen him the least bit on edge. Even stranger, there was a hint of urgency to him that confused me further. "The, um, well, can't you feel it?"

His brows furrowed, instinct at war with the need for action. Slowly I saw the anger drain from him, releasing the tension that had drawn his shoulders up upon Tara's unexpected arrival. He turned his face sharply to Liss, but she was already on the move. Without turning, I heard her voice and knew she was moving counterclockwise (Liss would have called it widdershins) around the circle, twisted twig in hand. Her voice, soft yet insistent, echoed in my ears:

"By the earth that is Her body,
By the air that is Her breath,
By the fire of Her bright spirit,
And by the living waters of Her womb,
By the Great Mother Herself,
I release this circle,
Open, yet unbroken.
All spirits who have made contact here
    tonight
Will here remain.
Where we go, you will not follow.
Merry meet, ancient ones, and merry part,
And merry meet again."

She'd released the circle at Marcus's behest. Immediately a cunning look transformed Tara's face. Slick as a whistle she bent at the waist to pick up the Ouija board and pointer, lurching as she took a step forward. Watching her, I shuddered as instinctively she reached out a hand to steady herself against the nearest headstone. She was a braver girl than I was, that was for sure. Or maybe foolhardy would be a more apt description. "Whaddaya think, Jamie? How 'bout by the big stone in the center?"

Of a sudden Jamie, despite his earlier bravado, didn't look quite so sure. His big booted feet seemed to have taken root. "I —"

" 'Kay, well, this seems like the spot." She had gone very still, and if a person had the ability to perk her ears, Tara's would have been standing straight up like antennae. "Geez-Louise, what have you all been doing? There's enough energy here to power a major-type TV station."

She sat down, losing her balance at the last moment and landing with a soft *phloomph* on her rump. Blowing out her breath, she reached for the Ouija board and set it atop her crossed knees, then twisted around when she discovered her friend had not followed her. "Jamie, what the hell's wrong with you? Are we doing this or not?"

The brashness the young man had arrived with seemed to have abandoned him. A shadow crept along the ground, seeping insidiously, darker, darker. He cast a fearful glance upward. My gaze followed the path his own had taken. A line of clouds had appeared as if from nowhere, overtaking the glowing moon and growing thicker by increments. Shadow upon light upon shadow. "Yeah. Yeah, sure," he said, jamming his hands into the hip pockets of his droopy jeans but not moving.

Ever attentive to the technology that was his raison d'être, Devin made a slow circle, a device in each hand. "Wow," he said under his breath. "Double wow."

While the rest of us stood by feeling out of place, Marcus walked over to where his more impulsive cousin had assumed the lotus position and was currently trying to induce a meditative state. His quiet words carried back to our ears. Most of us discreetly turned our attention elsewhere. "Tara, it's not safe here."

"In an old tumbledown graveyard?" she scoffed. "Get real, Marcus. If you're so worried, why are you here? 'Sides, we're in the middle of nowhere. You know you just want to tell me what to do."

"You've been drinking again."

"Right. So?"

Marcus blew out his breath and ducked his head as though counting to ten. When he could speak, he said, "You know as well as I do that it's not safe to work with energy or spirits when you're not in full possession of your faculties."

She snorted. "That's just a bunch of goody-goody hooha and you know it." Her gaze flicked to me over his shoulder. I transferred my gaze to the dark fields behind us so that she wouldn't know I'd been paying attention. "Oh. I see. You're doing it for the benefit of the Fluffster."

"I'll let that one slide, but only because *I'm worried about you.* For the gods' sake, Tara, one of your friends has been killed. It's not safe for you to be out here."

"I'm not afraid," she said, but her hands had gone still on the planchette. A glower pinched her brows. "And for your information, the Queen Bee was anything but my friend. I'm glad she's gone. I would have done the binding thing a lot sooner, if I'd known it would be that effective. Besides, I have Jamie. No one's gonna make a move as long as Jamie here is with me."

Marcus lifted his head and shot a measuring stare at "Jamie here," who had moved while the rest of us were pretending not to listen. He had made it all the way back to his rusting pickup truck. Hand resting on the old chrome door handle, he stood poised to fly at a moment's notice. As soon as he saw all of us looking at him, he jerked his hand from the handle as though it was iron fresh from the forge.

"Hmm," Marcus intoned speculatively. "I'm not sure old Jamie will do you any good. Looks like late-night graveyard forays aren't his thing."

Tara frowned in Jamie's direction. "Jamie! What do you think you're doing?"

The teen jumped, guilt making him whine. "Aw, come on, Tara. Let's just go get a burger or something, huh? This place is giving me the creeps."

"Coward," she muttered under her breath, then more loudly, "There's nothing to be afraid of."

"I'm not afraid. Just creeped out. If you don't want to leave now," Jamie offered, his gentlemanly instincts leaping unexpectedly to the fore, "I'm sure your cousin wouldn't mind if you rode back with him. Hey, man?"

"What!" Tara looked horrified. She scrambled with some difficulty to her feet. "No. No way I'm tagging along with Marcus."

"Well, I gotta go. Are you coming with or not?"

She hemmed. She hawed. She . . . "Oh, for the gods' sake! All right, already. You win. Let's go." She stomped-slash-weaved back to the pickup truck, which Jamie had revved into action before she reached the door. She settled herself into the seat, reaching for the bottle Jamie had held on to the entire time. "You're such a weenie, you know that, Jamie?" she accused as she shut the door, but Jamie was already backing up. Peeling back, in fact. Double time.

"Wow," I said, breaking the silence.

Marcus blew his breath out, shaking his head. "Uncle Lou is going to have a cow when he hears about this."

Marcus, I knew, was talking about her underage drinking and, perhaps, the ill-advised use of her natural skills. But I couldn't help worrying about what else Tara had revealed — that the binding spell I had witnessed her casting had somehow involved Amanda.

Was it possible? Could Amanda's death have been brought on by a spell gone bad?

CHAPTER 11

"Too bad Annie wasn't able to come tonight. It's probably too selfish of me, but I would kill for one of her brownies right about now," I told Evie as we approached the outskirts of town. We'd been silent up until then, and I was eager to do anything that would rid us both of the lingering vestiges of the energy that had clung to us since we'd left the cemetery. "Want a pop?"

Evie hesitated, but shook her head. "Thanks, but I'd better get home. My mom will be waiting up for me."

So I drove her home. A thought began to smolder and smoke as I navigated the nearly empty streets, growing more insistent with each passing block. I squelched it as long as I could, holding it in out of uncertainty, but as I pulled up into the Carpenters' driveway, I knew I needed to put a voice to the worry that was running through my head. I shifted

Christine out of gear and set the emergency brake.

"Evie?" I couldn't hold back any longer. "Evie, what do you think about Tara?"

She looked surprised. "Tara? She's all right, I guess. A little intense, but everyone deals with life a little differently. It's all good."

I nodded, not sure how to proceed. "She seems to have quite the dark side going on."

Evie cocked her head as though puzzled. "Everyone has a dark side, Maggie."

Well, it was hard to picture the young girl sitting beside me as being bathed in anything other than an angelic sheen of light, but I knew she was probably right. Still . . .

"I didn't tell you this earlier," I began slowly, "but the other day . . . Sunday — the day that everyone was out searching for Amanda before we knew anything had happened — I was covering my area and I ran into Tara, down by the river. She was practicing, alone —"

"Practicing?" Evie said.

"Casting," I clarified, "and I don't mean with a fishing pole. Anyway, I surprised her mid-spell, and . . . Evie, she said she was doing a binding, and if the power she raised was any indication, she meant business."

Evie frowned. "A binding? You mean . . ."

Come on, Evie, don't make me say it, I willed. After only a moment or two, her eyes grew large. "Oh. *Oh.*"

"Yeah," I said, grim.

"You think maybe she was hexing Amanda," she said slowly.

Tara was Marcus's cousin, for heaven's sake. Just considering the notion that she had meant Amanda harm felt traitorous to Marcus and his family. I looked down at my hands, still and white on the wheel. "Yeah, maybe."

"Do you think . . ." She swallowed once, hard. "You don't think she had anything to do with Amanda's death, do you?"

"I don't want to think it. I just don't know."

"But Amanda was already . . . gone . . . by Sunday."

"Who's to say that particular binding was her first?" I looked at her, sick to my stomach. "Do you think the police — maybe Tom — should know?"

She was quiet a moment. "Maybe there's more to it than we know. I think we owe it to Marcus to try to find out before we say anything to anyone else. Don't we?"

Maybe she was right. I was too confused, too worried, to decide just now. Which left me staring out at the streets as I meandered restlessly through town and wondering what I should do with the rest of my evening. I did a drive-by of the apartment house, but the Jag was there. Just my luck. I could have used a bit of girl talk to remind me that the world hadn't changed so much after all. A part of me felt like I was still back in that creepy old graveyard. Orbs. Magnetic fields. Spirit trails.

Feh.

But there had been something there, strong enough that even a newbie like me could feel it.

So, when she's feeling down and troubled and needs a steadying hand, but her best friend is, ahem, otherwise engaged, what's a girl to do?

My parents still lived in a onetime farmhouse on the edges of Stony Mill proper. Once, long ago, it was a working farm, but its acreage had been sold off over the years, piece by piece, until it became what it was now — the last bastion of old-time Indiana amid a sea of suburban sprawl. Well, as much suburban sprawl as can hit a town of six thousand–plus people. House after house bore the same color scheme, the same multilevel rooflines, the same recessed front doors flanked by pots that would have borne cheerful geraniums in the summertime but that now stood withered and gray in the December cold.

The old homestead was as far from that strange notion of sophistication as was possible. It was big and white with a seamed tin roof that had lulled me to sleep through many a rainstorm, and a deep wraparound porch that felt cool even on the steamiest July afternoon. Rather than a tiny manicured lawn, it had a sprawling length of yard that often sported more than its share of crabgrass and clover, old-fashioned rose arbors, and a vegetable garden that at this time of year was nothing more than a square of earth scraped clean of flora and flotsam. At the back of the property stood the old carriage barn that now housed my father's woodshop and a small efficiency apartment for my Grandpa Gordon, a rowdy old fart who managed to enjoy life despite the electric wheelchair the ravages of time had exiled him to. I could see a blue glow strobing through the windows of his ground-level apartment. Probably he'd fallen asleep in front of *The Tonight Show* again. I didn't have the heart to wake him up. My mom, on the other hand, rarely slept. Long after everyone else would have drifted off, she could be found sipping coffee at the kitchen table over an old mystery novel, or relaxing with the Bible in the sitting room, rosary beads and crucifix in hand.

Tonight I found her in the kitchen. With a décor last updated around the Brady Bunch era, right down to the Harvest Gold refrigerator, just being there was an exercise in nostalgia. I looked around, soaking in the feeling of the place. The stove had been cleared, the sink scoured, the floor swept so clean a field mouse would starve to death if left to its own resources. Typical Mom. At least she'd changed out of her clothes and had settled into her old pink chenille bathrobe and slippers. It was a little threadbare at the elbows, but it looked comfortable.

It was surprisingly good to be home.

"Hi, Mom," I greeted her, closing the door behind me and slipping off my shoes so as not to track in the white limestone dust so prevalent around these parts. "You're up late."

She glanced up from the pages of her book — Christie's *The Thirteen Problems,* a collection of short stories. The front cover featured a listing of the stories, and my gaze snagged on the last: "Death by Drowning." A fitting choice, given the circumstances our little town had found itself in of late.

"Goodness. The prodigal daughter returns. You stay away too long, Margaret."

For a moment, I worried that she was in the mood for our usual friendly mother-daughter argument, but after a moment's stare, she relented. "It's good to see you. Want some coffee?"

I was still hyped from the night's activities, so I said, "No, thanks. I just thought I'd pop in to see how you and Dad and Grandpa are doing."

She carefully inserted a beaded bookmark into the paperback and set it down with military precision, the edges of the book parallel to the edges of the table. "We're all doing just fine. Your dad's gone to bed, of course. He'll be sorry he missed you." My dad rarely stayed up late. Sometimes I think he did it to gain some peace from my mother's micromanaging. Speaking of, I told her I'd been to see Dr. Phillips.

She grunted. "I had to cancel my appointment with him today. Grandpa Gordon forgot to remind me about an appointment he had with the urologist this afternoon. So, it appears I need to find a new doctor sooner than I'd hoped."

"Everything changes, I guess."

"Leaving to go into administration, of all things, he abandons his patients," she fussed.

"I guess maybe he just needed a change

of scenery."

Mom was too beside herself to notice my inadvertent funny. "Well, I think it's very selfish of him." She sighed in resignation. "I mean, a woman gets used to —"

"Getting naked in front of certain men?" I finished for her, unable to smother my grin this time.

"Don't get smart, Margaret. A woman gets used to certain things, that's all."

"Well, buck up, Mom. Maybe Phillips will have another cancellation that you can claim."

"Have you talked to Melanie lately?" she asked, changing the subject to my perfect sister. "She and Greg were out here with the girls just last Sunday."

I shook my head as a faint nudge of guilt tapped me on the shoulder. "Well, no. I've been too busy with the store and things." Not to mention I'd been a little preoccupied on Sunday, as had most of the rest of Stony Mill.

"Greg has been offered a partnership with the firm. That little bit of news almost makes up for Dr. Phillips. Isn't it wonderful?"

"Mm. Wonderful. I'll bet Mel is over the moon." Actually, I was surprised my little sister hadn't called me herself. That was just the kind of thing she loved to lord over me. Maybe she was growing up. Was it possible? Had five years of marriage mellowed my baby sister?

"She's so excited. Greg's success is her success, you know. It reflects well on our whole family."

I was okay with Melanie's good fortune until I caught the not very subtle inflection in my mother's voice. Mom had a bad habit of comparing me with Super Mel, the Junior League Wannabe. But I would do myself no favors by pointing that out to her. Tonight all I wanted was a few peaceful moments of mother-daughter connection, something to remind me that the strangeness I had felt around our town of late could not reach everywhere. My mother, I knew, would never change. As infuriating as she could be at times, sameness breeds comfort. At least I knew where I stood with her. No surprises.

"How is Marshall?" I asked, deftly changing the subject. "He probably has loads of tales about life in the big city."

A frown pinched her brow and tightened the lines around her lips. "Your brother is nearly as hard to get ahold of as you are. Maybe even more so. At least I can go into town and hunt you down at the shop if you don't answer your phone. But he's all the way in New York City, and if he isn't answering his phone, I can't exactly force the issue. I might have to resort to phoning him at work if this keeps up."

"Maybe he's been busy."

"Too busy to call his mother?"

Ahem. I decided to change the subject yet again before she got started on what was, in her eyes, an unforgivable offense. Meet your number one offender. "So, Mom, you haven't said — how is Mrs. Roberson holding up? Have you had a chance to speak with her?"

Mom got up to freshen her coffee, her frown softening into thoughtfulness. "Poor Wendy. To lose a child . . . and in such a way. It's unthinkable. Simply unthinkable." She sat back down, but not before placing a plate of cookies on the table before me. Grandma Cora's sugar cookies, my personal favorites. If they weren't world famous, they ought to be. Ah, well, I didn't get that brownie I'd hoped for, so why not indulge . . . "To think, poor Amanda had bought her a gift the *very day* she disappeared," my mom continued. "Wendy found it on the dining room table that Saturday, but of course Amanda never came home that night. Oh! That reminds me. The gift apparently came from Enchantments, and I'm sure you'll understand why Wendy cannot keep it. I told her you'd be happy to refund the money. Maybe you could go over there tomorrow and pick it up. The poor thing, she's not doing very well. Not well at all."

Pick it up? Oh, God. It was small of me, but the thought of facing a grieving mother without someone else there to help me out if the poor woman broke down in front of me made me more than a little nervous. "Um, sure. I could do that."

"On the news tonight, they said that Amanda's death had officially been ruled a homicide. Can you imagine? Your teenage daughter leaves for her part-time job and never returns home." Mom paused to take a sip of her coffee, grimaced, then reached for the sugar bowl. "You probably think I'm being a maudlin old woman. Maybe I am. Maybe I am."

I shook my head. "No. I don't think that. Where did Amanda work, Mom?"

"Night desk at the old Lewiston Hotel. Poor Wendy! She's feeling guilty over that, too. It was Wendy who insisted that Amanda needed a job to teach her about real life, real responsibilities. Sid, he never wanted it. She could do no wrong in his eyes. Forever his little princess." She was silent a moment, then slowly said, "I guess she'll be that now for sure."

"But . . . the job, the hotel, wasn't the cause —"

"Not the cause, no. But it's difficult for a woman to be logical or even to think beyond the depths of her private nightmare when the child she has raised comes to such a horrifying end."

It made me ashamed to think I'd even stopped to consider my own discomfort. "I'll go tomorrow. The clock must be a terrible reminder."

Mom nodded her approval. "Just keep in mind, she might seem a little . . . strange. The shock has been terrible. You'll understand what I mean tomorrow. She's verging on a breakdown, I'm afraid. Of course she's being medicated. Poor Sid, right now he's dealing with the loss of Amanda while trying to hold everything together for Wendy's sake. I don't envy him."

The refrigerator beckoned, so I grabbed a cold Diet Coke as I mulled over what Mom had told me. Something tugged at the fringes of my consciousness, something that had been unusual enough to take note of on that awful day. It reared its head now with a vengeance. "Mom, how much could a teenager working a night job make, do you think?" I asked her, leaning a hip against the kitchen counter as I popped the top on the can.

"Not much more than minimum wage, I guess." Her eyes, hazel like my own but lined with the cares of a woman nearing the end of middle age, narrowed the longer she looked at me. "Why?"

"Well, I don't know. It's probably nothing . . ."

"Margaret, stop beating around the bush."

It couldn't hurt to put a voice to the thought, could it? It's not like I was trying to spread rumors. Just to clear up a nagging uneasiness. "All right," I said, feeling my way. "You know that I saw Amanda the morning that she disappeared at the store. I almost didn't recognize her, and she certainly didn't seem to recognize me. She came in with her friends to buy the clock. To get her 'out of the doghouse,' she'd said. With her mom, I'd assumed. But, Mom," I said, looking up from my pop into eyes that seemed suddenly older, wearier, "she paid for it in cash like it was nothing. The clock was worth nearly five hundred dollars. But that's not the only thing. Even after paying for the clock, the wad of money she was carrying in her purse was a thing to behold. She had at least several hundred left. I'm serious. Where does a teenage girl get her hands on that much money, and why would she just be carrying it around?"

Mom looked troubled. "Not from Wendy, that's for sure."

I nodded. That much, at least, made sense. "Mr. Roberson?"

"Sid doted on Amanda, but he wasn't a fool. No, I'm sure he wouldn't have. What sane parent would? In this day and age, ready access to cash can only lead to trouble."

So, what did that leave? Baby-sitting? Please. I'd done my share of baby-sitting stints. They weren't exactly high-end gigs. Enough to keep a teenage girl in all the glamour mags she could want and a ready supply of bubblegum-flavored lip gloss, but that was about it. Then again, Amanda and her friends didn't look the type to like bubblegum. Young rural sophisticates poised for world domination. But how?

Drugs? Could it be?

I didn't like the thought, given what had happened to Amanda, but times had changed since I was a teenager myself. Drugs had been available back then to anyone who really wanted them, but they were nowhere near as prevalent as today.

I couldn't think of any other way a girl from a good family could come by that much money, enough that she'd think nothing of carrying it around with her in her purse. Could she have been a dealer at the school? A distributor of sorts? I didn't like to think it, but things like that, unfortunately, did happen these days. Could a girl of Amanda's social stature be drawn into something like that? And was her dislike of Tara purely two personalities that clashed, or was there a deeper reason? What *was* Tara's connection to all this?

CHAPTER 12

Technically it was none of my business, but I couldn't stop thinking about it. The hows and the whys of Amanda's disappearance. One of the hazards of living in a small town, I suppose. When you know or come into contact with so many people on a daily basis and have heard of so many more, one person's death has the potential for a high impact, and Amanda's had proven just that. There was a black cloud hanging over our town, and it was more than just a prevailing attitude. Worry, suspicion, and fear were like dragons circling overhead, waiting for just the right moment to lay siege upon the people of Stony Mill. And as in stories of long past, they were hard to banish once they'd sunk in their claws for the long haul. What this town needed most was for the police to find the real reason behind Amanda's murder so that healing could begin. We needed to know. We needed to understand.

Those were the thoughts running through my head as I took a few moments to stop by the Roberson house the next morning. Liss had surprised me by arriving at the store before me, ending her self-imposed hiatus. By the time I arrived, the door was unlocked, the lights were blazing, and the warm and nutty scent of coffee permeated the shop. In the hour before the store officially opened, we had a heart-to-heart talk, the kind that I'd longed for weeks to have with her. Gosh, it was good to see her there! And better still to be able to talk to her, live and in person. There was something about Liss's eyes that made me incapable of holding back. I found myself spilling out everything that had happened, every last disjointed thought. Liss listened attentively, murmuring responses that were, as usual, the perfect things to say. When at last the words had stopped gushing forth, she told me how grateful she was for my hard work, even more grateful for my friendship. Then she told me — ordered me — to take a well-deserved day off. At first I refused — Liss was newly back, I'd much prefer enjoying her company for the day — but in the end I gave in. There *were* some things that I needed to do, and I never seemed to have enough time to get to them. Of course *I* knew I'd probably end up back at the store when all was said and done, but I would humor Liss for the morning at least.

First things first: I would pay my respects to the Robersons.

I'd already cleared the return with Liss. "Of course," she'd said, sympathy shining in her clear silver gray eyes. "The poor woman needs no reminder of what happened. These next months will be difficult enough for her." She'd given me the cash from the till without a moment's hesitation.

My next move was an afterthought that suddenly seemed like a terrific idea. I dialed my mother's number with gusto.

"O'Neill residence."

"Good morning from your oldest and most loving and appreciative daughter," I said.

"Well. Good morning to you, too. A visit last night and a phone call this morning? I'm overcome. To what do I owe the honor?"

"I have a favor to ask."

"Somehow, I knew you were going to say that. What did you need, Margaret?"

"Your company. I don't suppose you happen to be free for the next hour?" I told her I was following through with her plan to pay my respects to Mrs. Roberson and to pick up the clock, and for once Mom didn't fuss. She even seemed to think my doubles approach was a good one. "Great. I'll be over in ten minutes," I told her, ringing off.

True to form, Mom was ready and waiting at the door when I pulled up outside the old farmhouse, her coat on, hair combed, and purse slung over her crooked forearm. She hesitated only a moment before opening the passenger side door and settling herself into the sagging bucket seat.

"Have you considered looking into a new car for yourself, honey?" she asked politely as she eyed the faded dash. "This old thing looks to be on its last legs."

"Get rid of Christine?" I scoffed. "Hold your tongue, woman. She may be a little worn around the edges, but she's got a lot of life in her. Sturdy. Reliable. A true classic. They don't make 'em like this anymore."

"You won't think it's so reliable when it leaves you stranded along the highway in a storm. You should ask your father to help you look."

"Which way to the Robersons', Mom?" Notice the deft change of subject, a tactic I'd long since mastered. Self-defense, doncha know.

The Robersons had once lived in the same quiet subdivision that Evie's mom and dad called home. Sometime in the last ten years they had traded up for a more expensive home on the bluffs overlooking the river a few miles west of town. I couldn't help staring just a bit in awe as I turned off onto their paved driveway. Thoroughly modern in style, it was imposing with windows that stretched two stories high, fashionably bare and revealing a great room with a cathedral ceiling and a big marble fireplace.

Criminey.

I was suddenly glad that I'd worn my best work outfit that morning, a pair of black wool slacks that still fit me reasonably well and a charcoal gray turtleneck that clung to me in all the right places. At least I wouldn't embarrass my mother too terribly. Pulling the collar of my pea coat up around my neck, I came around to where my mom was struggling to extricate herself from the sucking motion of the bucket seat and pulled her to her feet. Together we scurried up the brick path to the recessed door and pushed the bell.

Two additional tries gained no more response than the first. "Maybe she's not home," I said. It was too much to hope. I wasn't sure that this was the best timing to descend upon the woman unawares.

"The TV's on," Mom replied, cupping her

hand to the glass of the sidelights and peering in.

"Do you see anyone?"

"No."

"Maybe she's stepped out."

"For what? The poor woman's being medicated, Maggie. I don't think Sid would leave her the car keys. Besides, her car's in the garage — didn't you see it when we pulled up?"

I had missed that, but then, Nancy Drew I most certainly was not. I didn't have the nerve for it. "Where are you going?" I called after my mom as she wandered toward the corner of the house. Her answer was lost in the whine of the wind, forcing me to follow her if I wanted to be sure she didn't break a leg slipping and sliding down the landscaping mounds.

Her instinct proved worthwhile, though. As soon as I rounded the corner of the house, my eye was drawn toward the back edge of the property. There, poised near the edge of the bluff overlooking the river with her back to us, stood Amanda's mother.

Mom was already in motion, her legs pumping as she raised her arms over her head to wave her friend down. "Wendy!"

For a moment, my heart was in my throat. The disconsolate stance, the stooped shoulders, the waves of despair that emanated from her . . . What if she meant to jump? What if she leapt over the edge right before our eyes? And then I was running, too, my feet carried by the potential urgency of the situation.

The cold wind beat at us, but I heard only the echo of my own harsh panting in my head as I crossed the wide expanse of lawn. Mom reached the danger zone before I did, taking Wendy Roberson by the shoulders and turning her away from the edge. Only as I approached did I notice the cardboard box a few feet away, next to a small hole freshly dug. A spade lay next to it, damp clumps of dirt still clinging to its blade.

"Come away from the edge, Wendy," my mother said. It was the same calm and soothing voice she might have used with me as a child, loving and reasonable, but firm, and it was no less effective now. "You shouldn't be out here. It's far too cold. That wind's enough to scrub the skin clean off your face."

"I was just looking at the water," the blond woman murmured, turning to gaze back over her shoulder. The day was unnaturally clear and bright, and sunlight danced and shimmered across the mosaic tile surface of the wind-stirred water. It also ruthlessly revealed every line on Mrs. Roberson's well-cared-for face. "It's pretty, isn't it? It's one of the reasons we bought this land, built this house. I never thought . . . I never . . ."

Her voice broke and she pulled away from my mother's hands. Mom and I stood by, helpless, as she wept silent tears, her thin shoulders shaking violently with the vast depths of her grief. Deep within me, I felt my stomach knot and twist with it. My breath hitched and caught in my chest. I bit my lip and closed my eyes in an attempt to strengthen my personal boundaries by willing the invasion of emotion away.

Abruptly the struggle for personal space stopped as Wendy Roberson took a ragged breath, straightened her spine, and lifted her chin. In the same moment that she reined in her sprawling emotions, I felt the tension within me ease. But while the tragedy had drained from her features, the calm mask that took its place was somehow even more horrible than the anguished tears.

Mom put her hand on Mrs. Roberson's arm. "Let's go inside, Wendy, shall we?"

She shook her head. "I have to finish this."

"Finish? Finish what?"

Without a word Wendy Roberson walked back to the box and took it into her hands. Carefully, calmly, she knelt before the hole and settled the box into place. I looked at my mom, my brows raised in question. Mom looked at me, a faint grimace tightening her brow, before she knelt beside her friend and took her hand.

"Your hands are freezing. You've been out here too long. Let Maggie finish this for you. Come inside and let me make you a nice strong cup of coffee."

Mrs. Roberson looked at me as though it was the first she'd noticed I was there. "Maggie."

"Yes, Maggie. My daughter, remember? She'll cover that up for you, and she'll do it up right, won't you, Maggie. Now let's get you inside."

This time Mom was successful. Mrs. Roberson allowed herself to be pulled to her feet and led off toward her expensive house. I watched as the two older women disappeared into the glass-walled all-season room that jutted off at an angle from the main shape of the house before I turned to my assigned task.

I've always been a curious person. As I may have mentioned, there have been times when that's gotten me into . . . trouble. So when the first thing that occurred to me to do once they'd passed out of sight was to dig my keys out of my pocket and slit the packing tape that sealed the lids shut . . . well, what can I say? I'm a bad, bad girl. I just couldn't help wondering what it was that she was burying at such an odd time.

I zipped my house key along the flaps, then, with a last glance up toward the house, I slid my thumbs beneath and revealed the contents.

Underwear.

Lots of underwear.

Frilly, frothy bits of lacy, feminine underwear. Silky low-cut panties, demi-bras, thigh-high stockings galore, and at least one garter belt. Now, Mrs. Roberson was a petite woman, granted, but these weren't the kinds of things that would flatter the figure of a woman that had borne children. And the panties were extra small.

Ten to one, they belonged to willow-thin Amanda. But why bury them?

Frowning, I closed the box and rose to my feet. It didn't take long to heap the dirt on top of the lot, mounding it up when there was too much left over due to the amount of space the box itself claimed. I used the spade to smooth out the dirt as best I could. As an afterthought I found a flat fieldstone and placed it on top as a marker. Who knew, maybe Mama Roberson would suffer a change of heart and want the items back. Stranger things had happened. And that done, I carried the spade back up to the house, eager to get warm again.

It felt weird just wandering into Mrs. Roberson's house, but no weirder than ringing the bell when my mother was inside and the owner already knew I was there. Or at least, she should. By the looks of things out by the river, she was a little loopy on happy pills, so maybe she wouldn't remember me after all. Still I stood the spade up on end on the patio and pushed open the French doors.

The doors led into a big, modern family style kitchen, with stainless offerings to the appliance gods, sleek countertops, and whitewashed cabinets. I slipped my shoes off by the door to keep from making tracks across the pale wood floors and wandered toward the next room, from which low-pitched voices emanated.

I'd been in Liss's house, which had been impressive enough, but The Gables had a cozy intimacy that this house was lacking. This house was built for effect. Everything was in some shade of white, from winter ice to vanilla, with punches of black and aubergine to break up the monotony. The contrast between it and my own apartment was more than a little depressing. How did people afford all of this?

Damn.

Then again, money wasn't everything. The Robersons had money, plenty of it, but it hadn't protected them from the ill winds of fate, and the energy of the house was all-consuming: despair, grief, gloom. The dark with no end.

Damn, damn, damn.

Mom and Mrs. Roberson sat together on a sofa. Mom was speaking quietly and holding her friend's hands in her own. She looked up as I walked through the doorway. "There you are, Maggie. See, Wendy? I told you she'd take care of it for you. No need for you to be troubling yourself over something like that at a time like this."

Wendy Roberson peered at me through eyes red-rimmed and damp. She smiled weakly. "Thank you, Maggie. Won't you sit with us? You must be freezing after that."

I perched warily on the very edge of a chair, hoping against hope that I hadn't spattered myself with dirt and grime.

"You're very lucky to have such a helpful daughter, Pat." She sighed heavily, dabbing a balled-up tissue to the corners of her eyes. "She must be a blessing to you."

"That she is. Hush now."

But she couldn't seem to stop. She looked

at me, her eyes eager. Hungry. "You baby-sat for my Mandy, didn't you? When she was a little girl?"

I cleared my throat. "That was my sister, actually, Mrs. Roberson. I do remember Amanda, though. She was a beautiful girl."

Mrs. Roberson frowned as though working hard to bring my sister's face to mind. "Two daughters."

"That's right," Mom soothed. "Maggie works at that gift shop, remember? She is going to take the clock back for you, if you still want to return it."

"The clock. Yes. My Mandy was such a good girl. You remember. Headstrong but good. My little girl was smart. She knew what she wanted. She was going places. She was going . . . places. Nothing was going to stand in her way. She was just like Sid in that way. Much smarter than me. Just like Sid. Daddy's girl." She took a deep breath. It came out with a little whine at the end, half sigh, half whimper. "She was going to be some kind of corporate executive. A woman with power. I knew it. Sid did, too. He was the one who made sure she was exposed to his world so that she'd be prepared for the future. Took her to the country club. Taught her how to network. Me? I insisted she get a job, something that would teach her a little bit about regular people. The real world. Well, she's seen more than enough of that now, hasn't she?"

Her words were getting slower. She was drifting away. I could feel that, too. In the harsh sunlight flooding through the sky-high windows, her face seemed to be made of paper that had been crumpled up into a tight little ball and then flattened out once more. I could see the cracks in the veneer of her well-cared-for face, tiny fissures ever expanding with the twin pressures of sorrow and guilt battling within her. But even worse were her eyes, vague and lost in the depths of her own private hell.

"Hush, Wendy. You really should rest. Where is Sid?"

Wendy looked around as though confused. "Sid? Oh. He had to go in to the office to take care of some urgent details. He's devastated, make no mistake," she said, suddenly defending her husband's choice, "but he has to keep busy. Yes, he does."

"Will he be home soon?"

"Mmm. Soon." But the airy answer wasn't convincing. In fact, I wasn't sure she'd even registered the question.

Neither was my mother. "Let's get you into bed. You really should have someone here with you, honey. It's not good for you to be by yourself just now. Come along," she said, gently urging Mrs. Roberson to her feet. "Maggie, you run on ahead and turn down the bed."

I did as I was bid, glad to do something useful. Mom, as usual, had everything under control, while my mind was just a jumble of confused thoughts and emotions. I was glad for a breather, no matter how short.

A wide hall ran the length of the upper story with open doors leading off on each side. Only one door remained closed. Amanda's, I assumed. The master suite occupied the entire south side of the second floor. Plush ivory carpet softened my steps as I stepped into a room stark in its simplicity, spartan in its design, containing only the most basic of bedroom furniture. Bed, sleek Oriental armoire, a wall of mirrors of all shapes and sizes, and two small ornate shelves serving as bedside tables. The bed, a massive wrought-iron offering, didn't actually need to be turned down — its many layers of white bedding had never been made that morning. I hurried over and pulled each up, one at a time, before peeling them back as one so that Mrs. Roberson could lie down unimpeded. I finished just as the two older women entered the room.

"Here we are. Now you just slip your shoes off and lie down, Wendy. We'll settle you in. There you are. That's the way." To me, my mom said, "Maggie, stay with Mrs. Roberson a moment. I'll pop down to the kitchen to make you a nice cup of chamomile."

With Mom for the moment gone, I stood beside the bed, feeling awkward and not a little bit useless. Mrs. Roberson was watching me through tired eyes. I tried a sympathetic smile. "I really am very sorry, Mrs. Roberson. I hope . . . I hope they find who did it."

I didn't know what else to say. What else was there?

She rolled her head on the pillow to look out the window, blinking at the brightness. "The sun is shining," she said, her voice as hollow as an empty glass. "I don't know why that should surprise me, but it does. I'm standing still, but the world keeps turning around me, and around, and around." She closed her eyes to it and turned her face away. "It shouldn't be shining, you know. It's impossible for the sun to shine this way when the light has left the world. It just goes to show you that what we're seeing isn't the truth. It isn't real. It just isn't."

Her breath caught, and for one horrifying

moment I thought she might let out a wail. I heard it inside my head, long and keening, before it sliced through my heart in one clean effortless motion. It took my breath away.

She grabbed my hand, staring at me with an intensity that unnerved me. "I should never have insisted she get a job. My fault. It was my fault, and Sid knows it. I see the way he looks at me. She would have been home, where she belonged. She would have been safe. She wouldn't have been exposed to unsavory elements. It must have been the hotel. It *must* have been. There's just no other way. No other —"

The last word was hiccuped out. Mrs. Roberson covered her face with her hands and cried silent tears, her shoulders jerking with the effort to hold them back.

"Mrs. Roberson . . . Wendy . . . It's not your fault," I soothed, hesitating a moment before reaching out a comforting hand to touch her shoulder. It felt right to do that. "Sometimes things just . . . happen, and there's nothing we can do to change them. There's no rhyme to it, no reason. It just is."

She let her hands fall away from her face but kept her eyes closed. "I think I do need to rest now. I have some prescription sleeping pills on my husband's side of the bed. Could you get them for me, please?"

"Sure, if it's okay."

I handed them to her. She took one from the bottle and dry-swallowed it before lying down again with a sigh and closing her eyes. I stood at the window, watching the wind push cloud shadows across the surrounding fields as I listened to her struggle to lose herself in sleep.

So much pain. So much heartache. So much guilt.

Eventually her breathing slowed, became more regular. She rolled onto her side beneath the heavy covers, tucking her legs up and cradling her hands up to her throat as a child might. The bedroom windows had no curtains and no shades that I could draw against the late morning light, but it didn't seem to matter. Almost asleep, I thought. With any luck she'd sleep until her husband got home from wherever he was. Mom was right — it didn't feel right that she was alone so soon after what had happened. She should have family around her, helping her cope.

"The boys . . ." she murmured.

Not asleep after all. I reached out a gentle hand to stroke her hair as tears leaked from her closed eyelids. "Hush now. Hush. It's all right."

"Not her fault. I should've taught her . . . better. Too . . . embarrassed. Stupid woman." The words came as though from the depths of her consciousness, slow and tortuous. "She was a . . . good girl. Good. It was too late . . . found out too . . . late. Jordan. She gave herself . . . to him. I knew. I . . . knew. Changes." She took a deep breath, letting it whistle out slowly. "So many changes. Too late. My fault. Mine."

She opened her eyes suddenly and stared straight into mine. Seeing me? I wasn't so sure. The dilated pupils and wild look only served to confirm my suspicions. Reaching over the edge of the bed, her fingers scrabbled, tugged. She slipped something from between the mattress and the box springs. "You . . . take this. Please. Take . . ."

I looked down at what she was pressing into my hand. A CD? By one of the latest teen divas, no less. "What —"

"It was Mandy's. Can't . . . open. Passwords. I don't want to see . . . anymore. But I can't . . . keep it. Might be . . . I don't know. Just . . . take it. Please."

Opening the jewel case, I frowned. Behind the teen queen's CD was a second CD, an unlabeled one.

"Found it . . . in her underwear drawer.

264

Hidden."

I had a sneaking feeling that she would never have considered handing over her daughter's things to me on any other day. The drugs talking, I guess. "Mrs. Roberson, I'm not an expert. I might know someone, but —"

"Please. If it's . . . important . . . police. But don't . . . don't tell . . ." Her eyelids fluttered, reopened, closed again, remained closed this time.

"Don't tell?" I prompted her gently.

"Don't tell Sid . . . about what we buried. He doesn't . . . know. He'll . . . hate . . . me. I should have . . ." Her voice was trailing away. ". . . should have . . . doesn't know . . ."

I watched her a moment longer as sleep dragged her back down beneath its waiting darkness. Her lips worked now and then as she slipped farther away, trying to form words, but only one emerged.

". . . baby . . ."

She said no more.

I frowned, lost in thought, as I closed Mrs. Roberson's door quietly behind me. Mom was just coming up the stairs. The aroma of hot coffee preceded her, fingers of scent that reached out to draw me in.

"Too late," I whispered, taking the cup from her hand. Ah, caffeine. Much needed. "She's out."

"Asleep?"

"Blessedly. Should we call her husband, do you think?"

"I don't have his work number. I'll just have to stay. You can go on, though, dear. There's no need for both of us to be here. What's that you have?" she asked, nodding toward the CD I still held in my hand.

I gazed at it somewhat bemusedly. "Something she wanted me to look into. I'm not sure that I should — she was really out of it — but in the meantime, what do you think about the clock? Should I still take it back today?"

"I don't see why not. Wendy did insist she wanted to return it."

"Okay . . . but where do you suppose it is? I don't exactly want to go snooping through their things."

We looked at each other and said at exactly the same time, "Amanda's room?"

I glanced over my shoulder toward the lone closed door leading off from the hallway. "I don't suppose it would hurt to check. What do you think?"

"Quickly, then. I'll stay here."

I gave her a look that said *coward,* which

she returned with an imperious lift of her brow. "Here," I said, handing her the coffee cup and the CD, "hold this, then."

I moved purposely toward the room I believed to be Amanda's and pushed open the door.

The room had a queer, disused feel even though only a few days had passed since Amanda's disappearance. It might have belonged to any well-to-do teenage girl. White wicker furniture, lavender bedspread, curtains for once, purple walls, dresser, armoire, desk — nothing strange or unusual about anything that leapt immediately into view. And yet . . .

I wandered inside and stood a moment to get my bearings. If I stood very still and reached out with my mind, I could feel something here. The remnants of Amanda's presence, perhaps. A vague emotional imprint stamped into the warp and fiber of the room itself. Maybe it was none of my business, but I felt a strong need to understand. Was there something in here that might give some insight into Amanda herself, and how she came to this end?

Clock first. Then if there was time . . .

I opened what appeared to be the armoire first, only to find that it was in actuality a combination bookcase/entertainment center hiding the room's various electronic components. TV, DVD player, stereo — little Amanda need never leave the deluxe confines of her own room. The drawer below held an assortment of DVDs. Typical teen fare, mostly juvenile comedies, some romance, a few scary selections.

The writing desk next to it was picked clean. It had space for a laptop computer, but the laptop itself was nowhere in evidence. The police, I assumed. Part of the investigation. I hoped they found something.

I moved on to the closet. Holy sheep, how many clothes did this girl own? Tank tops, sweaters, skirts, and pants spilled out of every free space, dangled loosely from hangers, filled the upper shelves. And where there weren't clothes, there were shoes, boots, sandals, flip-flops. Amazing. But no room for the boxed-up clock.

My searching gaze fell upon the bed. I got down on my hands and knees to lift the coverlet. A few dust bunnies (In a house like this? Perish the thought!), but nothing else that I could see.

I sighed and sat back against my feet. Obviously the clock was nowhere in this room. Now what?

"Did you find it?"

I looked up at the sound of the half-whispered words to find my mom in the doorway. "No, nothing. I don't think it's in here."

Mom seemed to have forgotten her intentions of standing watch. She wandered into the room, trailing her fingers over the pictures on Amanda's bedside table. "So young."

"I know."

She lifted one of the frames. "This must be her boyfriend? Handsome boy."

I came to look over her shoulder at the picture of the young couple some unseen photographer had caught in a playful moment, arms slung casually about each other's necks. So this was Jordan — Mom was right, he was a handsome boy. It was also obvious he came from money. Vintage or not, designer polos, with their beloved alligator emblem, did not come cheap. Neither did the confident way of carrying himself — it seemed to come as natural as throwing his arms around his favorite girl.

And apparently, if Mrs. Roberson's observations were more than just a mother's guilt-induced ramblings, doing more than that as well. Not that that was out of the ordinary these days. But what about all the sexy lingerie? Was that normal for a girl of not-quite-eighteen?

My ears perked up at sounds coming suddenly from downstairs. "Someone's here."

"It's probably Sid. About time, too. Come on."

We left the room and quietly closed the door behind ourselves. A peek inside Mrs. Roberson's room confirmed that she was sleeping soundly, so Mom and I made our way downstairs, where we found Sid Roberson in the kitchen, staring blankly down at his open briefcase on the table before him.

He looked up at us in surprise. "Pat. I'm sorry, I didn't know Wendy was having anyone in."

"We just stopped in for a moment, Sid, and she was having a hard time of it, so we thought we'd sit with her awhile. She's sleeping now. I'm glad to see you back, though."

"Thanks. It's been a rough few days, at that."

Quite the understatement, but I understood. Everyone seemed so dead-set against exposing themselves these days as having human feelings, human frailties. Maybe they thought to do so made them appear more vulnerable to the world at large, so avoiding it was a kind of self-preservation technique.

"Wendy had mentioned a clock that she wanted to return to the store my daughter works at. I thought Maggie could help her out while we were here. You don't happen to know where it might be?"

He looked around the kitchen a moment. "Well, I thought it was right here." He poked around in a few of the more emptier cupboards, then opened the door to the broom closet in the pantry. "Ah, here it is. It's still in its box — I guess our Mandy had started to wrap it but never finished. In any case, Wendy can't bear to look at it. She'll be very grateful to the store for the return."

"We completely understand, Mr. Roberson," I assured him, taking the clock off his hands. The look in his eyes told me he was loath to give it over and might prefer to keep it, but he seemed ready to defer to his wife's wishes. As an afterthought, I offered, "If you like, we can hold it for a while, in the event that either of you changes your mind."

"Thank you. You're very kind."

Securing the box under my arm, I opened my purse, removing the envelope that contained the money Felicity had given me. I handed it to him. "The amount that Amanda paid for the clock," I explained.

He took it in his hand and opened it. The frown that looked permanently etched between his brows deepened. "That's quite a lot of money. Are you sure there hasn't been some sort of mistake?"

"Oh, no, sir. I sold Amanda the clock myself. There's no mistake. In fact, I have a store receipt right here, if you need to see it . . ." I didn't tell him what I'd told Tom — that Amanda had had quite a lot more cash on hand that day. It wasn't my place.

"No, there's no need." He tossed the envelope onto the table.

Mom cleared her throat. "Well, since you're home, Sid, there's no need for us to stay any longer. Please tell Wendy to call me," my mother added, "if she should need anything. Even just to talk. You take care of yourself, too."

"I will. Thank you again."

CHAPTER 13

I dropped my mother off at home and then headed back downtown for a bite of lunch. Annie-Thing Good was calling to my rumbling stomach in a big way. I'd offered to buy Mom lunch for not making me call on Mrs. Roberson all by my lonesome, but she turned me down, saying that she wanted to get back to make sure Grandpa Gordon didn't fill up on Cheetos and licorice whips. Funny, the two of them together were like a fussy cat and an overly enthusiastic puppy, but it was becoming more and more obvious to me as the years went on just how much my mom cared for her father. She just didn't want *him* to realize that.

The lunch rush was nearly over by the time I pulled up, so I scored a prime spot in angled parking directly in front of the glass storefront and headed inside, blinking as my eyes were forced to adjust to the lack of sunlight.

"Be right with you!" Annie Miller's voice chirruped out from behind the saloon doors that led to the small restaurant's kitchen. The sound of it was as shiny-bright as a brand-new penny, but worth so much more. Height challenged as she was, I could just see the fuzzy top of her carroty curls through the window to the back. I held my tongue, hoping to surprise her. Between the Christmas rush at the store and everything that had been going on, I hadn't been by in a couple of weeks, and the heady rush of scents emerging from the kitchen were enough to send my olfactory reserves into sensory overload.

My mouth watered as I browsed along the glass counter. Not one, not two, but three different types of cheesecake were on the menu this afternoon, along with Annie's signature turtle chunk brownies. A sliver of demure raspberry swirl was calling to me, but the double fudge ripple blitz was appealing to my closet bad girl. If I stuck to something light like soup, it couldn't be considered completely indulgent, could it? Besides, I needed to think, and I possessed the kind of brain that needed to be fed regularly to be at its best. A little something special just might do the trick, and every woman knows that chocolate does it best.

I set my purse down on the counter beside someone's packaged lunch and waited for Annie to finish. According to the chalkboard, today's special was chunky chicken noodle with sage-butter bread, a hearty split pea with ham and shallots, or your choice of any regular sandwich. In light of my determination to have my cheesecake and eat it, too, I decided I'd better stick with the chicken noodle.

Annie appeared within moments, wearing one of her outrageous color combinations in the form of a mouthy T-shirt and long skirt for ease of movement, as always paired with her well-worn Birkenstocks.

Today's T-shirt: *I Love Everybody . . . Wanna Be Next?*

Soap bubbles clung to her hair and her freckled cheeks were pink with exertion, but she was all smiles as soon as she caught sight of me. "Maggie! I was wondering when I'd see you. How've you been, girl?"

"Hey, Annie!" I waggled my fingers at her. "I just came in to be fed, as usual. You know I like you even more than your food, right?"

"Oh-ho-ho, so you say," Annie shot right back, as good-natured as ever. She pushed back a damp curl that had flopped down over her face. "And yet I never seem to see you unless I supply dessert. I just don't know what to think."

I laughed. "I do. I think I can't get enough of your cooking."

"Some friend. Good thing I love my job. What's your pick for lunch today?"

"A cup of chicken noodle and, um, a slice of that double fudge cheesecake," I said sheepishly.

"An excellent choice, if I do say so my-self." Annie placed a foam bowl on a tray and started to bustle about the big tureens. She slid the tray across the counter before me, topped it off with a real cloth napkin, and then dished up a generous piece of the creamy dessert and set it down on the tray with a flourish. "Think that'll do you?"

"I think it might. In fact, you're probably saving my life. Hey," I said, remembering the reason she'd been missing from the cemetery investigation, "how's your cousin's baby? Was it a boy or a girl?"

She beamed. "A girl. Simmone Claire. Eight pounds, two ounces of pure love. She's perfect."

How nice it was to hear good news to counteract the effect of Stony Mill's latest tragedy. Smiling to myself, I took my tray to a booth in the corner and slid in, settling down for a quiet and peaceful meal while Annie went back to her kitchen chores.

With nothing else to hold my attention, the CD came out of my purse. It really was none of my business, that much was obvious. Shouldn't Mrs. Roberson have handed it over to the police with the rest of Amanda's personal files? Why would she have given it to . . . me? I mean, okay, granted, the sleeping pills had played a big part in her decision-making process — of that I was certain. But was that enough?

I stared at the mirrorlike surface of the unlabeled CD as I ate my soup, wondering what I was going to do with the thing. Not what I *should* do with it, mind you, but what I was *going* to do with it. Because a part of me already knew that if I could find a way to take a peek at whatever was on this CD, I would do it. Consider it morbid curiosity. Chalk it up to my inquisitive nature. Call me out for being a busybody, if you must. I preferred the term "concerned citizen" myself. Besides, whatever the reason behind Mrs. Roberson's oddly placed trust, I could not bring myself to refuse the call to arms. I would do my best to ascertain the nature of the information on the CD. For all anybody knew, it could be full of nothing more relevant than the Roberson family vacation pics. If it did prove to contain evidence, no matter how minute, I would turn it over to the police. And if not . . . well, then, I would let Mrs. Roberson decide its fate.

One thing was certain: I needed technical help for this one, for sure.

The door chimes tinkled, accompanied by a moment of street sounds and a billow of cold air. Shivering, I made myself a smaller target and waited for the chill to pass as I gathered up my tray. If I took the cheesecake to go, maybe I could catch up with Marcus. He was the closest thing to a computer guru that I could think of.

Annie sailed through the swinging doors, making them rattle on their hinges. "Afternoon, Randy. What can I get for you?"

Enchantments' across-the-street neighbor, Randy Cutter, stood at the counter, all six feet of him, a short wool pea coat giving him a naval flair. I rose to my feet and took the tray over to the counter, where Annie was taking his order. I held back, waiting my turn.

"Okay, so that's a double order of split pea, a Tuscan Chicken on Rosemary Brioche, a side order of Parmesan Peppercorn Bowtie, and a slice of apple pie. Oh, and a large iced tea."

"That's it. Thanks."

That's it? It must be nice, being a guy. I'd weigh a thousand pounds in no time if I ate like that. Dammit.

As Annie bustled away to the kitchen, Randy turned to acknowledge me with the customary nod. Neither of us really knew the other outside of our respective storefronts, so that's as much of a greeting as there would be. His gaze lowered slightly, involuntarily, as it so often does when a man encounters a woman in close quarters. Together we did the Step Aside Two-Step to get out of each other's way as Annie brought his tray to him.

"Here you are, good sir. Soup, bowtie, pie. I'll have your sandwich out to you in a jiffy." As Randy began to turn away, Annie snapped her fingers. "For heaven's sake! I'll forget my head, next thing you know." In an instant she reached below the counter for a checkerboard napkin, whipping it expertly open and draping it over his extended arm. "There you are," she said, smoothing and patting it into place. "Good to go."

He looked down at the napkin, then back at her.

Annie burst out laughing at his expression of incredulity. "Oh, go on with you, then," she said, shooing him away. Turning her motherly attentions to me, she took my tray. "What's this, Miss Maggie? No cheesecake after all?"

I shook my head. "I'll take it to go, though."

"I'll just get a box for you."

Annie whisked off to the kitchen. Randy Cutter gazed after her and just shook his head before stepping around me with his tray and moving toward the nearest table. Annie came back through the swinging doors, a small foam take-out carton in her hand.

"Annie, do you think I could use your phone?"

"Sure thing, sweetie. Here you go." She pulled a phone out from under the counter and set it down in front of me. While Annie slid the cheesecake into the box, I dialed the store.

"Enchantments Fine Gifts and Collectibles," Liss's voice sang in my ear.

"Good afternoon, Enchantments," I said lightly. "How is everything?"

"Just ducky, ducks. You know, I've so missed this. It's good to be here. How has your day been?"

"Fine. Listen, I have a question for you. How good do you think Marcus is at computers?"

"Aces. Really top shelf. Why?"

"I'll explain later. Promise. Right now I need you to tell me how I can find him."

Annie slid an Annie-Thing Good napkin and a Sharpie my way. I scrawled down Liss's directions and recapped the pen. "Thanks, Liss. I'll call you back later."

"I'll be counting on it."

Annie looked at me as I handed the phone back to her. "What's up?"

"I have to see Marcus about a . . . computer problem a friend of mine has. Password breaking, that kind of thing."

Annie's freckled nose crinkled. "Ooh, I hate that, when you password-protect a file and then can't remember what password you used! That's great that Marcus can help with that kind of thing. I'll have to remember that."

"Yeah, well, it's not that she forgot the password. She never knew it to begin with." At Annie's curious stare, I caved and lowered my voice to barely above a whisper. "The files belonged to Amanda Roberson. I'm just helping her mom out." I glanced over at Randy Cutter. He had been watching us, but the instant my gaze shifted in his direction, he looked down into his lunch. Men. Do they never tire of ogling the opposite sex? On second thought, I'd been doing a fair bit of ogling myself of late. Enough said.

Annie's mouth was forming a pained *Oh.*

"Maggie . . . you won't get into anything you can't handle, will you?" she urged in an undertone.

I shook my head. "Not me. Not this time. If there's anything important there, it's off to the police the thing goes. You have my word on it."

Marcus's bachelor pad, as I soon discovered, was a study in contrasts. Should I have expected any less? No grungy trailer stuck out in a run-down trailer park for this big, bad biker boy. Instead Marcus lived in a small, Craftsman-style bungalow in one of the earlier parts of town, complete with an old waist-high cast-iron fence in the front. The fence brought vividly to mind memories of *The Omen,* which I had sneaked into the theater to see when I was a little kid, contrary to my mother's strict orders. (I am, of course, woman enough to admit that I've had nightmares ever since. Score one for the moms of the world.) If the house was a bit Ozzie and Harriet for my image of Marcus, the garage out back was the perfect atmosphere for a Harley-Davidson lover, a converted livery barn that provided ample room for all the tools, spare parts, and even biker friends.

But that's not where I found Marcus.

I found him on his knees in the kitchen, elbow deep in soap suds while an old-school Seger tune blared from a boom box on the counter, more than audible through the back door. Kind of a more up-to-date Mr. Clean, except someone really ought to tell him that it's probably not the best idea to scrub the floor on hands and knees wearing leather pants. Oh, the chafing possibilities! Still, I took a moment to appreciate the image of him in total domestic bliss before I wiped the grin off my face and knocked on the door. I had to knock again — guess the music was up higher than I thought. Marcus glanced up the second go-round, and this time I did laugh at the look of chagrin that crossed his face. In one easy movement he pushed himself to his feet and motioned for me to enter while he reached behind to turn down the music.

"Hey there, tough guy," I greeted him as I closed the door behind me to shut out the swirling eddies of cold. "Worried about dishpan hands?" I nodded toward the yellow rubber gloves.

He glanced down at himself, and I could swear I saw a blush rise in his cheeks. "Er, yeah, well, you know how drying all the cleaning solutions can be."

"Oh, yeah," I sympathized, "they're terrible. You know, this is a side of you that I haven't seen before. I never really figured you as the Domestic Goddess type."

"Smart-ass."

I grinned. "Thanks, I do try."

He crossed his arms over his chest, doing his best to look imposing. All he accomplished was to bulge out his biceps under his white T-shirt. On second thought, he managed his objective quite nicely indeed. "Cleaning your home can have many benefits, you know. You can sweep out the negative energy with the dirt and dust. You freshen the air and clear the way for new and positive energies to join you. You can trace a power sigil into the soap suds and empower your wards —"

"And you get a super clean floor, too."

"Have I ever told you you're a —"

"Smart-ass, yeah." Circumventing the soapy puddle and bucket, I leaned up against the kitchen counter. "So. This is the place you call home."

He took a chamois cloth from his back pocket and began to dry the floor. "Yeah. It isn't much to look at, but it's mine."

"It's nice. It has a lot of character."

"Thanks."

"But I must admit, it *is* pretty funny to

see you doing this kind of thing. Do you cook?"

He looked up, his brow arching. "Doesn't everyone?"

Well, some of what I did probably shouldn't be called cooking. But that was beside the point.

"So what brings you out this way?" Marcus asked, crossing his arms and mimicking me, one hip against the counter.

I took the CD case out of my purse and set it on the counter, placing my hand over it for safekeeping. "This has to be kept under wraps," I cautioned.

"Scout's honor."

I took a deep breath and plunged in. "This belonged to Amanda Roberson."

He looked more closely at the two, but didn't make a move. "And you have it . . . why?"

"I visited Mrs. Roberson today. She was . . . distraught, and a little out of her mind with grief, I think, and somehow one thing led to another and . . . she asked me to take it. To help."

He slipped the jewel case from beneath my palm and looked at it more closely before handing it back. "Bubblegum pop. Pretty typical for a teenage girl."

"There's another CD inside. A copy."

"What's on it?"

"Don't know."

He quirked his dark brows at that. "What do you mean, you don't know? Didn't you look?"

"No time. According to Mrs. Roberson, the files are password-protected."

"Why would anyone password-protect a music CD?"

"I don't think it's a music CD."

Briefly I explained what had happened at the Roberson house and how I had come to be in possession of Amanda's property. To his credit, he listened to the whole tale, allowing me to ramble at will. "I think Mrs. Roberson was hoping to find someone who could tell her what was on the CD, and with luck, reassure her that it was something completely innocent. After what happened to Amanda, it's understandable that she might be suspicious of anything she thought was out of the ordinary. And apparently she . . . had her concerns about her daughter's, well, activities. You know. Sexually." I was a grown woman. I would not blush. I would *not* blush! "She had a boyfriend she was intimate with, and maybe more than one. Or at least that seemed to be the gist of her mother's worries. I wasn't completely clear on that. Whether the files on the CD are personal or not, relevant or not, who knows? It could be anything. But maybe knowing for certain will set her mind to ease, once and for all."

Still frowning he said, "I don't get it. What's the connection?"

"A daughter dead? A mother's fear? Guilt? Hope? Everything all wrapped up into one?" I shrugged. "Does there have to be more?"

He was silent, thinking. "These really should go to the cops, Maggie."

I squirmed, knowing he was right . . . and yet something held me back. "Mrs. Roberson just wants to know what's in the files for now. It could be nothing. If it's anything relevant, even potentially relevant, then they can have it, with pleasure. But if it's nothing . . . well . . . what's the point?" I looked him straight in the eye. "So. Will you try?"

"Do you even have to ask? Maggie. I might challenge you, but I will always be here to back you up."

Smiling at his loyal response, I handed him back the CD.

"Let's see what we've got."

I followed him through the little bungalow, through arched doorways from kitchen to living room to a dark little hallway. First door on the right, a bedroom that seemed to be taken up mostly by a very large bed

— I averted my eyes quickly, but not before I noticed with approval that the bed was neatly made. Next on the left, a cottage-sized bathroom with olive green vanity and bathtub, very seventies. The last door proved to be a small bedroom that Marcus had turned into his office-slash-computer room.

Actually it was more than just your typical computer. The setup he had tucked away in his dark little office was enough to keep a midsized company powered up and happy. It was a wonder the town hadn't nailed him for overloading energy capacities on this end of town.

Marcus the bad boy as technogeek. The very idea never failed to crack me up.

Marcus pulled up an extra chair for me and pressed a button on the computer. It flared instantly to life. He inserted the CD into the drive and opened the gateway to the CD drive. A list of the files contained on the CD appeared on his extra-large flat-screen monitor.

"No password to access the CD . . ." Marcus muttered to himself.

He double-clicked on the first file. Up popped a window prompting him for a password. He closed the file and selected the next. And the next. The same thing happened through the next five files. The sixth, however . . .

The sixth file opened without a prompt with his photo editor. Marcus and I both leaned closer to the screen as the JPEG appeared on the screen. It was a graphic design of hearts, interlocked with daisies and sparkles, very pretty, very girly, very . . .

Familiar.

"Oh my God," I breathed. The revelation was enough to bowl me over. I stared at the screen, dumbfounded at what had been under our noses all week long.

Marcus had, as usual, leaned back in his chair, his long legs stretched out beneath the table and crossed at the ankles. Now he sat up straight, his focus intense on the screen as he tried to discern the reason for my interest. "You recognize it."

I nodded, excitedly. "I think so, Marcus! You know the SunnyStonyMill website?"

"I like to think so."

"Did you know there is a kind of underground blog attached to it?" When he shook his head, I continued, "The high school kids have been all over it. No one knows who wrote it. I discovered it accidentally through Evie and your cousin Tara, the day that Amanda disappeared. At first I thought it might be a virus or something, because the SunnyStonyMill site didn't work properly when I accessed it through the history. Evie filled me in, but not before I reported the problem to the county M.I.S. department. The woman didn't believe me at first, but . . ." I shrugged.

Intrigue lit his clear blue eyes. "And you recognize this graphic from this underground blog page?"

"I believe so. Which means —"

"That Amanda is, if not responsible, at least involved."

"Exactly."

"So. What kind of blog are we talking about here?"

"Have you ever heard of Peyton Place?" At his nod, I explained, "Well, consider this blog sort of a modern-day version."

His right eyebrow lifted. "Is it still there?"

"I'm not sure. The blog was heavily firewalled against a preemptive strike, according to the systems person I talked to. I haven't talked to her since, so I'm not sure if she's found a way to take it down or not."

He turned back to the computer and opened up the Internet browser. With a glint in his eye and hands in position over the keyboard, he said, "Well, let's just take a look, shall we?"

"Not like that," I said as Marcus began to type in the SunnyStonyMill.com address with lightning-quick fingers. I dug in my purse for the scrap of paper on which Evie had written the address and various password commands, and handed it to him.

The familiar black-red-black strobing screen made its appearance. "I think it's still there," I told him. "This is exactly what it did for me. I guess the systems people haven't cracked it yet."

Marcus shook his head in awe as he keyed through the many password scenarios. A rueful half smile played at the corner of his mouth. "In a way I feel like a proud dad or brother or uncle or something. I always knew Amanda had it in her. This is amazing. I mean, I knew she was smart, but this is way beyond anything I'd ever seen from her. She was holding out on me, that much is obvious."

I had forgotten that he'd once told me he had known her. It occurred to me I'd never asked how. "What do you mean?"

"Amanda was a student in the extracurricular computer programming workshop I put on at the high school. She was quite good. Better than most."

Every time I turned around, this man was surprising me. "I didn't know you volunteered at the school."

"My uncle Lou got me into it. He's a history teacher at the high school, you know. Anyhow, he thought I could do the town a favor and teach these kids some stuff they would never learn in their regular computer classes. To keep things interesting for them. And it was fun for me, too. I've even been thinking about going back to school to finish up my degree to become a teacher myself."

His pride in Amanda's talent faltered slightly when he began to read about an altogether different sort of talent. The blog hadn't been updated since the day before she disappeared, which only served to confirm my suspicions. "This is pretty shocking stuff," he commented gruffly.

"Uh-huh."

"Little Amanda had quite the social life."

"Yup."

"And I'm only up to page three."

"Amazing, isn't it? I've only read the first ten pages myself. It was about all I could stomach at the time. But now that I know it was hers . . . well, I think it bears a closer look, definitely."

He pushed back in his chair, studying me. "Let me guess. You think maybe the blog contains some kind of information that might lead the police to her killer."

"It's possible, isn't it? I mean, it's more

likely than a serial killer bebopping through Stony Mill proper and choosing Amanda at random. What do you think?"

He assessed me quietly. "I think we'd best do what we can to preserve the information on the website before county systems support shuts it down." He began to systematically print off the text from the months' worth of entries. The printer whirred to life and started spitting out pages.

"Print one for me, too, would you?"

"Done."

"Marcus, you're at the high school — maybe you know these boys. What do you know of Jordan Everett and Charlie Howell?"

"As relates to Amanda?"

I nodded.

"All three of them took my workshop, so I guess I know them as well as any adult can. Jordan Everett was Amanda's boyfriend. You've heard of the Everett family, right? Jordan was typical of that kind of money. Big man on campus, athletic, good-looking kid, good student. He seemed to have it all together. Charlie, on the other hand . . . well, Charlie's family are old-time Stony Millers, but they don't have the right address, if you know what I mean. Good people, hardworking, but blue collar all the way. He's worked hard for everything he had, and trust me, it wasn't much. But what Charlie did have was a talent for basketball."

That's where I knew the name from. Charlie's name came up almost as often as Jordan Everett's in the *Stony Mill Gazette,* which faithfully reported on every single local game and most of the away games as well. Basketball was more than a sport in Indiana. It was a way of life. A Friday night game was likely to bring in a higher attendance rating than all of the town churches' Sunday attendance numbers combined, and that was saying something.

"How was he connected with Amanda?" I pressed, curious.

Marcus leaned back in his chair, steepling his fingers over his flat stomach. "Charlie had a crush on Amanda that would not quit. You could see it, every time he was within ten feet of her, as big and bright as the full moon. And she knew it, too, the poor kid. That girl led him around by the 'nads, no doubt about it. And he was the up-and-coming big leaguer on the basketball team, which kinda-sorta threatened Jordan's status as captain, I guess, enough that it got his blood up on a regular basis. Amanda liked to play with Charlie to keep Jordan in line."

Obedience by emotional blackmail. Nice.

"Could either of them be responsible for what happened to her?" I asked him quietly.

He closed his eyes and leaned his head back against the high back of the desk chair. "I don't know. No. Maybe. Ah, who the hell knows what anyone will do with the right sort of provocation? I suppose anything's possible."

Which brought us straight back to where we were to begin with. Amanda dead, and just about everyone within her circle of acquaintance a potential suspect.

I nodded toward the computer monitor. There were other files there that we had not checked. "How good are you at breaking passwords?"

Marcus opened his eyes and studied me. "Fair to middlin', I'd say. I trained for it in the military. A long time ago they used people as code breakers, but now they mostly use programs for it."

"I'd like to know what was on those files. Will you work on it?"

"If I can break it, I will. But if it's important . . ."

"Then off to the police it goes, straightaway. Scout's honor."

CHAPTER 14

The light on my answering machine was blinking when I arrived home at my basement lair, but for the moment I ignored it, instead throwing my coat and purse into the chair by the door and heading straight for the refrigerator for my daily indulgence of an ice-cold can of Classic Coke while I made my dinner. I probably shouldn't, taking into consideration the piece of cheesecake I'd treated myself with at lunch, but then again, I hadn't finished it, so the Coke wasn't going to do any harm. Or at least not much.

Tonight's entrée was going to be canned ravioli à la microwave and a side of peppered cottage cheese. Large curd, of course. Nothing fancy, but it would do the trick. I wielded the can opener like the pro I was and popped the ravioli into the microwave, waiting for the *Ting!* of completion before assembling a tray and carrying it to the living room.

My evening plans were tragically interrupted — *Magnum* had been preempted by a college basketball game. Now, I know it's the state sport, but it gets pretty bad when it's the topic of conversation on everyone's lips, men and women alike, not to mention in every newspaper and on every news broadcast. Enough is enough.

And the romance novel I'd borrowed from the library left a lot to be desired.

The topping on the cake was the message on my machine. It turned out to be from my sister, Melanie, whose perfect life left a lot to be desired in mine. "Hey, sis, it's me, Mel. Did Mom tell you the news? Greg made partner! And it's about time, too, I say. After all that he's done for the place, it should have happened years ago. But at least they've corrected their oversight now and are willing to make up for past mistakes. They're sending us on a trip to Hawaii! All expenses paid. Can you believe it? Of course, this means I might need your help in watching the girls. Mom can't do it all, and I know you won't mind, since this is such a special occasion and you have no real ties of any kind. Thanks, Mags! I'll let you know the dates as soon as I have them. 'Kay, well, gotta run. There's a sale on at

Sugarland Crossing, and I've got swimsuits to buy! Talk to you later!"

I was not going to obsess. I was not going to waste time wishing I had even a quarter of her good luck.

Instead, I sat there, calmly chewing my canned ravioli until I no longer felt like the poor relation. There were times, though, when I wondered whether Marshall had had the right idea after all. My older brother had left the house for college upon graduation from high school and had never looked back, except for holiday breaks and summer vacations. And after his second year, business internships came into play, which meant summer vacation had been eliminated as well. He didn't have to deal with the day-to-day minutia of living a hop, skip, and a jump from a family that liked to be involved in his every thought. He wasn't stuck having Mom organize his life every time he turned around. Hell, he didn't even have to answer the phone if he didn't want to. He was leading the quintessential bachelor life. I could learn something from him.

With dinner over and evening monotony stretching ahead of me, it was natural that my mind began to wander. I picked up the copy of the blog that Marcus had printed for me and flipped through the stack of pages, but I couldn't bring myself to read through more of Amanda's sexcapades tonight, no matter how much it needed to be done. Tomorrow. Tomorrow would be soon enough for me to read the whole sordid lot of it in its entirety before handing it over to the police. Maybe by the time Marcus broke the password (Or was there more than one? One for each file?), there would be even more information to give them. Or was that too much to hope for? I should have asked Marcus how long he thought it might take. Marcus was a guru, but realistically speaking, it seemed to me that it could take days.

If only there was something that could help things to go faster.

Sighing, I went to my bedroom, pulled off my boots, wriggled out of my clothes, then stood staring impassively into my closet. Normally I would have pulled out a pair of sleep pants, a camisole tee, and my fluffy robe and bunny slippers, but something held me back tonight. I sat on the edge of my bed, held in place by a burgeoning feeling inside me that seemed to be trying to tell me something. But what?

Close your eyes . . . breathe deeply . . . find your center . . .

What do you feel?

Eyes closed and moving on autopilot, I grabbed a pair of jeans, a hoodie, and a pair of tennies and began to dress again. As I pulled on the shoes, I began to understand that I was supposed to go back to Enchantments. Why, I didn't really know, but I knew it would come to me by the time I got there.

The store wasn't dark, as I had expected it to be. Liss was still there. I saw the lights in the upstairs loft as I pulled up even before I saw the low-slung black Lexus brooding in its usual parking space. Things clicked into place like the inner workings of a lock under the magic fingers of a master locksmith. I was looking for something, anything, to give us an edge in making the investigation process move a little faster. I was willing to suspend my supernatural skittishness enough to try just about anything. Maybe a finding spell, to aid the police in their quest for information on the assassin. Or maybe there were crystals Marcus could use while trying to break Amanda's passwords to help him make the necessary connections. At the very least, Liss would know what was possible.

I let myself in the back door and headed through the dimly lit storefront toward the stairs. "Liss? Are you up there?" I called.

Liss popped her head over the stair rail.

"Is that you, Maggie? Come on up!"

"Are you sure? Is it okay?" A moment of uneasiness made me cautious. Liss in the loft alone, on a dark winter's night, almost certainly meant one thing: She was practicing, and I didn't mean practicing for karaoke night at the Little Nipper Tavern. I was okay with what I had witnessed in her presence, but thus far that had been limited to the friendship and protection circles we participated in on N.I.G.H.T.S. extravaganzas. Nothing sinister in that.

Nothing sinister in any of it. I knew Liss too well to worry that she might be involved in anything dark. It just wasn't her style. My only defense for my chariness was the strangeness I had felt in the air last night at the cemetery. Swirling currents of energy, and though I was far from expert in matters of the supernatural, it didn't feel all . . . good. In fact, some of it felt downright threatening. I'd have to be a lot more certain of my ability to fend off negative energies before I'd feel more at ease.

"What I mean is," I amended before she was able to sense my uncertainty, "are you sure I'm not interrupting anything . . . important?"

Her tinkling laugh could have broken any dark spell. "Of course not. You're a welcome distraction in anything I do. Come on, then."

I started up the stairs. "If you're sure . . ."

"Really, Maggie, you'd think you were afraid of me."

I shut my mouth and mentally tried to push the wariness from me. Liss was too psychic for her own good, and the last thing I wanted to do was to hurt her feelings. "Of course I'm not. I just didn't want to intrude, that's all," I told her as I rounded the bend to the landing. "Sometimes people just want to be alone, even if they pretend otherwise to spare your feelings."

"Since when have you known me to not speak my mind?"

Hmm. Good point.

The loft glowed with the soft golden lighting of upward of twenty candles on various stands situated around the open space. It was a large room that spanned the entire length and breadth of the storefront below. One end was crammed with tall bookshelves, back-to-back library style, filled to overflowing with books on every arcane subject imaginable. Along the sides of the room stood a goodly number of glass cabinets which housed crystals and jewelry, mostly of Celtic design. Still more cupboards held the witchy herbs that didn't quite fit in with the mainstream bulk herbs we sold downstairs in the giant apothecary cupboard. Most people just didn't expect to find mugwort and belladonna next to their cinnamon and cloves. Better to keep them separate than to raise the eyebrows of those who might object to finding pagans and witches living in their own backyard.

Liss stood before an altar stand in the center of the large circular braided rug, her arms raised in a V of reverence to the moon, just visible through the skylights high above us. Mesmerized by the sight, I slid onto a low bench that stood against the gallery rail, unwilling to break the ribbon of energy that I knew surrounded the circle. Liss in mid-ritual was a sight to behold. I literally couldn't take my eyes off her. Even at an indeterminate age, with her auburn hair streaked liberally with silver, her alabaster skin remained smooth and for the most part unlined, and her eyes glowed with life. No, it was more than her eyes. The very room vibrated with it the moment she walked through the door. Liss was the most alive person I'd ever known, and people flocked to her like a moth to a flame. Me, included. Whatever elixir she'd found through her religious practices and unique approach to life had given her an internal peace that was extended to whomever she came into contact with, and it was addictive. Had I really been afraid to come up only moments ago? At that moment, I never wanted to leave.

In her blue silk ritual robe and silver bracelets, Liss conducted her ritual with the serenity and passion of a Dianic devotee from long ago. On her forehead, just below the hairline, she wore a circlet I'd never seen before, cast in silver, the crescent moon at its center tipped up so that the crescent became the horns of a steer. The circlet only served to accentuate the otherworldliness of her appearance.

As the ritual went on, I recognized it from my reading as a personalized self-blessing and dedication to the divine spirit she thought of as the Goddess. When it was done, Liss solemnly released the energy to the heavens and reopened the circle. Taking a moment to compose herself, she knelt to ground the remnants of energy, then turned to me with a smile.

"That wasn't so bad, was it?"

Drat her intuition. Sheepishly I put down the purse I'd been clutching to my breast and said, "It was lovely. It's obvious you take great joy in your beliefs."

"If one's beliefs are not a balm to one's soul, why should one waste one's time?"

From anyone else's lips those might have been fightin' words, but from Liss it just sounded like calm, cool reason.

"So?" At my inquiring glance, she cocked her head. "Why did you come? I assume you aren't here simply to witness my rededication to the Goddess."

"No. No, I guess I'm not."

"Why then?"

"I'm not sure. Something told me to come here. Crazy, huh?"

Her laugh tinkled in the air. "Maggie. After everything I've told you, I'm going to think you're crazy for having feelings?"

"Hmm. Well, I guess you're right. Besides, I'd be lying if I said I wasn't starting to listen to those little nudges and hints. So touché to you."

"And what are the nudges and hints telling you tonight?"

"That there might be something witchy that can be done to help in the quest for finding the person responsible for Amanda Roberson's death. Got any ideas?"

"Hmm." A glint in her eye, Liss leapt to her feet and ran over to a cupboard. She unlocked it and withdrew from its depths a battered, leather-bound book the size of a business portfolio. She dragged its sizable portions with her and plopped back down on the floor with it as though she were a teenage girl about to share a glamour mag with her best friend. "Let me flip a moment. There's something in here that might help."

" 'Kay." As she flipped, I made conversation. "So, what exactly is a rededication for?"

"I haven't been practicing much since Isabella died. Started feeling sorry for myself, I suppose. Wallowing in the regrets of a misspent lifetime, and all that. So with the moon still being full tonight, I decided to do a little ritual for myself, to thank the Lady for her patience and for her wisdom in giving me time to myself. Isabella, I think, would understand now. There's no room for judgment in the spirit world. Just an assessment of whether a soul has learned the lessons it set out to learn and the preparation for life anew."

That swung far, far from the Christian viewpoint where the soul was judged after death, whereupon it was cast into the nether regions of hell or ascended into the realms of angels. "No fiery damnation?" I asked, curious. "No cotton candy clouds and plucking on harp strings?"

She shrugged. "Death means different things to different people. But no, I don't believe in that."

I was still a moment, thinking about that.

"Did you know that the original meaning for the Hebrew word for sin meant 'to miss one's mark'?" Liss continued. "I believe that a person sets out to learn certain lessons in each lifetime they choose to inhabit. Failing to meet that objective because their soul resists the forces that drive the universe, that's what gives you 'sin,' only not in the way most people believe. That meaning stems more from the minds of men, in my personal view. Men who desire power to wield over other men. Men who would cast human failings upon their God because they cannot conceive of what it means to be above that. To be a spirit of light."

"I'm not sure what I believe." It was the first time I had admitted that to anyone. The first time I could say it without fear of reprisal. "I've not been sure for a while now. I'm really confused. Most of the time I just don't want to think about it at all."

Liss reached over and patted my hand. "I think the important thing is that you allow yourself the time to discover what your God means to you, without the pressure or demands of outside forces. Listen to your own heart. You know the truth. It's there inside you. Inside each of us. Waiting to be remembered."

I shivered at the mystical words that filled me with a tingle of energy. Of awareness.

To distract myself, I told Liss, "Did I happen to mention the strange blog that was attached to the SunnyStonyMill website?"

"Hmm, no, I don't think so. Why? Was it anything interesting?"

"I'll say." Briefly I related the discovery of the blog, and the connection Marcus and I had happened upon just that afternoon.

"Maggie, that may just be the first real clue that's come out since Amanda was found. Have you mentioned this to your police friend?"

Feeling sheepish, I shook my head. "Not yet. I was hoping to be able to give him just a bit more at the same time."

"Ah." She gave me a speculative glance. "To be helpful? Or to show him up?"

I squirmed beneath her probing gaze. "You do see a lot, don't you? To be *completely* honest, I suppose there is a part of me that wants to show him up. Just a little bit. A woman scorned, and all that. Crazy, I know, but I can't seem to help it."

"Not crazy. Human. His rejection hurt you. Aha!" Liss cried out abruptly, pulling her hand back to hold the book open to the flickering light. "I knew it was in here. This is a finding spell to be used when an object has been purposely hidden or obscured. We could, of course, write our own and it could be just as effective, but I've always trusted the wisdom of my ancestors and see no reason to stop now. We'll just customize it, personalize it for this specific situation. How does that sound?"

"Sounds good. Do you think it will work?"

"I'd bet my broomstick on it."

I opened my mouth as surprise washed over me.

She winked. "Just joking. I would never bet my broomstick. How on earth would I get around town?"

An hour later, we had something we both thought we could work with. I helped Liss collect the various bits of herbs and other components she would need to perform the spell ritual.

"Would you like to assist?" Liss asked me.

I hesitated. A part of me thought it would be cool, very cool, but another side of me wasn't sure I was ready to actively participate in real magick. I also didn't quite see how it fit into my Catholic upbringing. Technically speaking, it didn't at all, and that was part of the problem.

"If you'd prefer, you can just lend me your energy by being in circle."

Being in circle. I'd been in circle before.

That I could do. "Sure."

We'd placed the components on a square silk scarf in the center of the braided rug, a pillow on each side of it. Liss motioned for me to take a seat on the velvet pillow across from her.

She cast her circle in an instant, without words. I felt it the moment it closed around us and rose into a protective bubble over our heads. Quickly she summoned the four elements, earth, air, fire, and water, to attend the ritual, then immediately began assembling the spell components in order — rather like following the recipe from a cookbook, I observed. While she placed the items in a copper pot in the center of the silk cloth between us, I sat in a lotus position and closed my eyes, concentrating my entire being on finding my center. The soft darkness enveloped me, and I embraced it, gratefully reaching for the elemental nothingness that made everything else disappear. Once, briefly, my thoughts meandered sideways in the abyss as I wondered what Tom would think if he could see me now, lost to the waves of power I didn't entirely understand. My skin tingled. My nose itched. My scalp prickled. My mind locked on its target and held, until thought and body and spirit merged as one.

Liss spoke the words we had written, once, twice, thrice. The energy swirling above our heads rose to a fever pitch.

I felt her take me by the hands and lightning zipped up my arms. Though we were separated by a space of at least two feet, I could feel our breathing as it found a mutual pace, faster, faster. When it felt as though I could bear the buffeting of the energies no more, Liss threw our hands upward above our heads and released the power we had channeled back to the universe. Then we both sank to our cushions, our breath coming as giggles of release.

"Wow," I said, leaning back on my hands. Liss smiled tiredly at me. "Indeed."

We were silent a moment as we allowed our pulses to settle. I rolled my head against my shoulders to look over at her. "How do you think we did?"

"I think it went brilliantly, ducks. You'll see. Give it time. I think you'll be speaking with your special police friend soon."

I looked up at her in surprise. "What do you mean?"

A sly smile curved her lips. "Let's just say I put in a little cosmic nudge in his direction. Think of it like ringing his doorbell."

"I didn't want . . ." I started to deny, but the knowing glint never left her eyes. "Okay, so maybe I did, just a little."

"I could whip up a love spell for you," she offered, the picture of well-meaning pseudo-maternal innocence. She was tired, but not too tired to take advantage of an opportune moment. "Nothing that would remove his free will, of course, that would go against the Rede, but perhaps a little something to open your heart and mind to the possibility of love."

What was it about women over the age of forty that made them want to pair up any unattached younger female within their circle of acquaintance. I had never really thought of my heart and mind as problem areas. "Thanks — really — but in love I think it's probably better to let things happen on their own, if they're of a mind to."

"If you change your mind . . ."

But I knew I wouldn't. Tom already had a low opinion of Liss and anyone else who practiced the Craft. Casting a spell on him wasn't going to help matters at all. Even a cosmic message might be pushing things.

"Oh! I almost forgot." Liss leapt to her feet and went to one of the glass cabinets, returning a moment later with an expectant look on her face as she handed me a small package. "I have something for you."

"For me? What is it? Oh, for heaven's sake,

you don't have to give me presents, I . . ." I had untied the string and began to unwrap the plain brown paper. Out rolled a glittering arrow-shaped object on a slender silver chain. A pendulum, crafted of deepest purple amethyst, balanced on the opposite end by a beautifully worked silver bead. My breath caught. "Oh — my — it's gorgeous."

"I'm so glad you like it, sweets."

My eyes flew to her face. "Oh, but I can't keep it. It's much too expensive. It's —"

"I've always loved this one. Amethyst is marvelous for psychic connections. And I wanted you to have it, Maggie. You've worked so hard for me and for the store, it's the least I can do. I've never used it much anyway, and I'd like it to go to someone who might take some pleasure in it. You seem to have a knack for this particular tool of divination, whereas my tool of choice is a scrying mirror. Besides, a thing of beauty should always be appreciated, not tucked away in some old box, gathering dust."

I let the pendulum roll back and forth on my palm, marveling at the glitter of its faceted point. "Oh, but Liss —"

She slid another item onto my lap while I was distracted. I glanced down. It was a piece of oiled canvas, printed with a semi-circle graph intersected by a number of radial lines, a series of two letters or numbers at the end of each. "It's a diviner's chart," she explained at my blank look. "To help you take your divination to a deeper level."

I turned it this way and that, trying to make heads or tails of it. "How do you use it?"

She spread the cloth on the floor and held out her hand for the pendulum. Supporting her elbow to keep it steady, she suspended it so that the tip of the amethyst hung directly over the center of the half circle. "Ideally, you say a prayer of protection — the Lady of the Light is a good one, but you can, of course, use Lord in Her stead, or substitute whatever prayer you wish to use — and then center yourself. When you feel you're ready, you run through your usual questions to ascertain that you've accessed your spirit guide, or your inner self, or even an ascended being, just as Eli instructed you. And then of course, you begin asking questions. Except for with this method you're not restricted to 'yes' and 'no' questions only — the pendulum points toward a line to spell out an answer, and then you clarify the letter or number by asking it to show you a 'yes' answer for the correct letter. Slow going, but not nearly as slow as running through the entire alphabet to obtain the correct letter."

Fascinated, I cocked my head and squinted at the graph. "Does that work?"

"Why don't you let me know? As I said, the black mirror is my method of choice. I've never been much good with a pendulum." As though to prove her point, the pendulum in her hands hung stock-still over the center. "Oh, and one other thing, Maggie. Until you become more proficient, holding the point of the crystal over your opposite palm may help to open your energy pathways, at the beginning of a session especially. You should be able to feel the energy running though the chain, through the crystal, and into your palm."

I had felt it, the other night, and it still amazed me. Truth be told, I was excited by Liss's gift, and I couldn't wait to test out this new aptitude a bit more. "All right. Thank you. I'll just consider it an early Christmas present, so long as you allow me to return the favor. Er, do witches celebrate Christmas?"

She threw back her head with an engaging laugh. "Well, in the witching community I think you'll find it more commonly referred to as Yule or Yuletide, but yes, absolutely. Many of the modern Christian celebrations hearken back in actuality to pagan rituals, traditions, and beliefs, and for good reason. The people could not give up their beloved traditions that stretched back into antiquity. Eventually, when they couldn't abolish the practices, the church absorbed the most persistent of them into their own theology."

Food for thought, anyway. "It's supposed to be about the birth of Christ," I murmured pensively.

"The birth of the god, yes. If you believe what church theologians have to say, the birth of Christ was supposed to have taken place in mid-April. Early church leaders moved the date back to coincide with the old celebrations of the rebirth and renewal of the god figure, to convert the masses who still followed the Old Ways. More followers equaled more money in church coffers, and money always equals power. It's a universal truth. Then of course, there's the fact that they demonized the old godface of Pan or Dionysus, giving them Devil horns and cleft feet to convince those who clung to bits and pieces of their old beliefs that the Old Ways were the way to evil. They used fear to manipulate. To dominate." She shook her head with a rueful chuckle. "Having one church, one belief system, ensured their continued prosperity and power. But it has nothing to do with the divine spirit that created us all, by whatever name. Only human failings."

A cynical viewpoint, perhaps, but it made sense given the psychological makeup of man. A person could see it happening firsthand in a smaller way, right in his or her own church. What was it about human nature that made jockeying for position such an important facet of our psyches? Human weaknesses. Would they be our downfall? They certainly hadn't served Amanda Roberson well. "So you celebrate Yule, then."

"Yes. Well, some do."

"Only some?" I asked, a little confused.

"Yes, you see, there is no one way to practice the Old Ways. Ancient traditions are as varied and individual as the people who brought them into being. There are so many traditions that one could never say, this is the one *true* way. It would be arrogance at its most overbearing. Which means, there are no two pagans or witches exactly alike. Spirituality is a very personal thing, and our sense of individuality is something we all fiercely defend. All paths of Light lead to the Divine."

But were all people entitled to salvation? I wasn't so sure anymore.

CHAPTER 15

I spent most of Thursday, in between customers, hunched over the counter at the store, practicing with my new toy. It was better than the Crazy 8 ball I got for Christmas when I was seven. Hours of entertainment, fun for the whole family. But this was specific to me, and there is something very appealing about that. Something I didn't have to share with anyone. My little secret.

So while Liss caught up on paperwork and made plans for the summer line, I began to familiarize myself with what it meant to be a dowser. I discovered that the crystal wouldn't start to respond until I asked if anyone was there. I learned that sometimes the connection was better than others. Most intriguing was the realization that by the end of the day, whomever or whatever I was in contact with was responding to questions I thought through in my head *before I spoke them aloud.* Which left the skeptic in me wondering: Was I somehow subconsciously causing the pendulum to move, even though I was consciously making an extreme effort not to affect it? Could I trust the answers that the pendulum gave? Or should I assume they came from the depths of my psyche, so far buried that even I didn't know they were there?

If that wasn't twisted, I didn't know what was.

I also discovered that using the dowsing chart was going to take practice. The yes-no questions were easy to discern, once you'd attuned yourself to your particular pendulum, but using the chart required a still hand and a perceptive eye. Sometimes it appeared that the pendulum point followed a certain path, but when asked to clarify, it wouldn't specify any of the letters indicated. Of course, I hadn't asked it anything important either, so maybe my spirit guide was just tired of answering ridiculous questions, like, *"Is the sky blue?"* So as the clock rounded 2 p.m., marking the customary afternoon lull, I smoothed my hands over the cloth chart and focused my thoughts on the black nothingness within before taking up the pendulum once more and pouring my energies into the crystal point. It was working — I could feel the vibrations pulsing through the crystal. I balanced my elbow on the scarred wooden countertop and let the pulsing waves flow through me.

"Spirit guide?" I said in a low voice.

The pendulum swung clockwise in generous circles, motioning *Yes*.

"Spirit guide, I'd like to ask you a question or two about a death that occurred here in our town within the last week. Is that all right?"

Yes.

Encouraged, I continued. "Do you know who was killed?"

Yes.

"Can you spell out the name of the person who was killed?"

Yes.

Okay, now we're getting somewhere, I thought. I dipped the pendulum to allow it to stop moving, a clearing motion so that it would start with a clean slate. "All right, first letter."

M

I frowned. "Is the first letter an M?"

Yes.

Hmm. I dipped the crystal to clear it. "Second letter."

The pendulum began to move, settling into the direction of the N.

Double hmm. "Is the second letter an N?"

I asked, my skepticism in this particular method growing.

Yes.

This was getting me nowhere. "Third letter?"

D

Something clicked in my brain, and I stopped breathing. "Is the third letter a D?" I asked faintly.

Yes.

M-N-D. "Are there any other letters?"

Yes.

"Fourth letter . . . ready?"

The pendulum swung in a wide circle, again, and again, then elongated its orbit to settle on a straight line path toward the A.

M-N-D-A. Amanda. God, I was slow.

Excited now by my success, I thought about what I should ask next while the pendulum moved back into its powerful back-and-forth motion that indicated a waiting pattern.

"Spirit guide . . . do you know who killed her?"

The pattern did not change.

I frowned. "Spirit guide, am I not allowed to ask that question?"

No.

I blew out my breath in frustration. Why the blazes not? Wasn't it for the greatest good? I tried again. "Spirit guide, can you tell me anything that will help the police find the person who killed her? The person who killed Amanda Roberson? Anything at all?"

The pendulum began to alter its orbit again. "First letter?"

W

"The first letter is a W. Second letter?"

T

"Second is a T. Third?"

R

"Third is an R? Are there any more letters?"

Yes.

"Next letter?"

A

W-T-R-A. "And the next?"

The pendulum slowed until it resumed the short, choppy waiting motion.

"Are there any more letters?"

Nothing.

W-T-R-A. Well, the A had been out of sequence in Amanda, so maybe it was in this word, too. Or maybe my spirit guide just couldn't spell. I knew lots of people in the here-and-now who couldn't spell to save their lives. Maybe that didn't change once a person passed over to the other side. I thought through what words used those four letters. Amanda had been found in water, perhaps that was what my spirit guide meant. Or maybe . . .

A waiter?

Did Amanda know anyone named Art?

Dammit. This was useless. Liss never mentioned I'd have to be proficient at unscrambling anagrams.

I meant to put the pendulum down. I did, really I did, but the pendulum had started to move toward a letter again. Unable to do anything else, I watched, held captive by the flowing energies that made my hand feel paradoxically heavy and light at once. "C" — a pause as the pendulum circled, and then made a line drive once more — "C again?" — I held my breath — "L?" — "K" — nothing. "Is that all? C-C-L-K?"

Yes.

This one wasn't as hard, or at least it wasn't if I was interpreting it correctly.

My eyes swung toward the end of the counter, where I'd left the box I had carried in from my car this morning.

Clock.

I set the crystal down carefully in the center of the dowsing chart and went to the box I'd transported from the Roberson house. I slipped my fingertips under the flaps we'd crisscrossed to hold the box shut in lieu of packing tape and flipped them up. The clock rested within, its cracked face giving testament to the passing of many years. I lifted it out of its padding and set it carefully on the counter, brushing away some stray bits of Styrofoam that remained stuck to its dark wooden surface. It was a beautiful specimen, elegant lines of polished wood giving testament to great care being afforded it over its lifetime. But it was only a clock. There was nothing that could be viewed as evidence against her killer. Nothing on its back, or underneath.

I tipped it, angling it carefully backward so that I could look at its face. The winding key was in a tiny, shallow drawer that was typical of clocks of this style. I took it out and decided to wind it up, just a little ways. There was something so comforting about the muted *tick-tock* of an old windup clock. Some people hated the sound, a reminder of the relentless passage of time, but it had always made me think of long summer nights spent on Grandma Cora's lumpy horsehair divan, the sounds of an old clock playing counterpoint to the singing of crickets and whirring buzz of a million cicadas.

But when I turned the little key, nothing happened. The clock didn't tock. It didn't even tick. What it did do was clunk.

The inner pendulum must have come loose. I turned the clock around on the counter until I could get to the door in the back. The mechanism refused to budge. I twisted it carefully, but it would not twist. Yeesh. Had it come loose while I was transporting it?

"Uh, Liss? Can you come out here a moment?"

Liss stuck her head between the velvet curtains, her usually sleek hair a trifle disheveled and reading glasses stuck on the end of her nose. "Did you need something, Maggie?"

I swept my hand toward the counter. "The clock Mrs. Roberson returned . . . it isn't working. I think the pendulum has come loose, but the door mechanism doesn't appear to be working either. I know the clock was working when Mrs. Roberson first looked at it, and I know it was working when Amanda bought it, but —"

She waved her hand at me. "Don't fuss, Maggie. I'm sure it's something quite simple."

She placed her hands on either side of the clock and shook it gently back and forth. Something shifted inside. Instead of reaching for the knob I'd been trying to twist, she ran her hands over the carving around the base of the clock like a blind person reading Braille. I heard the tiny sound of a catch releasing, and to my amazement the door fell open the tiniest fraction of an inch.

"How did you know what to do?" I asked her, incapable of hiding my admiration. "I would never have guessed that release was there."

She smiled at me. "This clock takes me back to my childhood. My grandmother had a clock just like this. My gran, she was a village wisewoman in Scotland, you know. She was quite lovely."

"Scotland?" For the first time I realized that there might be more to the lilt of her accent than I'd realized. "I thought you were English."

"I am both, I suppose, technically. I was raised in Callander before moving to London with Geoffrey when I was in my twenties. But I do have family still in the Trossachs around Loch Lomond, whom I've been missing desperately of late. Perhaps I should arrange a trip home soon," she mused. "Springtime in the Lowlands is lovely in a way that Indiana, as pretty as it is, cannot possibly manage."

Such a view might be denounced as elitist, but we were talking about Scotland here, so I was inclined to forgive her.

We turned as one toward the clock, bending at the waist until our heads nearly touched.

There was the pendulum, lying on the floor of the clock case. Liss withdrew it easily, but hooking it back up proved a little more difficult.

Finally Liss bent down even farther and craned her head to see inside. "Well, well. What have we here?" She poked her fingers into the space. Frowned. Got down on her knees in front of the counter. "Could I trouble you for the needle-nosed pliers from the tool chest?"

"Of course." Hurriedly I retrieved the tool from the chest in the supply closet and brought it out to Liss. "What do you see?"

She didn't answer. By then she was needle-nose deep in the case, pulling at something inside that I could not see. Something on the hidden ceiling of the cabinet.

"There! By Jove, I think I've got it." From the small space she withdrew a small piece of what looked like plastic, about an inch square.

"What is it?" I asked, a little breathless at the discovery.

"It appears to be a kind of disk. Like the

sort one would use to expand the storage capacities of a digital camera." She held it in the palm of her hand, and we both stared down at it, then brought our eyes up to lock gazes.

"Does this kind of thing fit into more than one kind of digital camera?" I asked.

"I'm sure I don't know," Liss answered, gears clicking in her head.

"Do you think Amanda hid it in the clock?"

"Well, it does make sense, doesn't it? The antique dealer I bought this lovely old thing from wouldn't know a digital camera from a didgeridoo."

"It could be Spring Break pictures, or pictures of her friends."

"Certainly it could. Only if that was the case, why should she hide them at all?"

Neither of us could fathom it, but on one thing we both agreed: We were dying to know what was on the disk.

Liss ran off to the office to find the digital cam she kept in the drawer for the sole purpose of taking shots of merchandise for the Enchantments page.

"Do you know how to work it?" I asked her when she returned with the camera.

"It can't be too hard, I shouldn't think." Liss turned the camera over in her hands until she had found the necessary slot for the plug-in disk. "There we are. It appears to fit."

We exchanged an excited glance. "Can we upload them to the laptop?" I asked her. "It might be kind of hard to see detail on the camera's viewing screen."

"One laptop, coming right up."

The first few pictures we skimmed through. A picture of a car, Amanda seated playfully on its hood, a knowing look in her eye. A group shot at a lake, her with the boy I now recognized as Jordan, surrounded by a few other couples. Several pictures of her and Candace and Lily, the Troublesome Trio, arms around each other's necks as they mugged for the camera. Jordan, playing basketball. Jordan, dressed for Halloween as the Grim Reaper. One of the Trio, also from Halloween, who all seemed to be channeling your modern-day streetwalkers (or perhaps they were imitating the latest Hollywood starlets, heh).

There was nothing strange about any of them, especially, unless you counted the odd pic of another basketballer, identity unknown, who was looking into the camera with an incredibly soft look in his eyes.

Until . . .

A boat. Sid's?

The pictures weren't very good, as pictures go. Off-center, a tad blurry, and shot through a leafy veil, they seemed to have been taken with no real sense of focus, and at first glance, no purpose. I leaned forward, trying to make sense of what I was seeing. A pontoon boat with the somewhat uninspired name of *Shady Lady,* tied up to a typical wooden deck on a quiet, nondescript lake. The boat was white with blue and green trim, and on the large size for the overgrown puddles we boasted around here. Hanging from the railing were what appeared to be a pair of men's swimming briefs (very), and next to them an itsy-bitsy bikini top in a bright Kelly green with white polka dots.

Interesting.

The pictures continued, a whole series of them, the minute differences the only indication that they must have been shot in sequence on the same day. If my first thought was to wonder where the owners of the suits were hiding, the final photo answered the question in vivid Technicolor detail. In this snap the cabin of the boat had caught a stray beam of sunlight. Even slightly out of focus, it was impossible to mistake the sight of a pair of human bodies intertwined in the throes of some kind of sexual gymnastics. Most impressive of all was the height of the girl's legs. That had to hurt. It also answered the question of the missing bikini bottoms. They were dangling over the man's right shoulder, swinging from the girl's ankle.

"Is that what I think it is?" I asked, knowing the answer already.

Liss straightened, her face inscrutable. "If you're thinking it's a photographic record of someone's love affair, then I would have to say yes."

"Someone's. But whose?"

"Can't you guess?"

I didn't have to. Assuming the only person who had touched the clock from the time it left the store until the time I'd retrieved it from the Roberson household was Amanda herself, there really wasn't much guesswork involved. "Can we zoom in?" I asked her.

Zooming in served only to pixilate the photo beyond recognition. Damn. "Who is it?" I muttered under my breath. "Who is she with?"

The camera disk wasn't offering any immediate answers, but that didn't stop my whirring brain from posing more questions.

Why did Amanda secrete this disk within this antique clock? To keep the photos safe and sound in a place no one would guess to look? But in a clock she was giving to her mother, she had to know that they might run the risk of discovery. Or was that the point? Did she hide them in the event that something *might* happen to her?

"It isn't your usual high school photographic record," Liss mused aloud. "I wonder who took them."

"And why," I added. "Was it someone she was afraid of?"

"The man in the pictures?"

"Maybe. Or someone close to him?"

"It could have been someone else," she posed. "Someone related to the man in the photos. Because it is a man full grown, yes? Do you agree with that?"

"Rather than a high school hottie, you mean? Absolutely. Body shape and thickness is all wrong for a young man in his teens. Which means it could have been —"

"A jealous wife, perhaps —"

"Or girlfriend. Although we can't rule out a jealous boyfriend," I reminded her. "Still . . ."

"Yes?"

"Well . . . we're assuming the girl in the pics is Amanda. And while I suspect that's exactly right, to be fair, we really should find out for sure."

"Mrs. Roberson?"

"Mrs. Roberson."

"And if it is?"

"Then I think we need to hand this over to the police."

After placing a BE RIGHT BACK sign on the door, I once again found myself driving out West River Road, this time with Liss riding shotgun. "I hope she'll see us," I said as I rounded the last curve. The Roberson house loomed atop the bluff, like it was waiting for us.

"Don't worry, she will."

We found Mrs. Roberson in a much more positive frame of mind than I had seen her in yesterday. She opened the door to us, bland curiosity the only light in her pale eyes — but at least it was more than the dead look it had replaced. "Maggie. What a surprise," she said, her gaze flickering to Liss. "I didn't expect to see you here today."

"I'm sorry to intrude, Mrs. Roberson —"

"Wendy, please."

"Wendy, then. I'm really sorry to pop in on you like this, but we found . . . something . . . and I wanted to ask you a question or two about . . . well, about Amanda."

Her pale face went even paler. Her grip on the door tightened, knuckles going white, as though she couldn't decide whether she wanted more to hear what I had to say or to send me packing. "You found something?"

"Yes."

After a tense moment or two, she released the door and backed away. "Come in, won't you?"

We followed her into the white-on-white great room. She sat down on the edge of a chair, then stood back up again. "I should offer you something," she said vaguely. "Tea? Coffee?"

"Nothing, thank you. Wendy, this is my boss, Felicity Dow."

"How do you do?" Mrs. Roberson murmured.

"Very well, thank you. I hope you will allow me to tell you how very sorry I am for your terrible loss."

Mrs. Roberson inclined her head, receiving the lament with a wordless acceptance.

"About the clock that Amanda had bought for you," I began, softening my voice as I went.

"The clock? Yes?"

"Your husband had mentioned that he thought Amanda had been in the process of wrapping the gift for you when she left the house."

Mrs. Roberson frowned, confusion etching her brow. "Yes. The box was partially wrapped, and it even had a gift tag for me. All that remained was to tape down the flaps of paper on either end. I guess . . . I thought maybe she was interrupted. Maybe she was called away or maybe she was late and had to leave before she was done, I don't know."

"Wendy, I had wrapped the clock at the store, before she left," I said softly. "She had to have unwrapped the clock, and then started to rewrap it. The gift wrap is the same."

"But why?" Mrs. Roberson worked to process the information. "Why would she do that? That doesn't make sense. Does it?"

"It does if you take into account what she had hidden inside the clock's case."

Taking her cue from me, Liss opened her purse and withdrew the tiny storage disk.

Mrs. Roberson stared blankly at the device. "What is it?"

"It fits into a digital camera. Think of it as a kind of storage device."

"A storage device. For photographs?"

"Yes."

"Are there pictures on it?"

The time had come . . . "Yes, there are."

Mrs. Roberson swallowed, visibly. "I . . . I don't know . . ."

Liss reached out and put her hand over

Mrs. Roberson's. "If you'd rather not see them . . ." she said, her voice as soft and gentle as a warm blanket.

Mrs. Roberson was trembling. "I have to know," was her simple answer. "You can understand that, can't you? If these pictures contain information, anything at all, about Amanda's death, I have to know."

"We've brought a laptop with us," I told her. "Since they're already loaded onto the store laptop, we thought it would be easiest to show you this way."

She had us set up on the low-slung coffee table, with the laptop screen angled away from the tall windows. As Liss powered up the computer, I could see the cracks in the veneer of Mrs. Roberson's well-cared-for face deepening, tiny fissures that were expanding with the twin pressures of sorrow and guilt battling within her. She looked ancient, weary, and utterly, desperately alone.

She relaxed a little when she saw the first pictures. "Jordan's car. He's very proud of it. Oh, but doesn't my girl look pretty. Some of her friends. Candace and Lily there. Don't they all look lovely. Halloween — that seems like only yesterday. Oh, but it wasn't. It wasn't."

"Do you recognize this boy?" I asked her,

showing her the photo of the second basketball player.

"That's Charlie, a boy she worked with. Always trying to get her to go out with him. Seemed a nice enough boy, but Amanda wasn't interested, really."

"Charlie Howell?"

"Yes, I think that's right."

It was time for the big reveal. My heart began to pound.

"A boat?"

"Do you recognize it?" Liss asked quietly.

"No. No, I'm sure I don't. Why, do you think it's important?"

I couldn't answer. I had to let the last picture speak for itself.

Mrs. Roberson went quiet. I don't think she was even breathing. She leaned closer to the laptop. "Is . . . is that . . . ?"

She couldn't seem to finish. Tears had formed in her eyes, and all I could think was that no mother should have to have that image of her own daughter burned onto the fabric of her brain. Rivers of despair coursed through her, as palpable in the air as any physical force or substance. That old saying about wearing one's heart on one's sleeve? Well, the sleeve is more a person's energy field, but the concept is pretty much the same. Mrs. Roberson's heart might as well have been a ten-foot beacon that spelled out "CALLING ALL EMPATHS" with flashing red lights.

"Wendy, I think we need to know for certain whether the girl in the photo is Amanda," Liss murmured as gently as possible.

Mrs. Roberson gave us a short, wooden nod. "Yes, it's her."

"Are you sure?"

"The shape of the . . . the legs. The suit . . . yes, it's her."

"Amanda owned a swimsuit like that?"

Mrs. Roberson nodded.

Liss looked at me. "Then that begs the question: Who took the photos?"

"I suppose . . ." Mrs. Roberson bit the inside of her lip. "Well, it's possible that Amanda took them herself."

"Herself?" I frowned and sat up straighter. "But these were taken *of* her from a little ways away. How could she —"

"Amanda took a photography course at Grace College the summer before her junior year. She's been notorious with her camera ever since. She was always setting it up in different places, trying to catch people unawares. You know, just silly kid stuff."

"Setting up the camera is one thing — but someone still has to take the picture."

Mrs. Roberson nodded, tearful once more. "She begged her dad for a wireless remote control for her camera, and of course Sid bought it for her. Daddy's little girl, you know. It seemed innocent enough at the time."

We were losing her again. To bring her back, I reached over and gently placed my hand on hers. "Wendy . . . Is Amanda's camera equipment here in the house?"

She blinked away the fog of memory and regret, and took a steadying breath. "Yes. The police, they checked the camera for any relevant photos, but it was wiped clean. It's upstairs in her room."

"Could we see it?"

She stood. "I'll just get them, then."

When I was sure she was out of earshot, I turned to Liss. "Wireless."

"Point and click," Liss said, nodding.

"Do you think it's possible? Did Amanda take the pictures herself?"

Liss looked pensive. "Assuming the remote works in the way that we think it might, I would say not only is it possible, but it's almost certainly the most sensible assumption. It would certainly explain a few things, at least."

"Like why the pictures were slightly out of focus, why they weren't better planned, or even pointed directly at the subject in question — the boat. Because even moored, the boat is on water and will shift around with the wind. So," I summed up, "if you have a fixed object — a camera — pointed at a shifting object — the boat — what do you get?"

"Blurry, off-center photographs."

"Exactly."

"I wonder how far away a camera can be and still have the remote work."

We went quiet again when we heard Mrs. Roberson's footsteps descending the curving stairs. Before her she carried her daughter's camera equipment with the reverence one might afford a church offering plate. She set it down on the coffee table next to the laptop.

"Here it is," she said. "And this is the remote."

She placed a small black object next to the camera. Liss and I exchanged a glance. The size of a matchbox, only thinner, it was easy to see how simple it might have been for Amanda to conceal the device in her hand.

I picked up the remote. It seemed fairly straightforward — a pressure-sensitive button for taking a picture, another for controlling the power on the camera. According to the label on the back, it worked within a range of up to fifty feet. And, most importantly, no telltale wires to disguise or conceal.

Mrs. Roberson took the tiny storage disk in hand, staring down at it as it lay in her palm. Without a word she turned the camera over. "Where would this thing go?"

I pointed out the slot and watched as she did the honors. The disk slid into place. That solved that question.

"Mrs. Roberson — Wendy — think back. Have you ever seen that boat before?"

She frowned at the photo displayed in all its lurid glory on the laptop screen. "I don't think so. Sid might, of course — oh, but he mustn't know about these pictures."

Liss and I exchanged a glance. The photos had been shocking enough. Was she strong enough to handle the reality of the blog? Liss shrugged, leaving the decision up to me.

I took a deep breath and reached for my purse. "Wendy, there's something more we need to tell you. Do you remember giving me a CD the other afternoon, when my mom and I stopped in to see you?"

"Yes," she mumbled, scarcely able to meet my eyes, "I remember. Vaguely, but I remember."

From her answer, I couldn't tell whether she regretted her actions or not. "Most of those files were password-protected — I have a friend helping with that — but there was one file that came up without entering a password. A file with some computer art."

Her relief was instantaneous. "Oh. Is that all? Yes, Amanda was always fiddling about on her laptop when she was home. She was quite adept at things like that."

I took a deep breath. "Actually, that isn't all. You see, I had seen the graphic design before. I just didn't associate it with Amanda until the CD. I don't know quite how to tell you this."

In the end, I didn't. I couldn't. I just removed the printout of the blog from my purse and handed it to her. Mrs. Roberson hesitated a moment before taking it, her hands shaking hard enough to rattle the papers. She read slowly, painfully, through a few pages, then squeezed her eyes closed and set the printout down on the coffee table.

"I'm so sorry," I told her. "I couldn't think of a better way to tell you."

She opened her eyes again and looked at me. "Not your fault. If it was anyone's fault, it was probably mine. I suspected, you see. I suspected that Amanda had been . . . free

. . . with more than just her boyfriend. I would overhear her sometimes, on the phone with her friends, when she thought I was downstairs. But I chose to pretend I heard nothing. It was easier that way." She fell silent, lost in thought. "The clock . . . She was going to give it to me and hide these there, under my very nose. In my own bedroom," she said quietly, shaking her head. "How did she get so smart?"

"Smart?" I echoed.

"She was always hiding things from me, you know." Wendy grimaced. "Whenever I worried about her, I would go into her room. Sift through her things. To, you know, see what we were dealing with. Or even just to reassure myself. Sometimes I'd find something, and then I could talk to her about it and she couldn't sweet-talk her way out of things. I hadn't found anything in a while. I thought maybe that meant she had less to hide, that she was growing out of it, but I guess I was only kidding myself. She'd just gotten smarter about her hiding places. God! How could I have been so blind?"

I, too, was quiet a moment, trying to decide how best to explain. "Wendy, the photos and the blog might be important. We're going to have to turn them over to the police."

"But Sid —"

"We won't be the ones to tell Sid, I can promise you that. But I can't promise that the police won't want to talk to you both about the photos and the blog. I don't think you're going to be able to keep this from him indefinitely. I'm so sorry."

"I just . . . I just want to know how all of this could have happened to my little girl. I don't understand why it happened at all. What did I do wrong?"

It was a question I knew she would be pondering for some time to come, and I didn't envy her the heartache. What do any of us do wrong, when it comes to love? We love too much, and the best of us are blinded by its brilliance. How are any of us to know when love has begun to go very wrong until it is too late?

CHAPTER 16

We left the Roberson house shortly after Mrs. Roberson handed us a list of personal trivia she had compiled at our request — things like Amanda's date of birth, middle name, favorite pet, Wendy's maiden name, et cetera. In other words, anything she could think of that might possibly be something Amanda had used for a password. It wasn't much, but it was a start.

That done, I drove back to the store. "What I really need to do is catch up with Marcus," I told Liss. "I know he probably hasn't had enough time yet to break much of anything, but I really want to show him these photos and give him the list of personal data that Mrs. Roberson was kind enough to give us. Keep all of our discoveries in the same basket."

"Tonight's your early night, and this afternoon is Marcus's computer workshop at the high school. You should be able to catch up with him there."

They say once you leave high school, you can never go back again. As I pulled into the mid-twentieth-century brick building's parking lot later that afternoon, I had to wonder at that little nugget of misplaced logic. Of course you could go back again. You just couldn't have the tight little butt you had when you were sitting in Mrs. Ochmonek's English class, doodling the football captain's name on the inside cover of your spiral notebook, and daydreaming about the day he'd finally come to his senses and recognize you for the love of his life.

Who was I kidding? I'd never had a tight little butt. Wanted one, but never had one. And I still didn't.

Some things never change. Dammit.

At least Christine blended into the surroundings. I cozied her up between a rusting Ford Escort and a GMC pickup that had so many different parts from so many different eras that its true age was no longer discernible. Mostly it seemed to be held together by rust and Bondo and a goodly bit of duct tape.

It was just past four-thirty when I walked through the front doors into the long, glassed-in hall we'd nicknamed Eyeball Alley because that was where everyone who was anyone went to observe the comings and goings of everyone else. From the gym doors at the north end of the hall reverberated the constant slaps of leather basketballs against the polished gym floor and the rhythmic chants of the cheerleading squad. I turned away from the noise and headed for the stairs and the computer lab I knew I'd find on the second floor.

When I was still in school, the computers had been oversized metal monstrosities with monitors the size of boulders, and they took ten minutes to power up. (Okay, so that is a slight exaggeration — but not by much.) As I reached the open doorway to the computer lab and stuck my head in, I was at once impressed by how things had changed. The current lab was decked out with recent versions of the top-model Macs, enough for a computer for each student in a class, as opposed to the measly ten we'd had to duke it out over. Either the school had discovered some previously untapped government grant, or someone in Stony Mill was being very good to our school system.

My bet was on the latter. In the last few years the school board had been soliciting funds to expand the curriculum in ways meant to draw even more big-city tax refugees to our borders. One unfortunate by-product of this was the pilfering of tracts of farmland for the kinds of houses the rest of us could never hope to afford.

Big-city people with big-city expectations had made for bad feelings among the old-time Stony Millers, who saw the newcomers as intruders upon a way of life that would never be again. That Stony Mill was suffering growing pains was an understatement. Each side faced off on a nearly daily basis over a river of convictions a mile wide, each certain of the rightness of their personal missions, and neither giving an inch. Not even a centimeter.

I guess so long as it benefited the students of Stony Mill, did it matter who was right?

Marcus's computer workshop appeared to be, for the most part, over, with only a few students milling about in the back of the room. Marcus looked up from the computer station he was fiddling with as I knocked on the open door.

"Hello, Sunshine," he greeted me, waving his hand for me to come on in. "Liss called to let me know you might stop in."

"Did she now." The kids in the back didn't seem to be paying attention, so I circumvented the first row of tables and set my purse down on the Formica desktop beside him. "Are these your kids?" I asked, nodding toward the loiterers in the back.

"A few of them. The rest headed out already. These are my diehards."

I shook my head, smiling. "I still can't believe you're a teacher."

"Some days, neither can I. But I'm not, technically. Just a volunteer. One day, maybe."

The three kids in back slung heavy backpacks over their narrow shoulders and made their way toward the door. Two cast a curious glance my way as they left, but said nothing. The third waved and said, "See ya, Mr. Quinn," in the same semisheepish undertones used by insecure teens worldwide. Poor kid. He looked to be about fifteen and a little on the small side at that. Something in his eyes made me want to hug him and tell him that none of what he was going through now mattered one whit in the grand scheme of things, to stick with it and stay true to himself, because ten years down the road he'd be signing paychecks for the nimrods who had made his high school life a living hell.

Marcus waved back at him. "Have a good one, John. And good work today! That game sequence you programmed was just awesome. Very advanced stuff. You keep that up and you'll be VP at Microsoft someday."

The kid lit up like a two-hundred-watt bulb, his shoulders straightening with pride. He was cute, in a geeky way. Give the boy some confidence in his own abilities, and he'd have no problem attracting the opposite sex. Especially once he'd left SMHS behind and entered the real world.

As soon as the room had cleared, I slid onto the desktop, swinging my feet back and forth over the edge. It was something I would have done as a teenager, and it felt remarkably good. Just being here was like a step back in time. Can't go back again? *Piffle.*

"So, what's on your mind, Sunshine?"

Every time I saw him, he seemed to have a new nickname for me. I had to admit, I kind of liked it. In that way, he reminded me of a younger version of my grandpa. "The plot thickens in Amanda's murder," I told him.

"News?"

I shook my head. "Nothing that's gone through official channels. Or at least not yet."

He stopped checking cables and looked up at me, waiting for me to elaborate.

"Liss and I found something. Inside the clock Amanda had bought for Mrs. Roberson from Enchantments on the day she died. Mrs. Roberson didn't want the clock around, so Liss took it back as a return."

Marcus looked intrigued. "What was it?"

"A tiny little storage disk for a digital cam. One of the pics showed Amanda and . . . someone . . . in a compromising position."

He didn't laugh. I'd half expected him to. He was a guy, after all. "Could you tell who the man was?"

I shook my head. "They were on a pontoon boat called the *Shady Lady*. It was a recent model, by the looks of it, fairly posh."

"Hmm. I'd like to get a look at those pics."

I slugged him. "Marcus!"

Surprise flickered over his features, then he laughed. "Not for that. To see the boat, you goof. Do you have them with you?"

"No, but Liss has them on the laptop at work."

"Hold on a sec. I can have her e-mail them to me."

I waited while he whipped out a cell phone, dialed the store, and spoke briefly with Liss.

"Bingo," he said, ending the call. "She'll shoot them over straightaway. Who knows, maybe someone around here will recognize it."

"Only we won't really be able to show them around, Marcus," I cautioned him. "I have a feeling these pictures are important. I think we're going to have to hand them over to the police ASAP."

"Huh. That bunch of boobs couldn't detect their way out of Sheehan's Corn Maze," he said, referring to the county attraction some crazy farmer had gotten into his head to plant every year.

"That's probably not quite fair," I pointed out, even though I had at times come to the same conclusion. "It's not that they're boobs. It's that they prefer to take a" — I scrambled, trying to recall Tom's exact words — "more methodical approach. There's a protocol to investigation, Marcus. Logical. Orderly."

Ahem. Was word theft a crime? Well, what Tom didn't know . . .

"Yeah, except logical isn't a word I generally associate with our honorable boys in blue."

"Tsk, tsk. Such animosity."

He made a face at me. "Maybe I have good reason."

I didn't say anything, just sat there, swinging my feet back and forth.

"Or maybe I'm being a fool. Wouldn't be the first time. Won't be the last."

I laughed, and he grinned back at me.

The computer next to me sang out,

"You've got mail!"

"Let's have a look at these pics."

I slipped down off the table while Marcus pulled up a second chair.

Liss had only sent over two. Marcus pulled them up on the computer and whistled out a long breath.

"Do you recognize the location?"

"It looks pretty isolated to me. Can't tell the size of the lake at all from these pictures, but there doesn't seem to be much around. It might not even be in this area, you know, although I would bet it is. Needle in a haystack."

"What about the guy with her on the boat?"

He leaned back away from the pictures and shook his head reluctantly. "It could be any middle-aged man with money."

I looked at him curiously, amazed that he'd come to the same conclusion that Liss and I had already decided on. "Why middle-aged?"

"Because a younger guy isn't going to go for a pontoon boat, is he? This is some guy who's accepted that he's getting older. He's beyond the need for speed."

Perhaps Amanda was filling that need.

"Plus, no self-respecting younger dude is going to flaunt his jimmies in a Speedo outside of a swim competition. Count on it."

Well, I hadn't thought of that . . .

"Can you zoom in to get more detail?" I asked.

He made a few adjustments with the program controls and tried, with the same pixilated result that I had obtained. He shook his head. "These are lo-res versions. Did you change the sizing or the resolution?"

"Erm, I'm not sure. Liss did the honors, I'm afraid. She might have changed the size of the photos. I wasn't paying too terribly much attention to that part of things, I hate to admit."

"Well, without a higher resolution, I'm just not going to be very much help. I would need a hi-res scan in order to zoom in with any detail, and even then they might need to be cleaned up. Do you have the storage disk with you?"

Regretfully I shook my head. "It's back at the store. Liss thought we should probably put it in the safe until we are ready to hand it over to the police. But I did bring this for you." I handed him the list which Mrs. Roberson had made. "It's everything her mother could think of that she might have made into a password. I was hoping it might help with the files on the CD. Who knows, maybe something on it will be of use."

"Thanks. I have something for you, too."

With an admirable flex of his shoulder muscles, he reached behind him and snagged the handle of a lumpy satchel I hadn't seen on the floor beside him, so scarred and rustic that it might have been an antique at Enchantments but for its disreputable appearance.

"Where on earth did you get that thing?" I asked, giggling in spite of myself. "It looks like it died a slow death a few decades ago."

He looked down and quirked his brows in mock disbelief. "What? This fine bit of leather craftsmanship? Surely you jest, woman. Actually, it's from my uncle Lou. It's my good luck briefcase."

"And does it bring you good luck?"

"Hasn't let me down yet."

While he dug in the depths of the bag, I said, "I don't suppose you got anywhere with the files on the CD."

From his magic satchel he pulled out a pair of CDs. "I haven't broken the code yet — but what I did do first thing was make a duplicate of the CD, which will allow you to turn the original over to the police in all good conscience while allowing me to keep working on it. I made a copy for you, too.

Just in case."

Just in case of what? I shivered at the turn of my thoughts. Sometimes it was easy to forget that there was a man out there, walking the streets, who had killed a teenaged girl. "Marcus, you don't think . . . you don't think that it's dangerous that we should have these, do you?"

The look he gave me was quite serious. "Does anyone else know that you have the CD and the camera disk besides Liss and me?"

I shook my head. "Just Mrs. Roberson. And I don't think she would tell anyone — she didn't even want to tell her husband."

"Then for the time being, I think it's okay."

"You will keep working on breaking the code, won't you, Marcus?"

"As if you could stop me."

Technology, I decided as I tucked both my copy of the CD and the original in the teen diva case into my purse, could be a very useful thing. I really needed to get comfortable with it, for my own good.

Shouts echoed up the hallway, interrupting my thoughts. Marcus shot to his feet and ran to the door. "What is it?" I asked breathlessly.

"I'm not sure. Come on."

The noise seemed to be coming from downstairs, so we hurried toward the stairwell, bursting out into Eyeball Alley straight into the source of the commotion. A ring of shouting basketball players, cheerleaders, and students circled what was obviously a scuffle going on in the center. Several someones were chanting, "Fight-Fight-Fight," egging it on and proving that the human race really hadn't progressed much.

Marcus charged into the melee and tried to part the shoulder-to-shoulder high schoolers. "Out of the way. Let me pass!"

I stood on the fourth stair and tried to see over the heads and shoulders into the flying arms and fists in the center.

From the direction of the gym, Coach Abernathy came charging toward the skirmish, all barrel chest and testosterone. The crowd parted for him like the waters of the Red Sea. "Everett! Howell!" he barked. "Break it up. *Break it up!*"

Coach and Marcus reached the boys at the same time. With the help of a couple of other boys who had been nudged from immobility with the arrival of their coach, they managed to pry the boys' straining bodies apart. It took the lot of them to hold them down.

"What's gotten into you two?" Coach Abernathy said in his cheese-grater voice. "Jesus-Christ-in-a-box, do I have to tie you two up to get you to settle the hell down? Christ Almighty."

The two boys — hardly boys, almost men, with their long, lean muscles and flaring tempers — glared daggers at each other, chins set in loathing.

"You want to tell me what started all this today?" Coach pressed. "You two have had your mad on for months and managed not to lay each other out. Come on. What gives?"

The jaws set tighter.

Coach raised an out-of-control salt-and-pepper eyebrow. "Okay, then. Barnes. What were they fighting about?"

A tall freckled redhead sank into his shoulders. "Aww, Coach . . ."

"No hard feelings, right, guys?" Coach said, pinning the two combatants with a stare that would have stopped a semi. "See, Barnes? Spill it."

The poor kid was stuck fast between a rock and a hard place. He had to do what the coach asked of him, but if he did, he'd be snubbed for weeks by his high school cohorts for ratting out his friends. He hemmed and hawed, but he knew he had no real choice. "Amanda. Okay? They were fighting about Amanda."

I would never have expected compassion to exist within the coach's grizzled heart, but it was written in every crease on his rugged face. He turned to the crowd and waved his hands over his head to get everyone's attention. "Show's over, folks. I want you all to go home. Go on. Nothing to see here."

The crowd began to break up and melt away in twos and threes, leaving only me standing on the stairs, Coach Abernathy, Marcus, Charlie Howell, Jordan Everett, and the two boys holding them back.

Coach stood there with his hands on his hips, gazing down at the two boys with the same gruff authority he might use when solving altercations on the court. "Look, why don't you two ease off. Huh? Hasn't there been enough tragedy around here? Huh, Howell? Everett? Talk to me now."

Of the two, I would have been able to pick out Charlie Howell in a heartbeat. Both Charlie and Jordan were tall, good-looking boys, well muscled in a way that only constant physical activity and youth can achieve. But in Charlie's eyes I saw a glimmer of fire, an intense desire to prove himself that Jordan Everett with his money-eyed background would likely never have. I saw fire, and something more.

At the coach's words, tears sprang into Charlie's eyes. For a moment, he went limp. Then in an instant his entire body stiffened and he let out a howl of pain that tore at the very fiber of my being, so intense that it was all I could think of.

And then my world went black.

I came to moments later lying on a cot in the coach's office, my feet lifted high by pillows. Gazing around at the institutional gray walls and the office littered by sporting equipment, dirty Ace bandages, and what looked like a million used towels, I lifted my hand to my head with a groan. My head felt strange, fuzzy, and if I wasn't mistaken, I had a lump on the right side that was the cause of the pounding headache currently making my life a living hell.

"Howell, Quinn, get that ice in here!" Coach Abernathy barged through the door, and stopped short. "Oh. You're awake. How are you feeling?"

"Fine, fine." I struggled to sit up. The edges of the room wavered a bit. I gripped the edges of the cot until they caught and held. "Where — where did everybody go?"

"Maggie! Thank the go— er, thank goodness!" Marcus came through the door bearing one end of a big plastic cooler, Charlie

Howell on the other end. Marcus dropped his end and knelt by my side. "How are you feeling?"

"Everyone keeps asking me that," I said with a shaky laugh, running my fingers through my hair.

"That would be because you tumbled down the steps head first," Coach Abernathy said, throwing back the lid of the cooler and dipping a Ziploc bag into a mountain of ice. "You've got a nasty lump there just above your temple. Scared the bejesus out of all of us. Especially in light of everything else that was going on." He gave Charlie Howell a pointed stare. Charlie had the good manners to look apologetic.

Coach wrapped the closed Ziploc in a wrinkled towel and handed it to me.

"I'm fine. Really," I said, gingerly taking the lumpy mass from him. I couldn't help wondering if the towel was wrinkled from sitting in the dryer too long, or wrinkled from use.

Eeeeeh.

"Well, I think you'd best be seeing the doctor for that bump, just the same," Coach told me in his no-holds-barred way. "Who's your family doctor? I'll call the office and see if they can see you before they close."

"No, really —"

He raised his eyebrows, stopping my protest short.

"Dr. Phillips," I mumbled, feeling foolish.

Coach nodded approvingly. "Good man."

He moved into the outer office to make the call. I looked to Marcus for help, but he shrugged helplessly. "You should probably go, Sunshine," he told me.

Men. They always stick together. I huffed out my lower lip and settled my back against the painted cinder block wall to wait.

Charlie stood in the doorway, shuffling his feet. I glanced over at him. "You okay?" I asked him.

He shrugged, his face turning a dozen shades of red.

Marcus looked up at him, too. "That was some fight, man. You wanna talk about it?"

Charlie gave a swift, short jerk of his head in the negative.

"That's too bad. Sometimes talking about what's bothering you is the best thing you can do. All that emotion that's bottled up inside of you washes away, not forgotten, just acknowledged and accepted. Your feelings are valid and real. They should be treated with respect."

If Charlie's face got any redder . . .

My head was spinning again. I leaned it back against the cool cinder block and closed my eyes.

Anger . . . red, hot, searing fury . . . seething rage . . .

My eyes flared open as I recognized the sudden influx of emotion into my brain and body. I didn't have to ask where it came from. It was an echo of what I'd felt just before I blanked out.

Charlie.

I blinked at him, grief and loss crushing into my heart with tidal forces. I clutched my arms to my breasts, swallowing hard as the sensation filled my throat with choking tears.

"Sunshine? Maggie, snap out of it!"

Someone was shaking me. Big hands crushing my shoulders, shocking awareness back into my system. Oxygen surged into my lungs as I sucked in breath, long, searing, wheezing gasps that beat down the racking sobs. *Damn, damn, and double damn.*

I closed my eyes, dissolving at least one connection. "Charlie? If you're going to be in here with me, I need you to do me a big favor. I need you to take a few big, deep breaths and relax your muscles. And whatever you do, try not to think about Amanda or Jordan for the next few minutes. Okay?"

The teen looked confused. "Oooo-kay."

Coach came through the door. "Good

news. Doc Phillips has agreed to fit you in before he goes home, so Quinn here'll want to get you over there right away."

I pushed myself away from the wall. "Well, there's no reason for 'Quinn here' to do any such thing. I drove myself."

"And he'll be driving you to Doc Phillips's place." He held up a hand that had seen many a jammed knuckle, by the looks of it. "And don't try batting your eyes at me. It doesn't work for my boys, and it won't work for you. Your mishap happened on school property. Thusly and therefore, you, missy, are an insurance liability waiting to happen. Quinn'll drive you and that's that."

Oh, the indignity of it all as Marcus and Charlie Howell made a two-handed cross-seat for me between them and insisted I throw my arms around their necks as they carried me, litter-style, out to Christine. Coach Abernathy, in good form, followed with my purse and Marcus's satchel. He raised his grizzled brows when we arrived at Christine.

"She's more dependable than she looks," I began defensively.

Coach nodded, not really agreeing with me. His skepticism doubled when Marcus fitted the key into the lock and the tumbler wouldn't move.

"She's old," I tried to explain. "Sometimes she gets a little bit touchy."

"Right, then. Quinn, where's your transport?"

Marcus cleared his throat and nodded toward his bike.

The coach's eyebrows lifted further. "Jesus-Christ-in-a-box. Howell!" he barked. "You got your dad's Buick here today?"

Charlie's face remained carefully neutral. "Yes, sir."

"Got any plans tonight?"

"Work later at the hotel."

"Son, do you think you can drive this pretty lady down to Doc Phillips's office? I'd be doin' it myself, except Mrs. Abernathy's flight comes in tonight and I need to be getting out of here. I'll be in the doghouse for sure if I'm not there on time, no foolin'."

"Yes, sir, I can do that. I don't have to be to work until seven, so I got plenty of time."

"Well, then, hut to, son! Why don't you bring your car around? Marcus, you gonna follow on your bike?"

And that's how I found myself in the backseat of an old Buick, being chauffeured across town by a boy I didn't know to a doctor's appointment that I didn't make.

Welcome to my weirdo life.

Charlie didn't appear to be any more comfortable than I was feeling. "How you doing?" he asked me in a gruff, trying-to-be-mature voice. "Okay?"

"Fine, just fine. All better, actually. I don't suppose you'd consider turning this thing around and taking me back to the school?"

"I don't suppose that would do much good, considering that your friend is right behind us."

"Oh, yeah. Good try, though, huh?"

He grinned at that.

He stopped for a red light at Green and Watkins, once again distant, brooding. I couldn't help myself. "Charlie? Do you mind if I ask you something?"

His eyes met mine in the rearview mirror, wary but respectful. "Um, sure."

"What were you and Jordan fighting about?"

A surge of crimson drifted up the back of his neck. "Well, I guess there's no harm in saying it. Pretty much the whole world knows how I felt about Amanda Roberson anyway, and there's no use hiding from it now." He ran his hand over the back of his head and neck. His hands were surprisingly big, the fingers long, the knuckles and wrists knobby and oversized, as though he'd not quite finished growing into them. "I loved her. I would have done anything for her. And that son of a bitch knows something about her death."

A surge of rage. I swallowed convulsively. *Breathe* . . . "Jordan?"

"Damn straight. Jordan Fucking Everett. Fucking rich boy with his perfect house and perfect family."

So much bitterness. So much resentment. But was this simply a case of the have-nots versus the haves, or was there something more to his story?

"I don't understand. Why do you think he knows something about Amanda's death?"

The light changed, and his foot went down on the accelerator a little too hard, enough to make the sedan lurch forward. I flinched. "He and Amanda were arguing the night before. They'd been arguing a lot. He was always hanging out at the hotel, trying to catch her doing something wrong. Bastard. He didn't love her. Not like I did."

He had tears in his eyes. I could see them in the rearview mirror. My throat tightened instantly. Tears in his eyes and pain in his heart. It was a compelling combination. What was it about a man's tears that always made me want to hug him and make every-thing all better? But I resisted the urge to reach out and touch his shoulder, knowing I'd just end up embarrassing the poor guy. Besides, his emotions were so raw, they were beginning to overwhelm me again. He was doing a better job of containing them this time, but I could still feel my body winding up like a coiled rubberband. I blew out my breath and concentrated on relaxing my tensely strung muscles. My head was throbbing, but at that point in time I could no longer be certain whether it stemmed from the lump or from the emotional onslaught I was subjecting myself to.

"It must be hard for you," I said softly, "losing someone you loved. But I was under the impression . . . well . . . that Amanda and Jordan were an item."

His jaw clenched, lean and hard with youthful muscles. "They were together for a while, yeah. But they were on the outs. Amanda told me so."

"When did she tell you that, Charlie?"

"She told me that lots of times. We were friends. More than friends. We really talked about things. We used to . . . We —"

He turned off the road suddenly. I looked up, surprised to find that we had arrived at Dr. Phillips's office already. How time flies when your senses are being overloaded.

"We're here," he said unnecessarily.

"Thanks," I told him as I opened the car door, "for everything. You're a good kid. Your mom must be proud."

He nodded, the picture of humility. "Ms. O'Neill? Can I ask you something?"

"Sure." I paused with my hand on the doorknob. "Shoot."

"Girls are . . . I don't know. I think . . . no, I *know* Amanda liked me. It was all in the way she talked to me, you know? She'd *tell* me things. And she really trusted me. Not like Jordan. He . . . he didn't understand her like I did. God, do you know how many nights she cried on my shoulder because of the way he treated her? He didn't deserve her."

I nodded and patted his shoulder sympathetically. "What did you want to ask me, Charlie?"

He opened his mouth, closed it, shrugged uncomfortably, then finally blurted out, "I think she wanted to be with me, not him. But I'm not sure now, you know? I mean, how's a guy supposed to tell? She hugged me, she'd hold my hand when she talked to me, but she never . . . you know . . . kissed me or anything. Because she wasn't like that. She'd never do anything like that if she was with someone else. But maybe . . . once she'd let Jordan go . . . I think she might have . . ."

He met my eyes in the rearview, just the briefest flash, then cast his gaze down to where his knuckles were turning white on the steering wheel. "I'm sure you're right about that," I told him with only the barest glimmer of conscience for the little (oh, all right, *major*) white lie. "It's just too bad she'll never be able to tell you herself how she really felt about you."

He clenched his jaw and nodded, miserably.

"That's why it's so important that the police find who did this to her, Charlie. No one should be allowed to get away with what was done to Amanda. I know the police talked to you as her friend, but . . . if you know anything about any of the people Amanda hung out with . . . anything at all . . ." I let my voice drift off, my meaning clear.

"I wish I did know for sure who did it," he said after a long pause. "I just wish I did. There'd be no need for a trial by jury, that's for damn sure."

And on that note . . .

"Ready, Sunshine?" Marcus appeared at my elbow, bending down to slip his arm around my waist.

Embarrassed, I waved him away. "I'm

371

perfectly capable of doing for myself, you know."

"Now, Sunshine," he said as he helped me to my feet and settled me against his side, "when a man goes out of his way to play knight-in-shining-armor, the least you can do is humor him. Am I right, Charlie?"

Charlie grinned. "Right, Mr. Quinn."

"That's settled, then. Thanks, Charlie. I'll take it from here."

I thought of something as we got to the door, and turned back. "Oh, Charlie? One other thing. You don't happen to know anyone who has a pontoon boat, do you?"

He looked at me as though suddenly wondering if I might have hit my head harder than they'd thought. "Yeah, sure. Lots of people."

"White one, blue and green trim? Goes by the name *Shady Lady*?"

He appeared to think for a moment. Then he shook his head. "Nope, it's sure not ringing any bells. Why?"

I shrugged but kept my eyes on his face. "Nothing important. Just some photos Amanda had. I was just wondering where they were taken, is all."

"Oh, okay. Glad it wasn't something more serious." He raised his hand to wave at Marcus. "See you around."

"Smooth," Marcus drawled as we watched Charlie back his Buick out of his parking space.

"I was just checking. Mostly I wanted to see if he knew about the pics."

"And? What do you think?"

I shook my head. "He didn't seem to be lying. At least, I didn't sense it if he was. And the boat's too expensive for Charlie's family, based on what you've told me. Ah, well."

As Marcus guided me through the door, his arm a comfortable weight around my waist that was not at all unpleasant, he shook his head and muttered, "Mr. Quinn. *Mister* Quinn. Who'd'a thunk it?"

"Sounds good, though, doesn't it?"

"Maybe so," he mused, grinning. "Maybe so."

CHAPTER 17

The mid-December air had grown a toothy bite, its icy breath swirling around us as we stepped into the lobby before the glass door settled back into its aluminum frame. Marcus made me sit in a chair before heading up to the counter to wave at the receptionist. "Hey, Kate, how's it goin', girl?"

"Things are great," I heard the receptionist purr. Same old Katie. "God, I haven't seen you in ages, Marcus. You're looking good. Still making the bar scene with that band?"

"In my off time, yeah."

"And what are you in for today? I don't see you on Doctor's schedule."

Marcus angled his thumb over his shoulder at me. "We had a little accident over at the high school. Coach Abernathy called it in."

Katie stuck her head out through the receptionist's window. "Well, well! Maggie

O'Neill. Long time no see."

I waggled my fingers at her. "Hey, Katie."

"So you're the accident at the high school."

"Guilty as charged." I made a sheepish grimace. "I'm afraid it wasn't exactly in my plans to be back here so soon. I was forced."

"Bad luck," she agreed good-naturedly. "You're our last appointment for the day, so I'm sure the doctor will see you shortly." Her duties thus discharged, she angled a sideways glance in Marcus's direction. "Soooo, Marcus, where are you playing now? Maybe I'll have to get out to see you. I just love watching you . . . fiddle."

I had never seen Marcus blush before, but the color that crept up his cheeks certainly qualified. He mumbled the name of a bar two towns over, but mentioned he'd have to check his schedule to be certain. Before I knew it, he had joined me in the uncomfortable lobby chairs, slouching his long body down as though hoping to disappear.

"Margaret?" A nurse wearing white pants and a surgical-style shirt covered in pink teddy bears came to the door to call me back.

Marcus made a motion to assist, but I placed a staying hand on his arm. "I can make it, Marcus, thanks."

His sideways glance toward the avid-eyed Katie made me think this latest show of chivalry was somehow less than altruistic in nature. Ha. It was his own fault for being so intriguingly dark and dangerous. Let him suffer.

The nurse showed me into a different examination room this time, but it had the same requisite examination table, twin metal folding chairs, scrub sink, and bio-hazard box. "Doctor will be in with you in a moment," she told me, placing my file in the letter box outside the door and gesturing for me to climb up on the table. "You're our last patient today."

Terrific.

Going to the doctor, even when I was as sick as a dog, had always felt uncomfortably like complaining. Not to mention the fact that I'd just been there the other day. Two trips in a single week were enough to give any healthy girl the heebie-jeebies, right?

With a resigned sigh, I edged onto the examination table, feeling the pristine paper liner crinkle beneath me. At least the nurse hadn't forced me onto the scales first, like they usually did. Thank God for small favors. I mean, really, how many women needed the reminder that they were no longer their lean, mean, teen selves?

The only window in the exam room was small and too high to see out of, so I turned my attention to the personal photographs lining the industrial gray walls. This exam room had even more candids than the room I was in the other day. They were the only signs of energy in the otherwise airless room, all of Dr. Phillips at various stages of his illustrious life. As a college graduate, waving his tasseled hat over his head. Several pictures of fish of varying shapes, colors, and sizes, jubilant male faces mugging for the camera. A favorite dog, a yellow Lab that almost appeared to smile, all soft eyes, big teeth, lolling tongue. Next came a couple of pictures of the doctor's beloved lakeside home, viewed from the water, double-hung windows glowing golden with light from within. It was gorgeous, just the right blend of wealth and comfort and down-home charm. Last, a picture of the lake itself, fall reds and golds reflecting back on the still water. Sheer heaven.

There was a knock at the door. "Everyone decent?"

"Come on in, Dr. Phillips."

Dr. Phillips entered the room, looking every bit as brawny and barrel-chested as always. He consulted my chart. "So, what happened to you, young lady?"

"Nothing, really." I tucked my hands between my knees and sat up as tall as I could. "I had a little fainting spell and bumped my head. That's all."

"Fainting spell, hmm?" He came near me and took a small penlight out of his pocket, switching it on with a flick of his thumb. He held it up in front of my eyes. "Look off to your left, please. Mmhmm. Now your right. Good. Now, what do you suppose brought on this fainting spell?"

I shrugged, knowing there was no way I was going to tell him the truth. He wouldn't believe it anyway, so there was no sense in making myself look like a loon. "I don't know. I guess I shouldn't have skipped lunch today, huh?"

He took out his stethoscope and warmed it in his palm before placing it above my breast. "Any chance you could be pregnant?"

I coughed, embarrassed to admit it. "Um, no. No chance at all."

"Okay, okay. I had to ask." He used his big hands to probe against the glands beneath my jaw and in my neck. "You've been feeling all right lately? No inner ear problems, no headaches, nothing at all to report?"

"No headaches before I bumped my head, but I have a little one right now. Nothing else to report."

"Mmhmm . . ."

While Dr. Phillips scribbled on my chart, I turned my attention back to the photo of the lake house. The water was so smooth, it was really rather amazing. I could see the outline of every leaf on every tree, the detail of the bark on each tree trunk, the glimmer of clouds skipping across the sky above.

"That's a beautiful lake house you have, Dr. Phillips." And just for the heck of it, I wondered aloud, "Don't suppose you have a boat."

"Hmm?" he said distractedly. "My boat? Well, it's not entirely mine — I own a part of it with a couple of my friends — that's them there." He pointed to a picture lower on the wall. I could just make out a few middle-aged men — doctors probably — on . . . a pontoon boat. My heart started pounding when I saw the first few letters of her name. S . . . H . . .

I squinted, trying to make out the rest.

"I just call her my Shangri-La on Lake Casper," he continued. "It's a silly thing, I know, but I really think that place is just about perfect."

Shangri-La. Of course. I breathed a sigh

379

of relief. "It sure sounds perfect." I looked closer at the picture he'd indicated. "That almost looks like Randy Cutter."

"You know Randy?"

I nodded. "From the store."

"We've been friends for years. He loves fishing just as much as I do. We try to get out whenever we can. Not often enough with my schedule here and at the hospital." One last flourish of a scribble. "Well, young lady, there doesn't really appear to be anything wrong with you. Plain acetaminophen for the headache. If it doesn't improve, or if you begin seeing double, get ahold of me through the physicians' after-hours desk at the hospital. Other than that, a good night's sleep should do the trick."

"Thanks, Dr. Phillips."

"You're quite welcome. Take care."

Marcus was pacing by the time I came out. "How'd everything go?" he asked me, taking my elbow and escorting me toward the door.

"Fine, fine, everything's good."

"See you later, Marcus!" Katie was calling as the door shut behind us. I guess I didn't rate a good-bye.

"Soooo," I drawled as he hurried me along, "I guess Katie's going to be hitting the bars, looking for love, hmm?"

"Very funny." He stopped suddenly on the sidewalk, looking stricken. "Oh, crap. All I have is my bike. Do you need me to call Liss to come pick you up, or do you think you can hold on to me long enough for me to get you back to your car?"

"Well, I am pretty feeble, I know, but I think I can manage for the ten-minute ride across town."

Sarcasm was apparently lost on him. "Good, good. It's going to be pretty cold, too. Damn, I should have driven the truck today. Sorry about that. Anyway, here you go."

He handed me the spare helmet he kept strapped to the back. I took it gingerly. I looked terrible in helmets, hats, anything that flattened my hair to my forehead. It was the one bit of vanity that I almost always catered to. Combined with the bump, this helmet was a recipe for disaster. "Ow."

"Sorry, forgot about the lump. How is it?"

"Throbbing, but so long as you don't run into anything, I think I'll be fine."

"You question my driving? Foolish mortal."

He nearly killed himself kick-starting his bike. Bemused, I glanced up and nearly wet myself laughing. Katie was hanging out the glass door, calling something to him and waving like a madwoman. As we zoomed out of the parking lot, I couldn't stop giggling. "What was she saying?" I yelled over the engine.

"Don't ask!" he yelled back.

Back at the school, Christine opened right up for Marcus — no lock shenanigans in sight. I waved Marcus away and closed the door myself. He nudged his bike up beside me and motioned for me to roll down the window.

"I'll follow you home."

"You don't need to, I'll be fine."

"Humor me, wouldja?"

It didn't appear that I had much of a choice. He'd have followed me anyway.

On Willow Street, he pulled up behind me as I came to a halt behind Dr. Danny's omnipresent Jag. Before I could set foot from the Bug, he was there, ready to open my door.

"Goodness, a girl could get spoiled with all this attention."

"Shut up and enjoy it," he growled, putting his arm around my waist again and slinging mine around his shoulder.

"Marcus, someone's going to think I've broken something," I said, laughing. "I'm not an invalid, you know. In fact, I'm feeling fine now. Just a little headachy."

"I repeat: Shut up and enjoy it."

I've always been a practical girl. I had the full attention of a hot guy. So I shut up. I enjoyed it.

Marcus took charge of the keys before we reached the sunken stairs to my basement apartment. The stairs were too narrow to allow both of us down together, so I let him go first, feeling my way down at a more leisurely pace. At nearly six-thirty, the sun had long since set. The stairs were a well of darkness, the security light having apparently taken a holiday.

"Maggie. Go back up."

The sudden change in Marcus's voice stopped me in my tracks. "What's wrong?"

"Get the hell up the stairs, Maggie," he said in a voice terse enough to chill my blood.

I couldn't move. I stayed there on the fifth step, frozen in time and space, my heart in my throat as I watched Marcus burst through a door that had been left ajar by someone other than me.

Within moments, he was back out of the apartment and pulling me along behind him up the stairs to Steff's apartment. I thanked my lucky stars that it was too early for us to have interrupted much — Steff answered the door within seconds. Her hair was a teensy bit mussed, but only a best friend would notice the difference.

"Maggie! What's going on? Are you okay?" Steff looked back and forth between me and Marcus, alarm pinching her cheeks pale.

Marcus didn't wait for me to answer. He pushed me half into Steff and caught the door handle, pulling it closed as he told her, "Call the police. Someone's broken into Maggie's apartment."

"Marcus, wait —"

It was too late, unless I meant to follow him, and the fierce look on his face had been enough to prevent that. I glanced at Steff, and it occurred to me that Dr. Danny hadn't made an appearance yet. "Where's the squeeze?"

"Sleeping. Long day at the ER," she said, running to grab her phone to dial 911. "You would not believe the crazy things people have been doing! To themselves and to others. It's just plain wacko." She stopped, staring at the phone in her hand as though trying to remember why she had it. "I'm sorry, Mags. You must be all up in arms over this whole thing. After what happened last fall!"

Sirens and bubblegum lights splintered the serenity of the evening within moments. From Steff's window, I watched Marcus meet the cruiser three stories below. A second cruiser pulled up behind the first. After a brief word with Marcus, it pulled away from the curb spitting gravel, tearing off down the road with a blaring siren.

"What on earth is going on outside?" Dr. Danny emerged from deepest slumber at last, rubbing his eyes and jawline with the heels of his palms. He yawned, big enough to make his jaw crack.

Steff went and put her arms around his waist. "Someone broke into Maggie's apartment," she told him. "Can you believe it? By the way, it's about time you two met. Danny, this is Maggie O'Neill, my best friend. Maggie, this is Dr. Daniel Tucker, my genius boyfriend."

I dragged my gaze away from the window long enough to size him up. Tall, good-looking, boyishly rugged. Nice. As usual, Steff had impeccable taste. I nodded at him. "Charmed."

"A pleasure. Well, it would be under better circumstances. At the moment, all I can think of to say is, I'm sorry," he said. He put his hand on my shoulder, the briefest of touches, and in that instant I sensed great compassion in him. The medical profession had chosen well. So had Steff. She could do a lot worse than to hold on to this one. I made a mental note to pin her down on the subject later. But just now . . .

I buttoned up my coat. "I'm going down there."

"Maggie, wait," Steff said, grabbing my sleeve. "Do you think that's wise?"

"What can happen with two cops on the premises?" I left the two of them scrambling for their own coats and hightailed it down the steps before anyone else could think to stop me.

Elevated male voices slowly reached my ears, as though carried aloft by the popping red-blue lights. I shivered as the cold tried to invade the confines of my coat, listening.

"I'm telling you, we just arrived. The apartment was like that when we got here." Marcus, sounding frustrated. "No one was around. And by this time whoever did it is long gone."

"You didn't see anything. Hear anything."

My footsteps faltered on the steps as I recognized Tom Fielding's voice, terse and commanding as he stepped into his favored role as keeper of the collective peace in Stony Mill. I don't know why, but it never occurred to me that Tom might be the one to respond to our SOS tonight. Holding on to the railing with an iron grip, I peered cautiously over to the ground below. I might have known — the two of them were standing nose to nose, their stances stiff with dislike. A second cop was poking around in the winter-dessicated landscaping. Not one of them appeared to have noticed they had company in the body of a relatively calm and able-bodied victim.

Marcus pointed his nose even farther into Tom's face. "Why don't you go find who did this? Take a run around the neighborhood. Ask the neighbors whether they saw anything? *Do. Your. Job.*"

Uh-oh. Time for this able-bodied victim to open mouth and insert body between two hardheaded men.

The door was yanked open above me. "Maggie! Don't go down yet," Steff called. "Wait for me!"

The stairs reverberated as she hopped up and down on one foot trying to get her other boot on. Dr. Dan grabbed the back of her pants to keep her from pitching forward.

I sighed as two faces swung upward. So much for the element of surprise. "Is it safe to come down?" I called.

Tom gestured the all clear, so I hurried down, Dr. Dan and Steff hot on my heels. "Is it bad?" I asked. "My apartment, I mean."

"It's been completely tossed." Marcus put

his arm around me. "It's pretty much a mess."

I saw Tom's gaze light briefly upon Marcus's hand on my shoulder before dropping down to the notepad in his hand. "Maggie, I'll need you to walk through and see if you can identify whether anything is missing."

"You think this was a burglary?"

Tom shrugged. "What else?"

What indeed? But I didn't exactly have high-class digs or top-of-the-line things. Who in their right mind would want to steal from someone like me? It didn't make sense.

My eyes widened when they finally allowed me into my apartment. I followed Cop No. 2 down the steps while Tom spoke into his handheld radio mike. Steff grabbed my hand from behind as I stepped into the main room. Tossed, Marcus had said. It was an apt description. Ransacked might have been better. Completely and utterly demolished might be the best yet. There wasn't a single drawer that hadn't been dumped, a single shelf that hadn't been swept to the floor, a single closet whose contents weren't strewn one by one across my room. Even the mattress and box springs had been pulled from the bed and were now resting haphazardly against the wall. Under ordinary circumstances I might have been embarrassed by the colony of dust bunnies that had taken shelter beneath my bed, but there was nothing ordinary about what had happened here.

Someone had been in my home. The sense of violation and vulnerability was overwhelming.

Slowly, painfully, I moved through the rooms, trying to assess the damage. There was surprisingly little, other than the mess factor. Things had been rummaged through and strewn about, but nothing had been broken.

More strangely, nothing seemed to be missing.

"Nothing?"

I shrugged helplessly at the disbelief in Tom Fielding's voice. "I don't have much to begin with, and it's all there. No. Nothing is gone."

He narrowed his eyes at me and flipped his clipboard shut. "Which leaves me with only one question."

"Why."

"Yeah. Why. Why you, Maggie? Why your place?"

"I don't know."

"Yeah? You sure about that?"

The answer that eluded us came much sooner than we might have thought. Sometime after Steff, Marcus, Dan, and I began the unenviable job of sifting through my ransacked things and trying to make some semblance of order from the chaos, and while Tom completed his paperwork standing at my kitchen table, a call came through the radio Tom had hooked back on his belt.

"Fielding. You reading me?"

He glanced over at me. I had been surreptitiously watching him for a few minutes, hoping to get a chance to talk to him in private before he left. Pretending to be engrossed, I busied myself replacing the kitchen utensils in the big brown bean crock that usually kept them corralled.

His voice kept purposely low, he muttered into the walkie-talkie, "Yeah. Whatcha got?"

"You're not gonna believe this. I think we got the guy."

"Come again?"

"This guy was sitting in his car just down the street, watching us down here. I kid you not. He didn't even duck down when I drove past, the dumbass. Guess he thought he looked normal enough. Forgot all about the fact that he was wearing a ski mask."

"You're shitting me."

"Just like some goddamned cat burglar, straight out of the movies. Look, I'm taking him in for questioning. Meet me down at the station, why don't you. My guess is, those boot prints we found outside of Miss O'Neill's windows are going to be a perfect match."

"Who is it?" I heard Tom ask in a hushed tone.

"Name's Cutter. Randall J. Cutter. Owns a shop down on River Street."

Tom's attention whipped my way when I sucked my breath in through my teeth. "Copy that," he said, while his brow furrowed and his eyes assessed me curiously. "I'll meet you there just as soon as I get things wrapped up here."

I waited for him to sign off, my thoughts moving a mile a minute. Randy Cutter? He did this? But why? How? I couldn't seem to wrap my mind around it. Randy Cutter was a businessman, a former vet, an upstanding member of our community. I'd seen him nearly every day for the last few months, performing his ritual sidewalk sweeping. He'd never made any untoward comment, never looked at me sideways other than to wave hello. I mean, I'd seen him, just the other day at Annie's café. We'd exchanged pleasantries, the same as always . . .

Tom, I came to realize, was watching me. "I guess you heard that," he said with his usual economy of words.

I nodded, still frowning.

"Got anything to add?"

I shook my head. "I don't understand it. Randy Cutter? I just don't get it."

"You want to tell me what kind of contact you've had with him?"

"From the store, mostly. Your usual stuff. Most of the people who work down on River Street know each other. Randy's store is right across from Enchantments, so we'd see each other on the sidewalk from time to time. But that's about it."

"When did you last see him?"

I didn't have to think. "I saw him at Annie's café. Yesterday. I was just finishing up lunch and he came in as I was leaving. Before that, I guess it was the Little Nipper the other night. I don't think he saw me, though. He seemed pretty down in the dumps."

Tom frowned. "The night I was there?"

I nodded. "Amanda's body had just been found, remember? Everyone in town was feeling pretty down that day."

"And that's it? There's nothing else?"

"Nothing that I can think of."

"Hmm." He marked something down in his flip pad. "What do you remember about yesterday at Annie's? What were you doing?"

"Nothing. Honestly, Tom. I was getting ready to leave, and I asked Annie if I could use her phone . . . I needed to find Marcus for some help with . . ." My voice fell away as the moment came rushing back to me. "He was listening to us," I said as realization struck. "Oh my God, he was listening to us."

He took a step toward me, the very stance of his body watchful. "Listening to you . . . why?"

Feeling as though I was moving through a dream, I went to my purse and pulled out the original CD Marcus had just given back to me. I held it out to him.

He looked down at the face of the teen singing sensation in bemusement. "Thanks, but . . . it's not really my kind of music."

"No, it's . . ." I opened the case and extracted the real treasure. "It might be important to your case."

"My . . . ?" The cloudy look he was so good at had returned. "You mean the Roberson investigation, don't you."

Pointed enunciation, the kind that made me feel all of twelve years old. I opened my mouth, but no words came out.

"Well? Are you going to explain, or aren't you?"

"It was Amanda's," I confessed in a rush,

willing the right words to come forward. "There are files on it that are protected by passwords. I was talking to Annie about needing some help in breaking them open . . . but instead I decided that it should go to you ASAP." Okay, that was a teensy white lie, but self-preservation was a pretty strong human impulse. I was fairly certain that if I told Tom the truth, that we weren't originally planning to hand the CD over to him until we were able to break the passwords and access the files ourselves, I could probably kiss any potential future relationship with him permanently good-bye. "You know, because it could be important."

Without saying a word, Tom tucked the CD into his jacket pocket while the lines of his face morphed from surprise to shock to cold, hard fury. "Where did you get this?"

The room had gone perfectly, utterly still. No more banter between Steff and Dr. Danny, no more one-liners from Marcus. Just the kind of cringe-worthy stillness that made me wish I was someone, anyone else.

My mouth was dry as I cleared my throat. "From Amanda's mother. She — she asked me to . . . Oh, hell. She was out of her mind with a combination of grief and sedatives, and she asked for my help. I didn't know what to tell her, so I took the CD." I plunged on before I lost my nerve. "Apparently Mrs. Roberson found the CD hidden in her daughter's room, wasn't able to access the files herself, and got worried because of other things she had discovered about her daughter."

"And the reason she didn't come to me with this was . . . ?"

I shrugged helplessly. "It could have been nothing, you know, just a girl's silly scribblings. Oh, I don't know, maybe she should have turned it over immediately, maybe she wasn't thinking clearly, but somehow she convinced herself you would only want to see it if it obviously pertained to Amanda's death."

"That's a load of crap, Maggie, and you know it."

"I know, I know," I moaned, wishing I could rewind the last two days like a tape recorder. Where was life's redo button when you needed it most? "You really need to talk with her more, Tom. She was worried about Amanda's relationship with Jordan Everett, and — I'm not entirely sure about this — it seems she might have been worried about other boys as well? Maybe you know all of this already. You probably do. Oh, but just so that you know, I promised myself that, if the CD turned out to be more, I'd turn everything over to you, no matter what Mrs. Roberson wanted or didn't want. I did. Really."

"Well, that's just great. That's just perfect." He closed his eyes, his jaw working as he strove for patience.

It had been a fool's errand. I could see that now, though my heart had been in the right place. My head, well, I guess that was another story.

Tom slammed his hand down against the kitchen counter, hard, and my heart leapt into my throat. "What in the hell were you thinking, Maggie? Withholding evidence is a crime! Jesus H. Christ, I should book you for this, just to teach you a lesson."

I winced and bowed my head. He was right, and I knew it.

"And don't give me that puppy dog look, either," he added, scowling. "Now. Is there anything else I should know about, while we're practicing for your next reconciliation?"

Marcus took a step toward us, but I gave him a slight shake of my head as discouragement. Defending me would only make matters worse. I cleared my throat. "Well . . . if you're wanting me to be *entirely* truthful . . ."

"Oh, I do, I do."

"Well . . . there *is* the blog."

He narrowed his eyes even further at me. "The blog? You mean one of those online diaries?"

I nodded as Marcus came to stand behind me anyway, a protective force hovering at my shoulder. "Authored by Amanda and uploaded secretly onto the SunnyStony-Mill.com website. No one from the county knew it was there, and no one knew who wrote it. Marcus and I only just discovered the link to Amanda —"

"Quinn?" Tom's eyes flicked left. "You mean, you discussed it with *him* before bringing it to the police? To me?" His mouth tightened. "Who else knows, Maggie? What'd you do, share it with the whole goddamned town?"

I could feel his sense of betrayal, his anger. It was pouring off him in rolling waves, each stronger than the one before it. "Tom, the high school kids . . . they had been visiting this web blog for months apparently before Amanda died."

He looked at me, irony and hurt drowning his eyes. That was it for me. That was the extent of my honesty. I would have to leave the pics on the digital storage disk for another time. There was such a thing as too much too soon.

"So the whole town did know." He shook his head and sighed in exasperation. "I want everything that you have, and I want it right now. Consider it confiscated."

"All right."

He took out his clipboard and scribbled something in big, bold letters. "One last thing, Maggie. What is the connection with Cutter?"

"I don't know." I wasn't sure that he believed me.

It was probably terrible of me, but I handed over the original CD without a qualm *because I knew that Marcus had made copies.*

I probably definitely almost certainly should make time for confession to clear my conscience.

One of these days.

Tom left with the CD and the blog URL and passwords and headed off for a night of interrogation and investigation. I would have given anything to have been a fly on his shoulder, but all I could hope was that he and the rest of the Stony Mill PD managed to get the goods. Steff and Dr. Dan invited me to spend the night in Steff's apartment, but I demurred — three is company only in TV land. Marcus went home only after I forced him out with the reminder that the police had the man who'd broken into my apartment and I was now completely safe. I'm not sure he believed me, but I insisted. There was nothing left to do but to try to get this mess of an apartment put back together.

It was as good a plan as any.

As I sifted through papers and books and the flotsam that had collected in out-of-the-way places, I couldn't help thinking about all that had happened. Most of all I couldn't get Randy Cutter's face out of my head. I couldn't get over the fact that he had invaded my private domain and risked his freedom all at once. It was almost too much to digest. A man I knew, someone I'd seen on a day-to-day basis for months. Why? What reason could be strong enough, dire enough, to bring a careful, disciplined man like Randy Cutter to the edge? What secret would he be willing to throw everything away to protect? I frowned, knowing the reason for Cutter's irrational behavior must be clear.

He had acted out of fear.

The only answer was that he thought he might be implicated in some way in Amanda's files. But how? Why?

For that I had no answer. Only a lot of

speculation.

If one was to run with the assumption that Amanda had penned the lascivious tales on the blog (and at this point, I was 99.999 percent positive that was the case), then it became clear that Amanda was fairly sexually active. Okay, well, so, maybe "fairly" was an understatement. "Amazingly" might be more accurate. She had done the deed with her boyfriend, Jordan, but who else had received the, um, gift of her benevolence?

The blog was obviously the answer, but how to decipher the key?

Leaving the mess for the moment, I dug my printout of the blog from the voluminous depths of my purse, settled onto the sofa with my knees tucked beneath me, and began to read.

It was a task I should have undertaken before. Why had I not taken the time to go beyond the first ten pages? My only real excuse was the icky feeling that came over me the farther into the opus I ventured. The first few pages were the most innocuous, dealing primarily with boys at the high school. Lots of panting, lots of backseats. Typical kid stuff.

The bonfire following the big Stony Mill–Ouabache North football game more than a year ago seemed to be the kickoff for a whole new Amanda. Holy G-string, batgirl! The girl had certainly been making the most of her senior year, in more ways than one. It was at this point that Amanda began naming her conquests — not with real names, nothing as easy as that. No, Amanda had been too smart by half. She used aliases — Alligator Man, the Mole, Papa Bear. All the easier to make fun of them, my dear. But what was not clear to me was how many conquests Amanda had made in total.

I flipped through more pages, mesmerized by the tale that was unfolding before my eyes. At first it seemed to be a high school version of a secret swingers' society, taking place at parties, raves, school dances, after games. All recorded faithfully in Amanda's signature irreverent voice.

More disturbing, however, was an encounter that seemed to predate many of the others. Her first? A repeat encounter with someone Amanda described as Papa Bear. Someone considerably older than her. Someone who gave her gifts and who encouraged her Princess-perfect behavior, until . . .

When did the relationship stop? Or did it stop at all?

More importantly, did he know about

Amanda's tell-all blog? Did any of them? How many were out there, walking around Stony Mill waiting for the guillotine to drop?

So many questions. So many men. So little time.

The blog was overwhelming me. Darkness clung to the words, festering in the hidden nooks and crannies, sour and stale with the undercurrents of corruption and vice. I made myself stop after a time. It was simply too much for this small-town girl to swallow in large doses.

My phone rang at ten-thirty as I was restacking my collection of *Magnum* tapes on the shelves next to the TV.

"Hey, Sunshine. Are you doin' okay?"

I smiled into the receiver. "You know, Marcus, you're a real worrywart. Has anyone ever told you that?"

"I just wanted to see how you were holding up."

"I'm fine. Just finishing up here. Have you heard anything more about Randy Cutter?"

"Nada. As in, *not-a-thing.* Oh, by the way, the news about the break-in at your place is out. Not sure how, but you know how people around this town are. My mom heard about it at the gas station tonight, of all places. And apparently Randy Cutter's name is being bandied about as well."

"Bandied about, how?"

There was a moment of silence, and then he admitted, "As Amanda's murderer."

I blinked, not sure I had heard correctly. Randy Cutter? Could it be? I thought of what I knew of him. It wasn't much. A man in his mid-forties, ex-military, whose bearing still demonstrated that stiffness of spine and stature. How long he had lived in Stony Mill, I didn't know, but I didn't think he was an old-time resident. Perhaps one of our nicer big-city expatriates who came for the lower property taxes and business opportunities that our expanding population provided. I knew he was neat. Precise. A seemingly upstanding citizen. Was it all a front for deviant behavior? Could he possibly have killed to keep secrets safe? "What do you think, Marcus?"

"Unfortunately, I don't think it would be the first time a man has killed to save himself a little hardship."

Neither did I.

"Liss and I are coming over on Saturday," Marcus was saying, "to give your apartment a good airing with sage and incense. It will clear out any residual vibes from Cutter's intrusion."

I glanced around me with newly wary eyes. I had been so focused on cleaning up

403

the mess that I hadn't really thought about subjects paranormal. In fact, I'd been home so little in the last week that I'd scarcely thought about the strangeness I had encountered in my own apartment in the last two-plus months. Would Cutter's intrusion make it worse? "That sounds like a very good idea," I said, quick to agree to anything that would head wayward energies off at the pass. I was nothing if not slightly chicken.

"Great. Sure you don't want me to sleep on your sofa and keep watch until then? I make a pretty mean cheese omelette, too."

"Hmm. Tempting," I said with a grin, "but you have your own life to live, and I know I'm safe with Cutter in custody. I'll stick it out on my own."

"All right. Promise to call if you need me?"

"Promise."

I hung up with a bemused smile on my face. If I didn't know any better, I'd say Marcus had feelings for me . . . *Naaah.* Ridiculous. He was just being nice. Brotherly, even.

I was brushing my teeth when the next call came.

"Someone breaks into your apartment and you don't even bother to call your mother to let her know you're all right?" was the greeting.

"Hi, Mom. I'm fine. Really. I didn't want to worry you."

"Margaret! What have you been up to? What aren't you telling me?"

I shrugged. "I have no explanation, really. I'm just thankful they have the man in custody. It was luck that made that cop —"

"Officer."

"— Officer, then — pick up on Cutter's presence on the street. I'll sleep just fine tonight knowing he's down at the station."

She hemmed and hawed over the phone line. "Well, at least you're safe. I'm sending your father over tomorrow to install a dead bolt on your door and to check all the window locks. No sense in having the instance repeated, and we'll both sleep better if that's been done."

I was feeling all warm and fuzzy, basking in her motherly concern for me, which was really quite touching, when she ruined it all with:

"Are you quite sure this doesn't have anything to do with that woman you work for? She's foreign, isn't she?"

"What's *that* got to do with anything?" I asked, exasperated.

"There's no need to take a tone, Margaret, I was asking a simple question. And it's not that there's anything wrong with being foreign. It's just that we don't really know her people, do we, and with some things in life, a person's history must be taken into account."

My mother had a funny thing about knowing everybody else's business, past, present, and future. "Well, I'm sure even outsiders have history, Mom. We just aren't always privy to it."

"And that's really part of the problem, isn't it? People move around sometimes to hide who they are, don't they? Would you rather place your trust in the person you've lived next door to your whole life, or someone who could be a drug lord or a bank robber or even an axe murderer in a town across the state line?"

Considering that the neighbor we'd lived next door to for the majority of my formative years had spent hours on end shooting at all the squirrels, groundhogs, and chipmunks, and even cats and dogs, who were unfortunate enough to wander into his yard, I wasn't so sure that proximity was a fair measure of the reliability of a person's nature.

"Well, good night, then, dear. Just remember to jam a chair up underneath the doorknob of your outer door for now."

"All right."

All right? What was I saying?

A chair? Was that really necessary?

I was starting to feel jittery again, and I knew there was no need, dammit, not with Cutter in police custody.

I didn't use a chair, but I did check the locks again. Twice. And then I sat up against the pillows on my bed, my knees tucked up under the blankets and my teddy, G.T., clutched to my breast as I stared bead-eyed into the shadows.

There was something in my apartment. I would swear to it. Something small and shadowy, about the size of a cat. I could see it darting around the outer edges of the room. Like a rat (*gulp!*) but noiseless. In fact, completely silent.

There was more than one.

Worse, I could stare right at the shifting shadowy bodies, then switch on the light, and there would be nothing there.

Well, I say worse, but I think that was probably better. I'd have peed my pants if there did prove to be little creatures peering back at me, blinking in the sudden light. Of course, when I turned the light back off, they would reappear, darting helter-skelter around the baseboards and across the floor.

I tried to remember what I'd read about the shadows, and the debate about what kinds of creatures or entities they actually were. Some said they were brownies, some theorized fairies, some said they were the spirits of animals. I didn't know what to think, except that I wished they'd find someone else's home to hole up in.

Crap. Maybe I wouldn't be sleeping tonight after all.

With a sigh, I switched both bedside lamps on. At least with the lights on, I didn't have to see the creepy little buggers.

Had they always been there? Had I just not noticed? Was it the same with all of the otherworldly things I had seen or witnessed in the last few months? Had I been blinded by the popular modern belief that such things were figments of a collective imagination?

I had a feeling it was going to be a long night.

CHAPTER 18

The ringing of the telephone woke me up.

I opened my eyes and blinked in confusion at the lights. *Oh. Oh, yeah.*

More insistent ringing.

Phone. Right.

I threw the covers back and swung my legs over the edge of the bed in one quick movement that sent a sheaf of papers flying. The blog. I'd spent the wee hours avoiding shadows of one kind by immersing myself in shadows of another. An interesting diversionary tactic, but one that seemed to have worked. Judging by my current level of grogginess, I'd fallen asleep at some point during the night.

I stumbled out to the living room and grabbed the phone receiver before it could shrill again. " 'Lo?"

Tongue. Not functioning. Definitely not enough sleep.

"Maggie! I just heard! What happened?

Was it really Randy Cutter? I've been in his store downtown. That's where I bought the armoire in Greg's and my bedroom. I can't believe it. What on earth was he thinking? Do you really think he was involved in the Roberson girl's death? Well, the town will sleep easier at least. It's better to know than to not know at all. At least now I don't have to worry about letting Jenna ride her bike on our sidewalk."

"Hi, Mel," I said in a tired voice. There was something about my sister that never failed to wear me out.

"Is that all you can say to me? I mean, you didn't even call. I had to find out this morning from Margo Dickerson-Craig."

Margo Dickerson knew my business? Great. Randy Cutter was probably the only person in town my mom's circle of influence had not reached. Considering that he'd recently had his hands in my underwear drawer, not to mention all my other drawers, I counted that as a blessing.

"What time is it?" I craned my neck around to see the clock on the stove.

"What do you mean, what time is it? It's just after seven."

Oh, good. An excuse. "I have to go to work."

"Oh. Sure. Better be sure to bundle up.

They're calling for snow today."

Usually going into work was easy, Enchantments being my favorite part of my so-called life, but today I felt distracted and preoccupied, a testament, no doubt, to the events of last night. Liss gave me a curious glance or two, but said not a word when faced with the coins I dropped, nor my forgotten light-up Santa hat, not even the time I knocked over an entire stack of gift bags and sent them scattering to the floor. When five o'clock rolled around, she hovered by the counter a moment until I looked up at her.

"I'm going to be heading home now," she said, slipping into her coat. It was a crimson replica of a velvet opera coat, complete with ermine (at least, I *thought* it was ermine) collar. If the look she was going for was Edwardian opulence, she had achieved it and then some, especially when the coat was combined with what amounted to an ankle-length hobble skirt. I couldn't have pulled it off in a million years, so I guessed I'd better stick to my usual, no matter how boring it might seem to me. "Are you sure you'll be okay?" she asked me. "You've been a million miles from here today."

Rising from the box I'd been emptying, I

smiled at her and pushed the hair out of my eyes. "I'll be fine. It's just everything that's been going on lately. I guess I'm feeling a little out of whack."

"Ah. Perfectly understandable. The last week has been a bit trying, hasn't it." The glint of a plan came into her eyes. "I know! We'll close the store for a few days after Christmas, so that you can rest. With pay, of course," she added swiftly, as though I'd protested. "I don't want you wearing yourself out completely. After all, I have asked you to pull far more than your share of the weight with regard to the store. In light of that . . ." With a little flourish, she produced a small gift-wrapped box from beneath the counter's chintz skirt. "A gift, my dear. Something small that I think you can use."

I stared at the package in her hand and bit my lip. "Oh, but . . . but Christmas is a week away!" I protested. And I hadn't yet decided what I was going to give her. I mean, what do you give the woman who seems to have everything?

She arched her brow at me with a mysterious smile. "This isn't your Christmas gift, dear heart. It's my way of saying thank you. For everything."

"A thank-you? For what, doing my job? The pendulum you gave me was more than enough, Liss."

Half frowning, half laughing at her refusal to back down, I carefully began to unwrap the gift. After I spent nearly five meticulous minutes attempting to unknot the ribbon, Liss clucked her tongue and took the gift back.

"Life, my dear, is not all caution and wariness. Sometimes it is better to shred the paper and love the present to death than to tuck the salvaged gift wrap away and set the gift on a shelf somewhere to be admired from a distance." To demonstrate, she ripped at the colorful paper she'd obviously taken some effort with and laughed at my open-mouthed *Oh* of distress when it tore noisily.

My *Oh* turned into a squeal of delight a moment later when a cell phone box was revealed. A deluxe model, with the ability to text-message; take, send, and receive pictures; and even download e-mail.

"Liss, you really shouldn't have, you know. That sounds trite, doesn't it, but it's true."

"Why shouldn't you have one?" she asked lightly, smiling at my obvious appreciation for the gift. "You never know when a thing like this might come in handy for a young woman of the world. Marcus helped me pick it out — you'll notice we have even

413

gone to the trouble of placing our numbers in your directory. This lovely little thing is fully activated and ready for your dialing pleasure. And don't worry about not being able to fit it into your budget. This one is charged to the store account. Now," she said, catching me with her piercing gaze, "are you sure you don't want me to stay? I'd be happy to keep you company."

"You go. And have a good evening. Although I hope your plans include sticking close to your fireplace, the way the weather is looking."

The snow had begun to fall around one that afternoon, big, beautiful flakes, and store traffic had fallen off quickly after. I'd phoned Evie's house and left a message for her to stay home. Not a bad thing for a teenager on a Friday night, although I doubted it would be spent popping popcorn and watching a movie with the folks. Nowadays an evening stuck at home was more likely to mean hours of Internet chat and online games with friends.

Liss took a long look out the front window. "It does appear to be getting a bit slick, doesn't it? Ah, well, it's all very good for business. Once the snow stops, at least. I don't suppose tonight will be very busy. It never is in weather like this." She tugged on her gloves and headed for the back, only to turn before she entered the office. "Maggie . . . you *will* call me should you need anything, won't you?"

She said it so strangely that I had to laugh as I patted the gift she'd given me. "Of course I will. Now, stop worrying, woman, and go!"

She left after a last admonishment to close early if the weather warranted. There being no customers to speak of, I picked up my brand-new cell phone and began to play.

The first thing I did was to ring up Steff. "Hmm, 'lo?"

"Given up sultry and sexy now that you have a new man, I take it?" I teased.

"Hey, girl!" came the sunshiny voice I knew and loved. "Sorry, I was just taking a bite of peanut butter when you called. Hey, I was hoping to hear from you today. How are you doing? I wish you'd have stayed with me last night. Danny wouldn't have minded, you know that."

Somehow I wasn't so certain Dr. Dan would have wanted one of Steff's friends horning in on his romantic evening, and God knows he'd spent enough of the evening helping to straighten out my mess of an apartment. "It was okay. Really. I'm fine."

"If you say so. Hey, can you believe this weather? WOWO is saying this is turning into an actual winter storm. My mom said the grocery store is a madhouse. No bread on the shelves, no milk. Stripped bare. The usual routine. And we'll probably get the usual couple of inches and everyone will feel stupid."

"An actual storm. Maybe we'll have a white Christmas after all. Speaking of Christmas, guess what I'm holding in my hand right now?"

"Let me get out my crystal ball. Umm, I'm going to take a stab in the dark here and say . . . a phone receiver."

"Ah, but not just any kind of phone. Liss gave me a cell phone! It's so cool. I know, you're thinking *It's about time,'* but I really haven't been able to afford one. The Toad wasn't exactly forthcoming with the raises, you know."

"I know. I'm really glad your new boss is treating you better, Mags. You deserve it."

"Aw, thanks, sweetie. I'm glad you seem to be enjoying your new romance."

She giggled. "I am, at that. Danny is something special, that's for sure."

It was the way she said it more than the words themselves that made my breath catch. "Steff!" I exclaimed. "You're in love!"

"Maybe. It's too soon, really. I know that I enjoy being with him. I know that we have a lot in common. I know I can't wait to see him every day, and my day doesn't seem right when something happens that I can't see him. He's just really, really great. You know?"

Actually, I wasn't sure that I did, outside of my dad and my grandpa. And that just wasn't the same at all. "I'm happy for you. Really happy."

"Me, too," she said with a blissful sigh. "I mean, I'm not sure if he's The One or not. Only time will tell."

Time wouldn't tell me anything I didn't already sense. A pinkish red haze filled my mind when I closed my eyes and pictured my redheaded best friend with her man, and I smelled roses. Big, lush, blooming pink cabbage roses. Sheesh, all that was missing were the squiggly little hearts and silvery fairy twinkles, and really, I didn't need them to know that Dr. Dan was The One. I knew it with every fiber of my being. But I wasn't about to tell Steff. Better to let her enjoy the path every step of the way.

I hung up trying not to let myself feel down about the whole conversation. To distract myself, I spent the next several minutes figuring out how to program numbers into my phone list. Steff, Evie, Annie, Gen, Devin, Joe, Eli, Mom, Mel, and Marshall, who had broken my mom's heart by telling her he wasn't sure he could make it home this Christmas. With deference to Steff's romantic success, I even added Tom, though that seemed like a hopeless case of wishful thinking at this point in time.

With that out of the way, all that was left was testing out the camera feature. Which was way cool, as I soon found out. I even took it outside to take a picture of the falling snow, coming down even faster now. The streetlamps had come on, beaming down yellow spirals filled with swirling snow. I stood a moment in the cold, silvery otherworld conceived by the worsening storm, feeling the snowflakes hit my upturned face. A snow grader went past, its driver bundled to the hilt and sipping coffee from a quart-sized insulated mug as the heavy equipment barreled along past me, pushing the three inches of snow out of its path. I gave him a hearty wave, and he waved back. Life in a small town. It's a good thing.

Back inside the store, a silence had fallen that was so complete that it was almost as though time had stopped. The traffic on River Street was next to nothing, so I locked the front door and turned the OPEN sign to

CLOSED. I doubted anyone would know the difference if we closed early tonight. Right now all of Stony Mill was battening down its hatches in preparation for possibly the first winter storm of the season. This was one Christmas shopping day that would go unshopped.

But instead of calling it a day myself and going home, I turned down the lighting to security lamps only and brewed myself a strong cup of tea. Chamomile, to soothe, with lemongrass for clarity. Sitting on the cushioned stool behind the counter, I sat in the semidarkness and tried to unwind. Something had been nagging at the back of my mind all day, and I needed to find out what it was. I closed my eyes and let the fragrant tea steal into my brain. I'd found that it seemed to work even better than drinking it down. I just held the warm cup between my hands and let the steam work its magic.

I knew it had something to do with Amanda. That much was clear. She'd been on my mind from the moment I'd found out that she had disappeared virtually from Enchantments' doorstep. All the whispers and rumors and secrets that had engaged and titillated the town. The blog. The pictures on the disk in the clock . . .

The blog. The pictures.

Sliding off the stool, I retrieved my purse from the office, taking the printout of the blog from its voluminous depths. There in the darkened store, the words of the blog whispered to me, challenging me to understand, to open my eyes, to see . . .

I flipped through the pages a few times, back and forth, but I kept going back to where I first noticed that Amanda was using aliases for the men in her life.

The nicknames. What had they meant to her?

I sat down on the stool again with the cup of tea steaming away in my hand, staring out the windows at the lowering gloom. Snow was gathering in the corners of the windowpanes, blown there by the rising winds. I would have to leave soon . . .

Jordan.

Jordan was her steady boyfriend, and we knew with a fair level of certainty that the two of them had been intimate. But did she write about him?

And what about Charlie? He'd sworn they had never, that Amanda wasn't like that. Or was that a lie, something to cover their tracks?

Jordan, Charlie. Charlie, Jordan.

The two boys-but-almost-men. Both basketball players. Strong. Athletic. Young men, still inexperienced at handling the testosterone surges that could turn them into stark raving lunatics at any given moment. I could see them in my mind's eye, grappling about on the floor of Eyeball Alley, their muscles flexing, faces contorted with intense dislike. There had been an awful lot of power, both physical and metaphysical, swirling about that afternoon. Either one of them could have lost his grip on reality in the split second of a jealous rage, had Amanda pushed him to it.

Cut to the picture of Jordan that Amanda had kept on her desk, looking for all the world a young man in complete possession of himself. A young man of means, in his casually expensive clothes and easy confidence.

And in that one split second of time, my mind leapt the chasm of the unknown.

The Alligator Man.

Jordan's shirt had sported an embroidered alligator logo on the left breast pocket. It looked like the kind of casual chic clothing a young man about town would be expected to wear.

Excitement volleyed through me as the connection gained importance in my mind.

Could it be? It was as good a presumption as any.

My hands trembling, I picked up my phone and dialed Evie's home number. No answer. *Damn.* Who else could I call? Who else might know?

Tara might. But would she answer my questions?

I had to try.

Louis and Molly Tabor were listed in the phone book. I dialed the number and waited, holding my breath.

"Hello?" A male voice, presumably Uncle Lou.

"Hello, this is Maggie O'Neill. You don't know me, but I'm a friend of Marcus's."

"Oh, hello, Maggie. Yes, Marcus has spoken of you. How are you this evening?"

"Just fine, thank you. I was wondering if I might have a word with Tara."

A pause. "This isn't about the books that Tara took from your store, is it? Because I was operating under the assumption that she had paid you back for the books, and if she hasn't, I'd like to kn—"

"No, sir, this isn't about the books," I hastened to assure him.

"Oh. Well, then, just let me call Tara for you."

On the other end of the phone, I heard a

series of muffled sounds and knew he had placed his hand over the mouthpiece. But soon I was rewarded with, "Yo."

"Hi, Tara. It's Maggie O'Neill. Marcus's friend."

"Oh. Hi."

"Hi. Listen, Tara, this is going to sound a little strange, I'm sure, but . . . I need to ask you a question. Is that all right?"

"Shoot."

"It's about Jordan Everett. I need to know if he likes to wear a certain kind of shirt."

"Is this a joke?"

"No. No, it's not."

I heard a small intake of breath. "You're serious, aren't you. Is he all right? I mean, he isn't in any sort of trouble, is he?"

There was something in her voice that I recognized from that teen-girl part of me still lurking within. "You like him, don't you?"

Instant withdrawal. "So what if I do? That's not a crime, last time I looked."

"Is that why you were binding Amanda that day?" I asked, suddenly sure of the answer.

"Yeah, I admit it. I was trying to do a spell to get him to see what she was really like. He was blind to it, you know. Men always are."

I felt better, suddenly, knowing that Tara's ritual that day wasn't meant to cause physical harm to come to Amanda — no matter that she would have been a day late and a dollar short at the time. "Yes, they always are, aren't they."

"Lessee, the shirts he wears most often are LaCoste, I think. I'm not much into designer duds, you know, but I'm pretty sure that's right." She paused, then confided, "He sure does look good in 'em, though."

I laughed, but I was already heading back toward the office laptop. "That's what I needed to know. Thanks, Tara. I appreciate your help."

"No prob."

Within two minutes, I had my answer. Gotta love those Internet image searches. LaCoste was known for its alligator emblem. Jordan was known for wearing that kind of shirt.

Therefore, in my mind, Jordan Everett was the Alligator Man.

But what about the rest of them?

I tried to apply the same sort of thinking to the others, but the only one that came to me was Chicken of the Sea. It *must* have been her code for Charlie Howell. Not only was his name the same as the goofy tuna from that old advertising slogan, but hadn't she thought of him as some sort of pushover, the kind of boy she could lead around by a string?

Randy Cutter, I supposed, could have been Buzz Lightyear, a friend of her father's. He had the right haircut for the job. I flipped through until I found the first reference. There it was, a description of a mermaid bop in a swimming pool with Buzz Lightyear. Apparently, either Amanda had the lungs of a sea turtle, or else the man was a quick, um, study. No wonder he was willing to risk life and limb. No man would want that kind of rumor to get out.

But as for the others, especially the one she referred to as Papa Bear? I had no idea. Without knowing the intimate details of her life, how was anyone to know? What we needed was a diary, or a key, or a box full of photos with captions.

Photos . . .

Again, that nudge that felt almost as physical as it was mental. There was something I wasn't putting together. Something . . .

Hi-res. Marcus said we needed high-resolution versions of the photos so that the pics wouldn't be pixilated so badly when zoomed. But Marcus had spent the afternoon hauling me to Dr. Phillips's office, and the evening cleaning up my trashed apartment, so we'd never gotten around to it.

I reached for my cell phone again, selected Marcus's number from my phone list, and pressed SEND.

Marcus picked up quickly. "Hello, Sunshine. I was just thinking about you."

"Hey, Marcus. How'd you know it was me?"

"Caller ID — it's a wonderful thing. I just got home, this weather is crazy. Are you okay?"

"Fine, fine. Marcus, did Liss send through those original picture files to you in e-mail?"

"Yeah, they just came through. I should be able to open them with a higher resolution. Why?"

"I need you to send those picture files to my phone. Can you do that?"

There was a pause on the other end. "Well, yeah, of course I can. What's up, Maggie?"

His voice contained an alertness I attempted to soothe. "Nothing, really. I just wanted to see them again, Marcus. Something has been nagging at me, and maybe if I see them, I'll figure out what it is."

"Do you think you —"

"It's probably nothing. Can you send them?"

"Coming right up. You know, I've been thinking. We need to get that picture disk to the cops ASAP. We are officially withholding potential evidence, and that makes me a little nervous."

"I know, I know," I moaned into the phone, covering my hand with my eyes. "I've been thinking the same thing. But I just couldn't bring myself to tell him last night, not after everything else. One thing at a time. I'll drop the storage disk by the station tonight on my way home."

"Tomorrow's probably soon enough — no sense endangering yourself in this storm. Hey, I want you to be extra careful tonight."

"Sure. Why do you say that?"

"Randy Cutter's lawyer got him released on bond today."

I felt my heart give a little quaver of nervousness. So *soon* . . . "Even after breaking into my apartment and with a dead girl on our collective hands?"

"He had no history, and his lawyer used that to his advantage. And as for Amanda's death, even if he was responsible, the cops have to make sure they have every base covered. Whoever did it, they have to make sure the charges will stick. They'll need out-and-out proof."

He was right, and I knew it, but that

didn't make me feel much better. What about keeping the general populace safe from would-be stalkers?

"Listen, call me if you need . . . anything. I mean it. No worry is too small. And stay warm!"

One by one the pics came over the airwaves. I saved them using the instruction booklet to guide me, then began reviewing them.

By golly . . . no, it couldn't be . . .

I knew what I had to do to be sure.

Scratching a note to Tom, I retrieved the picture disk from the safe and tucked both the note and the disk into an envelope that I addressed to him. I sealed it tightly, trying not to give in to the feeling that I was sealing my own fate.

CHAPTER 19

One last call to make while I waited for Christine to push the oil through her pistons.

I dug out the phone book and looked up *Coolidge, Kathleen.* Dialing the number, I held the phone to my ear and listened to the sound of the ring. *Please be home, please be home, please be home,* I willed over the airwaves. *Oh, please be home.*

She picked up on the fifth ring. "Hello?"

I pressed the earpiece close against my ear so as not to miss a thing. "Hello, Katie? It's Maggie. Maggie O'Neill."

Katie paused a microsecond before responding. "Oh. Hi, Maggie . . . I wasn't expecting to hear your voice. What can I do for you?"

I gripped the phone harder. "I . . . I was wondering, Katie, if I could ask a favor of you."

"Um, sure. Shoot."

God love the midwestern need to be polite. I took a deep breath. "Okay. I was wondering if I could ask you to take me back to Dr. Phillips's office. I . . .." I what? What should I tell her? That I suspected her boss of carrying on an affair with a seventeen-year-old girl and possibly having information that might contribute to the police investigation of her death? Gee, that would really work in my favor of convincing her to help me break into the doctor's office. "I lost an earring when I was there today, a very expensive earring. It was my grandmother's," I invented as I went along, "and it means an awful lot to me. My mother would kill me if I lost it. I've retraced my steps everywhere else except Dr. Phillips's, and it just makes the most sense now, doesn't it?"

"Well . . . sure," she said, though she sounded as if she were trying to convince herself as much as I was. "Um, how so?"

"I'm sorry?"

"How does that make the most sense?"

"Oh! Well, because I know I was wearing it yesterday, and all I can think is that the missing one must have come out when I was changing out of my clothes." She didn't need to know that I'd never changed out of my clothes at all for the impromptu appointment. That little nugget of info was between me and my conscience.

"Oh. Oh, of course. That does make sense."

"So, you see, I was hoping . . . I mean, I know the weather is terrible, and I hate to ask, but . . . do you think I could convince you . . ."

"Well . . ."

"It would mean so much to me. Put my mind at ease, you know? My mom has a kind of sixth sense for this kind of thing, and I'm afraid she's going to ask about them before I find it. And" — inspiration struck — "and if you like, to repay you I'd be happy to put in a good word with Marcus." Was it mean of me, knowing that Marcus had no interest in Katie at all? I no longer knew. I only knew that I had to see the photographs on Dr. Phillips's wall again.

Katie's voice came, eager enough to make me feel guilty. "Oh! Well . . . If we go now, the streets should still be okay. We'll drive slowly. If you get to the office before me, just wait with your lights off. I don't want to attract attention."

"Thank you, Katie. I really, really appreciate your help."

And that's how I found myself not quite breaking into Doctor Phillips's office at just past eight o'clock that night. Er, was it considered breaking and entering if one had the permission of someone and a key to aid the way? I didn't think so.

We stood in the little hillock of snow that the wind had pushed in front of the glass vestibule. Katie's hands shook with cold and excitement as she struggled to insert the key into the lock of the glass entrance door as I lit the way with my keychain flashlight.

"Marcus is *sooooo . . . hawt,*" she enthused, hardly seeming to notice that the wind was whipping snowflakes the size of quarters into our faces. I turned my back to it and tucked my chin into my old wool scarf. It might not be pretty, but it did the trick. I wished she would hurry — the darkness and the storm were making me a little nervous.

At last we were wrangling our way into the glass vestibule. We managed the lock on the second door much more quickly with the problem of the wind on the outside of the building. The difference between the glassed-in space and the outside was incredible. Had the temperatures really fallen so quickly? I blew on my gloved fingers and rubbed my hands together.

"I'll just wait for you here," Katie said, holding the inside door open for me. "That way I can keep watch. God, I hope no one sees us."

"No one will see."

I switched my tiny LCD flashlight to perma-ON and stepped into the dark waiting room. The light was bright enough to see where I was going, but it left the eeriest shadows that seemed to move on their own accord as I moved forward. I circumvented the rows of uncomfortable chairs and headed straight for the Dutch door that separated the waiting room from the inner sanctum.

It was even darker in the hallway, away from the faint lamplight sneaking in through the waiting room windows. Darker and creepier. I headed straight toward the rearmost examination room, the room I'd been in a few days before for my yearly. This part of the office was even colder than the lobby. I felt the air pushing past me as I moved through the darkened hall, so I shrugged deeper into my wool coat, glad that I had left my gloves on. Passing by the first two closed doors on the right, I paused before the last to summon my courage.

My little flashlight did an admirable job of dispelling the gloom when I finally summoned the nerve to push open the door. Good thing, too — I was getting a little creeped out by all the closed doors. Somehow they seemed even more ominous closed than they did open and yawning with shadows and secrets. Too many secrets hide behind closed doors. I didn't even want to think about what secrets I might discover here. A part of me was almost afraid to find out, but another part of me knew I could not turn back. Not now. After withholding information about the blog and the CD from Tom, I was afraid to go to him about the photo storage disk without something more than an inkling of nervous suspicion. Either I needed proof, or I needed to prove my suspicions wrong so that I could sleep at night.

Somehow I found the courage within me to shine the light beam directly into the dark space. I wished I dared turn on the overhead fluorescents, but the last thing I wanted to do was to draw attention to a presence in the office, snowstorm or no. Best to get this over with quickly, before Katie gave up on me and went home.

The picture glass caught the beam of light and flashed it back at me. Faces swam into view in the peripheral light as I moved the beam to the next frame. The picture I was looking for was on the right-hand wall, but I began with the one closest to the door, working my way back. In a way, I suppose I was trying to convince myself of Dr. Phillips's humanity. That the balding, graying, slightly paunchy man I saw in these pictures, this good-natured man I'd known my whole life, could not be Papa Bear. He could not be sucked into an illicit relationship with a young girl. And he could never be capable of taking the life of another human being. He was a doctor, for God's sake. He'd taken an oath to protect life. Surely he couldn't have gone against that solemn vow.

Surely not.

I moved from picture to picture, pausing less and less over each one until I'd worked myself around the room to the one I remembered. It was a blurry photo of the doctor and two friends on what must have been a deep-sea fishing expedition based on the size of the fish the three of them were supporting. But it wasn't the fish or even the friends that had caught my attention. It was the tattoo he sported on his right arm that had barely registered on my consciousness at the time, just enough to nudge me into alertness now. Could it be? A bear?

If you're here, come to Mama, Papa Bear . . .

Reaching a hand into my pocket, I drew out my new cell phone and unfolded it. Its luminescent glow filled my hand with a reassuring blue light. With shaking hands, I worked my way through the menu until I found the picture files that Marcus had sent to me. I pressed the SELECT button, and the picture came into view in full, living color on the screen.

There it was, the *Shady Lady* with its embellishment of red swimming briefs and snappy polka-dotted swimming bra, and in the next, the murky snaps of the illicit meeting. It took me a few minutes, but I managed to zoom in somewhat toward the part of the photo where the blur of arms and legs could be seen. It wasn't the best picture, and I wasn't an expert, but . . .

Damn, damn, damn.

Why did it have to look the same? The head of a grizzly bear, open-mouthed in a menacing snarl, right there on the man's bicep.

There was just one more thing I had to do.

Replacing the photo on the wall, I closed the door behind me and made my way down to the examination room I had been shown into yesterday afternoon. This time I walked straight to a candid I wanted to see closer up — no roundabout delay tactics were needed or wanted this time. Dropping my phone into my purse, I carefully took the photo down from the wall, shining the LCD beam down on its glassed front.

There, looking at it close up, I could see what I'd not been able to see earlier.

Reflected in the water, the name of the good doctor's pontoon boat.

It was the *Shady Lady.*

Shangri-La, my ass.

I don't know how long I stood there with my hands on either side of that photograph, staring down at the evidence that would have gone unrecognized forever had Liss and I not found the pics in the clock. Even seeing it confirmed, I could scarcely believe it. Doctor Phillips had been involved with Amanda. Deeply involved. Enough that she had secreted away pictures relating to the affair. Had she seen him that afternoon? The details of what had happened to Amanda may be hidden, but I knew it had something to do with those photos. I *knew* it did. It's the only thing that made any sense at all, but more than that, the truth of it sank into my gut with a certainty that hummed along my nerve endings.

When at last I snapped out of it, I took a deep, quaking breath and resolutely turned the frame over to remove the back. A few muffled curses later, I decided the picture was not coming out of the frame. So with a muttered apology to my late Grandma Cora, I stuffed the picture, frame and all, into the depths of my purse. Then I crossed myself and cast a pleading glance heavenward for forgiveness.

Old habits do indeed die hard, if they ever truly die at all.

I wasn't really worried about what Doctor Phillips would do when he found the picture missing. I hoped by that time that the SMPD would have a chance to find whatever further evidence they needed to nail his ass to the wall. Whatever it took.

With my feelings toward the doctor hardening with each passing moment, I flashed my little light around the room one last time before turning to go.

"Maggie?" Katie's voice came faintly from what seemed miles away, surprising me to a halt. "Maggie, look who showed up."

The room suddenly closed around me, and my heart began to thunder in my chest. I shut my eyes a moment and forced myself to keep breathing. I wanted to believe it was one of the other nurses, just stopping in to check on things, or even whatever town cop happened to be on duty. I wanted to believe . . . but I didn't. Not for an instant.

I stepped quietly to the door and listened.

"She must not be able to hear us," Katie was saying. "I hope you're not mad, Doctor. She said she lost an earring. I didn't think it would hurt anything."

"Of course not." The voice was unmistakably gruff, unmistakably male, and it unmistakably belonged to Dr. Phillips. *Shit.* "You're sure she's back there?"

"Uh-huh. Looking for her earring."

I flattened my back to the wall, my breathing shallow. *He doesn't know anything,* I tried to tell myself. *Just act naturally and everything will be fine. To him, you're just a silly young woman willing to go out into a snowstorm to rescue a lost earring.*

Put that way, it did sound silly. I couldn't believe Katie had gone for it.

"I don't know what you were thinking. You girls shouldn't be out in weather like this."

They were coming down the hall; I could hear their footsteps. Thinking fast, I set my purse carefully down on the floor by the door and got down on my hands and knees with my flashlight, just as two sets of snow-covered boots appeared in the doorway.

The harsh beam of a giant Maglite put my LCD flashlight to shame as it shone in my face. I winced as it hit my eyes.

"Oh, sorry 'bout that," Dr. Phillips said,

pointing it away too late. "Miss Maggie, fancy finding you here. Katie tells me that you've misplaced an earring that you are desperate to find."

I blinked, but it was a lost cause. White spots had completely replaced the center of my field of vision. "Hello, Dr. Phillips." *Good girl, just stay calm and cool and collected and you'll do fine. He doesn't know.* "Yes, I lost one of the earrings my grandmother gave me before she died. Great sentimental value. I thought I might have lost it here."

"I see. Must be terribly important to be out at all hours in weather like this. Have you found it yet?"

"Well, no. Not yet."

He roamed the big beam of light along the floorboards and at the base of the room's utilitarian furniture. "There aren't many places to hide in here, that's for sure."

It was an innocent thing to say, but given what I *knew* . . . I stood up. "Well, I'm sorry to have taken up your time, Katie. I thought for sure the earring would be here."

Dr. Phillips rose as well with an agility that made me take a surprised step backward. "No harm done. Maybe someone else will find it and turn it in. If you leave a description of the earring with Katie, we'll keep an eye out for it."

He leaned a hand against the doorframe and bent down. My eyes traveled the path of his reach a moment too late to realize what he was doing.

His hand closed around the strap of my purse. As he straightened more slowly, a frown settling around his brows, my racing heart seemed to stop altogether.

The picture frame was poking out of the unzipped interior. Just a corner, but it was enough.

I could see it on his face. Recognition. Confusion. Questioning. And above all, a stillness that made me very, very nervous.

If I had had any remaining doubts, they dissipated entirely. The energy surrounding him had changed in a way that played havoc with my nerves, which were already on edge.

He didn't hand me the purse, but kept it dangling from his hand as he gestured us through the door. Having him at my back was not a comfortable feeling, but I managed to hide my discomfort long enough to hurry Katie up the hall toward the waiting room. All I could think of was how I was going to get us both out of there safely. I hadn't meant to endanger her, and yet somehow I had managed to do just that. The poor girl was completely oblivious to the fact that, at that moment in time, we were alone with a potential killer.

Ignorance can be bliss. I had the burden of knowledge, and the burden of obscuring that knowledge, for both our sakes.

To my surprise and relief, Dr. Phillips handed me my purse without a word as we reached the glass vestibule. Maybe I'd been mistaken — maybe he hadn't seen the picture after all. While Katie and I pushed away the snow that had built up against the outer door, he locked up the building, then followed us out.

"Let's get you girls home, hey?"

I breathed easier once we'd both reached the safety of our cars. But one thing neither of us had counted on was the small incline that precipitated the way out of the parking lot and onto the road. Katie's car, a minuscule foreign model, hadn't the wherewithal to make it up the grade, no matter how slight it seemed. When her tail end swerved sideways for the fourth time and her tail-lights flared, I knew I had to back Christine down.

Dr. Phillips appeared at my window, smiling amiably beneath a thick woolen beanie cap. I rolled the glass down a couple of inches. "She's not going to make it up without a little push," he told me. "It would

442

be safer pushing if I had some help. Would you mind?"

I didn't want to agree, but I didn't want to alert him to my reluctance, either, so I found myself saying, "All right." After backing off to a safe distance, I set the emergency brake, but I left Christine running with her lights on, pointing the way to safety, before getting out and crunching over in the snow that now reached above my ankles. Wind swirled the snow in circles around us. I shivered. My winter coat and boots were your standard cold-weather fare, made for weathering cold vehicles and walking from the garage to the house, not for long-term exposure. Cold from the snow seeped through my boots as I stood waiting while Dr. Phillips advised Katie to start in the parking lot before hitting the grade.

"You take that side, and I'll take this one, and we should be able to get her up there," he told me. "Just set your feet on edge in the snow for traction." To Katie he said, "Nice and easy, Katie, my girl. Keep your foot steady on the gas and keep going once we get you moving."

It worked far better than I thought it would. Katie's little car slipped only once this time, and she managed to work it out before taking Dr. Phillips's advice and continuing on. With his attention following Katie's departing taillights, I beat a hasty retreat back to my car. Crunching my way hurriedly through the snow, I didn't realize until it was too late that a layer of ice had formed against the ground. My feet slid out from under me and I landed on my rear, my hand out to catch my fall. Pain shot up my right arm, catching fire in my shoulder.

"Are you okay?"

My breath caught in my throat as Dr. Phillips appeared over me. "I'm fine."

He tried to help me to my feet, but I scrambled up on my own, eyeing him warily. "You're not. Here, let me take a look at it. Where does it hurt?"

I muttered something about my shoulder, and tried not to flinch as he made to unfasten my wool coat and peel it back. His hands were gentle, but I couldn't help wincing as he probed the aching area. "I don't feel anything broken or out of place in there, necessarily, but you need to have it x-rayed. Why don't you let me take you over to the hospital —"

I shook my head fiercely. "No. It's sprained or something, okay, I'll give you that, but it's not broken. I'm sure of it."

"Sprains can be even worse than breaks when it comes to healing. At least come

444

back inside and let me treat you. You can have your family take you in, if that would make you feel better."

I was stuck.

Dr. Phillips decided things for me when he went to Christine, switched off her engine, and returned with my keys and my purse. My mouth dry, I found myself supported on the arm of a killer as we maneuvered through the falling snow back to the office.

I stopped just inside the door and sat down decisively on one of the lobby chairs. "I'll just wait here," I told him.

He looked at me oddly as he set my purse down on the counter. "Suit yourself. I'll be right back with some supplies."

As soon as Phillips disappeared behind the Dutch door, I dug my cell phone out of my coat pocket and dialed Marcus's number. His phone rang, once, twice, three times. *Marcus, where did you go? Pick up, dammit!*

Frustrated, I pressed END, just as Dr. Phillips reappeared in the hallway, whistling like a madman. I tucked the phone away in the folds of my coat as I watched him make his way toward me down the hall.

"Here we are." Phillips sat down next to me and began to slowly extract my right arm from my coat. "I'm terribly sorry this happened. I feel responsible, in a way. If I hadn't asked you to help —"

"Not your fault," I said through gritted teeth.

"Perhaps not, but . . . Well. This brace should help until we can get you to the hospital for X-rays. And then I'll drive you wherever you need to go. Home, or your parents'?"

Drive me? "No, really, there's no need for that," I said quickly. "I can manage."

He smiled at me. "In an old Volkswagen? You won't be driving a stick shift tonight, young lady. Not with this shoulder."

Panic swelled within me, but I refused to give in to it. "It's feeling better already."

His eyes caught mine. "You're lying." He cocked his head, pale eyes assessing me in curiosity. "I wonder why?"

He rose to his feet and walked a few feet away from me, toward the glass door. A few moments ticked by in silence as he stared out at the falling snow. "Why did you come here tonight?" he asked. "Oh, I know. Your earring. But you were lying then, too, weren't you."

I opened my mouth, thinking fast, but he didn't let me answer.

"I asked myself, why would you feel the

need to come out in a winter storm to find an earring? You could just as easily have waited until morning. It's not as though the earring would be going anywhere, if it was indeed ever here at all." He paused and turned back toward me.

I opened my mouth, but no sound came out.

"Neither does it explain why you decided to take one of my photographs off my wall. No sense in denying it, you know. I saw it in your purse."

My gaze drifted to where my purse rested on the reception counter. I swallowed hard. "Dr. Phillips, I —"

"Yes? You what, my dear? What possible reason could you have for taking a personal photo? I'm afraid I don't understand. I might think kleptomania the culprit, but you took nothing but a ten-dollar frame."

And as I watched, he took a key out of his pocket and locked the inner door. The finality of the action touched home like nothing else had. "What are you doing?"

"Keeping my property from running away, as it seems wont to do."

"Are you going to call the police?" I asked. Hope against hope.

"Not yet. First we're going to take a look at that photograph that you seemed so

447

interested in."

He strode to the counter and picked up my purse. "Dr. Phillips —"

"Let's just see. Ah, yes. I love this picture. I took it just after we bought the boat last June. She's gorgeous, isn't she? But why would you be interested in this particular photograph?"

I was beyond thinking. My mind spun and spun, but nothing happened to get me out of this mess.

And then my cell phone rang. I pressed it protectively against my leg.

"Aren't you going to answer it?" Dr. Phillips asked me, standing over me with the frame in his hand.

Swallowing hard, I flipped open the case and pressed SEND. "Hello?"

"Hey, sweet stuff. You rang?"

My heart felt like it was going to beat straight out of my chest. "Marcus. What a surprise."

Marcus laughed, oblivious to the terror in my voice. "Sorry I didn't pick up. I was down in my office working on the files and I didn't want to give up to answer the phone. I think I'm close, Maggie. Very close. I've gotten a couple of them open, so far just copies of the blog entries, but maybe one of the others will be more enlightening.

One of these days I'll show you a little more how the code-breaking programs work. It's pretty fascinating stuff."

My breath caught as Dr. Phillips reached for me. But instead of grabbing me, he pushed the volume button on the phone, until Marcus's voice was loud enough that I needed to hold the phone away from my ear. I gripped the phone harder.

"What's wrong, Maggie? Where are you?"

I cleared my throat. "Nothing. Nowhere."

"You sound a little strange."

"Do I?" I forced a laugh. "Must be the storm. Listen, I'm going to have to go —"

"Did you get the pictures I sent over all right? They turned out really well after I cleaned them up a bit. The boat is pretty sharp and clear, you should be able to see it, even on your phone. I'm thinking they should be able to run a record check on the name —"

I cut him off quickly, my eyes locked on Dr. Phillips. "Yeah, I got 'em. Thanks, Marcus. Anyway, gotta go, places to go, people to meet."

A pause. "Yeah. Sure. Okay. 'Bye, Maggie."

"See y'around."

I pressed END quickly.

"Who was that? Marcus your boyfriend?"

I shook my head.

"Just a friend? You sure about that?"

I nodded.

"A friend in need is a friend indeed," he quipped, chuckling heartily at his own joke. With his rosy cheeks and big nose, he reminded me a little too closely of the jovial Santa who'd been hired to visit all of the River Street shops throughout the holiday season. I'd never see Santa in quite the same way again. "Just one more thing. What pictures did he send you?"

Crap. I tightened my hand protectively around the opened phone.

"Well, why don't you just let me see them, hm? I think it's a fair exchange. You looked at my photos, I look at yours." He held out his hand.

Short of throwing the phone at him and pissing him off, it wasn't much good for self-defense, and there was no way I could keep it from him if he decided to take it by force. Biting my lip at the loss, I handed it over.

I sat quietly, trying to still my thoughts, knowing I was about to be completely and utterly exposed.

The expression on his face as he flipped from picture to picture and back again was as bland and imperturbable as if he was surveying the breakfast menu down at Ivy's Truck Stop. "Well, well. Where on earth did you get these?" He sat down next to me, frowning when I flinched away from him. He sighed and moved opposite me instead. "You needn't worry. I'm not going to hurt you. I just want to know where you found these pictures."

I wasn't stupid. If he wanted to harm me, it wouldn't be all that difficult. Not only did he outweigh me by at least a good seventy-five pounds, but my injury was going to make fighting back difficult. Reasoning was my only defense. "From Amanda," I said at last.

"So you've found your voice again. That's good. How did you know Mandy?"

His pale eyes watched me closely. Curious, more than threatening. I relaxed, just a hair. "I didn't, really."

"She gave you these pictures out of the goodness of her heart, hey?" He leaned back in the hard lobby chair and steepled his fingers over his bulging stomach. "I doubt that. Mandy was hardly what I'd call altruistic. Why don't you just tell me where you got them. Did you steal them?"

"No. I didn't steal them. I found them. In a clock she'd bought that her mother returned to our store."

He closed his eyes wearily. "As easy as that. Good Lord, I wonder what else she's squirreled away."

He sounded so tired, I almost felt sorry for him. "There are files, Dr. Phillips. And her blog. The police have all of that now."

He lifted his brows. "Do they? I suppose they do. I should have known I couldn't trust her. Randy should have known, too. Did you know she'd been with him that afternoon? I followed her. Poor Randy will be the one they blame. I'll have to make sure of that now."

Of course I knew, too, but somehow I got the feeling that he didn't see me as much of an obstacle. I was starting to get that eerie feeling again. *Keep him talking . . .* "Why do you think the police will continue to suspect Randy?"

Again he cocked his head with that calm stare. "Why wouldn't they? He had the motive. He had the opportunity. You see, my dear, the easiest solution is so often the right one. No one believes in conspiracy theories anymore. And he did break into your apartment. Why, I can't quite figure. Did he know about the pictures?"

"I think it was the CD," I told him, knowing that information could not help him now. "I guess he was worried about what

452

might be on it."

"He should have been, too. Was she black-mailing him, like she did me? Or was she just using him to get what she wanted?"

"What is it she wanted, Dr. Phillips?"

"Money? Power? Sex? Who the hell knows what went on in that twisted little head of hers. All I know is that she held open the door, and fool that I was, I walked straight into her lair."

I wasn't about to ask what he had planned for me. Better not to know than to worry about how and when it would happen. I doubted he'd tell me the truth anyway.

"Why did you kill her?"

"Kill her?" His salt-and-pepper brows rose high. "I didn't kill her. No, she killed herself. Or might as well have. She killed herself when she tried to ruin my good name. To destroy a lifetime of good work. I couldn't keep paying her what she was ask-ing. Susan — my wife — had found one of the withdrawal slips and questioned me about it. I was able to explain that five thousand away, but I just couldn't risk hav-ing her find out the truth. Dear me, no. And then the damned fool girl went and got herself pregnant! Mine, so she said, but I think you and I both know the likelihood of that. But Mandy was threatening to tell my wife. She'd even come to the house a couple of times with high school fund-raisers. It was only a matter of time before she said something to Susan. Hell, she might have done even if I had kept paying her. For kicks. Mandy liked her kicks."

A baby, too! So Gen's intuition had been right. Dear God. That would mean . . . "How . . . how did you do it?"

"I didn't hurt her," he was quick to assure me. "It was very quiet, very easy, her passing. There are so many drugs that can immobilize a person. Things that are difficult to trace. But it wasn't supposed to kill her. Just to make her . . . go to sleep until I could get her in the water. That was a bit of a mistake, yes, it was. All water under the bridge, I suppose."

His sudden laugh at the unintentional pun chilled me to the bone. It was at that moment that I knew for certain his regret and sorrow only ran so deep. His sense of self-preservation was far better developed.

He rose suddenly and held his hand out to me. "Come on, let's get you home."

Home. Right.

I reached for my cell phone, but he took it and slipped it into his coat pocket before gathering up my purse and pulling me gently to my feet.

"Did you want something for the pain?" he asked me. "Your shoulder must be bothering you."

I hesitated only a moment before answering, "All right."

I palmed the pills, rather than swallowing. I knew they were meant to relax me into oblivion, but I left him his deception. Maybe he thought I was the type to go gently into that good night, submissive and docile. Whatever, by the time he piled me into the backseat of his SUV, I was playing in full sleep mode. Surprisingly gentle, Dr. Phillips laid me out across the backseat before throwing my purse in and closing the door. My shoulder was throbbing, and I would have loved to have had the benefit of medicine to dull the pain, but it was a risk I could not take. Every throb meant I was still alive. I would cling to that hope to get me through.

I would have given anything to have my cell phone back as I recognized that we were on a route that would take us out of town. Dr. Phillips's SUV performed beautifully in the snow, sliding only slightly in the rear as we took a corner. Through slitted eyelashes, I noted the roads — mostly state highway, until we turned off onto a county road that I knew circumvented a series of spring-fed lakes reputed by area fishermen to be bottomless. Like most of the smaller lakes in this part of the state, these were circled by aging cabins and run-down trailers, the vacation homes of the not-so-rich-and-famous, but my heart didn't exactly leap at the sight of civilization. These were summer places. The roads back around these lakes closed at first snow and didn't reopen until spring thaw, and most of the places were abandoned long before then. We weren't about to be overrun with potential witnesses for the defense or the prosecution.

My plan, if you could call it that, was to run. I was no match for the doctor's superior weight and strength, but what I did have on my side was the element of surprise. I'd stayed deathly still for the entire ride, allowing my head to bob with the motion of the vehicle along the rutted and snowy roads. Phillips was expecting a limp body for whatever end he had planned. What he was going to get was anything but.

It wasn't much of a plan, granted, but it was the best I had at present.

My heart began to race as I recognized the slowing of the vehicle. I opened my eyes as far as I dared and tried to get my bearings, but it was too dark to see much at all. At least the snow had slowed, and overhead the thick storm clouds had grown fitful and lacy, exposing a scrap of moon from time to time. The lake was a small one, from the looks of it, but I didn't see even a hint of light coming from the small domiciles surrounding it.

Phillips stopped the SUV and set the emergency break. I could hear him rustling around in the front seat, so as quietly as I could, I tried the door. The latch didn't budge, even though the locks weren't set.

Damned childproof doors.

He got out of the SUV, but left it running, thank you, God. I forced my panic down to a usable level and closed my hands over the armrest on my door. *One . . . two . . . three . . .* As soon as he put his hand on the latch, I shoved with all my might, ignoring the searing pain that ripped through my right shoulder. Phillips went over like a barrel of monkeys. I leapt from the SUV and slammed the door, immediately going for the driver's side latch. Hope surged within me as my hand closed on the cold metal. I was going to make it. I —

Had miscalculated.

CHAPTER 20

Phillips's arm came around my neck and dragged me backward down the steeply pitched boat launch. A scream ripped from my throat, aided along by the liquid fire rippling and pulsing outward from my shoulder. He clamped his other hand over my mouth and nose, hard enough to hamper my breathing. I tore at his arm and his hand, at anything I could reach, but came away with little more than a bit of skin and a renewed effort on his part. My world was going a little hazy. The more I kicked and yanked, the more oxygen I consumed, until I thought my head was going to explode with the effort. His grip relaxed slightly when his feet slithered beneath him.

We were on the ice.

New ice.

It cracked and shuddered under our combined weight, a groaning sound that sent a shiver down my spine. I made myself focus. How far out were we? Too far. The shore seemed a distant memory. Oh, God. *Mother Mary, pray for me,* I pleaded. *Give me strength.*

With the last reserves of energy I possessed, I wrenched and twisted from his grasp, falling to the ice with a painful jolt and rolling away from him across the ice and snow. Phillips stopped where he stood, watching my desperate movements with a patience born of dominance.

"You can't run, you know," he said, his quiet voice unnaturally loud in the stillness.

My own vulnerability infuriated me as much as his certainty. "Neither can you," I spat, facing him down.

He just eyed me sadly. Resignedly.

"You're not thinking clearly. Katie will suspect. She knows you were there tonight."

"I took you home. Dropped you off. That's the last I saw of you. I'll even make sure there are footprints in the snow leading from the curb to your apartment." He took a step closer, forcing me to move farther out on the groaning ice. "Listen, why don't you just give in? I won't hurt you. I'll make sure of that. I wouldn't have hurt you before, but you left me no choice."

"Is that what you told Amanda," I flung back at him, "before you killed her? Did she beg and plead with you? Did it make you feel good?"

"You're overwrought. I'm sure if you just took a moment to think clearly, you would see that I'm not the villain here. I'm a victim. Just like you."

Fury raged through me, powerful, cleansing, uplifting in its strength. Power filled me, spreading inch by steady inch, like ice in my veins. "I am no man's victim," I grated out before yielding myself and letting the electric power take control.

In the next instant I found myself leaping upward, bringing my feet together and down with as much force as I could muster.

"Waters!" I cried in a voice that was not quite my own, *"Heed me!"*

With a rumbling sound that began as no more than a gentle vibration, the ice rippled beneath my feet like Jell-O.

Phillips threw his hands out sideways for balance. "Stop that," he said, confusion and disbelief in his voice. "What are you doing?"

I did it again. And again. Each time, the thundering groan that answered became louder, the enraged cry of an elemental water spirit roused from slumber.

They say these lakes are bottomless . . .

Phillips had fallen to his knees and was now on all fours, holding on to the ice as though he could steady it. "Stop it, stop it now! What in God's name is happening?"

But the energies that flowed through me from the ice and sleeping water would not be denied. I felt them surge through the soles of my boots, into my feet, up, up through my veins. A breath of ice lifted my damp hair, freezing it in a Medusa's snarl of jagged curls. A spectral voice came, from within me, from beyond me. The voice of the Great Mother:

"Blessed are the precious and preserving waters, the blood of Life, the keeper of the mysteries of intuition, the place of magick from whence all life sprang forth. Wash away our troubles. Free us of darkness of spirit. Waters! Heed me!"

I threw my hands into the air, and through that same cold, dark air came the sound of rending, splintering ice. Phillips stared at me in abject horror as the ice beneath his feet seemed to dissolve into snow crystals. He sank into the waters, his grimace of surprise freezing into a mask of terror as he was dragged under by cold, unseen fingers.

My energy spent, I dropped to what was left of the ice around us, panting, and closed my eyes, waiting for the waters to take me, too. I don't know how long I lay there on the ice, too cold for even pain to overcome.

I think I dreamed, of a place warm and bright with love, a place of angels and gardens and the Mother. Mary, bathed in spectral light. Mary, Queen of Heaven. That must be where I was. Heaven, or someplace like it. But when I opened my eyes again, I saw my cell phone lying in the snow four feet from me. I took a deep shuddering breath, wondering if I could summon the energy to reach for it.

I could.

My fingers were so numb I could hardly make them work, but somehow I managed to find my way through the menu to my phone book, then I pressed SEND, knowing the phone would select whoever was first on my phone list. I no longer could remember who that was.

And then I closed my eyes and wept.

I was in the place I had dreamed of, the warm place filled with light. Except the pain had followed me there. I frowned, trying to chase it away. It didn't belong there — only love belonged there, love and light. I writhed and gnashed my teeth, but it wouldn't go. At last I was forced to look it in the face, to see it for what it was.

My eyelashes fluttered open.

I was strapped to something that I could

feel but could not see, a strange kind of blanket covering my entire body, and the light was a giant lamp shining down on me from above. I could sense things moving around in the background, but just then I had eyes for one thing and one thing only: Tom was staring back at me, his gray-green eyes only inches from mine, his face distorted by fear and worry.

I felt something warm and soft against my cheek. It was his hand.

"Hey," I croaked, trying to smile.

A shadow crossed in the depths of his eyes. "Hey," he said softly.

"You must have been the lucky one, huh?" I said, meaning the random cell phone call I'd made from the ice.

He swallowed mightily, then leaned forward to press his forehead against mine, his breath warm and silken on my skin. "Yeah. I'm the lucky one."

It was much later that I found out exactly what had happened that night after I'd lost consciousness. How the ice had stopped cracking, miraculously and literally, at my feet. How my answers to Marcus earlier from Dr. Phillips's office had been mysterious enough to drive him to call out the cavalry — or in this case, the Stony Mill PD — on a countywide manhunt when he

463

discovered I'd never reached my apartment. How my random dial to Tom had been the final piece they'd needed to pinpoint my location. How Tom had found me in the open SUV over an hour later, kept alive by the low-running heater despite the open door. How I got there, no one knows.

Dr. Phillips's body, as it turned out, wouldn't be found until the spring thaw.

There was justice in that, somehow.

Christmas came and went, much as Christmases tend to do. I stayed close to my family, taking solace in the mundane. In the normal day-to-day tedium of life. At my folks' house on Christmas Day, my older brother, Marshall, called me from New York, eager for the details of my narrow escape, and told me I was his new hero. Mel revealed that she and Greg were expecting. Again. My nieces, Jenna and Courtney, had given the day a sweetness that made me long for a family of my own. And Tom . . . well, Tom had made the declaration that he wanted to date me, looking after me in the days following my near miss in a way that left no doubt as to whether he cared for me or not. In a way, things looked brighter than they had in a very long time.

So why couldn't I believe it?

New Year's Day dawned pure and cold, but bright and cheerful. I got out of bed and dressed for the weather before anyone could tell me not to drive myself. It wasn't easy shifting with my left hand, but I was a woman with a mission, and I would not be denied.

There was something I had to do.

I stopped at Wal-Mart and picked up a trio of white roses before heading for the cemetery. The snow from the storm had melted away on Christmas Day, but the recent dip in temperatures had left a crust of frost on the recent graves. There was a bite to the air that said the ground wouldn't be brown for long.

Best get this over with.

My mother had told me where I could find Amanda's grave. As I steered Christine toward the back of the cemetery where all of the newer graves could be found, I marveled that I had somehow found the reserves of personal strength to do this, alone, when once I avoided cemeteries like the plague.

How things change.

Still, I shielded myself with protective light before leaving Christine's sheltering confines. No sense in breaking entirely with tradition.

Amanda's stone was a big, rose granite affair that sparkled in the sunlight — I think she would have liked that. As I read her name and the span of dates below, I laid two roses on the stone, then closed my eyes and said a prayer for her and for the unborn child no one would ever know about. It was her mother's wish, one I could understand, even if I didn't agree with it.

Secrets. This town was all about secrets. I guess, in a way, all small towns are.

The last rose I left on a stone at the far end of the row, a stone that had been newly erected just this week. *In memory of Doctor Newton Phillips, beloved father and husband.* There was no body to be found within, but that would come in time. All things come to those who wait.

The CD had been the one piece of evidence that would have blown the whole case wide open, if Doctor Phillips had not acted. Not only had little Amanda kept a list of receipts for cash she'd managed to trick him out of, she also had kept a running list of dates, times, places, and activities. Little Amanda was nothing if not enterprising, but she'd made the mistake of believing utterly in her own immortality and power. Poor, misguided girl.

Was it the blackmail that had pushed Dr.

Phillips over the edge? Or the baby? Was it really Dr. Phillips's child, or someone else's? Was it even important anymore?

One thing was for certain — Sid Roberson would probably regret introducing his daughter to his country club cronies for the rest of his life. Poor man.

Funny how every day we are given choices to make in our lives. Some are just more far-reaching than others.

I gazed down at the doctor's newly erected stone. *Rest in peace, Dr. P. Please, rest in peace.*

As I turned to leave, I caught a movement out of the corner of my eye where no movement should be. Overhead, the big oak trees shifted in the windless morning, cold branches chattering together. I looked up, just in time to see a ball of silvery light zip between the branches only to disappear into the trunk of a giant specimen itself.

Secrets and spirits. This town, it would seem, had plenty of both.

ABOUT THE AUTHOR

Madelyn Alt is the author of the Bewitching Mysteries. A born aficionado of all things paranormal, she currently spends her days toiling away in the mundane world of business and her nights writing tales of the mysterious. She loves chocolate, Siamese cats, a shivering-good ghost story, the magic in the world around us, and sometimes, more chocolate.

Madelyn writes from her 1870s-era home in a small town in northeast Indiana, and is currently at work on the next installment in the Bewitching series.

For more information, please visit her website at: http://www.madelynalt.com.